Magic lurks in every world in *Isaac Asimov's FANTASY!* . . .

- A mysterious tuxedo-clad man buys the evening paper and takes a walk through the park—into a secret, enchanted world where his lover and his enemy are waiting for him . . .

- F. Scott Fitzgerald leaves his Long Island mansion and travels back to his hometown, where he is haunted by creative failure—both figuratively *and* literally . . .

- The sight of a delicate swan unearths long-buried memories for a young prince . . . and the swan's sudden transformation leads to a painful truth buried even more deeply . . .

A collection of incomparable stories
by fantasy's greatest talents.

ISAAC ASIMOV'S
Fantasy!

EDITED BY SHAWNA McCARTHY
Abridged Edition

ACE BOOKS, NEW YORK

This Ace Book contains the
abridged text of the original hardcover edition.
It has been completely reset in a
typeface designed for easy reading,
and was printed from new film.

ISAAC ASIMOV'S FANTASY!

An Ace Book/published by arrangement with
Davis Publications, Inc.

PRINTING HISTORY
Dial Press edition published 1985
Ace edition/January 1990

ISBN: 0-441-05499-4

Ace Books are published by The Berkley Publishing Group,
200 Madison Avenue, New York, New York 10016.
The name "ACE" and the "A" logo are
trademarks belonging to Charter Communications, Inc.
PRINTED IN THE UNITED STATES OF AMERICA

10 9 8 7 6 5 4 3 2 1

Copyright Notices and Acknowledgments

Contents

The Storming of Annie Kinsale

Lucius Shepard

IT WAS ON a rainy Thursday morning, just the odd speckles of rain staining the front stoop, but the sky over Bantry Bay nearly black and promising worse to come, that Annie Kinsale caught sight of the soldier's ghost. She was standing at the kitchen window of her cottage, half-listening to the radio, idly debating whether to add cheese or butter to her shopping list—a body couldn't afford both what with prices these days—when she saw the gray figure of a man waving a rifle and running, stumbling, and then, as he passed the point where her primrose hedge met the country lane, vanishing like smoke dispersed by a puff of wind. Annie's heart went racing. There was no doubt in her mind that he had been a ghost, and she had known him for a soldier by the curious shape of his rifle. She crossed herself and peered once more out the window. Gone, he was, and considering the paleness of his substance, the poor soul had likely been at the end of his earthly term. Her first thought was to hurry into the village of Gougane Barra and tell her best friend Eleanor Downey what had happened; but on second thought she decided against it. Though Eleanor was the only person in whom Annie had confided her secret, though she was trustworthy in that regard, she would be quick to spread the word of this, and Annie's reputation for being a "quare one" would suffer an increase. Sure, and wasn't her name this moment dancing on the tongues of those red-nosed layabouts who were welcoming the morning in at Henry Shorten's pub.

". . . livin' out in the midst of nowhere," that hulking stump of a man Tom O'Corran was saying—his static-filled voice was issuing from Annie's transistor radio. "Six years, and nothin' warmin' her bed but that damned cat! It ain't natural for a woman like herself.''

'' 'Twas the manner of Jake Kinsale's passin' what done her,'' said old Matty, rheumy-eyed, with hardly a hair between the tips of his ears and the porch of Heaven. "The heart is rarely wise, and violence will never enlighten it. But I'll grant you she's a pretty woman.''

Pretty, was she? Annie stared at her opaque reflection in the window glass. Her skin was that milky white that turns easily to roses, and her hair was a dark shawl falling to her shoulders, and her features—undistinguished, except for large brown eyes aswim with lights—were at least expressive. Pretty enough, she supposed, for a bump in the road such as Gougane Barra. But thirty years old, she realized, was not the first bloom of beauty, and lately she had accumulated a touch of what Eleanor—with a giggle—had called her "secretarial spread."

"I'll not argue that she hasn't reason to grieve," said Tom. "Well I know that the friction was hot and strong 'tween her and Jake, and he was a soul worth grievin' over. But six years, man! That's time enough for grief to go its rounds."

"It's not grief that's taken her," said Henry Shorten; his voice faded into rock music, then swelled as Annie adjusted the tuning dial. "She's settled into loneliness is all. Her mother and grandmother, and as I've heard, her great-grandmother before them, were women who thrived on loneliness."

"Och!" said old Matty. "I was only a scrapeen of a boy when her great-grandmother was alive, but there was a force of a woman! 'Twas said she had unearthly powers, and that the divil himself had tied a knot in her petticoats. Maybe Annie Kinsale is not so alone as you're thinkin'."

"Well," said Tom, laughing, "be it diviltry or loneliness or grief that keeps her shut away, before winter's end it'll be myself she's hearin' at her bedroom door."

Irritated, Annie switched off the radio. That blustering fool! Then she laughed. At the heart of Tom O'Corran's bluster was a great shyness, and like as not, if he ever were to reach her bedroom door—a most improbable event—she'd have to instruct him on how to insert the key.

For the remainder of the day Annie put aside all thought of ghosts and Tom O'Corran, and—also putting aside the idea of going shopping, because the storm that soon blew up from Bantry Bay was as thunderous and magical-seeming as the one that had carved the name of St. Kieran on the wall of Carrigadrohid Castle the year before—she went about cleaning the cottage. With muttered phrases and flicks of her fingers, she set the tea-kettle boiling and rags to polishing and the bed to making itself; and when the water had boiled, she sat herself down at the kitchen table with a steaming cup, her marmalade cat Diarmid curled beside her, and turned in the radio to a Dublin station, hoping for some music to drown out the pelt and din of the storm. But there had been trouble in the north that day, and all she could find were reports of bombings and fires and pompous editorial expressions of concern. She switched it off. Ever since Jake had been cut down by an errant bullet on a Belfast street, she had not allowed any talk of war within the confines of her home. It was not that she was attempting to deny the existence of violence; it was only that she thought there should be one place in her life where such concerns did not enter in. The cot-tage, with its feather pillows and hand-me-down quilts and con-tented cat, was a fragment of a cozy, innocent time that had just faded around the corner of the world, and she meant to keep it so despite the ghosts of soldiers and bad news from the north.

A stroke of lightning illuminated the smears of rain on the window; beyond the glass, the lawn was momentarily drowned in yellow glare, and Annie saw a primrose torn from its stem and blown away into the night like a white coin thrown up to appease the fates. It made her shiver to think the wind could be so particular, and she switched on the radio again, tuning not to the Dublin station but to the cottage belonging to Mrs. Borlin who—foul weather or fair—told the cards of an evening for those uncertain of their paths.

"... faith," she was saying, "and isn't it a fine life I'm seein' before you! What's your name, girl?"

"Florence."

Thunder crashed, static obliterated their voices.

"Will you listen to that!" said Mrs. Borlin. "Praise be to God, at least the hay's in. Now, Florence, there's yourself there, the queen of hearts ..."

And Annie, comforted by this telling of a golden future, sipped her tea and absently stroked Diarmid's back.

If you haven't yet guessed how it was that Annie accomplished her housework, how she eavesdropped on her neighbors, it was, simply stated, because she was a witch. Not a flamboyant witch of the sort typified by her mother, who had once caused the waters of Gougane Lake to rise into the air and assume the form of a dragon; nor was she a vengeful sort like her grandmother, who had once transformed an English banker's eyes into nuggets of silver; and she certainly was not as renowned as her great-grandmother, about whom it was said that an eagle-shaped rock had flown up from a mountain in Kerry to announce her death in Heaven. The witch blood was strong in Annie's veins—and hot blood it was, too, for an Irish witch is a creature of potent sexuality, her body serving as the ground upon which her spells are worked; but her mother had undergone a late conversion to the Church and had preached against witchery, infusing Annie with an enfeebling dose of Christian morality, and she had never developed her powers. She was—except for a spell she'd nurtured over the years, one she might use if someone more suitable than Tom O'Corran happened along—limited to feats of domestic management and the like. She had as well the gift of seeing into people's hearts (though not into her own), and she could sometimes catch the tag-ends of people's thoughts, an ability that came in handy when dealing with Mr. Spillane the grocer, a thoroughly larcenous individual. Yet she was content with these limits; she had no need for more, and what she did have sufficed to ease her loneliness. Mrs. Borlin's readings were a special balm to her—their uniform cheerfulness reinforced the atmosphere of the cottage.

"Don't be despairin', Florence," said the old woman. "A girl like yourself will soon be marchin' at the head of a regiment of suitors. You might have 'em all if that's your wish, and . . ."

Suddenly Diarmid sprang to his feet and let out a yowl, and at almost the same moment there came a thump on the door. Then another, and another yet. Slow, measured knocks, as if the hand that sounded them belonged to an oak-limbed Druid stiff from centuries of sleep. Annie lowered the volume of the radio, crept along the darkened hall, and put her ear to the door. All she heard were branches scraping the stone wall. She peeked through the window beside the door, but whoever it was must have been sheltering under the lintel, out of sight. If it *was* anyone. Chances were it had been a bump in the night, a spirit blown by the storm from its usual haunts and flapping there a moment. To make certain, she cracked the door. An eye was staring back at her. Lightning bloomed, and she saw that the eye was set into a man's haggard, bearded face. She screamed and tried to close the door; but the man's weight was against it, and as his eye fluttered shut, he slumped forward, forcing Annie to give ground, and pitched onto the carpet. His rifle was pinned beneath him.

Annie bolted for the kitchen and grabbed a carving knife, expecting him to follow and attack her. When he did not, she peeked out into the hall. He hadn't moved. The skeleton stock of his rifle made her wonder if he wasn't the soldier she had seen earlier—yet he was no ghost. She flicked on the lights, knelt beside him, and rolled him over. Blood came away on her fingers, and there was a mire of it soaking his right trouserleg above the knee. Without further speculation as to who he was, she dragged him into her bedroom and hoisted him onto the bed. She slit his trousers, ripped them up the seam, and Whssht! the sight of a livid scar running the length of his calf stopped her breath a moment. The new wound was drilled straight through the flesh, with—thank God—no bones or arteries involved; after cleaning and dressing it, she took his rifle and hid it under some logs in the woodshed. Then she came back and sat in a chair by the bed and applied cold compresses to his brow until his tossing and turning had abated.

Annie kept watch over him late into the night, easing him when he cried out, rearranging the blankets when he tossed them off, and while he slept she studied the puzzle he was. He was in his thirties, olive-skinned, with black hair, heavy-lidded eyes, a cruel mouth, and a blade of a nose. Written everywhere on his features were the signs of great good humor and equally great sadness. A face like that, she thought, was as uncommon around these parts as a rose in winter. He might be an immigrant, but that didn't wash—something about him failed to blend with the notion of dark northern winters and bitter springs. She tucked a blanket around her legs, preparing to sleep. The puzzle would be solved come morning, and if he was legal, she'd have him off to the county hospital. If not . . . well, she'd deal with that as events dictated. The last thing that crossed her mind before she slept was an odd feeling of satisfaction, of pleasure, in knowing that the morning would provide a chore more fulfilling than the composition of a shopping list.

Be they strangers or lovers, there's an artful process that goes on between two bodies sleeping in the same room, a subtle transfer of energies, and who's to say how much effect this process had upon Annie and the soldier. One thing certain, though—Annie had not slept so soundly in years, and on waking, stretching out her arms to welcome the day, she felt her animal self uncoiling as it had long ago on waking after a night of love. The rain had diminished to a dripping from the eaves, dawn hung gray in the folds of the curtains. It was to be a clear day. She pushed off her blanket, and as she stretched again, she saw that the soldier was watching her. His eyes looked all black in the half-light.

"Quien eres?" he said. *"Donde estoy?"*

Annie had a queer, chill feeling in her chest. "Don't you speak English?" she asked, laying her hand on his brow, which was cool.

He stared at her, bewildered, as if he had not understood. But after a second, he said, "Where are the others? Where is this place?"

"There weren't any others," said Annie. "And you're in Gougane Barra, County Cork." Then, the chill feeling intensifying, she added, "Ireland."

"Ireland?" He said it "Ay-er-lan," repeating it—the way you'd try out a new word, mulling over its peculiar sound. "That can't be true." Suspicion hardened his features. "Who are you?"

"I'm Annie Kinsale." She went to the window and pulled back the curtains and pointed out to the green hills rising into a silver haze. "And that's Ireland. Where did you think you were?"

He couldn't take his eyes off the window. "I was in the mountains above the village of Todos Santos." He shook his head, as if to clear it of a fog. "There was a storm. The fighting was very bad, and the government troops were all around us. I was running, and it seemed I was running just ahead of the lightning bursts, that they were striking at my heels. Then I was running in a place without light, without sound . . . not running, exactly. My legs were moving, and yet I felt as if I were falling, whirling. I thought I'd been hit again. . . ."

He had started to tremble. Annie sat beside him and tried to steady him with a consoling touch. "My grandmother used to tell us that storms and wars were sister and brother," she said. "Children of the same chaos. She said they had a way of inter-actin', creatin' a magical moment between them in which things could pass from place to place in the wink of an eye. I'll wager that's what happened to you." He wasn't listening, his trembling had increased. "What country are you from?" she asked.

"Chile." The answer seemed to give him strength—he cleared his throat and squared his shoulders, ordering himself.

"Chile, is it?" she said, affecting sunniness. "Well, now!

That explains it further. Wasn't it an Irishman who freed your country from the Spanish? Bernardo O'Higgins. And wasn't it Chile that sent the first fuschias to Ireland? There's many a connection between the two lands, both physical and spiritual, and maybe the storm was part of that.''

"What year is it?'' he said wildly, lunging up, then wincing in pain and falling back.

"1984,'' said Annie.

He looked relieved. "I thought that might have changed as well.'' He inched up on the pillows. "Is there a newspaper, a radio? I must learn what has happened.''

"The local paper's more likely to have news of Cam Malloy's prize sow than of rebellion in Chile,'' said Annie. "And besides, though I'm glad to be of help to you, as long as you're here there's to be no talk of war in this house. I won't stand for it.''

A flush of anger suffused his face. "Is it that you find the idea of war repulsive, or is it just that you're hiding from the realities of the world behind your riches?''

"Riches! You call this shoebox of a cottage riches?''

"You have warmth, food, health. In Chile these are riches.''

"Well, here they're not, and I'm hidin' from nothin'! I've had a sufficiency of war in my life, and I'll not be takin' it into my bed!'' She blushed, realizing what she had intimated, and, angry at herself, she lashed out. "If you won't obey that simple rule, then get the hell out of my house!''

"Very well,'' he said stonily. "In any case, I must get back to my men.''

"Oh?'' said Annie. "And I suppose you'll be catchin' the next bus for guerrilla headquarters?''

He stared at her for a moment, dumbfounded, and then he burst into laughter. And Annie—never one to hold a grudge—joined in.

His name was Hugo Baltazar, and before becoming a soldier he had been a professor of comparative literature at the university in Santiago—thus his knowledge of English. Over the next two weeks as his wound mended, stormy, rainy weeks, he told Annie about his country; and she added each new detail to a picture she'd begun painting in her head. It was like one of those tourist maps with illustrations of parrots and golden beaches and cathedrals rearing up and dwarfing the little towns whose attractions they were—her version of Chile had so many attractions that it

was less a map than a collage of brilliant colors. Of course she
knew it was incomplete, that Chile was suffering a war the same
as Ireland, probably a worse war, and that those terrible images
might dwarf the ones she had pictured. But she liked thinking
of Hugo as hailing from a land full of fiestas and shade trees,
where an engraved and beaming sun rose out of a map-colored
sea, and the four winds had smiling faces. War did not suit him.
Not a man who carved flutes from twigs and sang and told stories about Indian ghosts and mysterious rites on Easter Island.
He was, she thought, a born Irishman. Perhaps there had been
some truth to that sauce she'd ladled about Ireland and Chile
having a spiritual connection.

Be that as it may, shaved and washed and dressed in Jake's
old clothes, he cut a fine figure. Now and again she would catch
herself looking at him, watching, say, the muscles bunching in
his jaw or his hair ruffling in the breeze; occasionally she would
find him looking back at her, and then she would blush and duck
her head and start peeling spuds or chopping lettuce or whatever
chore was at hand. She knew very well what was happening,
and even if she hadn't had the gift of seeing clear, she would
have known by a dozen different signs—the way they passed each
other in the hall, as stealthy as two cats on the prowl, being
careful not to entangle their tails; the way he jerked back his
hand after accidentally touching her, as if the prospect of touching her had been foremost on his mind; the way he tensed when
she reached in front of him to set down his dinner plate. Yet she
also knew that he was troubled by all he'd left behind, and one
evening, while she was still trying to figure out how she could
ease his mind, he brought up the subject on his own.

"Annie," he said, "I want to talk to you about . . . about
the disturbance in my country."

They were standing at the kitchen sink, her washing, him drying, and Annie set down a plate so hard upon the counter that
it split in two. "No!" she said. "I told you I won't have it!"

He balled up his towel and dropped it onto the broken plate.
"If we can't talk here," he said, "then we'll go outside." He
seized her by the arm, and, limping, fighting off her slaps, he
dragged her into the garden behind the cottage. There he let
loose of her arm, and she started to flounce back inside; but
before she had taken three steps, he said, "I love you, Annie."

She stopped dead in her tracks but did not turn to face him;
she could tell what was coming—it was spelled out in the droop-
ing stalks of the primroses, in the angles of a broken ivy trellis,

and in the stars that ignited cold and white like crystallized points of pure pain. "Do you?" she said. His hands fell on her hips, and they felt so heavy, they seemed to make her light, to drain away her strength. If he moved them, she would shatter.

"Yes," he said, "and I want to stay with you. But I can't. I have responsibilities I can't avoid. Friends who are suffering."

"Is it addicted you are to sufferin'?" Her anger became brighter and hotter with every word. "Is peace too stodgy a situation for your warlike soul?"

He tried to turn her, but she refused to budge. "I know you don't understand this kind of commitment," he said. "You haven't seen . . ."

"I've seen plenty, thank you very much! And one thing I've seen is that war changes nothin'. One dictator falls, and another pops right up."

"You can't stop trying," he said, "If you do, you risk losing your humanity."

She twisted free of his grasp and walked a few paces away. "How will you go?" she asked, her voice small and tight. "You've no money, and God knows I can't help. I'm barely scrapin' by."

He was silent a moment. "The other night during the squall, I had a feeling, a very strong feeling, that if the winds were blowing harder, if the lightning was striking down, I'd be able to walk out into it and find my way home. It sounds unreasonable, but it's as reasonable as my coming here." He moved up behind her and again put his hands on her hips. "You seem to have an understanding of these sorts of things. Do you think . . ."

"Yes, damn you!" She whirled around and pushed him away. "Go, if that's all you want of the world! Go, and good riddance to you!"

"Annie . . ."

"Leave me alone!"

"Please, Annie, I just want . . ."

"Will you for Jesus' sake quit tormentin' me!" Out of the corner of her eye, she watched him limp toward the door. She had an urge to call him back, but her temper got the best of her and she shouted at him instead. "All this time I thought I was givin' shelter to a man, and in truth I was just harborin' a Communist!"

"I should have known," he said angrily, pausing on the stoop, "I should have known you were the type to rationalize injustice, to cure a disease by sticking labels over the sores.'' He stepped inside and slammed the door.

Annie stood in the garden until the light in the guest room had been switched off and the moon—almost full—had risen over the roof of the cottage. She shivered a little with the night chill. She tried to hold everything inside her, to harden it into bitterness, but the bitterness caved in and she cried. The tears left cold, snaky tracks down her cheeks and blurred the sharp image of the moon—it seemed a weepy arch of moons was connecting her eyes and a distant point in the darkness beyond Bantry Bay. Finally she blew her nose and wiped her cheeks. There was no use in moping. Things were as they were, and the question was what to do about them. What, indeed?

She went into the cottage and leaned against the wall beside the door of the guest room; her fingers strayed to the top button of her blouse. ''Why not?'' she said to the empty hall. ''Better to know exactly what you're losin', if you're to lose it a'tall.'' In a matter of seconds her clothes were heaped on the carpet, and she was slipping through the door.

The room was ablaze with moonlight, so bright that she thought the arch of moons she'd seen must have been real, that they were beaming in from every angle. Hugo's head was a shadow on the pillow. He propped himself on an elbow, his breath sighing out. Annie came a step closer. She could feel the moonlight shining up her skin, and could see the shine of her skin reflected in his eyes, in all the stunned and stricken way he was staring at her; and she remembered a night twelve years before, how she'd stripped off her dress and gone dancing along the crest of a hill—a wild, slim girl taunting her first lover, Jake; and he'd stumbled after her, tripping over stones, afflicted with that same bedizened look. She could almost believe she was that same girl, the years peeled away by grace of the moonlight. She knelt upon the edge of the bed and stretched out her hand to him.

''If you're really leavin' on the storm,'' she said, ''we mustn't waste the calm weather.''

Magic—at least the contemporary Irish brand—does not consist of a pair of golden thimbles or a book of spells or secret brews or of anything so rigid and bound to a single set of principles. Mainly it consists of having an eye for the materials appropriate to the moment, having the talent to weave them together, and having the power to spark them, to channel their own natural powers into a symmetry that fuses opportunity and intent. Annie had all these qualities, and by five o'clock the next morning, she had all the materials as well—hair, a silver thread, a ruby pin-prick of her blood, and various other substances (which, for various reasons, are best left unmentioned). What she lacked, however, was the conviction that this was the proper course of action. Oh, she wanted Hugo right enough! Her senses were still stinging with him, and his smell was heavy on her skin. But her Christian upbringing was getting in the way. She wished now that her mother had let her develop her powers, that she had acquired a strong and helpful familiar rather than Diarmid—a fat old mouser with bad breath, a taste for porridge, and scarcely a flicker of animal cunning. She picked him up from the floor and gazed into his slitted yellow eyes. "What do you think, cat?" she said. "Will we have him, or should we let him fly?" Diarmid twisted his head to the side, trying to sniff the saucer that held the materials; he nudged it with his cheek, and the drop of blood slid down along the silver thread.

"Well," said Annie, deciding. "I imagine that's all the omen I'm likely to get."

She took the saucer and a lit candle and stole back into the guest room. Huge was asleep, his breathing deep and regular. She knelt upon the floor, held the candle above the saucer, and searched her mind for words that—though they didn't have to be particularly meaningful—would give the spell sonority. She sang them softly, each phrase stirring the candleflame.

"May all white birds and unicorns
Here find shelter from the storm,
May man's light strand and woman's dark
Knit together in a spark,
Singe their spirits, steam the flood,
And bind this moment in our blood."

She touched the flame to the materials. They burned separately at first—the hair crisping, the thread shriveling, the rest sizzling and smoking—and then a web of cold white light united them, flared briefly, and was sucked into the ashes. Annie smeared the ashes on her lips, rubbing them in until her mouth began to tingle. Hurriedly, before the tingle could subside, she slipped into the bed. Hugo was lying on his side, facing her, and she pressed herself against him; she rested her knee on his hip, reached down and guided him between her legs, fitting him to her. He mumbled, waking to the touch. She kissed him, mixing the tingling ashes with their saliva. And as his hands gripped her hard and he eased inside, their mouths still clamped together, she felt the charge go out of her.

In the morning Hugo told her he would stay. He seemed happy, yet at the same time confused and a bit depressed. To take his mind off the confusion, Annie suggested they go on a trip, a honeymoon of sorts. She'd borrow Eleanor Downey's car and they'd drive out into the country. She'd show him Cork. Still confused, he agreed.

For the first four days it was as if the Emerald Isle were intent on proving the accuracy of its nickname, flashing a different facet of its beauty around every bend in the road. Near Glengariff they saw what appeared at a distance to be a river of milk flowing down a dark green hill; and as they drew near, it turned into a scene equally as magical—a herd of sheep streaming over the hillside, with golden dogs barking, leaping, and men in bright sweaters shouting and running after. They picnicked in the Pass of Kimaneigh beneath steep, ivy-matted cliffs, the slopes thick with ferns and foxgloves and honeysuckle, and they listened to an old man tell a story about a skeleton that ran nightly through the pass, carrying a ball of yellow flame in its hand. They walked along mossy bridges and tossed pennies into the still rivers for luck; they bought an armload of crimson fuchsias and decorated the car with them to symbolize the union of their souls and blood; they made love all night in a country inn as quaint as a picture on a teacup, and in the morning they watched the sunrise stripe a nearby lake with heliotrope, rose, and silver—like the markings of an enormous tropical fish. But by the end of the fifth day, despite the beauty of Cork, despite their own beauty, Annie realized that she had been wrong to work the spell. No amount of sightseeing and lovemaking could diminish Hugo's confusion. That night, lying awake beside him, she listened to the fringe of his thoughts—there were screams in Spanish, anguished faces, bursts of gunfire, gouts of flame rising from the midst of jungles. Those thoughts were part of him, permanent, untouchable by magic. She understood that sooner or later, bound together in this way, all their brightness would fade, and she determined to break the spell. It would be better to lose love quickly, she thought, than to watch it linger and die.

Now the breaking of a spell is the sole constant of Irish magic. Every spell worked successfully—it's said—causes pain to the Devil (not the Christian Devil, but the old Celtic demon whose back was broken by Cuchulain, whose splintered backbone props up the Irish hills), and the only way to reverse the process is to take back the Devil's pain. All this requires is the will and the strength to bear it, and a knowledge of those places where His bones lie close to the skin of the earth. Annie was not afraid of pain. She'd borne Jake's death, and nothing could hurt her worse. And so, that same night, she left Hugo asleep in their hotel outside the town of Schuul, and climbed to the top of a hill overlooking Bantry Bay, a spot dominated by a standing stone—a head-high cylinder of moss-stained granite, tufted around by weeds and carved deep with both pagan signs and crosses.

The moon was just past full, wisped by clouds; its light made the grass underfoot and the surrounding hills look dead and gray. The sea was the color of old iron, and the wind and wave-sound combined in a single mournful rush. Nothing seemed alive. Even the distant lights of Schuul might have only been flecks of moonstruck mica on a rock face. Annie shed her clothing, her skin pebbled by the chill, and embraced the standing stone, crushing her breasts against the largest cross, pressing her hips to one of the pagan signs. The stone's coldness pervaded her, but nothing happened. After a while, she realized that she did not want anything to happen, that she lacked the will. Determined, she began to talk sweetly to the stone, teasing and charming it, building up inside her the weight of self-loathing and perversity that was needed in order to contact the Devil. She crawled over the stone, grinding her hips into it, licking it, tracing the deep seams of its carvings with her fingers as if it were a live thing and she was giving it pleasure. Then she felt a trembling in the earth, felt also an eerie lustful joy that was both hers and another's, and heard a keening note within her skull. It seemed that the pain and her scream were one substance, a white cry issuing from the rock below, a column of pale fire pouring through her, reducing her to a white frequency that shrilled along the crisped pathways of her nerves. She fell back onto the tussocky ground. Her limbs were quaking, and the muscles of her abdomen were writhing like serpents beneath the milky skin. She tasted blood in her mouth.

She lay there for a long time, debased, ashamed, foul with the act. Dawn paled the sea with a dingy yellow light. At last she put on her dress and went back into Schuul. She brought Hugo coffee and cakes, kissed him as if nothing were out of the ordinary, and told him that she wasn't feeling well, that maybe after breakfast they had better get along home.

* * *

It went unspoken between them that he was leaving. He knew she knew and vice-versa, so what was the point in talking? They made love sadly and spoke rarely and spent long hours staring at one object or another that they weren't really seeing at all. On the fourth night after their return, a mad black grandfather of a storm blew up off Bantry Bay, and Annie took shelter in her bedroom, lying on her back and gazing into nowhere. Every few seconds the walls were webbed with lightning flash and shadow; the porcelain vase on the bureau leaped forward from the dark like a plump little god garlanded with flowers, and evil energies winked in the facets of the crystal doorknob. It wasn't long, though, before she heard Hugo enter. He stood in the door, holding his rifle.

"I'm leaving," he said.

"Leave then." She turned away from him, wishing she was stone and trying to be so. "Mind you don't let out the cat."

"I can't part from you this way, Annie."

"Does that mean you'll stay if I keep up my sulkin'?"

"You know I can't." His footsteps came near. "For God's sake, Annie . . ."

"Is it for His sake you're leavin'? I thought it was to right the wrongs of the world that you were givin' me up." She sat up, tossing the hair from her eyes. "Don't expect me to be noble, to see you off down the garden path with a wave and a gentle tear. That's not the way I'm feelin'." She flung herself face down. "You'll be needin' all your concentration for the killin', so you'd do well to forget me. I'm startin' to forget you this very moment."

After a second, the door clicked—a vital, severing sound. She squeezed a handful of quilt hard as if she could make it cry out and lay motionless, heavy, full of dark thoughts. So this was to be her lot, was it? Growing old ungracefully in Gougane Barra, and, now that she'd wasted her one potent spell, settling for Tom O'Corran or some unsightly replica thereof, each night having the grand pleasure of watching his chin sink to meet his chest after a half dozen pints at Shorten's, and once a year—unless the weight of children was upon them—having a wild fling at the livestock fair in Killorglin. The storm lashed at the windows, raging, smearing the peaceful planes of her life with roaring light. God, what a fool she'd been to think she could shelter from it, not in fortresses or mine shafts and least of all in a rosebud cottage on a country lane. . . . Then the real meaning of that thought penetrated her, startling her so that she jumped up from the bed and went into the hall without—at first—having any idea where she was going. There was no shelter, no hiding. But there was a more profound kind of shelter in doing and sharing. It shamed her to be learning it at such a late date. She took a step toward the door and felt a surge of insecurity; but the bonds tying her to Gougane Barra had suddenly grown frail— they were ancient Irish bonds of habit and hopelessness, and she threw them off. She tore open the door and ran into the storm, with Diarmid streaking ahead of her.

Lightning was printing the world in negative, casting images of white electrified trees and palsied shrubs. Rain blinded her, thunder set her heart pounding. Where could he have gone? She spun in all directions, dizzy with the tumult. Then she spotted Diarmid prancing down the lane, his tail waving, as if the storm didn't exist in his universe. Shielding her eyes, she followed him. He turned off through a thicket, and Annie had to run to keep pace. Branches whipped her arms, eel-like strands of wet hair plastered to her cheeks, and she began to doubt Diarmid's instincts; but a few yards farther along she caught sight of Hugo standing on the slope of a hill, looking lost. A lightning flash showed his shocked face as she came stumbling up.

"What are you doing?" He grabbed her by the shoulders.

"I'm comin' with you!"

He shook his head and said something, but the words were drowned out by the thunder.

"What?"

"You don't know what it's like!" he yelled. "What'll you do there?"

"What am I doin' here? Nothin'!" She took his hand. "Come on!"

He pried her hand loose. "No!"

"All right! Be off with you! Or don't you know where to go?"

He didn't answer.

Another lightning burst lit the hillside, and Annie saw Diarmid perched on a stone farther up the slope. His tail was curled around his haunches, and he was licking a paw.

"This way!" she shouted, taking Hugo's hand and dragging him along.

Diarmid scampered off uphill. Beyond him, above the crest of the hill, the darkness was arched over by great forks of lightning that receded into the distance like the supports of an immense hallway. Shadows whirled through the air, briefly silhouetted by the flickering arches, and Annie saw that they were all bearing arms—rifles, pistols, knives. As she and Hugo drew near the crest, she felt the presence of these phantoms, the chill touch of their unreality, and it frightened her to think that she would become as insubstantial as they. But she kept walking. Ozone stung her nostrils, and the wind drove needles of rain into her cheeks. The darkness atop the hill now seemed to be flowing toward them, and though they were making a steady pace, they seemed to be moving faster, the toiling shapes of the bushes rushing past. She glanced at Hugo. His face was dissolving in a black medium; there were absences in his flesh—beneath his eyes, above his lip, in all the places where shadows might accumulate. And yet his hand was solid enough. He tightened his grip and pulled her around to face him.

"Are you sure?" he shouted. "Is this the right way?"

He didn't appear to notice anything out of the ordinary, and his dependence on her gave Annie confidence. She smiled and nodded. All the noise of the wind and rain and thunder were merging, resolving into a keening note that she heard inside her skull. The Devil's music. She wasn't surprised to learn that He was involved. She felt herself going dark, pressed thin and whirling by the union of two darknesses. Hugo took a step back, his face anxious.

"It's all right," she said, putting her lips close to his ear. "Like you told me—I've an understandin' for this sort of thing."

It was more than a year later in the dead of winter, a few weeks after the fall of the dictatorship in Chile—an event that had stirred barely a ripple on the still pond of Gougane Barra—when Eleanor Downey received a package from Annie Kinsale. There were exotic birds and Indian faces on the postage stamps, and inside was a letter, a newspaper clipping, and a vial of pinkish white powder. Eleanor read the clipping first. It was a sidebar to an article about the Chilean revolution, detailing the rash of minor upheavals that had afflicted the government and the military during the latter stages of the war—swindles disclosed, plots unmasked, infidelities revealed; two generals had been shot by their wives, and one of the wives—judged insane by the press—claimed to have been listening to a program of classical music on her radio, when suddenly she had heard instead her husband in intimate communion with his mistress. There were rumors of similar phenomena, all unsubstantiated. Eleanor laughed so hard that tears sprang to her eyes.

In the letter Annie said she was sorry to have run off without a word, but that she was happy with her marriage and work. Especially with her work—it was a joy to have a meaningful occupation. Things had improved immensely for her since leaving; even her powers were on the increase, what with the turmoil of war to stimulate them. And speaking of that, the one sight she wanted to see in Gougane Barra—aside from Eleanor, of course—was the expression on Tom O'Corran's face when he heard the news. If Eleanor would rub the powder on her eyelids and ears, and would read the pertinent parts of the letter to the boys at Shorten's, Annie would be able to see and hear all that transpired. Eleanor didn't waste a moment. She applied the powder and hurried through the snow to the pub, where she found Tom O'Corran, Henry Shorten, and old Matty gathered around a roaring fire and just lifting their first pints of the day.

"I thought she was dead," said Tom O'Corran after Eleanor had finished reading. His expression was that of a man who's swallowed something that didn't taste quite right.

"Chile!" said Henry Shorten. "She must have lost her wits to be runnin' off to a godforsaken place like that."

"True enough," said old Matty. "It's never the path of reason that leads you away from home, though . . ."

His voice trailed away to a mutter, and he stared off into the maltdark distance of his mug; Tom O'Corran sighed and lowered his head and scratched the back of his neck; Henry Shorten's eyes were misted and his Adam's apple worked; even Eleanor felt a bit gloomy, without knowing the reason why. It was a moment that comes often to Irishmen these days, when their souls understand what their minds will not—that Ireland is a poor, sad speck of greenery, pretty enough but losing its magic at a rapid rate, becoming a tourist map of unhaunted castles and mute stones and unhallowed darkness, lit only by the shining myths of its liars and the drunken glow of its poets.

"Well, she may be a fool, but still and all she's an Irish fool," said old Matty, recovering his spirits. He raised his glass, and the edges of his ears were made translucent and as red as fuchsias by the firelight behind them. "So here's to her!"

They all toasted her then, again and again, and before long the reminiscence was flowing. Hadn't she been a fine seamstress, and hadn't she had a grand touch with a tune, and couldn't you always count on her if you were a few pennies short of the necessary? And hadn't she been the prettiest flip of a girl in all of County Cork?

Halfway around the world, peering through the distanceless

pour of the magical moment, Annie laughed at the way they talked about her—as if she were casketed, covered up, and on the verge of being canonized. As if they never expected to see her again. But Annie expected otherwise. Once things were more stable in Chile, she planned to go storming again, this time to Belfast where she would take up her new vocation. She had a score to settle there. Her story was far from over, and the radios of the world had just begun to tell their tales.

Greek

Leigh Kennedy

MOST OF THE voices she heard murmured devotion.

Weeping and praying, a hundred voices chorused the one speaking a string of unhesitating syllables, flowing, without emphasis or inflection, a monotone chant.

Then, a change.

The background voices hushed to a whisper, listening to the voice of Apocalypse. The words were strange and difficult, but the voice was lyrical. Not praying, but revealing.

There were meanings behind the words—pauses, rising and falling of voice, but the story was buried by the hallelujahs of the Pentecostal Church.

Hannah turned the cassette player off. She dug through the papers and envelopes that cluttered her desk. "Uhm," she said, placing the tips of her fingers on her brow. "I took the tape and your term paper to Dr. Van Pelt in the linguistics department. He told me it was Greek, but he hasn't translated it yet." Apologetically, she looked at her student, who sat silently in the chair across from her. "I hated to tell him to hurry on it, you know?"

"Greek?" Candy said.

Hannah nodded. "Van Pelt says that this man probably knows the language fluently from the way it flows. Do you know anything about him?"

Candy considered. "Well, the preacher and everyone seemed pretty quiet whenever he started up. He sounded more like he was *saying* something than the others. When the preacher interpreted it, though, it was the same kind of thing he said for the other speakers. You know—God is watching and caring for us. Stuff like that.''

"What did the man do?"

Candy frowned. "Nothing. I mean, he just seemed like an old greaseball, anyway, you know?''

Hannah nodded. "Let me show you something.'' She went to her file cabinet and picked over the folders. She pulled out a newspaper clipping and handed it to Candy.

Candy read the clipping, which was an account from another city about an old black woman who seemed to have acquired the ability to speak Chinese, read ideograms, and had traded her few possessions for artwork, fabrics, Woolworth vases, that had a Chinese flavor. She had for years been living alone in the old family farm, living only off her garden, chopping her own firewood.

"That's weird," Candy said.

Hannah watched her face for a moment, hoping to see a spark of curiosity or connection indicating academic initiative. Candy looked at Hannah expectantly.

"Have you ever heard of xenoglossia?" Hannah asked, knowing well that one of the books she had supposedly read for her term paper had mentioned it, although briefly. In fact, the subject of glossolalia had to include the debate over whether the languages used were real or not. But then, Candy's term paper hadn't been much more than a definition of glossolalia and an explanation of her visit with a friend to the church.

"Xenoglossia," Candy repeated. "I think I saw it somewhere, but I don't remember . . ."

Hannah waited for Candy to do a little brain-wracking. She suppressed her whole stock of impatient feelings about students who no longer seemed to stretch their minds. They wanted everything told to them simply, then perhaps they would retain it. "What," Hannah said emphatically, "is an old man doing speaking ancient Greek in a Pentecostal Church? Where does an old woman alone on a farm acquire the Chinese language?"

Candy looked startled. "I don't know. Hmmm."

Hannah smiled. "It almost seems as though they could be the same kind of case, doesn't it?" In her teacher's voice, Hannah said, "I want you to think hard about how this could happen, perhaps in terms of environmental influences, unconscious influences, subliminal learning. Try to find out more about this man on your tape. Maybe he had Greek relatives . . . The old woman may have lived next door to a Chinese family when she was young and learned, then forgot, the language. The man may have a similar experience.''

Candy sat with attentive but unconvinced eyes. Hannah felt that she may as well tell her student that crossword puzzles were the key to knowledge.

"Well, okay," Hannah said. "I thought you should know about the man speaking Greek, in case you decide someday to borrow the work you've done on this paper for another term paper in the future."

"Thank you, Dr. Karel." Candy gathered her books in her arms, somehow not catching the long silk of her hair in them.

Hannah followed her to the door of her office, like a hostess, while Candy exited. "See you in class."

She read through another term paper, sitting on the bed, an afghan thrown over her shoulders, a cup of coffee on the nightstand. She sighed.

"What's the matter?" Ted asked.

"Nothing, really."

"You seem a little depressed or something."

She put her pen down and stared at the paper. "I'm too idealistic."

"Ah, burn-out," he said sympathetically. "And you're so young."

She laughed. "No, if I were burned out, I wouldn't feel this sad. I just feel that they don't seem to have much *umph*. I was so full of fire when I was an undergraduate. They don't even seem curious. They have no ideals, no heroes, no great aspirations—other than to make money . . . or have a good time."

"You're still full of fire," he said, putting his hand on her knee.

"I thought that the student who wrote the paper on speaking in tongues would be fascinated with the Greek, but it meant nothing to her. I suspected that any time she would ask me if I was going to give her a lower grade because she didn't match the others."

"It's probably always been like that, you just don't remember."

She looked at him, wanting to believe that it was true. He seemed to be able to stack up facts into orderly rows and give a convincing argument to any issue. But sometimes she mistrusted that, searching for the bridges that no one else had yet seen. Could it really be that students were deteriorating?

She shrugged. "Maybe," she said.

* * *

She paced in front of her classroom. "I just read an interesting article in the *Journal of Sociology.* I want you to think about this for awhile. There seems to be a decline of old, derelict poor living in the downtown areas of five major American cities. The facts were gathered in a similar way ten years ago and last year by the same researcher. He has presented his data thus." She drew a grid on the blackboard and filled in numbers, dates, and cities.

She looked at her students. Some seemed alert, some not. "I know that to do a proper assessment, you should read the article itself, and read other articles on the same subject. But, pretend you know a lot about it, and pretend that these facts are reliable—which they may be. Consider: is it possible that these are statistical facts and not real facts? If it is a reality, how has this come about?"

Silence. No eye contact.

Prodding them, she asked, "What happened when these people were young?"

They said nothing.

"What about those who lived through the Great Depression?"

"Maybe they're dying off," one of her more aggressive students said.

"Yes, maybe so." She calculated. "They would have been in their prime during the Depression. Do you think that would have been a significant factor in this population?"

No one disputed the idea. Most wrote it down in their notebooks.

Another student raised her hand. "What about social programs?"

"What do you think?" Hannah asked her class. "Do you mean social programs for those on the streets or for people before they get to this stage?"

"Maybe before," the girl murmured, not sure.

By the end of class time, they had discussed governmental budget cuts in social programs, the plight of the old and economically useless in an aggressively money-making society, changes in the family's role and self-expectations. Hannah had dragged every last observation out of them. She heard cynicism. They blandly discussed everything going down the drain, but not in the way that Hannah felt.

"Listen," she finally said. "It's nearly impossible to do

something that you think will be effective to make social changes. But if we all give up first, then what? We just have to chip away at it. It will *look* hopeless even if you work your whole life at it, but it *is* hopeless if no one cares. So, you," she tried not to, but did point at an especially flip student, "have to care or nothing of value will ever be done."

She let them go, and as they left, they all seemed to shrug past her.

Candy stopped by after class the same day that Dr. Van Pelt brought the translation by.

"I haven't had a chance to talk to that old man, you know," she said.

"Have you thought about it? What do you think?"

"I don't know," Candy said, wide-eyed. "I think he's a loon."

"That's not an answer," Hannah said. "Dr. Van Pelt said that he is reciting almost verbatim the *Iliad*." Hannah watched her student. "By Homer," she added.

"Boy, that's weird," Candy said.

"What church is it?" Hannah got out a pen and found a clear space on a file folder to write down the address. Candy paused, as if she realized that she was handing something over that was important, but couldn't manage the strength of carrying it. She gave the address and added a few landmarks. "I may drop by and talk to him myself," Hannah said.

"You can't just go barge in on him," Ted said to her over dinner.

"I'm not going to barge in on him, I'm just going to find him after church and talk to him."

"How are you going to find him?"

"I'll know. He sounds different from the rest of them."

"What do you think you're going to find out anyway?"

She shrugged. "I don't know. My Finnish grandmother used to tell me I was going to get in trouble all my life because I couldn't keep my nose out of other people's business. That's why I became a sociologist." She looked at him seriously. "Aren't you curious, too?"

He broke another roll from the basket. "I don't think it's going to be as exciting as *you* think. Besides, I agree with the Finns."

The church was not full of people but it brimmed with spirit. Hannah arrived late and hesitantly broke through that fullness into an empty space on a folding chair. The fluorescent light from ceiling panels shone harshly in the square room.

She was out of place, even though she had tucked her curly brown hair into a bun and wore the most conservative of her clothes. Her posture, expressions, and gestures marked her just as obviously as if she'd tied a gypsy scarf around her waist.

They sang and swayed, clapping in time. Some of the voices wailed, some were sweet, others profound. The preacher called out between clap-beats, "Love the Lord!" Bewildered babies cried. Hannah looked stiffly at the women's rounded shoulders and the men's shiny hair.

She put her hand in her canvas bag, feeling like a spy because of the small tape recorder hidden within. She fumbled with a hymnal, suspecting that she could hide her confusion by finding their song. All the while, she felt like a child again. The more enthusiastic they became, the more embarrassed Hannah was. Like being caught with a book that was trashy, or in clothes that were out-of-style but not defiantly so.

Maybe he's not even here, she thought. And it occurred to her that this could be a lot of discomfort for little reason. Ted was probably right. . . .

She didn't belong and every now and then a glance from someone reminded her. These fifty or sixty people probably knew each other well. She imagined them all turning at once to look at her, and in one big voice asking, "What are *you* doing here?" Or, running after her as an angry mob once they realized she was an intruder. Silly, she thought, these people are just worshipping God in their way. But she started to gather her things to go.

Then a sudden quiet bade her be still.

The preacher began to talk. His voice was pleading as he told of a man whose daughter had fallen dead only days after he'd denied God. Women wept as the preacher moved to and fro, retelling the anguish of the father. Men bowed their heads and worked their jaws.

Hannah was transfixed. She forgot herself and wondered at the effectiveness of his oration. Like a tidal force, he pulled his congregation back and forth with upturned palms full of accusing words. He pushed his prayer upon them, and drew prayers out as they began to murmur. Hannah could smell the heat rising out beyond their perfumed deodorants and after-shave. They were massive and weeping.

Someone moaned with a wide-open mouth, stood, stumbled forward, and then collapsed.

Hannah rose in her seat but kept herself from going forward. The man on the floor trembled and thrashed his head back and forth as he poured out single and double syllables. The preacher counterpointed. Someone begged for mercy. Someone else begged Jesus to come into her heart and her life. Others came staggering forward, pleading in sounds that she couldn't understand at all. Hannah felt oppressed by the God that they brought down through the roof and up through the dusty linoleum.

"N, ra kai egkos afeken, ekon d' emartanay fotos," he said.

Hannah jammed her fingers down on "play" and "record."

". . . pama shatama matama katoo shatami . . ." another said.

No, no where did he go? She stretched to see.

And then she saw him—wizened, looking like a reformed alcoholic in his lean raggedness. He gestured, telling his story.

Following him home, she was not subtle as she rolled and parked, every block—but then her subject was unsuspecting.

She watched him enter an old apartment building. Inside the dirty tiled foyer, she pondered before sixteen mailboxes. Eliminating the couples, the females, she was left with nine featureless names.

Of course, the first choice was wrong. She was still dazed from the intensity of the church and expected the young man at the door to conjure or chant at her. He leered instead.

"Uh, I'm looking for a friend of mine. From church. An older man."

"Oh," the young man said sourly, "you must mean number eight."

"Thank—" she said to the closing door.

She hurried down the hall. Through the lacquered door she heard his voice singing. Before she knocked, she flipped her tape cassette and turned the recorder on, then put it back in her purse.

The subject opened the door to her knock and Hannah was overcome at the realization of the man standing in his home.

"Hi," she said. "My name is Hannah Karel."

"Hullo?" His eyes were curious and thorough.

"I just came from the church. May I come in and talk to you?" She sounded unconvincing even to herself. "I want to talk about . . . speaking in tongues."

"Yes. Lord love you, come in."

It didn't fit. Hannah was disconcerted by his manner—a gentle-voiced alkie. But it wasn't fair to judge by his appearance. The room didn't fit either. Sketches and paintings of soldiers with spears and arrows, landscapes of rocky shores hung on the walls, most pinned with tacks. Ketchup, salt, and pepper had to share the small table with pencils, acrylics, and rags. A straight-backed chair stood by the window, which without a curtain allowed flat light to brighten the room. The furniture was broken and mean, but the strange art gave it a garret feel.

"Did you do all these?" she asked, seeing another portrait behind her. Though his hand was naive, Hannah saw power.

"Yeah. I just took up painting a few years ago. Would you like some orange soda?"

"Yes, thank you."

"Did you see my exhibition at the church last month?"

"Oh, no, I missed that," Hannah said uncomfortably.

He had gone into another room, which Hannah suspected was a small kitchen. Water rushed; she heard metal clinking glass, a gurgle of liquid.

"How long have you been painting?" she said.

He came back into the room and gave her a glass, and sat down in the chair by the window. Hannah wished she had brought her camera—she could see the black and white portrait with harsh light on half his face, all pits, furrows, and oil, defined at the border of sun, then the night side of grays. She liked the sound of his voice, his big clumsy-looking hands.

"I was a drinker, you see," he said. "I thought of nothin' but the bottle and how to get more when I was out. How to get more when I had enough. And one night, God came to me. He told me—this is true and I'm not afraid to say it—He told me that He was going to give me spirit because I was empty. And I began to speak . . ." He closed his eyes.

"Speak in Greek."

"Greek?" he said.

Hannah watched him.

". . . the words that God gave me to worship Him. And he gave me dreams to go with the sounds."

"But where did you learn Greek?" she asked.

"I don't know Greek. I don't know what you're talking about." He seemed puzzled. He sipped at his soda. "I love God and I love my dreams. That's why I began to paint. It was about five years ago now. I had to . . . to *do* something. Something to show how I see."

Hannah looked around at the paintings and sketches. She looked at the portrait of the woman, whose ringlets were dark on her forehead. The stark landscapes, the costumes he dressed his subjects in . . .

"What does '*aspairontos*' mean?" Hannah asked.

"What?" He leaned forward and wrinkled his nose.

" '*Aspairontos.* ' "

Again, he leaned forward, but this time his hands fell between his spread knees as if he'd just dropped something unimportant. "The words don't mean nothin', miss, between you and me, except they are the words that come to me. I see things when I say them. But they're just words."

Hannah nodded. She didn't doubt his belief. "Did you know you're speaking ancient Greek?"

He stared at her. "You're not really from the church at all, are you? I thought you'd come to talk about the Lord and pray with me."

"I'm a sociology professor. I was curious about where you learned Greek and why you recite it in the church as if you were speaking in tongues."

He looked away from her into the flat light out the window and was still. "No one else would listen and I have to say the words to see the story. Everyone else thought I was just crazy."

"The story?"

"The story in my mind."

But he would say no more about it.

Hannah sat in the kitchen with Dr. Van Pelt, his wife and their year-and-a-half-old, who clung to his mother's fingers as he sat on her knee.

"Well, it's definitely Homer, too," Van Pelt said, moving one piece of paper over another and back again. Sometimes he lifted a paper and peeked under it as if it were a young woman's skirt. "But not all of it. This isn't in place, at least, and I don't remember it in the work." He read: " 'The mind of man is dying, even their dreams have no substance.' "

Hannah sighed. "Trouble is, I really believe that he doesn't know what he's saying. Maybe his Jungian archetypes are coming forward."

"Come on, Dr. Karel," Van Pelt said. He gave her the look probably reserved for students who beg off exams. "You don't believe that, do you? Even with the human linguistic apparatus being an inherent part of our neurological structure, one must learn the ingredients—the vocabulary—at the very least.''

Hannah shrugged. "I don't know. Maybe it *is* God.''

Van Pelt and his wife exchanged glances. The baby said something like "lay-chay'' and reached for his bottle. "I doubt that,'' Van Pelt said.

"I was kidding,'' Hannah said defensively. "But imagine if Homer was a prophet and what's the difference between the *Iliad* and the Bible . . .''

"It's obvious you lack theological background, Dr. Karel,'' he said.

He was not a man that could see another side even for the sake of argument. Hannah had gotten so used to egging her students on to brainstorm a question that she'd forgotten the wall that learning could build around some academic individuals. "Well, what about random duplication of sound?'' she asked. "Just coincidentally, your interpretation of his sound matches closely . . .''

She stopped speaking as Van Pelt shook his head. He pointed to the pages of syllables garnished with dots, double dots, upsidedown e's, and vowels jammed together.

"I have trained for years,'' he said, then stopped, looking at her indulgently. He shook his head. "He's just lying.''

Hannah stared at the papers.

Why did she believe the old man more than Van Pelt and his years of education and research? Obviously, the professor was right.

Obviously.

"Thank you so much for your time, Dr. Van Pelt. I really do appreciate it. I'm sure it's probably a case of cryptomnesia. As soon as I find out his learning source, I'll let you know.''

Van Pelt smiled. His wife smiled, too. The baby babbled something. "I would be interested, for sure,'' Van Pelt said. "Keep in touch about it.''

Candy didn't come into her office. She stood in the doorway, her eyes restlessly glancing back into either direction of the hallways.

"I went to his hometown,'' Hannah said, rising to meet her student, since the student wouldn't come to her. "I traced his entire life history, talked to his psychologist at the veteran's hospital. I met his sister. I even went back and talked to the minister at that church, which was a difficult interview to say the least.

Nothing. No Greek neighbors, no leads that anyone knows of. He never did it before a few years ago. Nothing.''

Candy nodded.

"What do you think?'' Hannah asked her.

"Gee, I don't know.''

Candy looked exhausted somehow. She was probably trying to do too much. Remembering her undergraduate days of classes, boyfriends, and part-time work, Hannah felt a sudden sympathy. "Come on in, Candy,'' Hannah said. "Let's try to think of another approach.''

Candy hesitated. "Well, I really gotta go, Dr. Karel. I have to study.''

Hannah let her hands fall. "Are you all right? You look tired.''

Candy was mute for a moment, then looked at Hannah with sad, sad eyes. "I've been having these really weird dreams lately.'' Her chin fluttered. "They're so *real*. They're like a movie.'' She waited a long moment then burst into tears. "My mother thinks I'm crazy!''

Hannah shut her office door and listened to Candy's dream of living on a steep mountains, spinning raw wool that coated her hands with lanolin, and waiting for the peacock-colorful warriors to come home. Her mother told her she must be asleep; Candy felt she was awake.

But her mother would only put her hands over her ears and weep in alarm when Candy chanted all that gibberish.

She had always been comfortable on these streets where people lived out of garbage cans, used the sidewalks for their beds and urinals, lay their heads on bundles of newspapers at night.

She had been the kind of child that felt "missions.'' Her mother caught her carrying canned goods and blankets out into the suburban streets at night, believing that the poor children that Dickens had revealed to her were huddling in doorways, waiting for the good-hearted soul. She continued that into college, when she could be found serving up turkey and dressing to the homeless before going home to her own family. Even still, she sometimes resented the researching, the preparation for classes, all the peripheral things to the purpose of her life.

Even the old men who leered without shame, she pardoned—not excused—and remained tolerant of the greasy old women, carrying their load of tattered shopping bags from the best uptown department stores. Even through the years of studying social problems, structures, and conditions that lead to the rise, fall, or stasis in the lives around her, she had never let people elude her.

She came off a corner in a dawn chill, and saw an old woman across the street wearing several layers of clothing. The woman stood near the corrugated trash barrel, separating strips of greasy paper bags and torn cloth into piles.

The old woman muttered.

No. Not muttered. Sang. In a raspy old voice without any rhythm, she sang a phrase, paused with effort in her work, then sang again.

Hannah stood beside her and listened.

She knew the words, knew the tale that the old woman sang. As sure as any memory of her childhood, she remembered her Finnish grandmother reading the *Kalevala*.

"Siina kukkuos, kakonen, hekyttele, hietarinta, hiloa hoperinta, tinarinta, riukuttele!"

Hannah remembered the people of her grandmother's tales— Ukko swinging his hammer, wearing a skirt of fire and blue stockings. Aarni, guarding hidden treasures. Good deeds and bad done by colorful people who lived in a ripe land . . .

> Mastered by desire impulsive
> By a night's inward urging.
> I am ready now for singing.
> Ready to begin the chanting
> Of our nation's ancient folk-song
> Handed down from by-gone ages . . .

She looked around. The sun was a blazing red on the edge of a cobalt sky. Birds sang on blossoming trees. Down the street, a man played a flute. Others listened, their faces alive, alert, curious.

Hannah saw a grimy old man peer longingly from a dingy doorway. She turned back to the old woman poking through the trash. "Do you speak Finnish?" she asked in Finnish.

"Wha'?" the old woman said.

Hannah waited impatiently for her call to go through a maze of switchboards and secretaries in a university across the continent before she heard the good-natured voice.

"Dr. Taylor, my name is Hannah Karel. I wrote you a letter, but I decided that I really couldn't wait to talk to you. Look,

I've been downtown. Your article in the journal is wrong. There are just as many derelicts, aren't there?''

The voice laughed. ''Maybe in your downtown, but since I don't know where you are . . .''

''No, what I mean is—your article was deliberately wrong, wasn't it? To make us look?''

''So you've seen?''

''Yes.'' Hannah moved things on her desk with shaking hands. ''What do we do?''

''Enjoy it, I guess.''

Van Pelt shook his head. ''Someone once found a fountain pen embedded in sedimentary rock side-by-side with fossils from the Pre-Cambrian. There could be speculation that Martians dropped it during a tour in one million B.C. But there was an explanation.''

Hannah listened to his weary voice. He looked tired and empty to her. ''Yes,'' she said gently. ''But that doesn't mean nothing happened. An explanation doesn't wipe out the event. And to perceive the event, sometimes you need imagination.''

''I don't understand what you're getting at.''

''I'm sorry you don't,'' she said. As she looked at him, she had a feeling that, where in his brain he'd swept out magic and curiosity, now seeped ever so slowly, something old but bright.

A Surfeit of
Melancholic Humours

Sharon N. Farber

Letter; Wm Praisgode, M.D. of London, to Dr Tho: Sydnam
19 August, 1665

*Dear Sir; Never wold I reproach your Leaveing. You have
the Ladies and Children to protect and your Patients were
left before you. So Pitiefull is the Devastation of our Metropolis. Of this Weeke last did perish 5,319 Soules of which
3,880 were of Plague, acc. to the Weekely Bills. Any Distemperature is feared as Pest, and the Victim foresaken. Yes-
tereve was I summoned to Silver Streete to see a Man they
did wish to shut up with all his Householde. Seeing he had
rather the Dropsy, I took 3 oz. of Bloud, and he was much
relieved. Fair Nonsense is to be heard. Plague is, they say, a
Punishment, even as our Defeates with Holland, and they
hearken to the Omen of the Comet of Last Yeere. Our Friend
Mr Halley wold not term that a Portent, but he is fled as
well. You knowe me a Man of Science, not Superstition. The
Infection results of Miasmas from the Foetid Bowels of the
Earth and the Conjunctions of divers Starres and from
Odours of Carrion. Though the Dogges and Cattes have
been killed by Order of the Lord Mayor so that the Rattes
might be expected to Flourish, still do the Rattes die in great
Multitude, from the corrupt and poysonous Vapours. The
People are frighted and have turned against Jewes and
Quacks and Forraigners, saying they spread Pestilence. . . .*

WILLIAM PRAISEGOOD WALKED along Cheapside, past the fine
Tudor row of the Goldsmiths Guild, now closed and empty.
Houses were boarded up, deserted, or else had a red cross and

Lord Have Mercy Upon Us painted on the padlocked door, and watchmen without. Refuse lined the street, stopping up the gutters, so that the odor reminded Praisegood of the laystalls outside the city limits. The entire world seemed quiet, except for the screams of the ill and the lamentations of the healthy.

The doctor saw another figure approaching on the empty street, wearing a long-nosed bird mask, and carrying the gold-headed cane of the medical profession. The man crossed over to avoid a rat-gnawed corpse, then noticed Praisegood.

"Will?" called the birdman.

Praisegood halted some paces from his colleague. "Aye."

"Will—'tis I, George Thomson. What are you at, standing here with no mask or posie to half the effluvia?"

"What does it signify, George? Our physic is bootless."

The other studied Praisegood's ungroomed wig, his lined young eyes, his dejected stance, then backed away.

Praisegood gave a hollow laugh. "Fear me not, George. My melancholy is an old companion, not a symptom of the Pest." He spread his arms. "I am free of botch and token. But I cannot free my mind of the words of de Chauliac. 'Charity is Dead and Hope Destroyed.' "

" 'Sblood, Will, I cannot stand for this. There are few enough doctors left. You're needed! Look to your health. Send to me, friend—I shall give you of my own lozenges and preventative liquor."

Praisegood held out a reassuring hand. " 'Tis merely that my humors are imbalanced. I will bleed myself."

"Nay, you'll diminish your parts. Eat temperately, sleep well, and wear a powdered toad next your skin—my friend Sharkey has it so." He looked as if about to leave, then paused again.

"Will, I have a mind to anatomize a victim, that we may see wherein the Pest sits—in the organs, in the similar parts, whether it stops up the bile or inflames the dura. . . . Have you interest?"

"Aye!"

"Good; your friend Sydenham has not totally corrupted you. Now I must be off."

They parted, Praisegood headed east, walking aimlessly. Grass grew between cobblestones that had been worn smooth by coaches and porters, beggars and balladsingers. The setting sun cast a red pall upon the sky, reminding the wanderer of blood pooling under the skin of the doomed and dying.

"The Hand of God is upon us!" cried a voice. Praisegood

looked up to see a madman, wearing only breeches. "A judgement, a visitation!" He approached the doctor, arms outstretched, a fevered glint to his eyes.

"Keep back," Praisegood said, holding up his cane.

"Repent. Own your sins!" the man continued.

Praisegood spun about and fled, the delirious man close behind, calling out endearing words. Turning into a lane, Praisegood ran headlong into a link. The torchman pushed him aside, cursing, and his fellow took Praisegood and pulled him to his feet beside the deadcart. They held the torch before his face. "What do . . ."

Their mare tossed up her head and snorted. They all turned to see the madman run forward, ignoring Praisegood, and leap into the deadcart. He lay atop the piled bodies and crossed his arms over his chest.

"Now am I bestowed aright."

The driver rose from a body he had been stripping of its valuables. "Get off," he commanded, grabbing the man by the feet and tossing him onto the stones.

"But see my tokens. I am dead," complained the fallen man. He pointed to the blackened, swollen glands in one armpit.

"Dead soon, I'll warrant, but too lively yet for our lot," a link said.

The driver stroked his chin. " 'ee may follow us, lad, so when 'ee falls, we'll be right by and take 'ee to the pit." They tossed the naked body from the street into the cart.

Praisegood watched them go, the laden cart with the fevered madman stumbling behind. One of the links was ringing a bell, and the driver called, "Bring out your dead." They rounded the corner.

The doctor looked about. He was almost to Houndsditch. "Fool," he muttered. "Courting death as a man courts a maid."

He found an open tippling house near Aldgate. The tavern's former name was not known to him, but a freshly painted sign read *Deaths Arms*. There was a bright portrait of the patron, a crudely-drawn skeleton bearing an arrow and an hourglass. "Too many ribs," Praisegood muttered, and went in.

The tavern seemed as noisy and crowded as it might have been before the plague. It was filled with unemployed journeymen, ropemakers, seamen, porters, and bawdy women.

Praisegood paid for a mug of ale and found a seat, laying his handkerchief over the gilt canehead to preserve his anonymity. A large man was dominating the conversation, loudly mocking both the dead and the mourning survivors. Many of the drinkers had found employment as watchmen of quarantined houses or as plague nurses, and were openly bragging of the mischief they caused the captive families under their care.

A strumpet sat beside Praisegood. "Come with me, my gallant. I've the French disease."

He gazed at her through narrowed eyes.

"Ever'one knows pox keeps off the plague. Else why should we nuns still live and the schoolmaids not?" Finding no response, she put out a hand. "The pox lasts but a while, and 'tis easy cured by quicksilver from some quacksalver."

"Begone," Praisegood snapped, glaring until she complied. If only life were as simple as the woman seemed to find it, he mused. Paracelsus wrote that a particular remedy exists for every disease, even as mercury arrests the pox that beset the shepherd Syphilis. If Praisegood were a Paracelsan, he would at that moment be in an alchemical laboratory, searching hopefully for a specific cure for the plague. But while Praisegood admired Paracelsus' other views—that a physician should be ascetic, should travel widely, scorn money, and treat the poor for free—he doubted the existence of Specificks.

He looked up as a man came down the stairs, pressing through the crowd towards the door. The ruffian moved to block the path, crying, "But here's the real cause of misery." All were silent in anticipation. "Foreigners. Belike 'tis they as brought the plague."

"Forsooth, can one nation call down the wrath of God on another?" the man answered with a quiet voice, accented in some way unfamiliar to Praisegood. "More likely 'twas the virtues I see displayed here, than any intercession of mine own."

Impressed by the foreigner's calm manner and neat appearance, Praisegood stood for a better view. The man had deep black hair, but a complexion pale as parchment, his lips a dusky hue. He was dressed in the old-fashioned way, with doublet and long coat; all his clothes were gray or black.

"It an't right," the big ruffian called. "That honest Englishmen turn blue and die, while Frogs go unmolested."

He swung a massive fist. The small foreigner caught it, closing his hand about the other's. Praisegood heard a bone crack. The large man fell, shrieking. The others moved closer.

Praisegood banged his cane upon the floor. "Stay! Let this gentleman pass or, I swear't, thy friend shall be denied physic." They paused. "No physician nor chirurgeon nor the humblest

apothecary's prentice will give him aid, when I have published
his wickedness. But allow this fellow to pass, and I shall bind
up the hand myself.''

The black-clad man left the tavern, walking proud as a king
to his coronation. He stopped at the door, momentarily fixed
Praisegood with his eye, and was gone.

25 August

*Not an House in Twenty is unmarked by Plague, nor a
Merchant in an Hundred still at Businesse. You would be
surprist to see the River empty as it were with Ice, but for
Boates with Corn. I have heard even the Curator of the
College of Physitians is fled, and Thieves have made off with
the Strongchest and Silver. Dr Burnet as I told you afore,
Friend Thomas, took sick and declared it; and shut himself
up in his House, which was very Handsome of him. After
some Months, thinking himself well, he resumed Practise.
But Burnet took Feaver againe and has perished. I have
heard Laughter that a Doctor should die—of his own
Medicaments they say. Now do such a Multitude lie dead
that they may no longer be buried twixt Sun-set and Dawne,
and the Waggons are always full.*

William Praisegood walked homeward, his mind populating
the desolation with accusing ghosts. "You're a doctor," they
moaned. "What did you do for us?"

"I tried to help," his spirit rejoined. "I cannot stay the plague,
but still there are the usual patients. . . ."

"You cure them but to die another death," the ghostly voices
replied.

He thought of his patient Mistress Blackwood. Her two infant
daughters, Mrs. Sally and Mrs. Alice, had been sent to stay with
their uncle soon before that entire household fell to plague. The
news of her children's deaths had sent Mrs. Blackwood into labor early, going two days without the aid of a midwife, for all
those women were more lucratively employed as plague nurses
and searchers of the dead.

When Praisegood had at last been summoned he had been
forced to use the experimental forceps, a secret gift from his
professor at Leiden. The baby was large and healthy enough,
but Mrs. Blackwood had gradually lapsed into a hectic fever,
which was unrelieved by purging or emetics. Today the doctor
had called to find the babe suckling at a dead breast, and the

father hysterical with grief. He had bled the husband two ounces, but the infant was beyond help—there were no wet nurses to be found.

A year ago this tragedy might have brought tears to Praisegood's eyes. Now he only shrugged it off, numbed to any further horrors, like a sheaf in the harvest.

The low evening sun and the shadows of overhanging houses turned the streets as dark as night, few windows glowing to light the way. As Praisegood began to enter one shrouded lane, an old woman hailed him from the shadows.

"Stay, sir, an' you value your life."

"How, goodwife?" He could see now that she carried the white wand of an examiner of the dead.

"A pestilent lunatic," she replied, "lying in wait by the bakehouse."

"Most likely mad from pain," Praisegood said. "Let me come on him cautiously and give my elixir of poppy."

"Sich will not be soothed," the old woman cackled. "He will salute ye and by his kisses give release. Already he hath greeted his kin and friends until none be unmarked. But Deacon hath sent for his brothers who are already with token, and they shall make him fast."

Praisegood thanked her and hurried on in another direction, passing his parish church. Part of the yard had become a communal burying ground, a grave that had at first seemed ready to receive all the parishioners (save the parson, who had gone to the country as early as June). Surprised, the doctor noted that where that grave had been, now stood a hillock, and a new pit had been dug not far off. Ringed with warning candles, it gaped open like a lanced impostume, three men's height by four.

"Prepared to accept us all," Praisegood whispered.

A deadcart arrived. The bearer, beating his horse with a red staff, backed the cart up to the rim of the pit and discharged its load. Watching aghast, Praisegood saw the bodies tumbling down. The bearer appraised him.

"A cloak?" he asked.

"Pardon?"

"Buy a cloak, sir? Fine velvet for a gentleman," and he flourished the article in question.

"Knowest thou not, such articles carry plague? I've seen it oft."

"Dead men's clothes, their stinking carcasses, the air itself, matters not," the bearer shrugged. "Make the most of the breath you've left."

"Help!"

Praisegood leapt away from the cart. "How—"

The thin cry came again from the grave. "Save me. Is't there?"

The bearer snarled. "Another raving fool, b'God, masquerading as my stock." Noticing Praisegood's pallor, he laughed rudely. "Or a drunk belike, or oft-times a strick man thinks to save us the bother of burial and does it hisself." He took up a long shepherd's staff and walked to the pit's edge, holding out a candle.

"Bless you," the voice called.

"Take hold—Nay!" The bearer sprang back, making an old-wife's signal against the evil eye.

"Ar't ill?" asked Praisegood.

"The dead walk," whispered the man.

Praisegood took the candle from his trembling fingers. "No, 'tis as thou said'st. Some hapless victim entrapped in the ditch. . . ."

Wild eyes turned on him. "I saw him carried out from the inn, white as a virgin's shroud, cold as snow. When I took the buttons of his waistcoat, I cut him accidental—no sound or move did he make. No deader man have e'er I seen! The Warlock of Houndsditch . . ."

"For love of God . . ." came the voice. The bearer turned and fled. Praisegood looked uneasily at the gaping grave.

"Ha," he thought. "What would Tom say? 'Ghasties and spirits, Will? This is 1665!' " Taking a deep breath, he strode to the side of the pit and held up the candle.

"Who calls? Where are you?"

"Here," the voice quavered. Praisegood looked down into the noisome pit. The floor was a solid layer of dead bodies, naked or clothed or shrouded, each holding some haphazard position, the cadavers heaped at the edge where the cart had dumped its contents. Like a still pond they lay, with one half-covered man making feeble movements that set the other bodies quivering, ripples spreading along pale dead limbs. The man lifted up his head like a swimmer gasping for breath, and Praisegood recognized the foreigner from the Death's Arms tavern.

He lowered the shepherd's crook. "Catch hold." The man took the end. Footsteps sounded on the stones as the bearer returned with the deacon and another man.

"See?"

The deacon stood by Praisegood. "Thou'st been at the spirits, not seeing them, Alf." He nodded to the doctor. "You'll never land him alone." All together, they took hold of the staff and hauled up the man, until he lay at their feet gasping like a fish. Losing interest, the others left him with Praisegood.

Praisegood gazed after them. He had no wish to stay with a man so lately come from a plague-ridden grave.

"Will you leave me as well?" the foreigner asked. "I have not the plague."

"Why were you in the pit?"

"I have a—a sickness, that I sleep so deep I seem dead. The innkeeper must have come in against my orders." His voice had a sincere quality that raised Praisegood's pity.

"Shall I help you back to your inn?"

He shook his head. "No doubt they've stolen my goods, and would murther me before they'd welcome me."

"I can't leave you here." Praisegood lifted the man to his feet. He supported him along the darkened streets, the man holding up his hands to cover his eyes against the occasional glimpse of sunlight. They arrived at Praisegood's door to find a number of patients waiting. Seeing the doctor half-carrying a stumbling man in black, they backed away.

"Too much brandy," Praisegood cried heartily. "Here, lad, help me get him to bed." They deposited the man on Praisegood's own cot.

The apartment was dark and musty, the windows having been closed up against effluvia. Praisegood lit some candles and consulted with his patients, allaying their fears and ordering up medications. As he saw the last patient, a plethoric asthmatic widow, he heard some stirring in the bedcloset. He bled the woman from her right forearm, bound up the wound, and escorted her downstairs, barring the door behind her. It was deep night.

"Now for my final patient," he called as he came back up the stairs. "Come forth. . . ." He stopped.

The dark-clad man stood in the midst of Praisegood's room. His face flickered black and yellow in the dancing candlelight. His eyes were wide and red, and he held the bowl that had caught the old woman's blood.

The bowl was empty, and his lips were red.

"Madman," Praisegood rasped, backing to the hearth and taking up a fire iron. All was silent, except for the distant sound of wheels on stone, and a lone wavering cry of "Bring out your dead."

The man stirred, putting down the bowl. He took one step forward. Praisegood held the iron between them, like a sword.

"It is a cure recommended by the doctors of Prague," the stranger said softly. "I must apologize for not asking permission. . . ."

"It is barbaric."

The man continued soothingly. "I had planned to consult English physicians, but found plague here and was trapped. . . ."

"We'd never prescribe human blood," Praisegood said, trusting the man in black, though he could not say why. He put down the iron. "Tell me your symptoms."

"But you're exhausted—"

Praisegood smiled. "The doctor's health is unimportant. But you're right. Plague has made me busy as a bee in a rose patch, where before I had so few patients as to crave charity myself."

"If I might stay the night . . . I would sit up a while and read your texts."

Praisegood paused, then said, "As you will." He could not cast the man out onto a curfewed street inhabited solely by the dead.

The stranger continued, "My disease is called a 'Cyclic Catalepsis,' or by some a 'Coma.' I sleep only by day, and look as a dead man. You will find no sign of breath, not even with the most cunning mirror. My pulse is so faint as to be immaterial, and I will feel frigid and stiff. But see—I am always cold." He held out his hand.

Praisegood grasped it. "I am William Praisegood, Doctor of Medicine."

"Guido Lupicinus. Your name is well-chosen, Doctor."

Praisegood went to his bed, but caution demanded he bolt the door.

Upon rising the next morning he found Lupicinus in a chair, Culpeper's translation of *Pharmacopoeia Londinensis* open upon his lap. The doctor tried to take away the book, but the sleeping man's fingers were frozen about it. He was indeed cold, without movement, pulse, or breath. Praisegood's first temptation was to declare the body to the parish searcher, but the signs were exactly as Lupicinus had described them.

"I give you until this evening to wake," he muttered.

He walked to Smithfield, the heat already oppressive despite the day's youth. St. Bartholomew's Hospital was a hive of activity, but Praisegood found time to query the apothecary Frances Bernard on sleeping sickness.

"Never heard tell of it," Bernard said. "Ask Gray," and they hailed Thomas Gray, the chief of Barts' volunteer physicians.

"Sleep as if dead? I'll tell you what it is, Will. You and I have not had a virtuous full night abed since May. Perhaps Morpheus, god of sleep, has given our surpluse to your patient."

"Aye, 'twould be that," Praisegood grinned, and forgot the subject as he worked. While preparing to leave, he was summoned to see a young man with plague, whose buboes were firm and full of pus.

The surgeon attending him said, "An' we bring it out, he may live."

Nodding, Praisegood sent a messenger to tell his own patients he would be late, and he and the surgeon began the task of lancing the abscesses. The young patient screamed, fainted more than once, and lost much blood, but Praisegood went home pleased that he had rescued one man from a pestilential death.

His home was empty, his guest gone. Praisegood found a meat pasty and some ale laid out for him. "Not so dead after all," he said, and reread a favorite section of Burton while he ate. There was a knock at the door.

Lupicinus entered, bearing a heavy trunk. Praisegood helped him set it down. "You walk silently."

"A skill God has given me." He sat upon the trunk. "I went back to the tavern. They were displeased to see me. As I'd thought, they'd robbed me. Had I not already seemed dead, they would have split my skull as I slept." He grinned. "You see, I persuaded them to give me fair return."

Seeing Praisegood's guarded expression, he hastened, "Fear me not. I've been a warrior in my time, but have never harmed a benefactor, or a friend. Except once, of need, in Egypt when my comrade took a fever . . ."

"Egypt? You've been there?"

Lupicinus smiled, and began a tale of that far country. Despite his youthful appearance he was well traveled, with many stories that were only mildly embroidered, not the fantastic tapestries woven by those who travel only in wishes and in books.

The waning summer was as pleasant as it could be, with the heat and the plague and the record death tolls listed in the weekly Bills of Mortality. Each morning Praisegood went to Barts, leaving a dead man in his chair. Each night he saw his patients, while Guido Lupicinus either went out walking or else helped

with the physic. Then the men would talk of exotic lands and
better times.

The dropsical widow came again, barely able to labor up the
steps. Her son said, "She cannot lie to bed, but wakes gasping
for breath."

Praisegood shook his head. " 'Tis an ill disease. I must bleed
her now, to relieve her, but cannot revive the humors sufficient
to cure her."

"I'll get the lancet," Guido offered, and he held the bowl as
the blood rushed in, an eager cast to his face.

"See how thin and pale the blood is," said Praisegood. "You
must give her dark wine." The woman began to breathe easier,
and he sent her home with various medicinal powders.

The foreigner was still holding the bowl when he returned.
"Will th'art my friend and I would not disturb they sensibility.
Yet I must have this blood."

"The prescription was foolish . . ."

"There was no prescription. I lied to thee, Will. I must drink
blood because I am a vampire."

"Vampire?"

Guido laughed. "They would know me for this in Italy or
Hungary or even France, but your northern realm seldom hosts
my sort. A vampire is a dead man who rises each night to seek
blood."

Praisegood said, "You're delirious. Let me search you for
tokens."

"If delirium it be, 'tis a lasting one. How old do I seem to
thee? Thirty? Thirty-five? Thirty score years have I lived."

Praisegood smiled ingratiatingly. "And how did you become
this—vampire?"

"I was bit by one. A lamia, my cousin."

"Then it is spread by direct contagion, as is measles?"

"Do not mock me! I am not mad, nor a fool." He raised the
bowl to his lips and gulped down the red liquid.

Praisegood turned away in revulsion, speaking to the window.
"I was once called to consult with the parents of a youth who
suffered Lycanthropica. He thought he became a wolf, and would
get himself upon hands and knees, and howl and bay. He begged
me to lock him up, lest he kill a child and rend its flesh. This
was delusion, or 'hallucination,' we term it."

"Pliny wrote of men who truly became wolves," Guido said.
"Forgive me, Will. I did not wish to discover thee my curse,
but I needed the blood. I've not hunted these past few

nights. . . . I honor thy learning, but do not let disdain of superstition dull thee to the truth.''

He shrugged out of his waistcoat. The ribs stared through his pale, hairless skin. ''Find a pulse, physician, if thou canst.''

Praisegood took his friend's wrist. It was somewhat warmer than when he felt it that first morning, but there was no pulse.

He put his hand over the precordium, and at last laid his ear over the heart. There was no heartbeat.

The doctor sank into his chair and looked at the empty fireplace. ''There must be a scientifical explanation,'' he said weakly.

Thomas my Friend, I know your Scorn for Anatomisation. Would the Pest gone and we might take a Bowle of Coffee againe at Garways and heere of your Theories. —Take manie Patients with the Same Disease, observe the Coarse of the Diathesis, you have oft tolde me. Of late I have observed an entire Hoste with the Contagion, as manie as there are Leaves in a Forest, to no useful Expansion of my Knowledge, and so shall take Liberty of recounting you of an Anatomisation.

We gathered in George Thomson's Yard. Sharky was there, the Alchymist who has beene in America, and Hodges with a Posie ever to his great Nose, and an Antipestilential Electuary. Young Kreisell who was at Bologna was ever quoting those Masters; and divers Others of curious Temperament attended. The swollen putrifying Carcasse was of a Servant Lad, an. XIV, dead two Days. The Wether is still warm and dry (a bilious Time). With such an awful Heate and a Foetor of the Bodie, we welcomed the Sulphur which Thomson burned below the Table. Thomson wold not have me here for Feare I catch Pest, till I swore I was now well-fed and wanted not Sleepe. Then Dr Kreisell quoted Salerni, viz: ''Use three Physitians still, first Dr Quiet, next Dr Merryman and Dr Dyet.'' Sharky returned that Kreisell was wont to be Dr Merryman but had better been Dr Quiet. And so to the Anatomisation.

The Bodie was black and blew as if all Bloud was gone from the Veins into the Subcutaneal Tissues. We tooke first the Tokens, of which one in everie Groine, eache so big I cold not close my Hand round them, and More in the left Armepit and the Neck. They were firm and inside red without such Purulent Matter as dwells in most large

Apostems. The Similar Parts were swoll and red. Next to the Dissimilar Parts, first the Viscera. The Liver was engorged but without Blemish and the Gallbag without Feculence or troubled Chylus. The Spleene I wondered to beholde, and Kreisell could not containe but quoth Paracelsus much, to see it huge as the Head of a Mastiff. It was an uncommon red Hue and brake into small Bittes as we removed it. The Stomack was swoll and contained Clottes and the membrum was red. Hodges was disappoynted for he thinks the Stomack to be the Centre and Metropolis of the Bodie to which the Pest's Venom is channelled, the Plantation and Nursery of all Feavers he said, and yet we found it lesse Remarkable than any other Organ.

Next Kreisell quoth Wm Harvey that the Heart is as King of the Bodie, and prognsticked we should find much ill Health there. The Intestines were as such: the Gutt, especial the Ilion, was thick and soft with manie Places black with Gangreene, and much festering Matter. So foule the Odour that I knew, if ever an Atmospheric Effluvium should catch me, it were then. The Lights were heavie and sagging with Bloud, in parts like Liver, though only yellow Humour with manie small Clottes could be expressed. The Heart was seeming Normal, at which Hodges directed much Laughter at our young Colleague for quoting so manie Authorities but having no Sense. But unabashed Kreiseel quoth Horace— Nullius addictus jurare in verba Magistri. We dranke our Hostes Wine and so to our Homes and Practises. Of the Animated Wormes seen by Kircher in Plague, we found no trace not even with a strong Glass.

The windows of the crumbling half-timbered house near Exchange Alley were boarded up, but no cross or padlock graced the door to signify plague. Praisegood stared at the clapboard Merlinshead with its legend, *Here lives a Fortune-Teller.* The second word had been defaced to read *lies.* Another sign noted the availability of *Dr Sylvesters Universal Elixir of Sovereigne Virtue.* The doctor sighed, then banged his cane against the door. Receiving no answer, he called, "Sylvester! Ope'!" and thumped again. Finally a voice came from inside.

"Desist. I've a gun."

"I an't a thief," Praisegood called. " 'Tis I, Will Praisegood."

There was a sound of latches being undone, and the door

slowly swung open. Praisegood faced an old man with a raised blunderbuss.

"Ha. Will indeed. You can't enter."

"I've no wish to."

"This is my sanctuary. No plague will find me here."

"Keep your home, uncle. I only desire the benefit of your learning."

The gun lowered, and the man peered outward, a bag of herbs held to his nose. "You want my knowledge? My nevvy, the learned physician? Next you'll say the dead walk."

" 'Struth, I shall. Tell me of vampires, Sylvester. A—a friend thinks himself one."

"Vampires, heh?" The old man chuckled and came out one step further, blinking in the sunlight. His skin was pale and dry, and a filthy coat hung over his bony frame.

Praisegood sighed, remembering the last time he'd seen his uncle. The man had been resplendent in the costume of a successful fortune-teller, with velvet jacket and a black cloak. "Look, Will," Thomson had said, "one of those ungodly quacks who list in *The Intelligencer*." And Praisegood and Sylvester had each looked upon the other without acknowledgement.

"I do not feel at all well," Sylvester said.

"I have medicines . . ."

"And do I not, lad? If not my Universal Elixir, then I'd rather Anne Love's Pomander or See's Internal Balsam, than your approved pharmacopoiea."

"Peace, uncle. Vampires . . ."

"Vampires. Walking corpses who drink blood; accursed, evil beings. The French call them *Broucalaques*, and say they be men who have perished by violence, or were murthered unavenged, or took their own lives, or have eaten a sheep killed by a wolf. They say to stop them you must put a wooden post through their heart, or catch them in sun's light—you do that by scattering millet seeds, and the vampire is compelled to count them though the sun rises . . ."

"That's ridiculous," thought Praisegood, but he said politely, "What more?"

"The Roumanians say the vampire is the stillborn bastard of parents who are both bastards. The vampire's child will be a witch—on this, all agree. The gypsies think that a woman may marry a vampire, and he will help her with the cooking and housework. He is invisible, and only his child may see him. He must sleep each day in soil from his native land . . ."

"Ah," Praisegood thought. "A particle of truth. For what is earth but cold and dry: a metaphor for the melancholic humor that prevails in these vampires."

The door began to close.

"Wait. Is there anymore?"

"Yes," the old man laughed. "He who is slain by a vampire, becomes a vampire himself." The door slammed shut.

5 September, 1665

Still the Plague grows. I cannot tell of the Horrors I see dayly, lest I disturb your Sleepe, and give you Dreames to reflect mine waking Houres. In its stead, may I give Discourse on a certain Condition I have of late been discovered. Vampyres, the Animated Dead, do exist. I pray you, Thomas, do not set aside this Letter and say—Will is Distracted, he hath gone Mad. I have met a Vampyre, a Man who walks and talks even as you or I, yet his Bloud is cold and thick and flows not, and he lacks any Pulsations. But I write to refute Superstition. Vampyres are not Magickal, but Diseased. As with all Scientifickal Subjects we may from a Bodie of First Principles deduce the Particulars. I shall theorize in the Principles of the Schools in which I am learned, though I have read Van Helmont's Indictment of the Humours. Perhaps our Friend Master Boyle might convince me the Vampyre has a Derangement of the Hydraulico-pneumatical Engine which is his Bodie, or even a Disruption of his Attoms, but I miss the Company of Rob and must forge on myself. As none of the Authorities has touched upon this Matter, I must justify my Theorems by Conjecture and Inference alone, without benefit of Forebears, a Dwarf without a Giant's Shoulders on which to stand, Burton might say. And we have seen that the Authorities are not always Correct, for did not Dr Harvey shew that the Arteries carry Bloud and not Pneuma?

NOTES ON VAMPYRISM BY Wᵐ PRAYSGODE, M.D. (LEYDENSIS)

We know that there are basic Properties necessary to endow Life; these are an innate Heate, primitive Moysture, and innate Spirit. Also there are the four Primary Qualities, and any Derangement of them leads to Disese. Vampyrism is such a Disease of the Similar Parts and their nutritive Functions, being a Lack of Heate an Wetnesse (those Sanguine Qualities) and therefore a Compound Distemperature.

The Principle Cause of the Disease is an increase in Black Bile or the Melanchollic Humour. The Accessory Cause is a Lack of the Pulsific Faculty. The Indispensable Cause is a resultant Weakenesse of the Liver and Deficiency in Sanguinification. From these Causes we may understand the Diathesis.

From the Increase in Black Bile comes the Vampyre's Preponderance of the manifest Qualities of Colde and Dry, and his Melanchollic Temperament. The usual Source of Black Bile is Foode, but there must exist an independent Supply in Vampyres, perhaps generated in one of the Organs. Than to prevent more Black Bile, the Vampyre will not Partake of Foode. But as Chyle is made from Comestibles which enter the Intestine, and Bloud is generated by the Passage of Chyle through the Liver (which is here Overloaded with Bilious Matter), so there is a further Decrease in Heate and Wet by those very Attempts to increase them, for no Bloud is made.

Though no Blood is generated in the Vampyre, still does he Require it, and so he must take it by Drinking the Bloud of other Personnes. For I am tolde that the Bloud of Animals, nor Wine or Elixirs, may not substitute. Upon drinking the Bloud of Man or Woman, a Vampyre gains more Moysture than Warmth, and becomes Flegmatic. Thus do Vampyres differe from Ordinary Men in that they commonly have two Temperaments. After taking their Fill they are safe to other Mortalls, and are like to Sleepe.

> *—So dead their Spirits,*
> *So dead their Senses are*
> *Still either Sleepeing,*
> *Like to Folk that Dreame . . .*

To become fully Sanguine would require all the Bloud of manie Men's Bodies. I must note that my Vampyre Friend prefers the Bloud of Women, not only that they are Weaker and so easier persuaded to give up that which he Requires, but by the natural Instinct of a Male. Though he lacks the cruder generative Desires, I have been informed. Alas that Woman's Bloud is colder and moyster than Man's, and so gives less Warmth than a Vampyre might crave. And the Suns Light they avoide, as it warms but drys and so Desiccates the unwary Vampyre.

That there is no Pulsific Faculty is understood by the Purpose of such Pulsations. The Dilation of the Arteries (such as is called Diastole) draws in Ayre to the Lungs to temper the Bodie's internal Heate. This the Vampyre does not Require, as he is already Colde, and so the Heart does not beate and the Arteries do not carry their Bloud to the Lungs. But the beateing Heart, as has long been known, produces Vital Spirits and so the Vampyre is deficient in these, and tries again to Gaine them from Others.

Notwithstanding that the Vampyre is an Immortal Being, and so might seeme to have the perfect Balance of Humours. But as a well-paynted Hovel may seeme more attractive than a fine-built but less ornate House, the Vampyre's Superiornesse is an empty Facade or Shell, for it is based upon a pathological Dominance of Colde. The Vampyre is not a happy Creature, and because he may not Die except by Violence, does not carry the Hope of Heaven and is Abandoned to Salvation.

Moreover, Melancholly is a daungerous Humour, as all Physitians know, and leades to Destruction and Self-Destruction. As the Vampyre goes without fresh Bloud for longer than a few Days, he becomes Dryer, and the Surfeit of Melancholly makes him Mad.

> *—Both Sport and Ease and Companie refusing,*
> *Extreme in Lust sometime yet seldom Lovefull,*
> *Suspitious in his Nature and Distrustfull.*

So too the Yeeres of Melancholly may build an unwholesome and Evil Character.

I must treate on the Method of Spread of this Distemperature. Vampyrism is not disseminated by Miasmas, but seems to require a direct Contagion as does the Smallpocks and the Measles, as by the Seminaria of which Fracastorius of Verona speaks. That it is a poysonous Venom is shewn by this, that Garlicke protects from Poyson and from a Vampyre also, though this may result from the Odour of the Bulbe and from the acute Senses of the Vampyre, of which I shall another Time write. That it is Spread by Specifick Contact is shewn by this Fact, that he who is bitten by the Vampyre shall become a Vampyre in his Turn, but he whose Bloud is drank from a Bowle lives unscathed. By this we may suggest that Vampyres ought become Physitians and Chirurgeons and so earne their Day's Bloud in an honest and virtuous Manner.

The heat was oppressive and the air wet, heavy, and smelling of smoke. The sky glowed a soft red.

Guido closed the shutters. "These fires make the air intolerable."

Praisegood raised his head slightly. "The College of Physicians suggested it. Hippocrates ended the plague in . . ."

"He died millennia ago, Will, and thy College has fled like frightened puppies. See, here is written their other counsel. 'Pull off the Feathers from the Tails of living Cocks, Hens, Pigeons or Chickens, and holding their Bills, hold them hard to the Botch or Swelling and keep them at that Part until they die; and by this means draw out the Poison.' "

Praisegood leaned his head down upon his hands. His saturnine friend gazed on him with concern, then began again. "Oh, you scholars of physic—here are more cures you publish. Powdered toads and mastiff pups . . ." Seeing no response, he dug the knife in further. "Figs boiled in vinegar—Wait, here's a fine one." He waved one of Praisegood's favorite books. " '*Methodus methendi*: Take of Moss that hath growne on a dead man's Skull'—and thou wilt accuse me of dabbling in magic . . ."

"Enough," Praisegood groaned. "I will not rail with thee, Guido."

The vampire reached one hand out, and grasped his friend. "Thou wert always ever ready to dispute—Will! Th'art hot as a brand!"

"And thy hand is cold as death," replied the doctor. "George Thomson told me to live temperate, eat well, sleep aplenty, yet he would work to exhaustion. Now I hear he was taken plague and is closed in his house, as are others who were at the anatomization . . ."

Thunder split the stillness, and rain began to tap against the walls.

10 September

It was the first Raine since April, and in that next Day did die four Thousands of Soules. There are too Few to close the Houses or Bury the Dead or dig new Pits, so that Corpses lie in Publick, Fodder for Vermin and Birds, and floate in the River. Grass growes in Whitehall. Madmen run on the Streetes. I fear that soon no one shall Live to bury the Fallen, and all London shall be a Mausoleum. As to myself: I felt a Melancholly I thought my Usual, but then an Icy Chill taking holde, I knew it was the Ferment insinuating itself into my Bodie's Juices. Next I knew a grypeing of the Gutts and a Headayche as the poysonous Spicula did prick and vellicate the Membrums of my Braine. Soon came a Feaver with Palpitations and Unease. So did I eagerly search my Frame for Blisters of Whelks or an Apostem in the Groine, for oft these Tokens signal some feeble Hope of Survival. Instead I found the Stigmata Nigra, most ill of the Pest's Forms, saving only that which manifests with bloudy Sputum. And so I find myself a Dead Man soon. Ah veryly, Thomas, I would save myself an' I could, though all the World be so bleak. Few are the Physitians to treate the suffering People, fewer still now George and I are doomed. Would I might Rise from this Bed, and go my Rounds at Barts, see my Patients and deale out their Regimens. But now I am unable to do More than Lament and Regret. So swiftly now, before the Phrensy that strikes one plague-rid Man in two, I shall own myself in my Last Moments to be your Friend and to commend my Soule to your Prayers . . .

Guido lifted the man's head, placing the wine glass to his lips. "Drink, Will," he said, finally cozening the doctor into taking a sip. Praisegood half-opened his eyes.

"Guido?" he rasped.

The vampire laid one cool hand on the fevered forehead. " 'Tis I, Will."

"My blessings . . ."

"Will!" Guido shook him back awake. "List' to me, Will! Wouldst thou live?"

"My time is come . . ."

"Wouldst live?"

The dying man laughed. "Aye, I'd live. I'm a doctor, and the entire city my patient, now abandoned."

"Wouldst thou live, Will? To continue thy work? Even at the cost of thy soul?"

The man closed his eyes, and whispered. "I would live."

Guido undid his friend's collar. "Then sleep, Will," he said softly. "And wake to a better life than this thou leavest."

He leaned forward and placed his teeth to Praisegood's neck.

20 September, 1665

Tho: Sydnam from his Friend, Wm Praysgode of London Sir: I have by the Grace of God survived the Siege of this Epidemical Disease, and am in no way Impayred by having catched the Distemper. Furthermore am I returned to my Duties, though it seemes a Wonder there are any Patients to treate, as 8,297 died this last Weeke and 7,690 the Weeke before. But I am a Physitian againe, and shall live or die with the Citie, and my Hope is Renewed. The Plague may be defeated. If by the wondrous Mercy of the Almighty this Plague shall end, then I have a Minde to see the World, and perhaps to travel to other Cities so afflicted and work amongst their ill, for I feel myself now quite Immune to the Pest. Gwido Lupicinus has offered to be my Guide in any Travels I shall chose to Undertake. And so, my Friend Thomas, if we do not meete again in this World, be assured that I am

Yr humble and obdt Colleague and Servant

William Praysegode

Close of Night

Daphne Castell

IT HAD FINISHED raining by the time they drove through the first suburbs of Edinburgh, and a slate, disconsolate sky yawned hugely over the car, glimmers of sick yellow tearing the clouds to the west. Usually the wedges of Arthur's Seat, truculent slabs massing into view over the tall buildings, cheered Eva. Not this time, however—they seemed withdrawn a little from her, and less clear-edged. She felt uncertain of the city's welcome.

The Pentlands brooded over the coming night; and further north, the gaunt Highland line hunched its shoulders over the grey spears of the retreating rain, which had been chilly, whining, persistent, not easily cleared by a red evening sun.

Eva wanted nothing so much as to as to get to the hotel, and retreat over dinner from James's tireless, clacking, instructing tongue, which reckoned up business deals over the miles of travel.

They had stayed the night before at Carlisle. Later on this afternoon, the first meeting of the conference would begin, full of introductions and mistrustful back-patting. There was an evening sherry reception, to which wives were invited. "Commanded" would be a more appropriate word. Not for the first time in fifteen years, Eva wondered why she had married a businessman, to become almost a necessary part of an entourage. She had been a social worker, scurrying about desiccated city streets in constant trails of crises, too tired to eat, often; too discouraged by her environment to bother to dress well. Tall and slender, with a mass of floppy, bright brown curls, she looked well when she could trouble herself to search out something that suited her. She had done just that on the evening when

52

she decided to accept the invitation to the party at which she had met James. He was somebody's cousin, up from the country on a family inspection of the girl's lodgings, and invited only by hasty accident.

He was extremely presentable, but quite out of his depth, both in talk and attitudes. She felt sorry for him. He recognized it and was grateful. He invited her to leave the party and have dinner; she accepted, amused at his need to find a social substitute for his instinctive rejection by the party-goers, and somehow the meetings turned into a habit, while he remained in the town.

She had married him within the year, still not knowing quite why. Something to do with his more vulnerable spots, his need of a listening wife—his delightful manners played a part in it, too. She found herself honestly charmed by the habits of a man who always opened a car door, or any other door, for her, who pulled her chair back, helped her off with her coat. It was later on in their married life, and after they had discovered that they could not have children, that she also found out that charming manners cannot replace absorption—the absorption that stems from genuine concern with another, and intense interest in that being's every thought, movement, or action. She had had lovers, and if James had known of them, he had never said anything. But she had never found another person who looked into her face and watched her soul looking back at him, and waited for it to explain itself in speech and deed.

Perhaps there weren't many of them. Wealth formed a good cushion, she enjoyed travelling, and they travelled a great deal and in comfort.

She could concern herself with housework or not, as she pleased, for there was plenty of money to hire servants; she could work, if she wanted, voluntary, charitable work—as long as she was available to be presented as James's assured token of marital success and security.

She was a great deal better off than many wives. She was also bored, discontented, unhappy, and a little frightened.

"I know you're tired," said James. He prided himself, perhaps rather pathetically, on his perceptiveness. But who wouldn't be tired, after three hundred miles?

Eva shrugged, and regretted it—her neck ached badly, a series of sad, tenuous threads of pain that wound their way up into her brain.

"I think I'm probably hungry. I always feel like eating a lot when I'm in Edinburgh."

"Good food here, particularly the bakeries," agreed James. But Eva sometimes felt uneasily that it was because there had been so much hunger here in the past—whenever she entered the city, it was as if old odors called her to recognize them and include them with her own feelings. Odors of fear and hunger and sly passion without fulfillment and cruelty and blank incomprehension. She knew too much of the history of the place; she thought of no one famous or infamous individual—John Knox, Brodie, Queen Margaret—but of a nameless buzzing tumult of little people who had watched and suffered from the wings, while the great players strode and plotted and bargained.

"Walk-on parts," she said aloud, and James turned to look at her with concern.

"Having hallucinations, darling?" He chose jocularity rather than anxiety, and certainly he was perceptive about what irritated her. She smiled back, and he drew the car to a halt in one of the side streets. The Argonne was one of the better small hotels, but not the best. This meant that at off-peak seasons they often had it nearly to themselves, and the excellent, unobtrusive care of the proprietor and his wife, John and Ellen Dobree, was centered mostly on her while James was at meetings. She liked these journeys for no other reason than that she was lightly spoiled by a couple who knew nothing about her, but had been trained, and had practiced to give as much attention to guests as the guests themselves desired. She liked, too, the well-bred, shabby, dark furniture, and the unostentatious but plentiful comfort of the hangings and carpets. The walls were exceedingly thick, and it was very quiet, although the city center was quite close.

The food was excellent, as the best English home cooking can be, with recipes handed down over a dozen generations. There were not many Scottish dishes, but always superb bread, cakes, and oatcakes, and the best fish she had ever eaten.

There was time for a very hurried tea before James went off to his five o'clock session of introductions. She was to join him at the Great Britain at about half-past six—she was glad he had not booked them into the conference's main hotel. It would have meant more of the normal, rather tedious, social chores of joining women without common interests for coffee and shopping.

She unpacked efficiently, chose a green silk dress with a high curly neckline lined with peach, changed, and decided to walk into town, rather than catch a bus or call a taxi. Her shoes were not entirely practical for the purpose, glossy bronze with small thin heels, but they were comfortable enough, and it wasn't cold.

She arrived on the North Bridge with enough time to spare to look around her for a little while; she decided to visit St. Giles' Cathedral, and absorb darkness and grave silence for a while, before being thrust into the over-lighted, high-pitched gaiety of the sherry party.

The Cathedral was nearly empty, and she sat at the back, trying not to think, and above all, not to hear the sound of the car's remorseless engine, which was always so hard to get out of one's head after a long journey.

She thought someone whispered to her, and brushed her elbow, but turning she saw that her nearest neighbor was not only rapt in silent prayer, but many yards away. She read the notices near her—an organ recital, a string quartet from London, an appeal for those interested to take part in street theatre on the church's behalf. She noted the day of that, and thought that she might find an opportunity to watch it. She became aware that someone was watching her, and turned, half-smiling, to anticipate a remark from some friendly stranger—one of the vergers, perhaps. Did they call them vergers here? She must find out. Irritated and confused, she found that she had made that most familiar of mistakes—a dark old clothes-press, standing upright in a corner, had seemed to her, with her shoulder turned, to be leaning towards her like a human being.

There was a small metal plate set into the wall by her, and she read that, too. Jhonet Cowrey, it said, 1678, and nothing else. The clothes-press looked old enough to have belonged to one Jhonet Cowrey, too, though it was undoubtedly used for vestments, now.

A door creaked, and she saw the woman she had thought deep in prayer was slipping out of the Cathedral. A deep ray of light struck a tangle of red-gold curls above her neck, and the hand-woven cloth that hid the rest of her hair was a warm blending of purple and green, soft and blurred, like wet heather.

Eva thought it beautiful, and determined to try to buy one like it in one of the smaller, more expensive shops. It would not be anything like so attractive in a cheap make. Probably Princes Street would be better than the Royal Mile. She would ask Ellen Dobree.

As she rose to leave, an odd moment of half-suffocation overtook her, and for a moment she felt the Cathedral close its walls around her, with singing, and a rose and gold haze of bright candles, and a press of dark garments and dropped heads smelling of hurry and unwashed human flesh. It was as if her knowledge and her imagination had temporarily worked together to cast her back into some earlier time, when the life of mankind was the life of the church, and without the church there was not any authority or law or comfort.

The Royal Mile was almost as dark as the Cathedral had been, for a whole strip of street-lighting had failed, and she quickened her step, partly through nervousness, and partly because she had lost a few minutes during her dizziness in the Cathedral.

It was while she was passing the entry to a small dark flight of steps, quite close to a wine-bar she had often visited with James, that she heard a voice and this time certainly a touch on her elbow.

"Ye're late out," said a boy's voice, and a lad of about twelve went past her, turning to smile (but his face was half-hidden), and disappeared down the steps. She had not thought children so badly clothed still lived in Edinburgh—he was out at elbows, and, she was almost sure, bare-footed. She had seen the marks of some great burns on his hands as he moved—he must have scorched himself badly at home or school.

"I'll soon be indoors," she called after him, but he had gone. Moved by curiosity, she went down the steps a little way, and looked into the close where the boy had vanished.

She could not see very much, only enough to tell her that it was one of the unrestored old closes, not like the cleaned, renewed stone of Lady Stair's House, but dank and slimed, with pools between filthy cobbles, and strings of washing hanging high between the rooms.

There were obviously people in the houses, for many lights showed, and there was a smell of fish cooking, and whispers from a doorway, perhaps from a courting couple. Eva shuddered fastidiously at the thought of anyone sitting or laying on such stones. There was one single lamp in the close, tall and beckoning, like an iron lily. It shone with no warmth, but its light was singularly powerful, and lay in puddles of yellow beneath it.

As she turned back to go up the steps again, she felt her gaze drawn upwards, and found it met by a grossly fat old man who was sitting motionless in a bare window embrasure. He wore nothing on his arms—some kind of filthy white sleeveless shirt covered his bloated belly—and she could not tell whether he

could see her. His eyes were white-blue, filmed all over with
what might have been cataracts. It was like some obscene parody
of the balcony scene from Romeo and Juliet, and she leant sickly
against the damp wall, for the dizziness had come over her mind
again.

In the whitewash, scored deeply in black, near her hand, she
saw letters:

> Morag—gudewife—spaewife

and then much further down, large and hastily written:

> Nae wife

She went out, wondering what the unknown Morag had done
to attract praise and criticism of such different kinds on the same
piece of wall. A strange place, Edinburgh—some of the stories
were so well-known, and some so hidden. Had Jhonet Cowrey,
perhaps, known a Morag? It was a common enough name. That
was nonsense, though—they need not have lived at anything like
the same time.

When she arrived at the Great Britain, the party had already
overflowed from the conference suite, and slopped into the bars.
She could see James almost immediately, holding a drink, with
another by his side on the table, and talking earnestly to a fat
woman with too much make-up. He looked anxious and irritated, and his eyes constantly left her to roam round the room,
and then returned to pay painful attention. So this must be somebody powerful and important, and undoubtedly he had asked
her to meet his wife who would soon be here, and was already
wondering how to explain her lateness. Eva felt annoyed, but
contrite—this was what she disliked so much about James and
his business—her part-accountability for so many things.

She went and made her apologies, and was astonished to discover that she had somehow lost another fifteen minutes—she
was now nearly half-an-hour late for the sherry party, and James
was obviously exasperated, if worried. He introduced her to Mrs
Ferolstein, and was rather obviously careful not to ask her what
she had been doing, and how she had taken so long doing it.

Mrs Ferolstein proved unexpectedly pleasant and perceptive.
Whatever business connections, she was a devoted live-in lover,
as the dailies would have it, of Edinburgh.

"You were enjoying your little trek round the streets, were

you?'' she asked, in a soft rich voice, warmed with small Scottish inflections. "I never tire of her myself, the mysterious old lady of a town that she is!''

Eva smiled briefly, thinking of the night and the unexpected, unwelcome appearances.

"It's intriguing . . . I won't say I enjoyed it. I was lost for a while,'' she ended, looking apologetically at James, who merely shrugged, exasperated, before he set off to get them all another drink, and some canapés.

Over dinner, Mrs Ferolstein talked to her on one side about the historic glories of Edinburgh, and James lectured on the other about the dangers of getting lost in the dark and menace of the old town.

Eva had a sudden thought. "Mrs Ferolstein, do you know anything about the plates set into the walls of the cathedral?'' she asked, ignoring one of James's more vivid descriptions of a recent court case concerning a late woman walker and a mugger.

Mrs Ferolstein appeared to have an encyclopedic knowledge of the antiquities of St. Giles' Cathedral.

"Oh, Jhonet Cowrey!'' she exclaimed, when Eva had enlightened her. "Poor woman!''—as if she were talking about some distant and unfortunate relative—"Yes, they put her on trial for her husband's death—it seems she'd been worried about his health, and lack of—lack of energy,'' said Mrs Ferolstein delicately, "and she'd apparently asked for help from some woman in the neighborhood who had the reputation of being able to help in odd matters like this . . . some kind of a white witch, you may say. It was quite a celebrated case in the seventeenth century. The wretched man died, and of course, if you know the kind of thing that the herbal leeches of the day thought good for a complaint of that kind, you wouldn't wonder. There was some doubt, because she came from a good family, though they were poor, and everyone knew she was fond of him—naturally, or she wouldn't have been asking for the remedy. Nevertheless, they hanged poor Jhonet—the neighborhood woman was never known. I daresay there were a good many people who wanted to help Jhonet. She was well liked. But no one would risk their necks or the enmity of the medical-lady busybody who had put a good man into the next world out of kindness of heart, and out of a desire to save his wife from seeking consolation from someone more potent. So no one opened a mouth in the wrong place—after all, they might have had a need of their own one day, and a good spaewife is not all that easy to come by.''

"Spaewife?" Eva mused "I've heard it before—a fortune tell-ing woman or something of the kind. Would she deal in herbs and potions too?"

"Oh, for sure! And no doubt she would give a bit of good counsel, and along with a few charms, she'd explain to the nag-ging wife how to use the right words to her husband, or the timid young girl how to find confidence and make the best of herself for the boys."

Eva laughed. "A sort of primitive social worker-cum-psych too, then? Apart from the herbs and charms I've had to do some of that sort of talking in my time."

"Oh, were you a social worker, then?" Mrs Ferolstein's bright black eyes snapped with curiosity, and the talk turned to the rights or wrongs of the welfare state, and the ability of families in more ancient times to stand on their own feet, as compared with their acquired modern skill in knowing exactly what state body could be most easily called upon. "It's all a matter of survival," insisted Mrs Ferolstein, "only they have different tools and weapons now. They used to survive at all costs, on Nature's whim or bounty, or on their own sheer hard work. Now—" she shrugged off the indigent masses.

Before they left, however, Eva said, "It still seems odd that there should be a memorial in the cathedral—how could that happen if she was actually hanged? Surely—"

"Her family was a good one, as I've said. They couldn't pre-vail upon the authorities of the kirk to let her be buried in con-secrated ground. But the family waited, with its long memories, until most of the elders were dead, and the cause of Jhonet's posthumous banishment nigh forgotten. Then they asked for the plate, and gave a generous sum with it, for the rest of the souls of the poor of St. Giles. Nobody seems to have raised even the slightest demur. The date on the plate had to be the one that the rector allowed them to place it there—none of them wished to commemorate the day of her hanging. That might have been a bit too obvious, even for a church grown more easy-going. So the metal in the Cathedral may well be the only resting place her poor forgotten soul has to cling to."

As they walked down to the car, parked in a back street not far from Holyrood Palace, Janet pointed out the close to James. At least, she tried to—she was not absolutely sure, among the many, but she thought she remembered the marks on the walls nearby, and the colours of the paving stones and the patterns of the cobbles. A drift of seagulls rose up over their heads as they

peered closely together through the iron trellis-work that someone had drawn across the entrance.

Eva had not realized that entrances like this might be closed
off at night—James said that it didn't usually happen.

"The place looks derelict to me," he remarked. "I should
think they're rebuilding it—they're doing that with many of the
really old places. Extraordinary to think they used to be the
lodgings of large and noble families—ugh, look at that!"

Eva had seen nothing.

"A rat," James informed her, moving distastefully away from
the wall, "slipping along through the refuse as if it owned the
place. There's no one there, you know. Most of the windows are
broken or boarded up. I doubt if you really saw any inhabitants.
There could be some still left, I suppose. But it's pretty un-
likely."

Eva still saw vividly the gross white old man and his statue-
like corpulence—a pallid Buddha—and heard the whispers and
rustles and giggles, perhaps of lovers. But it was with the eyes
of her mind, and she took James' arm obediently, and left the
stairs to darkness and the night wind.

As they turned into the street in which the car was parked, a
woman brushed against Eva's shoulder. She stopped, and James,
irritated, stopped with her.

A pale, wrinkled face looked back at her, the patient smile on
it belonging to someone who was not old, but wrung through
by years of trial and near-hunger, and a whisper dropped through
the rising mists, as the woman went up to the higher part of the
road: "She said to come by tomorrow or the night after. He's
no just so weel—and my own bairns, if ye can. They're but
poorly."

"What on earth was all that about?" asked James, and Eva
could not answer, although she felt already that she might know
something more than her mind would bring to the surface.

"Must have mistaken you for someone local," James answered himself. "One of the panel doctors, perhaps."

"Doctors aren't the answer to every difficulty," said Eva, unaccountably annoyed.

"What an extraordinary thing to say!" James' eyebrows arched
in some displeasure. "I never suggested that they were. Aren't
you rather touchy this evening, Eva? And that was an odd time
to arrive at a function that you knew very well was important to
me. Mrs Ferolstein's a very powerful and a very intelligent lady—
fortunately she seemed to take rather a fancy to you."

Eva snapped, "And you find that odd?"

James sighed. "There you go again—and once more, I never suggested that. No, my dear, you do have an air of quiet self-sufficient competence sometimes. That would attract her attention. She likes people who can do things—solve problems, for instance. Perhaps it's because you used to do exactly that so much, at one time. She likes answers, without uneven ends hanging out."

"But I didn't know I gave that impression!" Eva laughed ruefully. "It's probably because I often feel lost in the kind of conversation your people have. So I sit quietly. Perhaps they mistake that for enigmatic knowledge. They must be rather stupid if they do."

"My kind of people," said James stiffly, "don't converse in such widely different terms from the rest of humanity. They go to plays and concerts, sometimes, like other people. Sometimes they even make jokes. It's simply that when they are engrossed in professionalism, they find it absorbing to the exclusion of everything else."

"Obviously." Eva's tone was slightly waspish, and they drove home to the hotel in a rather sulky silence.

James elected to have a whisky and ginger at the small hotel bar, which kept open till the most uncanny hours, and Eva cornered Ellen, who had been helping her husband serve, but was now quietly putting empty bottles in a basket, with one tired eye on the clock. Ellen at first professed no knowledge of the close which Eva had visited; but after a brief description of the shops in its neighborhood, some light dawned in her eyes.

"Oh, that's the Stirk Close—it was Butcher's Wynd, but there's a tale that one of the animals got loose from the slaughterer's, this'll be many years back, and rampaged round and got into the close, and couldn't get back up the stairs again. So round and round he goes, until he's tramped two-three bairns nigh to death. My, that was aye an unlucky place. My granny lived on the opposite side from them, at the start of this century, and she used to tell us about the sheer black fortune that seemed to hang on those folks' sleeve, and had for more years than any of them could remember. If it was hunger, there was always more there that were starving than anywhere else. If it was the sickness, they'd be down in droves. When it was bitter in the rest of the city, it was the Stirk Close that had snow piled up so they could barely get out, and there it stayed freezing, till it was gone from everywhere else. Some trick of the wind, maybe, that brought in the dust and the germs and the frost. But once people left the place, they vowed never to go back, and they always found themselves better off elsewhere.''

''I know,'' Eva found herself suddenly thinking of some of the past families she had thought of as ''hers,'' with the sheer arching pity she had always had for those who, bewildered, never did well, and could never seem to get the knack of it, somehow. There was always the next court-case or the next filthy disease, or the next bastard—they could never get clear of it, and they could never get away from their background. Call it what you would, unwillingness, lack of caring, inability to cope, the desire to yield, she had never been able to believe that it was entirely the fault of ''her'' families.

''Some of them said it was like a curse on it, my granny told me,'' said Ellen cheerfully enough, tipping up a bottle in which a tiny dram of cherry brandy remained, and licking it off her finger.

A full bluish moon had risen, and was edging the velvet curtains of the bar with watered silver. Eva looked from the warmth and smoky orange comfort of the small lamp-lit room to the austere fields of the sky, ridden by steely cloud bands, and felt a sudden yearning to be out in the night, breathing cold air.

James was affronted and astonished. ''But where are you going? You won't walk, will you? It would be stupid.''

''Just a quick turn in the car, round the road at the foot of Arthur's Seat, maybe as far as the water, and then quickly back,'' lied Eva.

''D'you want me—?'' James persisted.

''No, no!'' cried Eva, in almost hysterical impatience, as if someone was waiting for her who might soon be gone. She ran out of the hotel, fingering the car keys impatiently, and ducked into the driver's seat with a sigh of relief, while James stood on the steps, gazing at her with bewilderment.

As soon as she was moving, she felt a calm move into her excited veins, soothing down the blood that had been flowing at too hot a pace.

She drove rather slowly, knowing and savoring where she was bound, not the place so much as the adventure of assailing it by moonlight. The idea gave her short tremors of intense excitement at the pit of her belly, like the shivers that had shot through the depth of her being, sometimes, when she had looked down over high walls, and not quite been able to contain an unreasonable fear, yet longing, at the deep well of air and space that could so easily pull down her falling body.

The street was almost deserted as she drove down the steep slope, jouncing over the cobbles. Certainly the police would not trouble her, if she stopped just for a short while to see how the moon fell on the horrible place where so many of the poor had mourned and suffered, and asked vainly for help. But perhaps not always vainly—for there had been someone, had there not? Someone who cared, someone who was interested, who had tried to help Jhonet, even if it had been in error? The spaewife?

She stood by the steps, looking in and down, and, to her surprise, the gate had gone, the iron fretwork no longer interfered between her and what she looked for.

The stones were washed by the moon, and looked paler, and leprous, with trails as if slugs had been climbing them. But the windows, like wide open orange and yellow eyes looked at her, fully alive and clustered with people. She could almost see what some of them were doing—washing, putting children to bed, poring over pots or clothes and, in one window, a great old book with brass on its back and corners. There was faint noise, too, quarreling and crying, and fat gouts of obscene laughter from one room where a whore fondled a customer.

But it was the streetlamp that took her eye. It drowned out the moon, blooming yellow as a giant, stalked lemon stuck out in the middle of the close, a wrecking beacon for the dazzled eyes.

Its peaked head stood out belligerently, and round its foot was a magic circle of sharp-edged light, defined territory where nothing could creep or move, outside which there was indecision, chaos, dirt, and sickliness. Inside that circle, felt Eva, order and action functioned effectively and hygienically, like the functioning within the lights of a surgical ward.

The night closed off her excitement, and she felt suddenly sick and drowsy. She heard the voices, and they seemed to have some relationship to her, and to what she was feeling; but she turned from them and the lamp, and went back to the car.

"What are you doing with yourself today?" asked James at breakfast. The morning was clear and lovely, and sun gilded the caps of the small autumn flowers in Ellen's neat garden.

Eva liked the autumn versions of plants that bloomed more opulently in the hot weather. They showed restraint and a vivacious economy, like poor Frenchwomen attempting chic on small budgets. And the leaves smelt more spicy, especially the chrysanthemums. There was a brisk, herbal, curative effect about an autumn garden.

Ellen brought more oatcakes and smiled at them. "Good weather for a picnic, now—they say Cramond is lovely just now, and the wind not cold yet at all."

"It's an idea," said James, "you'll weary of the city if you stay in it all the time." Eva thought not; but she could see the sense of a trip to Cramond, as a time-waster. Did she really want a time-waster? She had an urgent sense of pressing hurry in her chest, as if there were something she had left undone, and that really ought to be done quickly. It affected her breathing, too, and she felt as if the fresh sea-wind off the harbor at Cramond might help her to relax and breathe more smoothly.

"The zoo's out in the same direction," said James doubtfully, "Isn't it? I suppose you won't want to—" he stopped. Eva was shaking her head, as he knew she might. She did not care for restraints for human beings or animals, even if they knew no better. Freedom ought always to be an option, even if it were only to be refused.

Ellen put her up a picnic: cake, and a couple of bridies, the pasties she liked so well, and fruit, and she bought herself a can of lager, and drove out towards the harbor. It was as she struggled with the twists of road and traffic at the bottom of Princes Street, that she caught a glimpse of red-gold hair, curling under a kerchief, and saw a pair of hands stretched out beseechingly towards her, and the anxious profile of a woman's face, and knew that she could not go out of the city that day.

James would not be home until late, and there was no party or reception, but she knew of other things she could do.

She was not needed just yet, but she must be within reach; it was a long time since she had planned her day to be within earshot, or telephone call, or walking distance of someone in just that way. Or on call? It was, again, a long time since she had heard or used that phrase. But she could go shopping for a while. At least part of the day was free to her; and nightfall was not yet.

The day passed remarkably quickly, as if it had simply hovered near her, and then been withdrawn. She bought a head-scarf of nearly the weave she had already seen twice, and ate her lunch in the gardens below the Scott Memorial; she watched the patient queue to ascend it, and the fuzz of black dots at the top that were heads peering over, and she listened to a band. She went into the gallery and looked at pictures, she visited the Camera Obscura and saw grey, dizzying windswept scenes, a panorama of half-real towers and houses; but she did not go near the Royal Mile. The time for that would soon be near, and she wished to feel the waiting and the excitement.

An elderly woman talked to her for quite a long time about the difficulties she was having with the nephew who lived with her—the illogicalities and thoughtlessness of the young, and the expense of having to feed them; and Eva answered so politely and sensibly that no one would have guessed that she heard hardly anything of what was said.

At last the sun sank, and grape-dark shadows bloomed in doorways, and thin mists began twining up from the long dank grass on the castle slopes, and stars pricked luminous patches in the evening sky, and Eva rose and stretched herself, from the bench she had been sitting on, and began to walk towards her close.

There were more houses than she remembered, and in better repair, and she missed the women carrying water, and the cries of the street-sellers, but she was content to be going back to the tasks she had to do, and to the people who needed her, every one.

She paused in the entry, and rubbed her hand lovingly over the inscription: 'gudewife—spaewife'; they had loved her, and had scrawled that over the stone. And never mind the spite of yon man whom she would not have in wedlock! She had better things to do with her time than to marry—look where it had led poor Jhonet. The healing gift was the greatest honor, and the greatest burden a woman could carry, whether it were of body or spirit.

The windows shone their usual homely good cheer to her, and she could hear the whispers of young Nan lying with her Willie, in the darkest patch, where the shadows were thickest. And what that child's clothing would be like the morrow, dear only knew!

The only man who saw her come in was old Master Wattie, who had been the best of all tailors, until he lost the use of his hand—she could help with the pain, but not the loss of movement. He inclined his head to her, and she knew others would soon hear of her coming home—those whose bairns were sick of the wasting disease, or the men whose warts and blains were made worse by their work in the mills, or the girls who wanted a love-spell, or something that would just disfigure a rival, not too badly, for a wee while. So, before she took up her abode again, behind one of those welcoming windows, she must sit at her old spot, and ply her old trade, and take care of their lives, for those that could not care for themselves.

The lamp pulled her, as it always did, into the safety of its covering glow, and all the faces came silently to the windows and watched her, as she sat down inside its limits, held safely and bound within the bourne and path of its globe; while outside the chatter and clutter of some other world, with which she had no longer anything to do, passed on and away from her.

What Seen but the Wolf

Gregg Keizer

"YOU SHOULD HAVE killed Sverri when you came across him outside Hofstadir, the blood from that farmer on his hands," Bjorn said, looking midships where the pitching deck was open. Sverri's screams still came from there, but they were quieter now. Heltevir, his wife, was by him.

The image came too freely to my eyes. Sverri had been hunched over the warm body of the farmer, his hands dipped over the man's face, as if he was trying to wake him. Blood was everywhere; across Sverri's cheeks and forehead, up to his elbows, down his trousers. His eyes had been mad, their circles too bright in the dim moonlight.

"Kill him for what?" I asked. Bjorn was Sverri's only brother, true, but he had no reason to question my actions. Eight days since the night I'd come upon Sverri, six since we'd sailed, and this the first time we'd talked of it. Perhaps that was part of the problem with the voyage. We should have said all this before we fled Ice Land. "Kill him for murder? That was what it looked like. Kill a friend when he could easily have paid weregeld to the sod's wife? How was I to know Sverri was thought a werewolf?"

Bjorn said nothing, only looked into the rain that clouded the horizon. The storm would be on us quickly. "Yes," he finally said. "You did not see him while he was a wolf, as the farmer's sons swore. If only we'd not found the wolfskin around Sverri's waist." I was silent, tired of trying to explain the wolfshirt Sverri had worn. They believed what they wanted to believe, and nothing I said changed it. "We could have stayed, instead of on our way to beautiful Groenland." The last word was an oath. We'd

67

heard of the lies of Eric the Red, the one who called a land of ice and rock *Groen*.

"It's too late for wishing," I said. "We are all here because of Sverri, but there are few of us who could not have stayed in Hofstadir. A few questions, perhaps some money spent, that would have been all. Everyone had a reason for joining Sverri in exile. Only you," I said, pointing to Bjorn, "and Heltevir had to run with Sverri."

"And you, Halfdan," a tall blond standing beside Bjorn said. I tried to put a name to him, but it took several moments. Thorvin. A friend of Bjorn's from his days gone aviking.

"Yes. It was unfortunate that the farmer's sons decided to fight." I rubbed the back of my head, feeling the lump only now disappearing. They'd held both Sverri and me until Bjorn had hacked his way into their longhouse and pulled us free.

"Enough," said a sharp voice. It was Eirik, his old, weathered face twisted in anger. Or perhaps fear. He leaned a hand on the afterboat, the small boat, large enough for six, perhaps, turned upside down on the deck of the ship. He seemed to touch it with care. Did he expect we would have to flee in it if the ship broke up in the storm approaching? "Enough talk. The storm will be on us soon, and then what? Already we are two days past landfall in Groenland. How are we to reach land if that touches our sail?" He pointed to the dark wall of clouds to the northeast, off our stern.

"Halfdan is sailing master," Bjorn said, looking at me.

"Sailing master?" I asked, wanting to laugh, but finding only fury instead. "On this pig of a boat? It needs a swineherd, not a sailing master." I watched Bjorn, half-expecting him to swing. Tempers were short.

"It was not my idea to sail in this," he said softly, gesturing at the small merchant ship we sailed. It was a knorr, wide and slow, not like the longships I was used to sailing. Its fifty-foot length had seemed enough when we'd left Ice Land, but six days with thirteen and one madman had shortened it by far.

Bjorn was right. We'd had little choice of ships when we'd fled in the night from home. I laughed and the sound seemed to surprise all those around me. "I have never sailed this far west," I said. "I only have heard of this way, that is all. There is a difference between sailing a passage, and only listening to another's memory of one."

"Four days is the passage," Eirik said, his voice sounding as if he was afraid of saying it. "We are lost."

"Then we will find land elsewhere," I said, my laughter forgotten, my anger again tight in my throat. "*Vikingr* have sailed around the world, and there always was land to be found. If we are lost from Groenland, what matter is that? Ice and bare mountains and little food is something I can do without. You?"

"We will try to find Groenland, Halfdan," Bjorn said, his voice an order that even I wanted to obey, for all my brave words. "I would not wish to be alone in the wilderness with my brother." He almost whispered the words. Those clustered around us glanced towards midships. I noticed Thorvin cross himself and wanted to spit. Christians among us, too. Wasn't Sverri Tryggvason, our werewolf, enough?

"Someone should stay with him when the storm hits," Eirik said nervously. He glanced towards me, then looked back to where Sverri was bound below the deck. "In case he is afraid, one of us could comfort him." It was too quiet when his words were gone.

"To watch him, you mean," I said loudly. "In case he breaks the bindings?" Eirik would not look at me. The men began to drift away, each to his own task before the storm. None stayed too long near midships.

"What of the animals?" I asked. There were two cows and four sheep huddled in the open well midships, their backs gray from the salt spray.

"Hope that they do not die of fright," Bjorn said, smiling slightly. "Hope that none of us die of fright." I smiled, but there was no laughter in me at his wish.

I looked at Bjorn and shook my head. "We'll live through this," I said.

"Will we?"

I listened to Sverri's distant screaming and wondered if I was right.

The storm came on us full of fury and horrible seas. The winds drove us south for three days, our ship wallowing in the troughs of the huge waves. It was impossible to calculate our course, for the sun was gone, hidden by the clouds, and the wind seemed to be backing; it came from a different direction than the sea ran. Then the fog smothered us. We were trapped in it for almost a day.

That was when we lost Ingolf, a cousin to Sverri and Bjorn. He went to the stern to piss, shrieked in a voice that made my heart cold, and was gone. We shouted for him, but the fog seemed to swallow our words. Bjorn found a spot or two of blood on the deck beside the steering oar, but that was all. Thorvin was at the oar, but he heard only a low moan before Ingolf yelled. Thorvin said it sounded like a pained animal, but it must have been only the wind, I thought. I stumbled in the dimness to Sverri's side, but the bindings were all in place, tight as before. It could not have been him. No one wanted to talk of it.

We let the ship ride before the wind, the sail furled and all of us sick from the gale. One of the sheep died and since there was no way to cook it, we had to simply skin it and heave the carcass overboard. Sverri quieted finally; the storm silenced his madness.

"Sverri, do you hear me?" I whispered to the shape in the dark. He stirred, then tried to sit up. I helped him edge back until he was against one of the knorr's ribs. "Sverri?" I asked, loud enough for only him to hear. I didn't think the others would want me talking to our werewolf.

"Hello, Halfdan," Sverri said, his voice even and sane. Where was his madness now?

"Do you remember?" I asked, sitting in front of him. Even so, it was impossible to see his face, for the clouds were still thick above us.

"How long has it been?" he asked.

"Eleven days since I found you on that farmer. Nine since we sailed."

He was quiet. For some reason, I wanted a light, so I could see his face. What if he was a wolf even now? I reached out my hand to touch his face, but stopped, unable to wish my arm to move further. My hand trembled, and I let it drop to clasp my axe.

"Groenland?" Sverri asked.

"We are off course," I said. "I don't think we will see Groenland soon." Again, Sverri was silent. "We are old friends. You have always been everything a friend should be," I said finally. "We have gone aviking together and you saved my throat that day in Frisia." I swallowed hard. "Did you kill Ingolf?" I put both hands on the axe. For the third time Sverri said nothing. "Sverri? Did you kill him as you killed that farmer?"

"Am I a simple murderer to you, Halfdan?" he asked quietly. "Is that all I am? Not even a madman?" I could not force the words to answer. "I have heard the others whisper of it, Halfdan. They think me mad, or worse. Do you?"

I shook my head, realized he could not see in the darkness and grunted a reply. Mad? I could not believe it. A murderer, yes, for I'd seen him hunched over the farmer's corpse. He had even had the madness in his eyes then, but all killings bring that on in a man. I'd killed, and knew that brief madness had glittered in my face as well. I remembered the sounds my voice had somehow made when the berserker madness caught me in battle. Sverri a madman? No. He had killed, but that did not make one insane, did not make one dangerous to old friends. How could Sverri be a madman for doing what I had done? How could he be mad, when I knew I was sane?

"Why don't you free me from these?" Sverri asked, and I heard the rustle of cloth as his hands appeared in front of my face. The bindings were tight, and even in the darkness, I could see they cut his skin.

"Do you believe I am a wolf, Halfdan?" I did not know what to believe. Everyone else seemed sure Sverri was a werewolf; the farmer's sons, Bjorn, all the rest of those on the ship. But we'd lived and sailed and fought together too many years for me to believe he could be a shape-shifter without my knowledge. The two years since we'd returned from Norway, where we'd been *ulfhednar*, wolf-shirted warriors for the King, had been filled with whispers of the frightened rustics of Ice Land. Sverri had not laid aside his wolfskin, as I had, and so the sods thought him strange. I knew him truly, and even though I too believed in the power of the wolf-shirt in battle, had proved it to myself more than once while fighting for the King, I knew it did not make one a shape-shifter. His *ulfhednar* wolfshirt was what they found on Sverri after his murder, and though I had tried to tell them it was nothing, they hadn't listened to me.

Yet, even still, in the darkness and quiet sound of the sea, I wondered and had small doubts. Could he be a werewolf? How could I not have those doubts. Only a god can be sure.

"Do you believe, Halfdan?" he asked again. Did he lean toward me in the dark? Were those shapes before me his hands? No, he was bound tight, I tried to remember. "If you believe I am a wolf, Halfdan, then that is what I am."

I left him then, afraid of his answers if I asked more questions. Did I believe?

"We are seven doegr south of the Groenland Western Settlement," I said, still holding the husanotra in my hand. Bjorn was in front of me, but in the darkness, even though the sky was clear, I could see only his outline. He took the husanotra, the quarter circle of wood, from my outstretched hand and held it up so that its bottom edge was level with the horizon, the line where the stars disappeared into the sea. He lined the Pole Star with the curved edge of the husanotra, marked the place with his finger, then counted the notches back to the straight edge.

"Seven doegr." He sighed. "Seven days of good sailing," he said, finally agreeing with me that we were far from Groenland. "Where are we?" he asked, his voice quiet. More out of secrecy from the rest than for fear of disturbing their snorings.

I shrugged my shoulders, then realized he could not have seen the gesture. "West of Groenland, south of Groenland, I would say. Lost."

"Still no land," Bjorn said.

"There are plenty of birds. We'll see land in a day, perhaps two."

"Go north when we come to land, then back east?" he asked. I wondered if he would let me make the decision, or if he was only asking me to soothe my injured pride. We were lost, after all.

"What if we left Sverri here, then sailed north to the Western Settlement?" I asked. The thought came suddenly. Even if Sverri was no danger to me, he was to the others. His kin and closest friend he might still smile on. But the others? Wouldn't it be simple to exile one, even though a friend, than to risk the death of several?

Bjorn snorted loudly, the sound waking the closest sleeper. I couldn't see who moved on the deck beside our feet.

"No?" I said. "Ingolf would disagree, I think."

"Ingolf fell overboard. The man could not hold his bladder," Bjorn's outline moved in the darkness. "Sverri had nothing to do with his death. He will come out of his magic once we are in Groenland. When he knows we are far from any of that farmer's kinfolk, he will cease his shape-shifting. Sverri is kin to me, remember that. I could not strand him."

I was silent. I'd decided Sverri had somehow murdered Ingolf. How, I didn't know; the asking of why was simpler to answer. Ingolf had most strongly claimed Sverri a werewolf. Sverri had not liked those accusations. That was what I'd decided. But it was not the time to argue, not when we were lost in an unknown sea none had heard spoken of.

"Sverri is inhabited by the White Christ's devil," a voice from the deck said quietly. Thorvin's voice. "That is what made him attack that farmer. That is what made him a werewolf.'' The voice was sure. I heard Bjorn swear under his breath.

"Only Christians could believe such foolishness," Bjorn said. Like myself, Bjorn had refused to take the cross in his hands and the White Christ into his heart. Thorvin, however, had not refused.

"Sverri is a murderer. Perhaps he is even mad enough to wear the wolfskin and think he could murder and not be found out that way. Perhaps he even thinks himself a wolf. But he has no devil within him.'' I had let my voice carry too loud, and more of the crew were waking. But I had little patience for Christians, even for the ones on board, the ones I knew.

"I will pray for him," Thorvin said. "I will pray for you as well, Halfdan Haukadale and Bjorn Tryggvason, so you will take the White Christ into you. Someday you will see that your gods are false.'' I heard Bjorn snort again. How many of the twelve sane on our knorr were Christian? I wondered. "If you had prayed for a safe voyage before we left home, as we asked, this would not have happened.'' Bjorn did not answer then, but I could feel his hatred in the air.

"I do not believe you are the same man who went aviking with me," Bjorn said after several moments. "You were not so pious then, Thorvin, for I saw you slit more than one Irish monk's throat. You have had more than one Irish nun under you.''

Thorvin was on his feet, his voice roaring in the darkness, the skittering sound of a blade pulling free of its scabbard filling my ears. But Bjorn already had a hand on his lance. He must have touched it before he spit his words on Thorvin. I stepped back, towards the edge of the deck, one hand grabbing a walrus-hide line to steady myself, the other reaching for the only weapon I had with me, my hand axe. It was unnecessary, for as quickly as it had started, it was finished.

Bjorn was standing, his foot planted on Thorvin's chest, his lance through Thorvin's shoulder, pinning him to the deck. Thorvin moaned softly; that was the only sound. I wondered if any of us even breathed during those moments. Then it was past, for Bjorn jerked out his lance point and threw the weapon to the deck. He was kneeling beside his friend, his hands wrapped around the man's chest. No one moved to help, or interfere, when Bjorn hefted Thorvin in his arms and carried him to the hold midships, then gently lifted him under the forward deck. Someone in the dark muttered under the sigh of the wind on the sail. Whether it was a curse, or a prayer to the White Christ, I could not tell.

It was not as if we did not have troubles enough to last us this voyage, I thought. Now we had to worry about this sudden division, as well as what Sverri had become, and the fact that we were far from the known world. It was too much for even a saga. Too much to live through.

The dawn came on us too slowly, for Sverri woke and began screaming once more, adding to the cries of Thorvin as he lay dying on a pallet below deck. Heltevir, Sverri's wife, tried to stem the blood from Thorvin's shoulder, but it was of little use. Bjorn's lance had probed too deeply. Bjorn stayed at the steering oar the remainder of the night, telling everyone who came near to go away. He would not even listen to me when I came to talk about our course.

My nose had been right, for when the light was strong enough, land loomed before us. It was not Groenland, for my sailing directions had said I would see high mountains with huge glaciers behind them. A coastline much like Ice Land, the man had said. But this land was low, only an occasional hill showing above the trees. That was the first thing I saw: the heavy green of the forests that stretched down all the way to the highwater mark, all the way to the cliffs that dropped into the sea. Even in the small bay before us, the trees walked almost into the very water, as if they were thirsty, or hungered for our ship.

"Thorvin is dead," a woman's voice behind me said. Heltevir would not look at me when I turned to her. Instead, her eyes were on the coastline off the port quarter. I could think of nothing to say.

"We will want to bury him here, I think," I finally said, to no one really, though Heltevir heard and nodded slowly. For some reason, though we had been out of sight of land for thirteen days, I did not want to step out of the ship onto that darkness of trees. Stupidity, I thought to myself, touching the hand axe next to me. There was no smoke curling above the trees, no savage Skraelings, the fierce natives the stories had warned about.

Then Sverri screamed again, and I touched Heltevir's arm, gently caressing it. What had we to fear from the land when there was a werewolf among us? I could not help but smile at the thought.

* * *

Bjorn threw the first handful of dirt into the grave. I watched as it covered the hilt of Thorvin's sword and splashed onto his sleeve. We'd laid him in a hole hacked among the roots of the trees towering all around us, and put the few things he'd brought with him alongside his body. A sword, two spears, his leather cap and shield, his axe, some meager food that we could ill spare. Bjarni, a Christian like Thorvin, had asked to bury his friend in their custom, but Bjorn had only stared him into silence.

"Could I say a prayer for his soul?" Bjarni asked. His words seemed to echo through the thick woods. Bjorn was silent, only watched as two of the crew, Kare and Ari, pushed the dirt back into the grave, then shoved more on top to make the mound. We'd gathered rocks earlier and I stooped down to set the first one in the soft earth, pushing it until it was half covered. Bjorn and the others helped make the outline of the boat that would carry Thorvin to Valholl, but three of the men, Bjarni, Thorstein, and Gudlief, stood to one side. Only three Christians still with us, I thought. Unless some of the others helping set the rocks had changed their beliefs suddenly. It didn't matter, I decided, as long as they didn't try to bury me in Christus style when I died.

"Say your prayer if you wish," Bjorn said to the three Christians. "Thorvin is safe from the eaters of the dead, and on his way to Odin's house. Nothing you mutter now will hurt him." And he walked toward the beach where the small afterboat was pulled clear of the water. I watched him, glanced at the ship riding on the short swells in the bay, and wondered if I should follow.

"Please, o Christ, listen to my prayer," Bjarni said, his voice too pleading for my liking. "Save Thorvin's soul so that he may see the gold of Heaven. Carry him to your heart and protect him from your devil. Save, also, the soul of Sverri Tryggvason and return him to the living. Banish the devil in his soul." I could listen no longer, and left the grave then, pausing only to kick a stone deeper into the dirt.

The air was cleaner once I left the shadow of the woods, and I could breath easier. Bjorn was sitting on the rock-strewn beach, flinging pebbles into the water.

"It's as if Sverri has cast a troll's spell over all of us," he said as I sat beside him. "Ingolf drowned, Thorvin murdered by my own hands. What will be next?" I shrugged my shoulders. "What is next, sailing master?"

"North, then east to Groenland," I said.

"Thorvin is the first one I have killed in manslaughter," Bjorn said. "Plenty of Irishmen, a few of those strange people south of Frisia, but those died when I went aviking. Not like Thorvin." I remembered the faces of those I'd killed, of the many that had perished under an *ulfhednar*'s axe. Only Sverri had made so many deaths, and again I wondered if he was truly a werewolf. Here, in the light, the thought almost made me laugh. In the darkness, I knew I might think different. Bjorn paused for a few moments, throwing more pebbles into the water. "Thorvin has two brothers and a father in Groenland."

That was why he worried. Not so much because he had murdered a friend, though that was enough to bother any man, but because of where we were to go. If Thorvin had living kin in Groenland, and they found out what had happened, as they surely would from Bjarni and the other Christians, then there would be a blood feud. Thorvin's kin would not rest until Bjorn and his family were dead. If it became bloody enough, it could extend even to those who had traveled and befriended a Tryggvason. Perhaps even me.

"I don't think the others will want to hear this," I said. The rest who had rowed with us from the knorr were still in the woods. How could they stand the darkness?

"You will stand with me," Bjorn said. "For Sverri, you will." He was right. I had left Ice Land because of my friendship with Sverri; I had done this much and could see little profit in stopping now. "We cannot go to Groenland," he said.

"What if we went to the Eastern Settlement instead?" I asked. Bjorn shook his head. I sighed and said, "They would find us eventually, I suppose."

"South?" he said, looking out into the bay at the ship. I could hear the voices of those returning from Thorvin's grave.

"If we did not have Sverri around our necks, we could go home. None of Thorvin's kin are there."

"You do not mean that," Bjorn said softly. I wondered if he was right, for Sverri's voice came back to me as it had two nights before, when we'd talked. A shadow fell over us and I squinted into the harsh light to see Bjarni. "Did you want to talk to me?" Bjorn asked him.

Bjarni, Thorstein, and Gudlief stood close together. Bjorn and I stood as well, and my hand went on its own to the hand axe in my belt. I noticed the others in the background. Heltevir in their front. She was brushing her hand through her long hair. Not for the first time, I thought of her hair in my hands, but thrust the thought aside. She was married, married to my friend, married to our werewolf.

"What is it, Bjarni?" Bjorn asked, his hands crossed over his chest.

"What matter is this of yours, sailing master?" Bjarni said, looking at me. "You are not standing with this murderer, are you?" I said nothing.

"You will be left to rot here, Bjarni," Bjorn said. "Put away your madness, and everything will be forgotten."

"Thorvin was buried a pagan, not as a follower of the White Christ should be. He was murdered by a pagan. We are here because of a pagan's crime in Ice Land. Thorvin has avengers in Groenland, Bjorn. You would not live long even if you did reach the Western Settlement." Bjarni stepped forward and pulled his sword free from his belt. Its blade glittered in the sunlight.

"Stop it!" a woman's voice shouted, and I saw Heltevir push her way through the three Christians. "Do you think this is Ireland, and you are all gone aviking? Listen then," she said as she stood between us, her eyes almost as dangerous as Bjarni's blade. I held my breath to listen, and heard Sverri's screams from the knorr riding in the bay. The sound echoed off the short cliffs bordering the sides of the bay, bounced from each of the thousands of trees. "Listen, stupid *vikingr*. That is why we are here in this wilderness. Do you think they will greet us with open arms in Groenland once they discover my husband? Do you think that they will welcome any of those who sailed with a werewolf? It doesn't matter if they are Christian or not, they will think the same. That we, too, may be like Sverri. We were stupid to think that we could escape. The first ship from home would tell them stories. It doesn't matter if Thorvin has kin or not; no one would have wanted us even if he was standing next to us now," she said.

Bjarni still held his sword, though the point had dropped until its tip was close to the rock and sand of the beach. Heltevir exhaled softly.

"We can only go south," Bjorn said. "We cannot go to Groenland, nor back home to Ice Land. We must go south, where it will be warmer for the winter. It will be here soon enough, two months, perhaps more if we sail far south." Bjarni still stood quietly. "If you wish, you may take the afterboat and sail north to Groenland, the three of you. Any others who wish to join them, as well," he said, his voice carrying over the water. "You can have your share of food, your weapons—"

His words were interrupted by another scream from the ship. It was almost a howl, Sverri's cry, almost like the sound of a wolf from the edge of the glaciers back home. But that was not what stopped Bjorn's words, for the screaming howl was not alone.

An answering cry came from across the bay, from deep in the woods it seemed. The answer was even throatier than Sverri's, and the hairs on my arms moved of their own will.

"Another?" Bjarni whispered, and all I could think of was the memory of Sverri bent over the body of the farmer he'd murdered, yet now the face was different on the corpse. I tried to wipe my mind clean, but the face remained. It was my face. By Thor, mine.

"More wood, Eirik," a voice from the other side of the fire said, and the old man tossed another twisted piece of driftwood onto the blaze. Sparks climbed into the night air and I moved closer to the warmth. We had slept on ship the past four nights, and even though I had been glad, had felt safer with water between us and the noises that crowded the shores, the fire was comforting. Perhaps it had been only my imagination, but each night on ship I had believed I heard replies to Sverri's wolf howls. None of the others would talk of it, but each day everyone was more nervous than the last.

Heltevir was curled beside me, asleep, her woolen cloak tucked around her. I recognized it. Sverri had taken the red piece of cloth from a girl we'd not been able to force in our boat. Sverri had killed her quickly, a blade thrust through her stomach, and laughed. Two years ago and more. It seemed like it had never happened.

"How many on guard tonight?" I asked the shape across the fire. We had seen no sign of Skraelings, the stooped and dark-skinned savages rumored to inhabit the unknown lands, but we would still post guard. There were other things besides savages to fear. Bjorn answered softly.

"Three. One by the afterboat, one near the fire, one by the treeline," he said. "Three hours and then wake another to take your place." The way he said 'your,' I knew he wanted me to take one of the first turns. But it was better than being on the ship another night.

The man next to me shuddered in the darkness. Not from the

cold, for we were so far south that when the midday sun shone, it was almost straight above us. "I never believed in trolls," he said. It was Bjarni. He and his Christians were still with us. Heltevir had been right; no one would have welcomed us with a werewolf in our company. Bjarni knew her reasoning had been sound. "It was not a devil of the White Christ, it had no horns like the priests have told me, so it had to be a troll. Am I right?" he asked. I didn't know what to say to him, for I had only heard the screams the night before, not seen what had crept on board.

"It was a troll," Eirik said, throwing more wood on the fire. Heltevir stirred beside me. "I saw it plain in the moonlight. It had huge shoulders, and long, stinking hair. Like the underside of turf when you dig it up for buildings. And his hands . . ."

"Shut up," Bjorn said, and in the sudden flame from the new wood, I saw his face. He was afraid.

"Let him talk," said Thorstein, the young man near Eirik. Even in the dim light, I could see Thorstein's auburn hair gleam from the oils he smeared into it each morning. He was a distant kin to Sverri, but a Christian friend to the dead Thorvin.

"It may help us all to talk of it," I said quickly, hoping to get my words out before Bjorn swore. But he was quiet this time.

"Trolls, yes, they were trolls," Eirik said again after some time. "And they had troll blades that gleamed in the dark." The old man was telling a story, that was plain. Who should know better than another saga teller? He had seen *something*, of that there was no doubt, but he was stretching details to hold us in his story. What matter, I thought, for the end was the same. Trolls or not, something had come aboard our ship the night before and slit two throats.

". . . and the blades seemed alive, in a way. I heard Ari cry out, struggle against the troll, but before I could get to him, he was dead. Then Thorvold screamed, but everyone heard that," Eirik whispered. "The trolls leaped back into the water and that was that."

"Perhaps they were Skraelings," I said, wondering at the same time if it had been Sverri. But I said nothing of that fear. He'd been bound with leather thongs since we'd sailed. How could he have done this?

"We've seen no signs of anyone," Eirik said. He was not going to give up on his troll stories so easily.

"That doesn't mean there is no one there. Just because we see no smoke, nor houses, doesn't mean Skraelings couldn't be about," I said. I stared into the flames for a moment, then jerked my head up as I heard a scream-howl from the ship. We'd left Sverri alone on the knorr. No one could stand his sounds any longer. Perhaps a troll, or whatever had killed Ari and Thorvold, would creep aboard again and rid us of our werewolf. That was not a friend's way of thinking, I knew, but I wondered how many of us still thought of ourselves as friends of Sverri.

"It doesn't matter who they were," Bjorn said and Bjarni muttered agreement. "We can't stay on the ship any longer. There's not enough room to swing a blade on it." He looked at the fire. *That* was something else we couldn't have on the knorr. The fire's warmth was comforting after so long sleeping cold, but the light was what made me feel safe. We might see what came to attack us this time.

"I'll take the treeline," I said as I stood and reached for my axe. Its haft felt good in my hand. The light from the fire quickly dimmed as I walked up the beach and towards the trees. The wall of them was complete; there was no break in their solidness. What kind of men crept onto your ship and murdered you in your sleep, I wondered as I sat on a fallen tree and tried to see through the darkness. Not a brave man. Not a man that had been aviking. Like one of those in Wales, who shot at you from afar with those strange bows of theirs.

Away from the voices of the others, I could hear Sverri's screams more plainly. Every time he howled, I winced, trying to will myself to stop, but it was impossible. The sough of the trees only half-covered his noises, and even when I pressed my hands over my ears, I could still hear him. For a moment, I thought of swimming out to the ship and slitting his throat, knowing that the others would think another troll came to us. But the thought passed by, and eventually, I fell asleep.

I must have fallen asleep. I must have been dreaming when Sverri walked from the treeline and sat down beside me on the downed log. I was dreaming, so I did not fear him, even when he smiled and spoke to me.

"Halfdan, my friend," he said, "how is it that you are out here?"

Since I was dreaming, I answered. What harm in that? "Guard for the others," I said.

"Don't you want to know how I escaped the bindings?" he asked. I shook my head. "Ah, you believe this is a nightmare. It isn't, you know,"

My axe was not in my hand; it must have fallen to the ground when I dozed. Now I wished it was in my hand, for something in Sverri's voice made me believe him. I touched his shoulder with my hand, and it was solid under his woolen shirt. He was no dream.

"How did you get off the ship?" I asked. I tried to look from the corners of my eyes for my axe, but I couldn't see it in the darkness.

"Do you believe, Halfdan?" Again the question of believing.

"In what?"

"In what I am."

"You talk with riddles, Sverri," I said, wondering if I could shout out for the others.

"It is in here, you know," he said, pointing to his head. There was light enough from the moon to see that. "Your belief is in here," he said again.

"Did you kill Ari and Thorvold?" Perhaps there were no trolls, nor Skraelings, who slit throats.

"Do you think I did?" It was useless, Sverri would never answer straight. My fright was past, and though I wished to feel my axe in my hand, I was not afraid of Sverri. How could I be? His voice was soft and sane, the same voice which had spoken to me for long years of friendship, the same voice that had comforted me in crazed battle for the King. What reason would he have to harm me? Even if he killed Ari and Thorvold—for whatever reason—I was safe. My friendship was my shield.

He stood and walked towards the trees, leaving me on the fallen log. Before he stepped into the woods, he turned back and looked at me. The shadows flickered over him, seeming to change his shape with every moment.

"I am what you believe me to be, that is all," he said and the shadows changed again as the trees behind him moved. For the span of a breath, as my doubts returned, I stared and thought I saw a wolf, the gray hairs on its neck gleaming in the moonlight, it eyes yellow and blinking, but then it was gone. I rubbed my eyes hard, but there was nothing there; only trees and shadows.

Shouts reached me. The night was bright, too bright even for the full moon. Then I saw it. The knorr was ablaze from bow to stern, and the only thing I could think of was how strange the woodsmoke smelled as it waved towards the beach.

"Get the boat into the water," Bjorn's voice shouted. "Fast, before it's to the keel!" I could see several figures shove the afterboat from the beach and then jump into it as it slammed through the breakers.

I ran to the beach and grabbed the first man I came to. It was Thorstein, and he stammered from the excitement.

"Sverri's l-loose," he said, pointing to the ship. "Bjarni said he saw him leap over the side and swim for shore, just before the ship caught fire. Who would have thought . . ." he said, but I didn't let him finish, and instead ran down the shore. It was too late for me to help fight the fire on board; the men in the afterboat would have to do. I had to find Sverri.

My eyes were wide now, not half-closed by sleep. But it was useless looking for him here on the beach. He had struck for the trees, away from the light and the fire he'd set to hide his escape. I began calling for him, yelling his name out every few moments. Perhaps he was sane enough still to come to his name.

A screech of a howl answered me, and I turned to the sound, my arms suddenly far colder than they should have been. He was there, in the forest.

"Sverri!" I shouted. "Sverri, it's Halfdan. It's safe, Sverri!" I waited, and within a moment, his howl reached me. It was farther away this time. He was moving deeper into the woods.

He was truly a werewolf. Until this moment, I had not believed it. No matter what those farmer's sons had said they'd seen attack their father; no matter what Bjorn said about the wolfskin around Sverri's waist. Even Sverri's own words had not convinced me. Until now I had thought it all just troll-stories, like the tales I'd spun enough times in a safe and dry longhouse. But for that brief moment I believed in werewolves.

I stood beside the first tree at the edge of the woods, and wanted to go in after him, but I could not force myself to do it. My legs were weak, and my throat was dry, and the axe in my hand was almost too heavy to hold. So I turned away from the dark trees and walked back to the beach, my eyes on the knorr, the fire still burning in it. Sverri's screams continued to weaken in the distance.

I joined the three who stood on the beach and watched as the ship burned. There were five fighting the blaze, then, for now there were only nine of us. Though the light from the fire was bright, it seemed smaller since I'd first seen it.

"I think it was only the sail," Heltevir's voice said beside me in the dark. "Hope that is all he did," she said. A man next to her grunted a reply. I put my hand on Heltevir's arm and she moved closer to me, her warmth pressed against my side. "What will we do for Sverri?" she asked quietly. No one answered her.

We waited on the shore, watching the fire dwindle on the

knorr, then looked hard into the half-dawn as the afterboat rowed towards us. The five men in it were soot-stained and singed around their eyes. Bjorn climbed over the afterboat's thwart slowly, almost falling into the water. I moved to help him and we stumbled onto the sand. He fell to the ground, rolled over on his back and breathed deeply.

"Can she sail?" I asked him, kneeling on the sand next to him. It took him moments to catch his breath.

"In time," he finally said. "The sail is gone, the mast is charred and weakened. It will have to be replaced. The animals are dead and part of the foredeck is burned through. It could have been worse." He paused. "Where is Sverri?" Bjorn asked, looking up at me. The light was enough to see his face now, though the sun had yet to rise over the water.

"Gone into the woods," I said. "I tried to follow him." Bjorn was silent. "I did not want to go into the trees to follow him," I said, and breathed easier when Bjorn and the others nodded. They would not have followed him, either.

"Sverri will return," Heltevir said in a whisper, her gaze on the forest to our backs. She was still pressed against me. "He will get lonely and come back to us before we leave."

I remembered my certainty that he was a true werewolf, and again had doubts. How could he be a shape-shifter when we had spent our lives together? How could he have hidden it from me? I recalled his voice, and the vision of the wolf I'd seen, and wondered which was true. What should I believe? Yet I knew that if Sverri came back to us, it would not be because he was lonely. If he was sane, and only a murderer, it would be because he was angry at the bindings he'd worn since we'd sailed; if he was truly a werewolf, it would be because he was hungry and could not find anything else to feed on. For the first time since we'd sighted this terrible land, I wished it held Skraelings. Sverri would prey on those before he came to us, I hoped.

The winds swept over the bay and thundered against the turf walls of the longhouse we crowded in. There had been little to do since the storms had come for the winter except spend our time telling stories, talking about the voyage and what we had done and seen. That was the only consolation; that we had done and seen things no other dreamed of. We listened to the wind, listened to the noises from the woods that were still troll-filled to us, listened to the howls of the wolves that roamed the edges of the forest. Whether the howls were from real wolves, or from

Sverri, it was impossible to tell. I tried to believe they were real, but it was not always easy.

We had pulled the knorr onto the shore long before and built low walls around her to keep the water out. It took several days, but we finally got her turned over and a vessel shed made so the ice would not split the strakes and make her unable to hold water. The new mast was cut and shaped, but not fitted. It would have to wait until spring.

The longhouse was not large enough for us all, especially since it was dangerous to venture outside for more than a few minutes at a time. The two benches that ran along the walls were barely large enough to hold us all when we slept, even when we had two guards awake during the dark hours.

Thorstein said he saw Sverri near the cliffs on the far side of the bay. He was in his human shape, Thorstein said, but he changed before his eyes into a wolf. I did not doubt his word. Signs of Skraelings were all about as well. Footprints along the shore, the glint of something bright moving in the hills behind us, a butchered caribou far in the trees. We had not been quiet as we cut wood, or fished from the afterboat. They knew we were here, but they did not show themselves. Perhaps they were afraid of us; though I wagered they were more afraid of the werewolf that haunted the edge of our camp.

"He has been gone too long," Bjarni said. I chewed on a piece of dried fish. "Three hours is too long," he said, looking at each of us in turn.

"Snorri can take care of himself," Bjorn said. Bjorn should know: Snorri was *his* house slave. "He had good reason to be gone this long. The snow is deep."

"We could look for him," Bjarni said.

"And get lost as well?" Thorstein asked, looking up from the piece of bone he whittled on.

"Something should be done," Bjarni said again, his voice quivering slightly. I wondered if he had renounced his faith in the White Christ yet. The other two Christians, Thorstein and Gudlief, had. Cold winds and werewolves were too strong for the White Christ, it seemed.

Another howl came from outside the turf walls and everyone looked up. It was close, that one. Very close.

I reached for my axe and went for the door. Bjorn was right behind me, and the others grabbed their weapons to follow us. The wind held the door closed for a moment, but I pushed hard

and forced it open, then stepped into the snow. Light and pow-
dery, it flattened easily, though even one step was work. The
paths we'd beaten down in the snow before were covered by the
recent fall. The howl came again, off to the left, in the trees not
twenty paces away.

"What are you waiting for?" Bjorn's voice asked from behind
me. I had stopped and not known it. My arms were cold, even
through the thick furs.

"What?" I said, looking into the dimness of the trees, believing that I saw two points of light blink once, twice, three
times.

"Move aside if you are going to stand and shake," Bjorn said
loudly, pushing me to one side as he lunged through the snow
for the trees. His lance was pointed up and in front of him, but
still he was lucky when the wolf leaped from the woods.

I closed my eyes for only a moment, my heart thick in my
mouth from my fear. I heard screams behind me, and the sound
of teeth in front of me. Then I was myself, my axe lifted high
above my shoulder, my eyes wide open.

The wolf had leaped onto Bjorn's lance point, and was struggling to escape. I could see the dull point jutting from the wolf's
back. Bjorn was under the wolf, his hands in front of his face,
warding off the death snaps of the wolf's mouth. I stepped forward, and swung the axe hard onto the wolf's neck. The axe
was still sharp and cleaved the head from the body easily. Only
then did I realize I was screaming like a beserker, only then did
I feel the sweat slipping down my back and sides under my thick
furs.

Bjorn wiggled from underneath the dead wolf, and yanked his
lance from the carcass. We all waited for the shape-shifting that
we thought would come when the dead wolf flickered into the
form of Sverri, for we all believed at that moment that the dead
animal was no more wolf than any of us. But the beast's shape
remained constant, and it was growing colder by the minute.
The wolf's open neck finished steaming and still it was only a
wolf.

A howl sounded across the ice of the bay. A dim chorus of
the sounds reached us all, repeated. The blood on my axe was
frozen, I noticed.

"Snorri is still out there," Bjarni said, his breath billowing
in the cold air. "We must find him before dark."

"Before more of these find him, you mean," I said, pointing
to the wolf on the snow.

"He is dead," Bjorn said. His voice was final.

"You cannot be sure," Bjarni said. "He could be close by, hurt perhaps by a wolf."

"Bjorn is right," I said. "Snorri is dead. He has been gone almost four hours. There are too many wolves to count around us." My unsaid words were clear to all; *Sverri may be near, Sverri may have killed again.* Was our friendship enough to protect me now?

"We could make sledges from the wood of the afterboat and pull them across the ice," Thorstein said, his oily hair glistening with the snow that continued to fall. The idea was ridiculous, but we were desperate. In the background, Eirik coughed quietly. He coughed too often, lately, and I wondered how long he would live before an illness took him.

"None of us would see home," I said, turning for the house almost lost in the swirlings of the snow. It was too cold, too dangerous, to remain here and talk. Sverri could be listening behind the nearest tree, he could be calling his new-found friends down on us within the span of a breath. I walked for the house, past the men who, like myself, had once called themselves *vikingr*, but who now whispered for fears of trolls and werewolves. If I had not been so frightened, I would have taken the temptation and laughed.

The next three days we spent inside, not daring to venture where the wolves could get to us. We even pissed in the corner, throwing dirt into the hole after each use. The smell was enough to force tears, but the fear was stronger. None of us wanted to end like Snorri, more likely than not buried somewhere in the forest under a snowdrift. We talked louder with each passing night, trying to drown out the sounds of the wolves, but it did no good, for sooner or later we had to sleep, or pretend to, and then the noises came through the walls.

"It's mad to sit here and listen to them, all the night and day," shouted Bjarni from his bedroll. It was dark in the house, the only light from the hearth at the center of the room. All of us were awake now. "They've got to stop!" he yelled, louder this time. "Stop it, make them stop it!" I was up and out of my furs, but there was already someone leaning over Bjarni, soothing him. Heltevir, perhaps. But it was doing no good. "Leave me be," Bjarni screamed and there was a thud of a body on the dirt floor. Then the door burst open and a needle-like spray of snow swept into the room. Bjarni was outlined in the doorway by the light of the moon on the snow. He had his sword in his hands, its tip pointed into the air.

"Sverri!" he screamed. "Sverri, you pagan, come to me. Come give your soul to the Christ, Sverri. You will thank me for it." He yelled each word into the wind, then ran from the doorway into the storm. By the time I reached the door, he was invisible in the snow, his tracks before the doorway already drifting shut. Thorstein, one of his once-Christian friends, wanted to push past me and follow, but I held him tightly.

"Are you as mad as he? He will be dead before he can breathe and shout another curse. Do you want to join the White Christ that much?" Thorstein struggled briefly, but not seriously. He knew I was right.

It was not as crowded in the longhouse now that there were only seven of us. We sat, most of the time in silence, and listened to the sounds from outside. Increasingly, we were on each others' nerves, taunting each other with silly things that should not have mattered.

Finally, the weather broke and the wolves disappeared with the storms. The snow melted quickly, faster than I had ever seen it in Ice Land. The ground seemed to swallow the snow in great gulps. It left acres of mud where the beach's sand and rocks ended. But at least Sverri and his kind were gone.

It was not yet spring, for the sun was not climbing high enough for that, but the clear, cold air made us feel human again, and we used the time well, getting things ready to sail once the ice in the bay broke. The sail was pieced together with what spare cloth we'd been able to salvage from the knorr, the hull was tarred with seal fat, and we split some of the immense birch trees for planking on the foredeck. Bjorn and I checked the knorr, looking for places where ice had gotten between the hull strakes, but the ship was sound.

We went nowhere without our weapons. Skraeling signs were everywhere, as well as wolf tracks which crisscrossed the mud and ended in the trees. Of Bjarni we found no trace, though we found Snorri's lances thrust in the ground at the edge of the forest. One was broken, another had pieces of fur and feather tied to its shaft. Both the fur and feather were colored red, the color of dried blood, Bjorn thought. It was not actually blood, for it flaked off too easily. It was some sort of smeared paint. Skraelings? We could not decide.

The fifth day after the weather broke, I was gathering firewood at the edge of the trees, one eye watching the green darkness, one hand on my axe. But he still surprised me. Sverri had walked up behind me, and I hadn't heard a sound.

"Hello, Halfdan," he said, and I shouted and whirled all in one moment, swinging my axe in front of me. He was several feet out of reach, and he smiled as I let the axe drop. It was Sverri, by the gods, and he wore an *ulfhednar*'s wolfshirt around his waist.

"Sverri," was all I could manage to croak.

"You do not believe still, Halfdan?" he asked. He spread his arms wide, as if he was inviting attack, then the smile still on his face, let his arms fall to his sides, his thumbs hooked in the wolfskin. I turned to see if there was any other in sight, but they were all in the longhouse, or the vessel shed. I did not want to cry out.

"What of Snorri and Bjarni?" I asked. "What have you done with them?" Sverri said nothing, only smiled. "Are you werewolf?" Again, no answer. I pulled my axe up to my chest and stepped forward toward him, but he only danced back slightly.

"I am what you believe I am," he said, speaking in riddles. Normally, I take fun at a riddle as easily as the next men, but not from this thing that was Sverri.

"And if I believe you to be a harmless rabbit that I can split with this," I said, holding my axe higher, "then that is what you are?"

"If you believe." He paused. "But you will not believe that I am a rabbit. I know you too well, Halfdan. You believe me as sane as you, a murderer as you've murdered. You believe me a friend who will not harm you. But not a rabbit." He was right. No matter how I tried to imagine it, he was not a rabbit. In the bright sun I could not even believe he was a werewolf. He seemed too much like the friend he had always been. I realized, even with my brief doubts, that I'd always thought him this. Perhaps mad at times, but a friend.

"Why did you burn the ship, Sverri?" I asked. I had the feeling that if I did not keep his attention with questions, he would flee. Or worse.

"The Skraelings think me a god," he said, ignoring my question. "They are like children, in a way. I am going to stay with them, did you know that?" I shook my head. "You will leave when the ice breaks?"

"If the ship is ready."

"With only six men and a woman to sail her?" He did know

Snorri and Bjarni were dead. We stared at each other for a long while before he spoke again. "Leave as quickly as you're able. Do not linger here. Tell Bjorn that for me." And he turned and was gone, almost as if into the air, for he moved so quickly into the trees that he was gone before I'd taken one breath.

I told no one of speaking with Sverri, just as I had not said anything of the first two times. No one felt love for Sverri, and I did not think any would take kindly to one talking to a mad-man. The madness might spread, they would certainly think.

But I thought long of what Sverri had said. He had spoken as sane as any of us, though his words and eyes had been unset-tling. Why did he treasure the Skraelings so? What did they give him that he needed? What was it that we could not provide him?

"Halfdan! Halfdan, here!" Heltevir shouted from the low door-way. I turned from the broken lance I was tying together and the look of fear on her face made me stand and run to her. She looked out the door, and I followed her gaze. Down on the beach Bjorn and the others stood uneasily as a crowd of Skraelings walked towards them. At least three dozen, I thought.

They halted once they were within a score of steps from my friends. I reached behind me for an axe and ran to Bjorn, but the Skraelings did not seem to even notice me.

"We will be killed if they want it," Bjorn said to me. He held his sword in one hand, a shield in the other. At least everyone was armed, I saw, looking down the short line to Eirik, Kare, Thorstein, and Gudlief. Six against thirty-six; a battle would not last long.

The Skraelings were tall, almost as tall as I. Their hair was dark and hung loose about their shoulders, as mine did. There the likeness ended. They were red, completely red, for they had smeared something over their hair, their faces, and their bodies. Its color reminded me of the paint spread on the feather and fur we'd found tied to Bjarni's broken lance. And their eyes. They were wide, wider than any I had seen, the brown circle inside the eye wider than my thumb.

One walked apart from the others, and as he stepped forward, I heard Thorstein hiss. "Kill him now," were the only words I could catch. But Bjorn stayed where he was and did not even raise his sword, for the Skraeling was stepping carefully to us, his hands held in front of him, the palms pointed up to show he held no weapon. He spoke in some savage tongue that I could not comprehend. Pointing to the ground, then to the forest, he nodded several times, then pointed back to us, all the while talking quickly as if we understood. He smiled, shook his head, smiled again, then pointed to the woods again.

"What does he say?" Heltevir asked from behind me. She had followed me from the longhouse. I wanted to tell her to go back, but I saw she held a lance. If the Skraelings decided to kill us, she would be as dead in the longhouse as here. Perhaps she might kill some herself if they threw themselves on us, so I said nothing. She wore the red cloak Sverri had given her long ago.

The Skraeling talked quickly, pointing to us again, then to himself. We were nervous, for it seemed he would order his people to attack, but he only motioned one man forward. The second Skraeling threw a pile of furs on the ground before us, then stepped back. Eirik leaned down and felt one of the pelts. "I've never seen anything like this," he said, and the first Skraeling grated a word or two out. The name of the beast whose fur it was?

I reached behind me to Heltevir, and pulled the cloak from her shoulders. Ripping a small piece from it before she could say anything, I walked to the Skraeling and handed it to him. He stared at the red cloth, held it against his own red skin, then waved it above his head. The red of the cloak was far brighter than the paint they'd smeared themselves with. The Skraeling seemed to think highly of the cloth for he motioned another man forward who threw more pelts onto the ground. We were already wealthy men, for I knew the furs would bring us enough silver to last a season of drinking.

The red cloth was quickly torn into enough pieces for all the Skraelings, and they in turn made piles of furs in front of each of us. One by one, each of the furs were named by the Skraelings, but the sounds were too strange and did not stick in my mind. Until the leader of the savages stepped forward, a wolfskin held out in front of him, and said "Sverri," loud enough for all to hear.

It was suddenly silent, the only noise the waves on the sand to our right. Gudlief crossed himself in the manner of the White Christ; Bjorn muttered under his breath and stepped backward without knowing it.

"Sverri," the Skraeling said again. The word was garbled, but understandable. It was certainly the name of our friend. The Skraeling held out the wolfskin again, expecting us to take it, I thought.

Thorstein and Gudlief whispered to each other, and I felt Heltevir's hand on my arm. "Can that be his skin?" I heard Bjorn ask, but no one answered.

"Sverri?" the Skraeling said, stepping forward and thrusting the wolf's pelt into Bjorn's face.

"By Thor . . ." Bjorn hissed, then moved back under the Skraeling's pressure. I saw Bjorn's sword moving in his hand.

"Sverri, sverri, sverri," said the Skraeling, stepping forward with each word. He pointed to us, then to the forest, then back to us, shaking his head, saying the name over and over.

"They want Sverri," I said, suddenly understanding the Skraeling's actions. He wanted to trade the wolfskin for our werewolf, for Sverri. The wolfskin they tried to give us was payment for Sverri, *was* Sverri in their minds. "Bjorn, they want to take Sverri from us," I said, turning to our werewolf's brother, but it was too late.

Bjorn was silent, but his face was blue with anger. His sword was above his shoulder and already arcing to the Skraeling's throat. I tried to reach for Bjorn's arm, but he was too fast, and before I could suck in a breath, the Skraeling's head was cut from his neck. Blood flew onto my shirt and the madness was on us.

The Skraelings screamed, and threw their hands into the air, but we gave them no quarter. At first I tried to stop Bjorn and the others, but it was useless, for the blood-lust was in them and they were mad. Then the Skraelings broke for the trees, and quickly the air was filled with arrows like the ones the Welsh shoot with their bows. Eirik went to ground, an arrow through his throat, and he flopped as a fish does before he died. Gudlief caught two in his legs and he screamed as he fell.

It was over as easily as it had started. The Skraeling were gone, all fled into the woods, all except the ones dead on the beach. Eight, I counted altogether. One stirred, pierced by a lance, but Thorstein drew his knife and put the man to sleep. Bjorn leaned over his knees and breathed heavily. His shield was full of arrows, and his hands were red from the dead Skraelings. I let my axe drop into the sand and knelt beside it and I was sick. I'd killed two of them, and they had not even raised their hands to shield their faces. Somehow it was different than killing Irishmen.

I dimly heard Gudlief moaning in the distance, and Kare's voice trying to comfort him, but did not concern myself with it. We had to leave as soon as possible, I knew now. The Skraelings

would be back for revenge, that was certain, and with their numbers, we would not live long in their attack.

"They have killed Sverri," I heard Bjorn say. I looked up,
and he was talking to Heltevir. "That was his skin they cut from
him."

"No," I said, wiping my mouth and the sourness from it.
"They wished to trade for Sverri. The wolfskin was ours if we
would leave Sverri with them. They think Sverri is a god."

Bjorn looked at me. "How do you know this?"

What could I tell him? The truth, that Sverri himself had told
me this? Or some lie Bjorn would surely see through? "I've
spoken with Sverri three times since we sailed. Last night he
told me this. He said they thought him a god, and warned us to
leave." It was the truth, though it did not sound like it, even to
my own ears, when I said it aloud. But Bjorn believed it; his
face showed that he did.

Heltevir spoke next. "You talked with him?" I nodded. "Then
he was not mad?"

"Not always," I said.

"We must leave in the morning," Bjorn said.

"The ship isn't ready. We have the mast to fit . . ." I began.

"The afterboat will do. Four men could not sail the knorr. If
we ran into any storms, we would drown." He was right. With
Eirik dead and Gudlief unable to stand, for his legs were surely
broken by the arrows, we did not have enough hands for the
knorr. The six of us would fit into the afterboat, though it would
be a tight sailing. "Everything but food and water and weapons
must be left," Bjorn said. "Even those," he said, pointing to
the furs still piled on the beach. A pity, for they would have
made us rich.

We spent the rest of the day burying Eirik and readying the
afterboat for the morning. All our possessions that we could not
take with us we threw in a heap next to the longhouse. The furs
from the Skraelings were tossed on top, then we added a layer
of wood. When we left, we would put a torch to it all. There
was no use leaving it for the Skraelings.

Night came too quickly, and we huddled in the longhouse, the
fire bright, our weapons in our hands. We tried to talk of the
battle, Bjorn even started to draw up a verse or two for it, but
his heart was not in it. We all thought too often of Sverri and
the Skraelings.

I waited until they were all asleep. Only Gudlief was awake,
but his pain occupied him. I didn't think he saw me slip outside.

The moon was new, and the darkness was thick around my eyes. I waited until I was used to it, then stepped away from the longhouse towards the woods. The trees were impossible to see. I could tell where they were only because they were darker than everything else. I stumbled many times, hitting my shins on logs, but I finally decided I'd come far enough from the house, and found a dead tree to sit on. I was not sure what I was waiting for, but I knew I had to wait.

"Sverri, old friend," I said to the shadow that moved in front of me. My arms were cold, and the axe heavy in my hands, but I kept my voice level. What if it was not Sverri, but a real wolf, or a vengeful Skraeling?

"Halfdan Haukadale," he said. It was Sverri, and I breathed easier. "You did not take my advice, Halfdan."

"We leave in the morning," I said.

"I told them that you would be dangerous," Sverri said. "But they wanted to see their god's companions, and trade."

"They offered skins for you," I whispered.

"I told them you were dangerous, but I didn't try to stop them. A god cannot stop his children from foolishness, can he?" Sverri paused. "Yet I did not expect your thirst . . ."

"It was over before it started. Bjorn thought the skin was yours, and he went mad. I could not stop him . . ."

"You tried so hard you killed as well," Sverri said.

He had been watching from the woods that morning, then. "We leave in the morning," I said again.

"The ship is not ready."

"We leave it behind. The afterboat will take us east. Perhaps all the way to Ireland. If we do not talk in our drink, no one there will know we sailed with a werewolf."

Sverri was quiet there in the darkness before me. He sighed and I wondered what he thought.

"Come with us," I said. "You are sane, Sverri. Come with us."

"Is that what you believe, Halfdan? That I am sane?" Still, the talk of believing. "The Skraelings believe me to be a god. A god who can alter his shape at will," Sverri said. In the darkness, it was difficult to see, but I can swear I saw Sverri's outline shiver, then slip into that of a wolf. Hot, sour breath came to my nose and the sound of an animal panting to my ears. Then the outline shivered again, and Sverri was there. "I am what is believed, Halfdan. In Ice Land, or Groenland, or even Ireland, what would they believe? That I was a god? I do not think so.

A murderer, perhaps, like those farmers thought me, but no god. It would be the same everywhere. Werewolves do not kill for food; they kill for pleasure. That is what I would have to do, then."

I began to understand his concern with believing. "Then Snorri and Bjarni, Ari and Thorvold?" I asked softly.

"Their beliefs were too strong to ignore," Sverri said. "They died of what they believed would harm them here. Ari and Thorvold wondered of trolls, Snorri and Bjarni believed I was a werewolf. They believed they would be murdered, so that was what happened."

"And the Skraelings do not," I said. I thought I saw Sverri nod in the dark. "You wish to remain here, where you will not have to kill." Again, I thought I saw movement. "What *are* you, Sverri?"

"What you believe," he whispered. "You believe me to be a friend, a man, a sane man, so that is what I am for you."

"For Bjorn? And Heltevir?"

"They believe other things. I would murder Bjorn and become a madman for my wife. That is what they believe."

"Were you ever a man, Sverri?" I remembered the days long ago when we'd gone aviking and he had laughed as he killed a girl in Ireland. "Were you ever human, Sverri?"

"While that is what everyone thought of me, I was a man." He was quiet for some time. "While we were *ulfhednar* for the King, I changed, Halfdan. Too many enemies of the King believed the *ulfhednar* power, that we were truly werewolves in battle, and so it all began. Too many believed to ignore. Home to Ice Land was no different. Even Heltevir thought me changed from those two years with the *ulfhednar*. I was a man until the Kind called for me. But beliefs change, Halfdan."

So they did, for in the darkness there with Sverri, I wondered what would happen if I had doubts of my beliefs. I thought him a sane man, a friend who would not harm me, and so he was. What if that belief slipped from me and I thought him a werewolf, as Bjorn so obviously did? My answer came swiftly, for the hot breath reached my nose again, and a low growl came from the shape I knew would be that of a wolf, if only I had light enough to see. The image passed, and again it was only Sverri.

"Your belief is strong, Halfdan."

"Luck to you, Sverri." I stood and held out my hand, groping for his shoulder. Then it was there and I felt his hand on my shoulder. His fingers gripped my shirt tight.

"Thank you, Halfdan Haukadale. You always thought me a friend. I had no desire to be anything else for you." And his mind slipped from me and he was gone, through the trees, heading to the Skraelings who thought him a god. And so he was one.

It was near dawn and I felt more tired than I had ever felt before. I wanted to sleep, forget everything Sverri had said. I knew I would not, and that thought tired me even more.

The wind and the currents were strong and though it had been only eighteen days since we sailed from Sverri's Land, already we had seen hints of land. First there was green moss in the water, and then several birds. They were the kind who lived in the south of Ireland, so that was where we would make landfall, I believed.

I believed. Two small words, but the difference between living and dying in the wilderness. I had tried to tell Bjorn, Heltevir, Kare, and Thorstein, even crippled Gudlief, of what I knew, but the words always came out wrong, and they only looked at me strangely, as if I was a Skraeling and spoke an unknown tongue. Whether they believed me was not my concern. Their beliefs were their own, after all.

As we neared landfall, I could only remember when we left Sverri's Land. It was gray, and colder than it should have been, but we waded into the water, pushing the afterboat in front of us. When the water was deep enough, we each climbed in. Bjorn set the sail while I held the steering oar.

We each looked back one last time, seeing the smoke from the pile of goods we had set afire rather than leave to the Skraelings. There was movement in the trees, and then a figure stepped out of the darkness and onto the beach. Heltevir cried out, and Bjorn swore, but I only looked.

It was Sverri, waving farewell to us, a group of Skraelings behind him in the woods. He had on his leather helmet, a lance in his hand. He was just as when we went aviking together so many years ago, before the King called us to become *ulfhednar*, and forced the change on Sverri.

What Bjorn and the rest saw, I had no way of knowing, though I had guesses I thought would have been on the mark. A wolf, a madman, what did it matter? He was what he was, that was all. Each according to his own desires.

I was happy with what I believed, and would not exchange it for all the gold crosses in the White Christ's heaven. *Beliefs change, Halfdan*, Sverri had said to me in the dark that last night. *I hope not, old friend.*

For if they do, who then would you be?

Galatea

Kristi Olesen

SPRING HAD COME, but the roses were still ugly, the new buds pinched off. When he ordered roses to be planted in the women's courtyard, Pygmalion had assured Galatea that their blossoms would be as exquisite as their thorny stems were misshapen. He pointed to one and then another, telling her which would be crimson, which dark-wine, which white, but she couldn't imagine the shiny red shoots and stubby round leaves producing anything but more thorns. Still, she checked them daily, waiting for the transformation. Pygmalion had told her to.

She examined the stems again, looking behind the leaves and studying the ground as best she could without bending or stooping. Nothing. Yesterday she had discovered the first tiny buds, three red and one white, tight-wrapped and fragile. She tried not to wonder who had plucked them. Or why. Pygmalion rarely visited this garden anymore.

Resting her hands on her huge belly, she sat carefully on one of the richly carved cedar benches that flanked the doors to the bedchamber. She gazed at her stomach, fingers tracing haphazard circles over the child that lay growing beneath. One more month. When Artremis again showed herself fully in the night sky, Galatea would be a mother. The roses would have many leaves then and the bushes of myrtle that crouched along the courtyard walls would be covered with flowers of pink and white. Or so Pygmalion said. Galatea had never seen spring.

Myrtle and roses, a dovecote and a pool for swans—all Pygmalion's way of honoring and thanking Aphrodite for her gift: for Galatea, the perfect woman, whose delicate skin was as unmarred as the ivory from which she had been carved.

"Will it be a boy or a girl, do you think Mistress?"

Galatea started and looked up. Drusilla stood before her smiling shyly, one sandaled foot rubbing at the other, her pale, straight hair straying from under her headband. Galatea returned the smile.

"A boy. Pygmalion says it must be a boy." She looked back at her lap. "Drusilla, do you know what happened to the buds? On the roses? I found the first yesterday and now they're gone. Who picked them?"

Drusilla flushed at the unexpected harshness in Galatea's voice. "I . . . he . . . I couldn't say, Mistress," she muttered, "maybe one of the gardeners took them. Shall I ask? I can ask if you want."

Galatea sighed and gentled her tone. "No. No, dear, don't bother. Silly to worry. They were so small. So small." She examined her hands, turning them over slowly as if she might find the missing buds hidden in them if only she didn't move too quickly.

Drusilla cleared her throat. "Mistress? Are you ill? Would you like me to rub your forehead? Can I get you anything?"

"No, thank you, Drusilla. I'm fine." She forced herself to smile again. "I was thinking about the banquet tonight. How exciting to have a guest after so long! I'm anxious to meet this bard and hear his singing." She had said the words to reassure Drusilla, but as she spoke she realized she *was* excited; a new face would help to break the long quiet of dinners in the great hall. And the tales! To others the poems were old, heard over and over since childhood, but to Galatea each was fresh, full of plots, heartaches and battles all the more intriguing for their strangeness.

"Go on, Drusilla," she said, her smile now a true one, "Go help the others with the preparations. I'll call you when I'm ready to bathe."

"Yes, Mistress. And about the roses? Ask one of the men. Maybe they can tell you." She bowed quickly and set off across the courtyard to the passageway that led through the men's courtyard to the kitchens at the rear of the house. Galatea watched the slave girl's frail back as she skirted awkwardly around the pond, the spindly rose plants and the chittering sparrows in their standing cages.

How simple the girl made it sound. Ask one of the men. But Galatea knew that, though Pygmalion had never specifically forbidden her to seek advice or guidance from the slaves, he would be displeased should he discover his wife on friendly terms with anyone other than himself, male or female. He tolerated Drusilla only because Galatea had to have at least one attendant, and the skinny blond slave, hardly more than a child, was too shy to have developed a talent for the wile and manipulations that made Pygmalion mistrust all females, save his own creation. He did not want his wife sullied by contact with the common run of woman.

She plucked an orange-blossom from the tree beside the bench and inhaled its fragrance, broad and sugary, without the subtle shifts and layers of scent in the white roses that Pygmalion so adored. He had given her white roses every day, back at the beginning. He had let her meet other people then, too—travelers, and occasionally family friends or other artists. They had all been kind though reserved, treated both Galatea and Pygmalion with the same mixture of reverence and familiarity that they used when speaking of immortals. The magic had happened right here, on their own island; even the slaves behaved as if this special couple belonged to them, handling Galatea both as a priceless pet and as a distant character from a bard's song. After all, she *was* a living miracle, and Pygmalion, the third son of a leading Cyprian family, had already been a celebrated sculptor when first he had begun to shape the now-famous tusks. Then, to be blessed by the personal intervention of Aphrodite, the Cyprian, the islander's most cherished deity: this was the fabric from which the poems were shaped.

Galatea sighed again and picked up her wool and carding-comb. She didn't *feel* like a poem. She felt much too human. With each passing day, as the ache in her back worsened, her apprehensions about the birth grew deeper. Oh, Hera, she prayed silently, please let it be a boy. Let the birth be easy. Let Pygmalion continue to love . . . But of course he loved her. He wasn't leaving her alone so often because his joy in her diminished; he was an artist, one of the blessed few whom the Muses chose to visit when they left their mountain. It would be sacrilege for him to ignore the nine sisters' holy gift. If only—

She pushed the wool aside and looked beyond the clay tiles of the low roof to the peaks of the northern range. Light from the late afternoon sun brought out muted ribbons of brown, ocher, and wine on the steep slopes and gilded the far-off thickets of cypress, oak, and cedar.

If only Pygmalion would take her walking in the mountains as he had when she was new, or let her go with him when he rode out to oversee the care of his groves, or take her on his calls to neighbors and family. There was so much she wanted to learn about Pygmalion and his world, but he kept her here, cloistered in this lovely, cool house in its pretty, fertile valley. He retreated to his studio, appearing only for meals. Then he ate rapidly and spoke little, mind focused inward, hands recalling the stone.

The sun angled past the roof and touched Galatea's cheek. Leaving the wool and comb tangled together on the bench, she rose and walked slowly to her rooms. Unveiled, she never stayed outdoors for very long. She had to protect her skin. Pygmalion noticed each tiny line, each mark, each discoloration, as he noticed every tremulous smile or blush, and every graceful movement of Galatea's full, matchless body.

Half-listening to the jabber of the sparrows from the courtyard, she sat on the edge of her bed to remove her sandals, recalling the way he had watched her at dinner last afternoon—the way he always watched her, of late. Rubbing his long, auburn beard, he judged and measured, the sinews in his arms jumping as his black eyes swept her form, searching for the inhuman perfection he had dowelled and whittled into a pale statue; searching for the unalterable innocence he hoped the goddess he had carved into this mortal woman's soul.

And finding what? Galatea stroked her stomach. He had not come to her apartments of an evening for many months. When she was new, she had known the Cyprian was with them, for the doves had cooed day and night, never leaving the cote, and the house had smelled of incense, roses, and myrtle. When Pygmalion made love to her, their light, shared laughter had frothed like the foam from which Aphrodite had sprung, whole and brilliant. He stayed at her side for weeks on end, shielding her from all other company, whispering into her ear, arranging and rearranging her hair and clothing, choosing the foods she ate and the wines she sipped.

He had told her everything—given her everything. She glanced about her bedchamber at the enameled friezes of hunt and harvest, at the plates of worked bronze on lintel and jamb. In every corner were whimsical statues of animals, carved from wood and covered in beaten gold, art to entertain a girl-child. And on every table lay shells and pearls, beads of amber and copper, belts of soft bright leathers, gleaming necklaces set with rubies and diamonds, golden chains, coronets, fillets, bracelets and anklets. Her bed and windows were draped in cloth of purple, dipped in the finest Tyrian dyes, her chitons all the most excellent weave, simply white or saffron.

Which would she wear tonight? She pulled the twisting cord near her pillow; copper chimes tinkled. Drusilla appeared in the doorway, brushing at the coal smudged on the front of her tunic.

She bowed, sniffling. "Yes, Mistress? Will you bathe?" By tugging at her headband she had managed to slide it down over one ear, making her hair bulge in sweaty clumps.

Galatea didn't let herself laugh. "Yes," she said, rising and unfastening her belt, "is the tub filled? I'll want myrrh for my hair and orange-blossoms in the water."

"I've already put flowers in, Mistress, and I'll get the myrrh right away. Do you need help with your chiton?"

"No, dear. Go ahead to the tubs. I'll come in a minute." Drusilla ran from the room, sandals slapping on marble. The poor girl wanted so desperately to please, a need Galatea understood too well. She picked up a long-sleeved pharos, wondering whether Pygmalion would rather see her arms covered or bare. Gold chains, or copper? As she undressed she inspected her reflection in the polished bronze panel near the window. No bruises, pimples, or cuts. But her breasts were so swollen, and her belly . . .

A dove flew past, flashing low over the orange tree, landed on the roof at the far side of the courtyard and began to preen its milky feathers. Galatea imagined Pygmalion's eyes and closed her own, arms crossed tenderly over her stomach.

The heifer stood docile under her gilded horns as the blade crossed her throat and blood splashed crimson on her white withers. Tendrils of purple-blue incense rode the breeze, twining with the sighs and prayers of unhappy lovers. The heifer shuddered and toppled. Priests swarmed, flaying the snowy hide, chopping portions from the thighs, setting them on the altars. Flames sizzled as the fat dripped and the red wine poured, roiling the hungry brown smoke. The priests chanted as they probed the entrails. Prayers grew fervent. Pygmalion stretched his arms skyward, tears on his tanned face.

The Cyprian's laughter filled the temple. Three times the fire burned white. Three times, higher and higher, up it leapt, floating above the altar. Six times in all the goddess showed her favor.

And the flames melted ivory to wax and wax to flesh, and each stroke of fire thumped at the pulse of a statue. Crimson blood beat in her forehead and forced her lungs into rhythm.

She gasped, sucking in sweet incense and the heavy smoke, her skin overrun with Aphrodite's pale, cold blaze. She waited for him, limbs still hard and leaden, until he took her and the last vestiges of stiffness dissolved. His warm lips were on hers, eagerly giving her his breath and water, so good, so strong—

"Galatea!" Pygmalion's voice rapped out from across the central hearth. "Our honored guest asked you a question. Shyness is becoming, but only in its place. Give an answer."

Galatea felt the copper-work of the divan digging into her back, felt the heat from the hearth, saw the table resting on its bronze tripod before her, tasted the bite of herbs on her tongue. She was not in the temple of Aphrodite. She was not fresh-made, wreathed in silver flame, receiving her husband's love for the first time. She was reclining in the great hall of her home, just having finished the oysters, listening to the bard, Doran, tell of his travels while they waited for the platters of meat and salt-fish to be carried in. How long had she been unaware? She had not relived her creation so vividly in many months. Did this mean that the Cyprian had returned? Was this a sign? She found she was panting, glazed in icy sweat. She swallowed, trying to calm herself and toying with her bread as she searched for words. The cloying incense of her vision clogged her throat.

The bard caught her eyes and gave her a kind smile. "Maybe your lovely lady did not hear the question, sir," he said, not looking at Pygmalion for a response. Galatea could not break from the bard's blue gaze. "I'll repeat it. What do you think of your husband's latest sculpture? Are you surprised at the change?"

Now she knew she must speak, for Pygmalion's annoyance was palpable. "I—I have not seen his work recently," she whispered. "I have not been allowed—"

"What? Not allowed to see such magnificent art? Not allowed to admire your husband's handiwork?" Doran's banter was a little too sharp. He bit off a hunk of crust and spoke around his chewing. "For shame, Pygmalion. Your charming wife should know that you no longer carve women—or men, for that matter, or any breathing thing."

Galatea looked from the bard to her husband, puzzled. Was this a jest? No, Pygmalion's mouth was sternly set. He was no longer annoyed. He was angry.

She inclined her head modestly. She knew she should remain silent, but curiosity goaded her. "What . . . what does my husband sculpt, then? I know he carves no women. I—I was the last. He stopped after me.'' Yes, that was the right thing to say. She sensed a slight shift in Pygmalion's humor. How she wanted to make him smile at her!

Doran sought for her gaze once more, but she refused to meet him. ''Indeed,'' said the bard, nodding. ''had I created beauty such as yours, lady, I would never sculpt another female. This I understand. And I understand why the honored Pygmalion never carves in ivory—no mere tooth, no matter how magnificent an animal it came from, could compete with the pallor of your skin.'' Pygmalion stayed motionless behind his table, ignoring the compliment. ''But your husband gives us only vegetation now—myrtle, and the thorny stems of roses without the blossoms. And only in the black stone of Hephaestus. Powerful, but uncanny. His muses show us no emotion—''

''My intercourse with the nine sisters is *my* business, bard!'' Pygmalion leaned forward on his divan, gripping the armrests. ''I create what they set in my heart. I do not question the immortals. Their gifts are too easily revoked.''

Doran's hands fluttered. ''Forgive me, lord. I meant no offense.'' His tone was warm, his smile conciliatory. ''I spoke only as one craftsman to another. I overstep myself. My excitement at being in conversation with so famous an artist makes me forget my manners. Please, accept my apologies, you and the lady both.'' Though he seemed to be speaking to Pygmalion, Galatea knew his words were for her.

For a moment the only sound in the hall was the faint hiss of the embers. Galatea tried to make herself small, trying to blend into the massive column at her back. The chink and clash of kettles and pots filtered down the hall from the kitchen, accompanied by the smell of roast mutton. The main course was on its way.

''No offense taken, bard,'' said Pygmalion finally. Galatea let all her breath escape. ''Galatea understands nothing of art; the discussion of it only upsets her. It is easy to forget what a child she is when looking at her womanly form. Remember, she is but nine months old. Why, her little slave-girl, Drusilla, understands more about the world than does my wife. Do not be misled by the ripening of her body. Her awareness is hardly more than that of the infant within her.'' He inspected her with an air of fond propriety. ''Did you know that her entire face was carved from a single tusk?'' Doran shook his head and arranged himself more comfortably on his divan.

Galatea relaxed. This she understood. Her childishness and

the art involved in her construction were favorite themes of Pygmalion's. On the rare occasions when guests were allowed to share dinner in the great hall, the conversation generally pivoted on the various qualities of Pygmalion and Aphrodite's perfect creation—her modesty, beauty, and complete simplicity. It was a role Galatea played with assurance, letting Pygmalion see only a part of what she had managed to learn when he was absent. She knew he enjoyed her most when she held her tongue and kept her eyes downcast.

"It was the largest single piece of ivory I have ever found," Pygmalion continued, warming. "They say there is only one other like it in the world. The beast it came from was ancient, perhaps the last of its kind. A huge creature, certainly. Akin to an elephant, but of a size to suit the gods."

Doran nodded and sat up, encouraged by Pygmalion's enthusiasm to launch into a description of the various fantastic animals he had come across on his journeys. Galatea reclined quietly, hands folded in her lap, glad to be ignored.

While the slaves brought in the steaming meat and cold fish, Pygmalion and Doran chatted amicably, comparing details of traveling, dissecting common acquaintances or the performances of other artists, and gossiping about Cyprian politics. Galatea listened and absorbed, trying to piece this new information into what she already knew. She hoped that one day Pygmalion would come to her for thoughtful discourse; she would please and surprise him with the amount of knowledge she had collected. He would begin to love her for more than her innocent femininity. And she needed to know as much about the outside world as possible to be a good teacher for her child when it came. She held her belly. She *would* be a good mother.

Pygmalion's habit was to call for wine only when the meal was finished, but tonight, in honor of Doran, the libations were poured early, and they all drank of a dry, gold vintage as they ate the main course. The bard kept the slaves busy filling the krater, frowning jovially when they mixed in too much water.

By the time the sweetmeats and fruit arrived along with Pygmalion's special wine, a strong, honied brew, almost black in color, Doran's voice was too loud, his gestures over-broad, and he giggled often—an odd sound coming from so large a man.

He began to watch Galatea, staring at her tapered fingers as she lifted her kylix and sipped daintily. Pygmalion did not like her to drink more than one well-watered cup of wine at any meal.

To her surprise, she discovered her distress at the bard's scrutiny changing to pleasure. His teeth were white and clean against his curly black beard. Tan, broad-muscled and unusually tall, his figure was even more imposing than Pygmalion's. Her husband, engrossed in a lengthy description of his last visit to the oracle of Apollo, did not seem to notice that Doran's attention had drifted elsewhere.

The bard caught her eyes over the rim of his kylix and again she was trapped by the steady blue gaze. He set his cup down and smiled slowly, shiny teeth biting his lower lip. His well-oiled beard reddened in the hearth's glow. A breeze slid through the smoke-hole in the low ceiling, carrying the smell of—roses? Galatea strained forward. Had she heard laughter? Yes. Yes, she felt the Cyprian's welcome mirth, but this time it held a dissonant lilt, a mocking edge. Teasing sweetness. Chilled, arms prickling, she looked away from the bard, knowing his hot stare had not wavered. The hall was quiet. Pygmalion had finished his story.

"It is time for you to retire, Galatea. You must remember the child. You need to rest. The bard and I have much to discuss. You will be bored. Drusilla?" His words were stone. Fidgeting with the hem of her tunic, the slave came out from her station behind a column. "Take your mistress to her apartments. She is tired."

Galatea commanded herself to rise, chided her limbs for their heaviness, but she did not move. Uncertain, Drusilla stood at the head of her mistress's divan, glancing unhappily at Pygmalion, whose mouth was a hard, straight line.

Anger. Galatea was feeling anger. Was it hers or Pygmalion's? She was shaking. "My lord." How loud her voice was! "I would be pleased to stay a while longer. I've not yet heard the bard sing. We haven't had a guest for so long. I would like to stay and listen—" She shut her mouth abruptly, awed by Pygmalion's reaction to her gentle dissension. He made as if to rise or speak, broad shoulders tensing, then all at once lost his strength and withered back like an old man or an uncertain child. He was diminished. She had hurt him. When she had thought he was self-involved, attending only to his story-telling, he must have been observing her exchange with Doran. He had been testing her.

The hall filled with the smell of roses, backed by a musk of decay and incense. The laughter came again, louder. Could Doran hear it? Or Pygmalion? Her husband stayed silent, unreachable, staring at nothing. The odor increased, a stifling perfume. Was she going mad? Doran's fingers drummed noiselessly against his thigh as he gazed into his cup. The laughter faded and disappeared.

Forcing her knees to unlock, she rose, awkward for the first time in her life, shivering so much that her pharos slipped off her shoulder, revealing the outer curve of her breast. Drusilla adjusted the garment hastily, but Galatea knew both Doran and Pygmalion had seen. The hall was too warm. She was dizzy and the child weighed too much, skewing her balance. She leaned on Drusilla.

"Forgive me, lord. You are right. I—I am unwell. I will retire. Good night." Pygmalion did not reply and she could not look at him. Without turning back, she and Drusilla walked unsteadily the length of the hall and out into the courtyard.

Behind, she heard the bard begin to tune his cithera; or was that the Cyprian's discordant laughter? No, it was Doran. He started to recite, the cithera's high tang accenting each verse. She couldn't discern the words of the poem, but the ponderous rhythm was clear. As Galatea went to her room, Doran, the bard, chanted an elegy and doves clustered on the roof.

Galatea slept badly, remembering none of her dreams, but knowing they had been foul. She woke early, her mouth tasting of soured wine, her temples throbbing. Outside her window she heard slaves calling to one another, grunting and cursing. Curious as to the reason for such commotion so soon after dawn, she wrapped herself in a purple cloak and went to the casement.

The sky was cloudless, the mountain peaks washed with gentle pinks and blues. Wild birds darted and hopped as they bathed in the pond, avoiding the pecks of the swans.

Two slaves, red-faced and sweaty, strained at a cart jammed in the courtyard's rear door. The load was shrouded and bulged oddly, making peaks and chasms in the dun cloth. Whatever was underneath rattled as the slaves tugged. Stone for Pygmalion's studio, probably: the black stone of Hephaestus, to be carved into a huge bush of myrtle or a dark, blossomless rose, thorns sharp and daunting. The workers pushed and pulled, rocking the cart back and forth until it rolled forward, tipped, and crashed on its side, spilling the load. The shroud fell away, revealing the material from which Pygmalion would work his next sculpture.

It was not black stone from the ugly god of fire. Across the shards and smaller teeth, wrapped and padded carefully, lay a huge tusk, the largest piece of ivory Galatea had ever seen. Poking through its covering, the tip shone dully, palest white, the color of innocence. A dove settled on the tusk, plumage a shade darker than the smooth surface; while the slaves righted the cart and began to reload, the bird fluttered off and rose, wings beating as it caught the sea-wind.

Galatea watched until it became an icy dot melding into the light sky. She did not look down until the workers had rolled the cart across the courtyard and into the hall. When they were gone, she studied the rose plants, unable to recall which had begun to flower white. She lifted her head and sniffed; orange blossoms and breakfast cooking, dew from the fields and fresh-turned earth in the furrows. By the time the crops were ready for harvest, Galatea would be one year old and the mother of Pygmalion's first child. She reached across the casement and touched a red-tipped shoot on the nearest stem, then pulled back to sit on the edge of the bed, bare feet dangling above the marble floor.

An hour later Drusilla came to awaken her mistress and found her sitting in the same place. Galatea's eyes were shut and her fingers traced endless circles over the perfect ivory of her belly. Sparrows chattered from their cages in the courtyard.

How F. Scott Fitzgerald Became Beloved in Springfield

George Alec Effinger

IT WAS ONE o'clock in the morning, and the gin was still flowing like a spring flood of melted snow. People had passed out, those whose constitutions couldn't keep up with the spirit of the fun-loving 1920s; they had been dragged from the parlor out onto the lawn. Pale clouds blew across the yellow moon, as if blown toward the ocean by breezes of jazz music exhaled by the great bright house. Laughter sparkled like champagne; amidst the ruins of the buffet, swans sculpted of ice sank slowly and sadly within themselves. And still people arrived looking for fun, finding instead gin and jazz and melting waterfowl.

For though the party was loud and blazing with electric life, it was curiously morose. There is nothing more common yet more uncomfortable than a party that turns thoughtful after midnight. The people who had arrived at eight had either gone home or were stretched out on the shadowed lawn; the new arrivals looked around, saw the false vivacity of the dancing drunken couples, and wondered if the long drive had been worth it. They looked at each other, wondering what had turned the wild evening into a desperate imitation of pleasure.

The answer was simple, but hidden from the guests. F. Scott Fitzgerald, the famous author, their extravagant host, had not attended his own party. Instead, he sat brooding in his study on the second floor, looking at a copy of his new novel, *The Great Gatsby*. The clinking of glasses reached him from the rooms below, the tinkling giggles of the blonde bobbed girls, the occasional tumult of lighthearted destruction. He heard nothing. He stared at his book, not truly seeing it, but seeing instead what he had wanted it to be, what he had wanted it to represent for him. Whenever he swept away the idealized vision and be-held what he had done, his spirit sank even more. He felt a great loneliness, a great lacking.

Zelda came into the study without knocking. She stood in the doorway for a long moment watching her husband, concerned for him. She came up behind him and put a hand on his shoulder. "The book has been published," she said. "It's too late to worry now. You can't change a thing about it."

"Oh," said Fitzgerald, "it isn't the book, really. I don't want to change anything in it. A word here or there, a phrase, you know. But it says what I wanted it to."

"Then what's troubling you? Our guests have missed you. They think it's odd of you not to greet them all night."

He smiled and tapped the book. "I'm becoming my own character," he said.

"It's too late for that." Sometimes Zelda showed how much insight she had into her husband's mind; she knew that he couldn't become his own character, because Jay Gatsby had been torn out of him in the first place.

"Then I don't know what it is," he said.

"Springfield," she whispered. "It was Springfield with *This Side of Paradise*, with *The Beautiful and the Damned*, with all the story collections. It's Springfield and Mamie Simon."

"Yes," he said, sighing. "I can't understand it." He stood, tossing the book onto his desk. "I want a drink."

Zelda smiled and took his hand. "Let's go downstairs and make a couple of drinks and say hello to our friends and throw ice water on the people sleeping on our grass. Just like in the old days."

Fitzgerald's face clouded. "The old days," he murmured. He shook his head. Somewhere, somehow he had become cynical about his own work; Mamie Simon was responsible for that, but he couldn't comprehend how she had done it to him.

"Come *on*," urged Zelda.

Fitzgerald let out one more heavy sigh, turned his back on Gatsby, and went downstairs with his wife. It was time to do something about Mamie Simon; it would take a while to decide exactly what.

In the morning, with the golden sunlight streaming in through the broken glass, the problem didn't seem any easier to solve. Fitzgerald moped around the house, picking up ruined books and putting them back on the shelves, kicking large shards of things into piles on the sodden carpet, feeling the wrists of comatose guests for signs of life. The atmosphere, though rich and gay and young, was oppressive. Zelda couldn't stand it any longer.

"What would Ernest do?" she cried.

Fitzgerald looked at her, a little astonished. "Ernest won't ever have this problem," he said. "I can't even imagine it happening to him."

"Then what about any of the others? You and Ernest are the top of the heap. If Mamie Simon can do this to you, the others lower down in the heap must have it even worse. Find out what they do about it."

"Say," said Fitzgerald slowly, "I might be able to learn something from them." He dug out his wallet and looked through the scraps of paper, his personal file of telephone numbers. He spent the morning calling his friends, other writers who might have a solution to offer. He talked to John Dos Passos, he talked to Theodore Dreiser, he talked to Willa Cather, and Edna Ferber, and Sinclair Lewis. Then he called up Ring Lardner and William Faulkner and Eugene O'Neill and (with a phone number that was a closely guarded secret) B. Traven. They all told him the same thing, the very thing that Gertrude and Ernest and Maxwell and all the others had told him: he should take Zelda and their daughter Scottie on a mad, wild trip to Europe. Then when he came back, the reporters would meet him at the boat, and Mamie Simon would never be able to ignore him again. And neither would the Dolphin Bookshop in Springfield.

"Sounds good to me," said Zelda. This was in the days when she was being a pretty good sport about everything.

So they packed quickly and got on the next liner to France. The story of that trip has been told elsewhere, and very little happened that is pertinent to this account, so with a kind of narrative magic we will skip ahead to the day when F. Scott Fitzgerald learned to his dismay that nothing had changed.

"Well," he said, "here we are, home at last." He carried his suitcase up to the front door. There were still people sleeping off that last party in the bushes. Zelda and little Scottie went inside, but Fitzgerald lingered on the porch. The vague distress that had bothered him so much before the vacation returned, more painful than ever. He knew what he had to do.

"Zelda," he called.

She came back outside and looked at her husband.

"Zelda," he said, "I'm going to Springfield."

"I knew you would," she said. "Go box their ears. Give 'em one for me. Let 'em know they can't treat you like this. I'll have the porch light on for you when you get back. I'm proud of you, honey."

Fitzgerald only nodded grimly. He kissed his wife and daughter goodbye, like Hector going out to meet Achilles, and grabbed his suitcase. He was more fiercely determined than ever before in his life, even more than when he was wooing his lovely bride. He was going to force his hometown, Springfield, to sit up and take notice.

Now, before we get on with describing the eerie events that occurred in Springfield, one fact ought to be pointed out: as many college sophomores know (but barely anyone else), F. Scott Fitzgerald did *not* come from a town called Springfield. He was from St. Paul, Minnesota. But the more astute readers will already suspect that this story is not really about F. Scott Fitzgerald at all. This whispered aside is for the benefit of the less astute readers, many of whom may still have some trouble figuring everything out. But there's a limit to just how much help you can expect from a story.

While we were speaking, Fitzgerald traveled from his palatial mansion on Long Island to his hometown of Springfield. It was a long, tiring journey by train and hired car. He checked into the best hotel, the Springfield Manor, and after he unpacked his suitcase he began to plan out his course of action.

First, he needed to take on Mamie Simon, at the office of the Springfield newspaper's weekly supplement, *Springfield-Match*.

Second, he was going to challenge the Dolphin Bookshop.

The only way to proceed, Fitzgerald sensed, was by the numbers and from the top. Mamie Simon came first; that required fortification, and that meant gin, which did not flow in Springfield in quite the rivulets and streams and torrents that it did in New York.

Indeed, Fitzgerald suspected that it was his blatant immoral glorification of alcohol, during these years of Prohibition, that had damned him in the eyes of Mamie Simon. Could that truly be his sin? If so, then it must be his salvation as well. After four quick gimlets, Fitzgerald had the desk clerk order him a taxi. It was time to beard the harpy in her den, so to speak.

Mamie Simon was eighty-one years old, but she seemed much older. She had been with the Springfield *Register-Pistareen* since her graduation from St. Athanasia's Academy in 1861. To say she was a feature on that newspaper is like saying that water is a feature of the city of Venice. In both instances the former pre-existed the latter, and in both instances the former had become, over the years, thick, sluggish, and just a trifle foul-smelling. The book review department had been given over to Mamie Simon's care in the Year of Our Lord 1866, in time to permit her to express her displeasure upon the publication of *Crime and Punishment*. In the next three or four years, she was privileged to cast her glum eyes upon the works of Mark Twain, Ibsen, Trollope, Flaubert, and many others. She disliked *Little Women*. She couldn't understand Wilkie Collins' *The Moonstone*. She considered *The Innocents Abroad* somehow distasteful. As for *Through the Looking Glass*, well, she followed it up to a point, but she confessed that after thirty pages she was hopelessly confused. And that only brought her up to the early 1870s. She continued to read and criticize, and she had put in a solid half-century of grumbling before Fitzgerald's first novel had made its appearance.

It was against this formidable foe that he had come to try his reputation. Even greater writers than he had feared to face Mamie Simon on her own ground. But Fitzgerald had an advantage in that the reviews of *The Great Gatsby* were overwhelmingly enthusiastic. Still, he wondered if that would carry any weight with the old bat at the newspaper.

He took the taxi to the offices of the Springfield *Register-Pistareen*. Just outside the building there was a large, round, shallow fountain that looked like it had never operated. A couple of empty bottles and several pages of newsprint bathed in the wind-rippled pool. Six wooden duck decoys floated on its surface. Fitzgerald wondered what they could possibly mean. He went up the stairs and into the newspaper's headquarters.

A secretary sat at a battered wooden desk and guarded the entrance to the weekly supplement's offices. She looked up at the author as if she were startled that someone wished to pass by her; perhaps it had been a long time since anyone had called on any of the paper's editors. "Yes?" she asked suspiciously.

"I have an appointment to see Mamie Simon at two o'clock."

The woman checked a typed list on a clipboard. "Mr. Fitzgerald? Just go right down there. Miss Simon is the third office on the right."

"Thank you." He took a deep breath and headed down the narrow corridor. He felt like a boy again, being sent down to the principal's office for discipline. He felt like he was back at Princeton, trying to overcome his feelings of inferiority because he wasn't rich and he was a failure at sports. He knocked on the frosted glass of Mamie Simon's door.

"Come in," she called. Her voice was as hoarse and dry as a desert bird's.

Fitzgerald entered her office and stood for a moment looking at her. She was just as he had imagined her: the blond wig; the deep maze of wrinkles on her face; the sharp, bright eyes; the folds of skin at her throat; the fingers like clutching claws. She was an old and bloodless bird, but she could still peck the life from any unwary worm that chose to disregard her. "I'm F. Scott Fitzgerald," he said, wincing to hear his voice crack.

"Yes?" she said, as if she hadn't the slightest idea in the world what that name was supposed to mean. As if he hadn't spent the last few years of his life on the top of every bestseller list that counted—every list but Springfield's.

"I have a new novel that's just been published by Scribner's," he said. He was dismayed that she didn't seem to know this already.

"How exciting," she said. "Are you from Springfield?"

"Yes," he said. He sat down slowly in a chair across from her desk.

"How absolutely marvelous that a young man from our community has had such good luck." She didn't sound the least bit enthusiastic. "What sort of book is it? A murder mystery or something?"

"Well, no. It's about a man who spends his entire life trying to win a woman he thinks he loves, even though his idea of her is idealized and completely unrealistic. It's a story about his determination, really, and the great lengths he goes to in order to achieve his goal."

Mamie Simon stared at him for several seconds, her mouth open a little, making small wheezing noises. "I see," she said at last. "Does it have a happy ending? Does he get the girl?"

Fitzgerald shifted uncomfortably in the chair. "Well, it ends tragically," he said.

There was another silence. "I see. Is your story set here in Springfield? My readers love books that take place here in town."

"No," said Fitzgerald, "it takes place in New York."

"Oh. That's exciting, too, I guess. If you have an extra copy of your book, I promise to take a look at it as soon as I can.

We're doing a series on local cookbook authors at the moment. Mrs. Lydon Healey has put together a rather beautiful collection of Springfield's favorite recipes and she's having it privately printed. But I will squeeze a mention of your novel into the column the first chance I get. I'm always happy to give a beginning author from our town his first review. From then on, though, your fate is in the hands of your readers."

"This isn't my first book, Miss Simon."

Her eyes opened just a bit wider. "It isn't?"

"I've had two novels that were considered rather successful. I wrote to you about them when they were published. I've had quite a few short stories printed in national magazines and Scribner's has brought out a couple collections of them. I sent them to you, too."

Mamie Simon looked thoughtful for a moment, then dismissed whatever conclusion she had drawn. "What is the name of your book again, Mr. Fitzpatrick?"

"Fitzgerald. *The Great Gatsby*. I requested that Scribner's send you a review copy."

"Well, then, it should be around here somewhere. We get so many books, you understand. I'll have one of the boys take a look through the closet. Even if we can't find it, I'll give your title a mention in the next few weeks. Let me know if there's anything else I can do for you, and good luck with your career." She looked away from him, at something more interesting on her desk, and he knew that he had been dismissed. He had failed entirely to make any impression on her at all. He stood up miserably and found his way to the door. It was time for another gimlet.

At four o'clock Fitzgerald went into the Dolphin Bookshop, the largest bookshop in Springfield. The shop was well-stocked with all the current bestsellers except *The Great Gatsby*. Michael Fell, the owner of the store, received Mamie Simon's advice concerning which titles were sure to be the season's better movers, and which titles to ignore. It isn't possible for a small store in a town like Springfield to carry every book by every publisher. Fitzgerald browsed among the lucky winners, searching in vain for one of his own books.

"May I help you?" asked Fell, when it seemed that the customer was not about to make a purchase without persuasion

"I'm an author," said Fitzgerald. "I was wondering if this store would be interested in ordering my new novel."

Fell's friendly smile disappeared slowly, like water evaporating from a birdbath. "Are you from Springfield?" he asked.

"Yes, originally. But I live in New York now."

"How wonderful." Fell's excitement was no greater than Mamie Simon's had been. "We don't carry vanity-press books here, only titles from the catalogues of major publishers."

"Oh, well, my book is from Scribner's."

Fell chewed his lip. "And we don't have it here?" he asked.

"You don't have any of my books."

"Let me have your name and the title of your novel, and when I send in the next order to Scribner's, I'll get a few copies."

"Thank you," said Fitzgerald. He wrote the information on a pad of yellow legal-size paper. He knew from Fell's attitude that it was too late for *Gatsby*, but he hoped the man would remember Fitzgerald's name in the future.

"We're always happy to help out local talent," said Fell, not bothering even to glance at Fitzgerald's name. Every day he had people in the shop trying to push their books on him. He listened only to the publishers' salesmen and Mamie Simon; authors knew nothing of the commercial value of their own work. Fell had learned years before never to trust an author's judgment. That was why middlemen were invented.

"I'm grateful," said Fitzgerald, feeling hollow inside, as if he had been caught at some petty crime. He wanted to get out of the store and out of Springfield as quickly as possible. He could live without the few dollars in royalties that would come his way if the Dolphin Bookshop began selling his books. He took a last look at all of his competition, smartly jacketed on the shelves, and his career seemed a pitiful thing. He forgot all of the enthusiastic reviews; he suddenly felt that he would never elbow his way to literary fame, at least not in Springfield.

He decided to walk back to the hotel. He felt embarrassed, like a huckster trying to swindle an innocent shopkeeper into buying an inferior product. Then the feeling changed to angry, as he realized again that *The Great Gatsby* was a good novel, a worthwhile book on which he had spent his entire skill and experience as a writer. He had let Mamie Simon and Michael Fell obscure that fact, but as he walked along Ridge Street his fury grew, and so did his determination. When he reached the Springfield Manor, he promised himself that he would not give up so easily, that they could deny him no longer.

It was easy to make the vow; it was much more difficult to keep it. Fitzgerald sat in the hotel lobby and wondered what he should do next. He had gotten nowhere in person. Perhaps the right thing would be to contact Scribner's salesman in the area; evidently the salesman had more influence than a mere author. Fitzgerald discarded that idea. He wanted *Gatsby* to succeed on its own merits, not because a salesman who had never read the book had persuaded a lot of bookstore mangers to buy it. He wished that Zelda were with him; he needed advice.

After dinner he retired to his room and tried to work. He fiddled with a half-finished short story, a piece whose premise had excited him a few weeks earlier, when the inspiration had struck him. He had been shaving, and suddenly the outline of a sad and ironic story occurred to him in its entirety, plot and characters and mood and everything. He had run to his notebook, the shaving soap drying forgotten on his face, and scribbled his idea quickly, intending to write the story as soon as he finished some work for the *Saturday Evening Post*. Now, with nothing but leisure and very little to distract him in Springfield, he discovered that he could not regain that initial flush of excitement. The story that had at first seemed so complete and balanced now eluded him. What had he intended to do with it? He couldn't even remember how the damn thing was supposed to end. His entry in the notebook read "story about beautiful woman taking over husband's career when he's hospitalized. He saves her." He couldn't recall what the point of the story was; as he read the few pages he had written, the woman seemed like a bubble-brained fool and the man was a lovesick sap. Fitzgerald didn't like either of them. He crumpled up the pages and threw them in the wastebasket. He didn't even bother to search for salvageable images or bits of conversation; that would require reading through it one more time, and he couldn't bring himself to do it.

He was famous for his facility in turning out short stories. The novels sometimes fought him as he struggled to comprehend their internal connections and complications, but the short pieces flowed from his hand as freely as the martinis at his Long Island home. He could hit on a new story idea, sketch it out, write the first draft, edit it, and turn out the final, publishable copy all within a few hours. He rarely suffered any kind of block when he was working on a short story. To Fitzgerald it was like telling a joke at a party; the story was all of a piece, each of its various elements implicit in the original conception.

It wasn't that the story had grown stale; it had rested in his notebook only a matter of weeks. It wasn't that the idea had been poor in the first place; he recalled his enthusiasm as he rushed to enter it in the idea file. It was that somehow he had lost some of the vital components. There was nothing to be done about it now. He scowled and paged through his notebook, looking for another story to work on.

He chose one of his favorite recent inspirations, a funny little account of three Yale men, a chorus girl, and a misunderstanding over an invitation. He had no difficulty remembering all the amusing lines of dialogue as he had heard them in his mind. The characters were easy enough to draw; he had been writing about these same people since his college days. Yet when he began to write, he discovered that he couldn't capture the story on paper. He was writing listless prose. He was aiming at a quick, light story and he was turning out such dull copy that he toyed with the idea of killing the Yale men in a terrible traffic accident, leaving the chorine and the reader to ponder the vagaries of the universe.

"Cripes," thought Fitzgerald, "I don't write this kind of stuff. What's going on here?" He tore the story into quarters, and it followed the other into the wastebasket. In the next hour he tried three other story ideas, and each of them was so dull or stupid or contrived that he wondered if his talent had left him suddenly and forever, without warning, like a case of three-day measles. Maybe he would have to get a job in a shoestore or something. Maybe he had become an overnight failure, a former author, fit now only for selling apples or lecturing at girls' colleges.

Finally, furious, Fitzgerald ripped the last sheet of paper from his typewriter. He had any number of excuses: the trip to Springfield had drained his creative powers; the interviews with Mamie Simon and Michael Fell had built a barricade that he had yet to overcome; his thoughts were back home on Long Island, instead of on the story he wished to write. He could have gone on, but these alibis were sufficient. He admitted to himself that he could do very little acceptable work in the state he was in, and some means of relaxation was advisable. There was a bottle of gin in his valise, and it called to him. He tried to resist, knowing that while alcohol is often the friend of inspiration, it is the enemy of good narrative. "But I don't want to work, anyway," he argued. "It would be good for me to take a little time off." So Fitzgerald crossed the room and opened the valise. The bottle of gin glinted in the lamplight, friendly and inviting. Hesitatingly, he opened it and promised that he would not finish the bottle that same evening.

When he had drained two-thirds of the gin, he began to feel sleepy. It had been a long and emotionally taxing day. He walked unsteadily to the bed and collapsed heavily on the covers, still clutching the sloshing bottle of liquor. Somewhere outside the hotel, a steeple clock tolled the hour. It was one o'clock in the morning. To Fitzgerald, it was still early evening. Nevertheless, his limbs ached, his eyes were unaccountably heavy, and nothing in the world seemed more wonderful to him than a short, warm nap. Unaware, he dropped the bottle to the floor, where the gin soaked into the worn, thin carpet. All was quiet except for the cries of the nighthawks outside. Fitzgerald's breathing slowed and became more regular. He was unconscious.

It was a restless sleep, filled with nightmares. He awoke once, crying out for a puppy that he hadn't thought about since he had been nine years old. He let his head drop back to the pillow. His temples throbbed. He dropped his right hand blindly over the edge of the bed, searching for the gin bottle, but he couldn't find it. He grumbled and tossed and rolled over on his left side. Again his eyelids slipped down, and he found himself in another nightmare. Giant copy editors from another world had seized control of his next novel and were incorporating all sorts of unearthly prose, and he was helpless to stop them. He moaned in his sleep. At last, when one of the monsters replaced the main character entirely with a large collie dog, Fitzgerald awoke with a hoarse cry. His heart was beating fast and loud, and his throat was dry. He needed a drink, but all the liquor he had brought with him now stained the threadbare carpet of the Springfield Manor. He had often pictured moments like this before; helpless, alone, repentant, cut off from all sources of gin; those moments always came at three o'clock in the morning, when for a quarter of an hour he could believe in God. He tried to compose himself again for sleep, but it was impossible. He knew that he would lie awake on the lumpy bed until dawn, and then he would rise and dress and slink away from Springfield in defeat, back to his secure palace on Long Island.

The minutes passed slowly. He watched the minute hand of his wristwatch linger between the six and the seven, between the seven and the eight. It was fighting gravity, he knew. He tried to force his mind to consider pleasant thoughts, plans for new stories, new novels, perhaps a theater piece or two. Yet his inspiration still deserted him. He wondered what he had formerly written about: who had those people been? What had been their problems? What made them funny or sad? It was all so empty to him now.

About four thirty, almost two hours before dawn, supernatural events began to occur. Fitzgerald didn't have much patience with the supernatural but, all alone in the hotel, he discovered that he was a captive audience. At first there were sounds. Loud moans, like a suffering patient on the verge of death, or a murderer who at last clearly realizes the horror of his crimes. The noises didn't seem to be coming from any particular place; they were all around, behind him, beyond the windows, from the direction of the closed door, beneath his bed. "Anxiety," thought Fitzgerald; he had experienced such nervousness before. "I'll put it all out of my mind and try to get back to sleep." He turned his pillow over and pounded it, untangled his feet from the covers, and lay back down with his thoughts concentrating on how happy he would be to get home.

The noises didn't go away. If anything, they grew louder. At one moment they sounded like the rising and falling of a hurricane's wind. At another time they resembled the awful grating of an out-of-tune carrousel. At last, it was too obvious to ignore. Fitzgerald lowered his feet out of the bed and put on his slippers. He began a slow, careful search through the hotel room. He found nothing. At last, fearful, he let himself drop into one of the room's plush chairs. He glanced from left to right, expecting to see the cause of his sleep's disruption. The moon beamed brightly through the white lace curtains; there wasn't a cloud in the sky. Everything outside was peaceful. For a moment, the noises disappeared. Fitzgerald considered calling the desk in the lobby and complaining, but now there was nothing to complain about. He felt a sick tightening in his stomach. As an author, he knew instinctively that the business was not over yet, not by any means. There was nothing to do but wait.

It did not take long. The white lace curtains, as pale as starlight, began to billow into the room, although there wasn't a hint of breeze. Fitzgerald found that he couldn't take his eyes from the curtains. They appeared to beckon to him. Then, as the curtains took on forms more familiar and tantalizing, there came a sudden slow rumble of thunder. The thunder spoke to him, saying, "Behold!" Fitzgerald was definitely upset now. He realized that the curtains had formed the shape of a human body in exquisite detail, and that the ghostlike presence did not flutter on the wind but remained in the room, just within the window. It gazed at him dolefully.

"Touch me, for I am real," said the curtain.

"No, thank you," said Fitzgerald from his chair. "Quite a few other people of my acquaintance claim to be real as well, and I habitually keep my hands to myself. Do, however, make yourself comfortable."

"Comfortable?" cried the ghost in a mocking voice. Its form was recognizable to Fitzgerald: the suit, the shirt and collar, the tie, the man's hat. Perhaps the author was only fatigued, or else he was truly asleep and dreaming; but the curtain-ghost seemed to Fitzgerald to look just like himself. He was meeting his own spirit. It was more unnerving than meeting someone else's. The ghost trailed a long chain that was clasped about its middle. It was endless, it seemed, and coiled about the wraith's body from its neck down to its ankles; the chain was connected to many odd things: notebooks, typewriters, galley sheets, magazines, books and cocktail glasses all forged from heavy steel. The lace curtain rippled and puckered, but the ghost's face never lost its utterly mournful aspect. Fitzgerald could see the thing as plain as cards on the table; he could feel the piteous gaze of the curtain's eyes upon him; he could trace the folds of the curtain as it wrapped about the ghost's head, like a bandage; he could discern a hundred different details, yet the whole experience was too impossible, and he searched for a more palpable explanation.

"You're not there!" said Fitzgerald. "It's just a trick of the moonlight and the breeze. But if you are here, what do you want?"

"Much!" cried the ghost.

Fitzgerald shivered. Tricks of moonlight do not often answer such questions. "Who are you?" he asked tremulously.

"Do you not know me? I am yourself. I am the chained and bound spirit of your own creativity. As you see, you have imprisoned me yourself."

"Please," said Fitzgerald, remembering his manners, "do sit down."

"You don't believe in me," said the ghost.

"No," said Fitzgerald, "I don't."

"Why do you doubt your eyes and your ears?"

"Because I dream like this all the time," said the author. "That's part of being a writer. My imagination works all the day while I'm awake, but does not murmur off into silence when I go to bed to take my rest. You are merely the hint of a story I haven't yet realized, or the lingering remnant of something I have already written and forgotten. Or else you are just the effect of one too many gimlets.''

The ghost raised a terrible cry at these words, shaking its chain and rattling its accoutrements with so fierce and horrifying a clamor that Fitzgerald grabbed the arms of his chair and forced himself to remain where he was. He wanted desperately to flee this room, to seek the company of more rational men. Yet as great as was his fear, so much greater did it become when the ghost removed the bandage from its head, and the parts of its hideous face loosed themselves one from another, to lie about broken and disfigured.

''Please!'' cried Fitzgerald. ''Why have you come to me?''

The curtain slowly raised one immaterial arm and pointed. ''Living man,'' it said in a deep, rumbling voice, ''you must believe in me.''

''Whatever you say,'' said Fitzgerald. ''But why do you trouble me? Surely there are lesser writers around who might benefit from such a revelation.''

''I come to you, Francis Scott Key Fitzgerald, because I *am* you.''

''And what is the significance of your chains?''

''I bear the bonds we forged together. We made it link by link, and yard by yard.''

Fitzgerald trembled. ''Like Marley's ghost,'' he murmured.

''Yes, a lot like Marley's ghost,'' said the phantom. ''Do you not know that any man at work in his particular field, whatever it might be, will find his earthly life too short? That at the end, no quantity of regret will counterweigh the misused opportunities of one's life.''

''You don't have to talk to me about misused opportunities,'' said Fitzgerald with a little bitterness. ''But I thought I was doing rather well, all things considered.''

''Indeed, so it appears,'' said the spirit. ''You are the toast of the literary crowd. In your home, luxury sits cheek by jowl with luxury. You have all the appurtenances of success: the clothing, the automobiles, the food and drink of the rich. Yet, then, why am I—why are *you* so bound and captive by this chain of unfulfilled promise?''

Fitzgerald was a trifle annoyed. ''Don't ask me,'' he said. ''Maybe you *enjoy* being chained up. I try to avoid making value judgments about people like that.''

The ghost wrung its curtain hands. ''Hear me! My time with you is nearly gone. I am here tonight to warn you, that you have yet a chance and hope of escaping this fate. I have come to make this visit to offer you that hope, Scott.''

"You are my creativity," said Fitzgerald. "You've always done right by me in the past. I'll listen. What must I do?"

"Do you not see it for yourself?" said the curtain, moaning. "What did T. S. Eliot say in his letter?"

"He said *Gatsby* is the first step American fiction has taken since Henry James."

"There," said the ghost. "See? Didn't that Chicago newspaper say that you had given a profound definition to the shifting of American ideals?"

"Yes, but I never understood what that meant."

The curtain looked impatiently up at the ceiling, as if a supply of strength could be expected from that direction. "It means, old chap, that America has turned its madly whirling eyes to you for leadership. It means that you are setting the tone and the style of this decade. You have been given a kind of power that is given to very few writers. You must awaken to this power, and use it to your advantage."

"I still don't understand," said Fitzgerald.

There came a long sigh from the curtain. "Didn't the New York *Herald* congratulate you on the invention of a new set of literary preoccupations? Didn't the San Francisco *Chronicle* say that it was as if you had written the script for the grand production of the Jazz Age? Didn't the *Times* say that you hadn't so much *captured* the mood and inclinations of our time, as *created* them?"

"So?"

"So you are not a reporter, in the way that Ernest is. You are the source of the trends other writers can only describe."

Fitzgerald smiled in the darkness. "I like that," he said.

"Sure," said the phantom, "but you haven't yet realized the full implications of such an ability."

"What do you mean?"

"Look to me no more; and look that, for your own sake, you remember what has passed between us!" Fitzgerald recognized that these were the very words that Marley's ghost had spoken before disappearing from Scrooge's chamber; and, as he watched, his own spectral visitor began to vanish. From the open window came the sounds of discontent, as if a crowd below were joining the curtained ghost in its dire yet curiously hopeful pronouncements. Fitzgerald heard self-accusing wailings; certain members of the crowd were as frustrated and angry as himself, but unable to remedy the situation. He could take action, or he could join the chorus of lamentations. The choice was entirely his own.

He closed the window and shook the now inanimate curtain. Now, in the quiet of the night, there were no signs of the spirit. All was peaceful again. Fitzgerald's mouth was dry, and he wished that he hadn't spilled the rest of the gin. He glanced around the shadowy hotel room and thought of the ghost's words. "Humbug!" he said, smiling a little; he didn't want to admit that he was afraid. He went straight to bed, and fell asleep upon the instant.

When Fitzgerald awoke, there was a germ of an idea in his mind. He looked quickly at the curtain, but it hung lifelessly from the rod. There was a faint alcoholic reek in the air, but otherwise there was nothing to indicate that the events of the night before had been anything other than a vivid dream. The author went to the window and opened it, and took a few deep breaths of the fresh air. He wanted to get to work.

He dressed himself in a maroon robe and worn felt slippers. He called down to the front desk to have a bottle of gin, a bottle of tonic water, and some limes sent up. Because of Prohibition, these drinks would be expensive. He shrugged; he had more important things to worry about.

He rolled a clean sheet of paper into his typewriter, ignoring the crumpled-up, stillborn stories of the afternoon before. "The Dolphin Bookshop," he typed, "is a pleasant little store situated on the corner of Lake Street and West 28th."

Fitzgerald stared at the sentence for a moment. "So I'm writing the script, huh?" he thought. He typed some more. "The business is owned and operated by a young couple, George and Tessie Brown, who allow their customers to browse comfortably among the current volumes, and are knowledgeable and courteous to every person who comes into the shop. They are eager to be of help, and they consider it their privilege to keep in stock all the titles of F. Scott Fitzgerald, who was born and grew up in Springfield. Whenever he visits his home town, the Browns treat him like a returning hero."

The paragraph made Fitzgerald smile; how he wished it were true. "I'm creating the inclinations, am I?" he thought. He began another paragraph. "'At the office of the Springfield *Register-Pistareen*, Carter M. Puurser, Princeton '12, is readying this week's book review column for the paper's supplement, *Springfield-Match*. The column is devoted to former Springfield resident F. Scott Fitzgerald's newest literary triumph, *The Great Gatsby*. Puurser, who with the novelist shares a love of Old Nassau, implores his readers to purchase *Gatsby* and savor its rich characterization, its celebration of America as we know it today, and its warning of where that same American spirit might find itself tomorrow. It will be a long while before anyone writes a novel to top *The Great Gatsby*, at least in the eyes of the faithful Springfield readership."

Although he had written less than a page, Fitzgerald felt exhausted. He let out his breath in a melancholy sigh and pushed his chair back from the desk. He read the paragraphs again, shaking his head. "This is just wish-fulfillment," he thought. If the ghostly curtain of the night before had been real—and could be trusted—perhaps there *was* something magic about his writing. In the harsh light of day, however, his doubts grew. He went into the bathroom and showered, shaved, and brushed his teeth. He dressed, unwrapping a fresh shirt and choosing a modest blue tie. He picked up the telephone and called the front desk. "I'll need a cab," he said. "I'll be right down."

His first destination was Lake Street and West 28th. He paid the cabdriver and approached the bookstore. He was startled to see a small mountain of *Gatsbys* piled up in the display window, and a hand-lettered sign, reading: *Springfield's own F. Scott Fitzgerald, the brightest literary light in America!* It was more than he expected; it was even more than he had hoped for. He grasped the doorknob with a sweating hand and went in.

A young man came toward him. Without the need for introduction, Fitzgerald knew immediately that this was George Brown, proprietor of the Dolphin Bookshop. Michael Fell was no more. "May I help you?" asked Brown.

Fitzgerald didn't know what to say. Yesterday, George Brown had not even existed. "I'm—"

"You're Mr. *Fitzgerald*, aren't you!" said Brown.

"Yes, I am."

"Just a moment, Mr. Fitzgerald. This is truly an honor. Please let me get my wife; she'd love to meet you." Brown hurried away toward the back of the store.

Fitzgerald nodded; this was more like it. It wasn't that he wanted to have shopkeepers fawning over him, but he desperately needed to be accepted here, in his birthplace. How often had he been reminded of his failure here? Whenever he wrote a check, or made reservations at a restaurant, or took a room at a hotel, and his name wasn't recognized. No one in Springfield had ever stopped him and said, "Aren't you the author of 'A Diamond As Big As The Ritz'?" All that was going to change, though. F. Scott Fitzgerald was writing the script now, and he was going to make a few pertinent revisions in the scheme of things. He began to relax; he even began to enjoy it a little.

"Mr. Fitzgerald?" said Brown, leading his short, slight, pretty wife by one hand. "This is Tessie. She's read every single thing you've ever published."

The young woman blushed. "I wish I had your bibliography, Mr. Fitzgerald. I'd just hate to think that I've missed a short story somewhere."

"I'm very grateful for your loyalty," said Fitzgerald, shaking her hand.

"Oh, everyone in town follows your progress," she said. "We all think it's so grand."

"Would you mind signing the copies of your books?" asked Brown.

"Not at all," said Fitzgerald, smiling. He reached inside his suit coat and took out an expensive fountain pen; Zelda had bought it at Tiffany's, just for her husband to use to sign autographs. The Dolphin Bookshop had so many copies of *Gatsby*, and so many copies of his earlier books, that he didn't get out of the store until nearly two o'clock. George and Tessie Brown were unwilling to let him escape, but Fitzgerald said he had another appointment, at the newspaper. At last they let him call a cab.

During the ride to the *Register-Pistareen*'s offices the warm glow faded, until Fitzgerald was left with a hard knot of apprehension in his stomach. One reptilian look, one syllable in Mamie Simon's grackle voice would destroy him. Despite his success at the bookstore, Mamie Simon was still the greatest threat to his happiness. Fitzgerald felt as he had on very few previous occasions: here, now, his life hung in some sort of balance. He would emerge from this last confrontation elated, renewed, and filled with great expectations or he would come out crushed in final defeat. It took a certain amount of courage to send the cab away and climb the steps.

The secretary sat at her battered desk, reading Sinclair Lewis' *Arrowsmith*. That was a good sign, Fitzgerald thought. At least she wasn't engrossed in some privately printed collection of household hints. "I would like to see Mamie Simon," he said.

"Who?" said the secretary.

"My name is Scott Fitzgerald. I was here yesterday."

"I remember," said the woman, "but whom did you wish to see?"

"Mamie Simon."

"Nobody here by that name, sir."

Fitzgerald felt a great joy grow in him. "Your book review editor—"

"Oh, you mean Mr. Puurser. He's not here now. Would you like me to take a message? He could call you later this afternoon."

"That won't be necessary; it wasn't anything important. Thank you very much."

"You're welcome. I really enjoyed *The Great Gatsby*, Mr. Fitzgerald."

He was startled. "Why, thank you. I'm glad you like it."

The secretary smiled shyly. "I'm looking forward to your next book."

"So am I," said Fitzgerald. He almost soared out of the building, inflated nearly to bursting with happiness.

The happiness, unfortunately, was not to last. Although he felt as Scrooge felt at the end of *A Christmas Carol*, Fitzgerald had overlooked something small and sad and vital. He ought to have assured his success in the same way he triumphed over his adversaries in Springfield. Rather, he was lulled by the sudden acceptance he had won in his hometown, and by the continued wonderful reviews for *The Great Gatsby*. He felt that he was Heaven's darling and, for a time, he was; but such moments cannot last forever, and even as Fitzgerald began to celebrate his victory, he began to lose ground. Across America, despite the reviews, the readers were not buying *Gatsby*. As quickly as it had come, as briefly as he had prospered, Fitzgerald's tenure as scriptwriter for the Twenties ended. No longer creating the attitudes of his contemporaries, he slowly lost confidence, and it showed in his work. He tried writing things like, "Once more on the top of the heap, F. Scott Fitzgerald laughs in the faces of those who claimed he has nothing new to show them." It didn't work; it was too late.

"There's nothing as fleeting as fame," Sheilah Graham told him on one drunken, rainy afternoon.

"Fleeting," agreed Fitzgerald bitterly. "I thought that meant years. I didn't know it meant *minutes*."

But that is the very end of this story. Fitzgerald guessed nothing of that when he packed his suitcase in the room at the Springfield Manor. That was a time of power and rejoicing, and he looked forward eagerly to returning to Long Island, to his great house and his beautiful family, to the company of his close friends and the warmth of adulation. In 1925, that was the theme of Fitzgerald's life, the way we should remember him: like Gatsby in more ways than one—rich, generous, and yearning. He became, in the end, even more his own character. He truly became Jay Gatsby, staring across the water at the green light, the emblem of the genuine and lasting bliss that forever eluded him.

All parties end, and all songs fade at last into silence; but Fitzgerald had something to cling to during his slow decline. He knew that whatever happened to him, however his fortunes fell, he was forever beloved in Springfield. At least in Springfield.

Chand Veda

Tanith Lee

How ILL-NAMED SHE was, he was thinking, in the moments before the train came off the rails. Gita—his 'song'. But she was not like a song, this fat, sullen young bride of his. It had been a terrible affair, the whole wedding. Because of the other girl, the one who had died before he could claim her, he had come to marriage later than most. Perhaps this, and perhaps the contagion of Western skepticism, made him feel ridiculous as he rode in his tinsel head-dress on the back of the tall red horse his foolish family had insisted on hiring (wondering all the while if he would fall off, his nervously gripped thighs aching horribly), while the band marched before and everyone else laughed and shouted.

Vikram had seen a photograph of the girl some months ago. He could tell it was a flattering photograph, even though it had not been able, actually, to flatter her very much. She was a lump of flesh, with small furtive eyes and, as he had found out only today, missing a top canine tooth on the left side. That could be fixed, of course. With his fine business, the book shop, on which everyone always congratulated him so vociferously, he could get money to buy Gita a false tooth. (Why then had her well-off family not seen to it?) But what else could he do? Starve her and work her, maybe, so the pounds of flesh melted away. There she had stood in her scarlet and gold bridal finery, and he had dutifully unwrapped her from her veil, wishing his short-sightedness, in that moment, were worse. And to make it more dreadful still, he beheld at once that she, too, thought herself cheated. If Gita was a poor bargain, so he supposed was he. Yes, it was all very well to talk of masculine pride, but a look

128

in a mirror got rid of that. Thin and ugly and blind wed to fat and ugly and toothless. What a pair!

And in that second, as he remembered, as if to compound the nastiness of it all, there was a wrenching and squealing, and a long juddering, during which the world fell over on its side.

When Vikram had opened his eyes, retrieved his glasses and found both lenses to be cracked—yet perforce put them on again—he discovered it was the carriage and not the world which had changed positions. From every side now, within and without the carriage, came a wailing and crying and shouting. Soon, lights were pouring down the track, and through the upside-down window, in the scream of the flares, legs ran about insanely.

"Are you hurt, Gita?" Vikram asked his wife, who was kneeling beside him with a look of gross ferocity.

"No," said Gita. And, as an afterthought, "Are you?"

"Bruised all over, but nothing broken."

She seemed to sneer faintly at this and he could have slapped her. Coupled to the bruising the horse-ride had already given him, the new, minor, all-pervasive and inescapable pain made him feel like weeping.

In a while, a demented official appeared at their upside-down window. After a lot of yelling, Vikram and another man, with some external assistance, succeeded in getting the door open. They, and others, were dragged out. They were not allowed to rescue their hand-baggage, and it was useless to argue. The scene outside was nightmarish, total chaos and confusion. The derailment was comparatively mild of its kind, and few had been hurt, but panic intransigently ruled. Nearby several Moslems writhed on the earth, praying. A goat, which seemed to have been on the train, skipped merrily down the line, butting and bleating.

Vikram stood and watched events through his cracked spectacles. At his side, a dollop of disapproving misery, Gita waited, immobile and witless. People pushed past them. "Well," said Vikram after a time, "shall we walk over there?"

"You are the husband," said Gita. "It is for you to say."

Vikram clenched his fists. He strode, stiffly, up the incline beyond the pushing confusion and the goat, and sat down on a boulder. Gita followed and sat down on another boulder. Beyond the fallen train and the red stream of flares, the night was very black, and far above the stars bloomed bright. Vikram thought of the nights alone, sitting or lying up on the roof of the shop, the stars floating high over the mist of the streetlamps. Waking to find the moon on his face, whiteness soaking through him like water into a sponge. He worked very hard in the book shop. Things were always going wrong. For example, there was the European who came in and stole the glossy paperbacks of temple erotica. One knew he stole them—after he had come and gone two or three of the editions were always missing, and besides he left his cigar-ash along the lines of the volumes, like a calling card. Or the young assistant who took two hours for a midday meal; always some excuse. Or the books which did not arrive on time, or came in too great quantities. And then there was that account which did not balance. And what was he to do about the electric fan in the ceiling, part of which had flown off and damaged one of the stands. Next time it might decapitate a customer, probably one with influential friends. Could he afford the new fan? Well, he would have to. And then all the expense and the time of this, which he had not wanted, this marriage to the other girl, the one who had died. She had not been pretty, but at least only plain. And he had met her, once, at her father's house, and she had not hated him and they had laughed together. She had had a lovely laugh; he could not help recalling it. It would have filled his life with silver bells. But there. She was dead and he was no catch and they had found him Gita, and here he was with Gita and a wrecked train, his body feeling as if it had been pounded between stones. It was no good looking at the stars, waiting for the moon.

Presently, another official came, closely pursued by a group of frantic people. Over the cries and imprecations, the official told them all they should follow the guard through the forest, to the station. No, they could not go up the line. There was a landslip piled across it; it was this which had caused the derailment. Everyone must go around. Yes, yes, they must.

An elderly woman clung to Vikram, sobbing. She was quite uninjured, but the despair of unforeseen, inevitable, mischance was upon her. He patted her. "There, there, my mother. It'll be all right. Look, there is the guard coming now, with his torch. And we will go to the station and they will give us tea, perhaps, free of charge." He glared over the woman's veiled head at Gita. Gita should have been the one to impart comfort. Who did she think she was, some princess? Had she no compassion?

The guard set off into the undergrowth between the tall trees and the tongued bamboos, his live torch flashing, disturbing

˙˙ngs. The woman detached herself from Vikram and scuttled after. Everyone followed, chattering or listless. The newlyweds brought up the rear.

Suddenly Gita said angrily, "Wait! My sandal is caught in something."

Vikram stopped and waited. Behind him, Gita panted and puffed, and the bushes creaked. He did not turn to see. Ahead the flare became smaller. "Hurry *up*, Gita."

"How can I hurry? The strap has caught in a root. I can't see what I'm doing." She sounded furious. It was all his fault, of course. "And you might help me."

So he turned and helped, not wanting to touch even her sandal and unable to see her, fortunately, in the darkness. When it was all attended to he straightened, and the light was gone.

"Quickly," he said then, and hurried forward, to fall headlong amid the eager claws of the forest. Scrambling up, scratched and hot with embarrassment that was invisible, while Gita stood like a rock, he muttered, "That way. Over there." And taking her arm, he pulled her after the memory of the wholly-vanished light.

All my life now is to be like this, thought Gita as she stumbled along with the thin ugly man, her lord. *Already he has brought me bad luck. The train has crashed. My sandal is broken. He dislikes me and may refuse to buy me a new pair.* She thought of her father's house, but without nostalgia. Her father and mother had not cared for her, either. It was the pretty daughter who had the attention, the bangles, the silk, the attractive husband. Gita did not blame her family. She did not blame Vikram. Although he was so graceless, bony and pock-marked, his squinting eyes full of reproach, it was a shame he had had to marry someone like herself. *But I am a good cook,* she thought defiantly, as a creeper smacked her in the face. *He doesn't know that yet.* Gita's aunts had encouraged her in the domestic skills, while the other sister had been taught everything more casually. After all, if the rice was, for the first months, sticky, the *nan* of an imperfect lightness, this would be forgiven a slender-waisted young wife with huge deer-like eyes. No, Gita did not blame Vikram. She only hated him for hating her, as was quite proper. She had a vague hallucination of their old age together, when she would withhold his favourite dishes (her culinary talent being all she could blackmail him with). Presumably they would have children. She shuddered at the idea of his reluctance or perhaps brutality. And the child, also, as it grew, would probably not like her.

She stopped brooding because Vikram had abruptly halted.

He stood there, an element of hotter denser substance in the hot black night.

"We're lost," he cried. He sounded in a rage.

Nervous, she could not, nevertheless, resist goading him.

"I knew we should be."

"It was your fault, Gita."

Her fault. Naturally.

He waved his arms, and she heard branches crackle and snap.

"Where is the station? Where? Where?" he shouted at the forest. "The guard has disappeared. I can't see anything. What is happening to me?"

It was true, there was no glimmer of light or movement anywhere, and no sound to be heard in any direction.

"Haven't you an electric pocket torch?" asked Gita innocently.

"A pocket torch? I? No, of course not. Did I think when I set out I should be in a train-wreck, abandoned in the jungle?" *But with my bad-fortune,* he thought, *I should have done.*

They stood then for a few minutes, gaping at the blackness to which Gita's eyes at least had somewhat adjusted. It was possible to see shapes, or to imagine they were seen, but not to be certain what they were. At last, Vikram decided. "We must go on." And he marched forward again, only to collide on this occasion with the trunk of a tree. As he scrabbled for his battered glasses in the undergrowth, Gita said, with an air of intolerable wisdom, "It might be better to remain where we are. Surely other people from the train will come by. Or if not, we shall see better in the morning light."

"Morning? Morning? You expect me to spend the night in the jungle?"

"I shall have to do so too."

"I must be in the town tomorrow. I have things to see to. You don't understand the modern world. My business— Already I've wasted so much time—"

"Yes," said Gita.

Something in her voice stayed him, but only for a moment.

"No," he shouted. "I intend to find the station. Come or stay as you please, woman."

As he rampaged forward once more, Gita picked her way after him. He presented a kind of whirling in the darkness, but mainly she located him by the noise he made, thrashing and crashing, and wild cries of pain and frustration, at length ornamented by swearing. Gita attended with interest, but presently even the oaths died. She came upon him suddenly, seated on the ground, nursing a foot all the toes of which seemed to him to have been fractured on a stone. As she loomed over him, he began to make a different noise, unlike all the others. It was a familiar noise, so personally familiar that she did not at once recognize it from another. Slowly, she realized he was crying.

The fool, she thought scornfully. *What does he think there is to cry about?* But she knew, and a wave of loneliness washed over her, terrible loneliness, for she too had shed tears very often, and now she could not help him, was as much the cause of his grief as anything else.

She sat down. She waited, listening to his sobs which, because they shamed him, he tried to quieten. She waited and waited, and listened and listened, and finally she said, "The moment the sun comes up, you'll easily see the way. It won't take long to reach the station. Then someone will take us to the town. They'll be very sorry. They'll be kind. And when we get there, you can rest. We'll send a message to your shop. Let them do without you one day. You work too hard. Let *them* work for a change. I'll make a *thali*. It will be very tasty. And you'll find I won't be a nuisance at all. You can be as free as you want. I shan't fuss. Visit your friends, write your poetry. I understand." She became aware he had stopped weeping and was listening to her. She said, "You'll have noticed, I haven't got a tooth at one side. When I was seven years old a boy from the next house used to run into our courtyard with my brother, and call out at me I was ugly. So one day I took a pan of milk that was curdling and threw it over him. He screeched and yelled, and I was beaten for wasting the milk. But the day after he threw a stone at me and it broke the tooth. So they took me to the dentist's shop and he pulled it out."

In the silence, Vikram gulped. "But that's—dreadful, a dreadful thing," he said.

"What did it matter? If I'd been pretty it would have mattered. But if I'd been pretty, none of it would have happened." She hesitated, then said, "You see, I know how I am. But I'm strong. Don't worry about me. I'll be a dutiful wife. In time, we'll get used to each other."

"Oh, Gita," he said.

How strange, he thought, astonished by her dignity, burned by compassion. He could not see her, and all at once, as her dismembered words were murmured in the blackness, he had become aware that her voice was beautiful. Yes, if he had heard her speak, on a telephone, say, never having met her, he would have visualized another woman entirely, a nymph with high, heavy, round breasts, serpent waist, dancer's feet, skin smooth as much-caressed marble. . . . Although Gita's skin *was* soft and smooth, he had noticed it, unconsciously, when he grabbed her arm so roughly. He had a sudden urge to reach out and touch her arm again, gently, investigate the soft smoothness, and if it were true. But he could not make himself.

He sighed. He must say something in response to her own brave effort.

"Yes," he said humbly. "It will be all right."

He heard her settle then, and he himself mournfully settled, a tree against his bruised and aching back. If only it *could* be all right, he thought, She was, after all, a decent girl. She had comforted his sorrow instead of mocking him. She had even mentioned his poetic writing with respect. He removed his glasses in order to wipe his eyes. And at that instant, a dim white glow appeared, far over his head. Too ethereal to be anything sent by the railway company, he knew it after a moment for the rising moon. The light swept like a silver blade through the roof of thinner foliage above them. He did not put on his glasses, simply allowing the light to come to him in all its mystery, formless. By his side, Gita did not say anything about the moon.

If only. But if only what? The dream of the moon knew. Soma, binding the earth to the sky by a cord of white fire and divine nectar. If only—Not meaning to, Vikram's glance fell on Gita sitting there passively. Viewed without the glasses, washed in moonlight—yes, that was it. A transformation. The light of the moon, *chand*, *chandarama*, the silvery, ever-altering one, altering all things—If only he and she might be altered, she for him, and he for her—for she had suffered. By magic, by prayer, by knowledge, by a wish.

He felt himself detached from the flesh, floating in whiteness.

By his side, Gita thought: *Let him sleep.* She lay back on the tree with him, and forgetting her punishments for his old age, mused, *He is a sad man. Ginger is good for sadness. I will put a little extra in the* thali.

When she woke, it was without haste, but with the sensation of something having touched her eyelids, a fingertip or a frond.

There was a lot of light now from the moon, which was directly before her, descending the arch of heaven and shining through the clearing. For it was, after all, a clearing they had stumbled to the edge of. Bushes of flowers were all about them, which she had not noticed before, exuding a delicate sweet scent. The warm moon seemed to bring out their perfume, just as the sun might do by day. Despite the discomfort and catastrophe of the earlier part of the night, Gita felt well, soothed, optimistic. She rose to her knees, and looked round to see if her husband Vikram was still sleeping. Then let out a stifled shriek. For Vikram was no longer there, had vanished. In fact, there was someone, deeply slumbering against the tree. But it was a stranger.

After a few seconds, Gita collected herself. There would be an ordinary explanation, no doubt. While she slept, for example, another lost traveller from the train had come by and Vikram had invited the man to join him. Then Vikram himself had had to go off among the trees for the normal reason. Meanwhile the newcomer slept and Gita awoke. That was it. She had only to wait a minute or so and her husband would return. And while she waited, she was at liberty to study the stranger, was she not?

Gita leaned a fraction closer, holding her breath.

The moon described him fully, the long strong length of him, relaxed in his sleep as some graceful animal, some panther out of the *rukh*. He was mature, though still young, his skin of a velvety darkness on the beautiful musician's hands, the arch of the throat, the face, into the hollows and over the plains of which the moon poured so completely. In all her life, Gita had never seen a living man so handsome. Asleep, soulless, he amazed her. But ah, behind the smooth discs of those closed lids, the thick fringes of those lashes, what eyes there must be— It was her desire to behold them, maybe, which caused her inadvertently to nudge against him. So he woke. So she caught a glimpse of his eyes, the eyes she had longed to gaze upon—large and gleaming, and filled by horror, by terror—

Gita sprang to her feet, gasping and humiliated. To wake him was to cause him to look at her. Yes, she was enough to make him recoil, leaning near enough to embrace him, with what emotions, what stupid desires scrawled across her hateful features? It was but too plain. In wretchedness, she longed to obeise herself in apology, but that also would be improper.

"There is no need for alarm," she said. "My husband will

return shortly. But I was surprised, and wondered who you were."

The princely man relapsed against the tree again. He breathed hard, staring at her, trembling, she thought, for his thick jet-coloured hair shivered to the momentum. What should she do now? Too late, she greeted him politely. He did not respond. He said hoarsely, "Your husband?"

"Yes, my husband. My Vikram. Didn't you come from the train and meet him by accident here?"

His mouth, that a fine chisel might have fashioned for a god-being on a temple, was ajar, showing the white teeth. Then his shaking hand came up and set in place on the carven nose, before the wonderful eyes, a pair of cracked and battered spectacles. They did not mar his beauty. Oddly, they enhanced it, a little pinch of the spice of humour, a tiny laughing flaw in his marvel: See, I am not perfect. I am human, too. I may be approached. Oh, one could love him for the silly spectacles perched on his god's face above his hero's body. It seemed he was half-blind, just like Vikram. Gita checked. For not only was he half-blind like her husband, but he had just put on the glasses of her husband. Then with a throb of terror all her own, curiously protective and tigerish, Gita cried at him: "Where is he? What have you done with him—" For surely it was madness that one man might murder another for the use of his broken spectacles, yet this was the forest and who knew what went on here by night— "Oh, Vikram—where is my Vikram?"

The man coughed. He said dully, "I am here."

Gita gave a scream of laughter. But the laughter was brief and left her. Then she sank down again and peered at him, fighting away the urge to cry, at which fight, in her seventeen years, she had become a veritable champion.

"You? How can you be Vikram?"

"See," he said, holding out his hands to her. She looked and saw rings that she knew. Then she looked again and saw the heroic body clad in Vikram's clothing which somehow fitted it. Then her eyes went back to his face, and the tears came despite herself.

"Oh," she whispered. "What has happened?"

"Don't cry," he said. He seemed to try to touch her, but his hands fell away.

She could not bear it. Some spell or curse had come about, and here she was, the most abject made more abject still. She turned her head and hid herself in a fold of her *sari*, instinctively.

"Gita," he muttered. "Are you Gita?"

Wild anger then in the *sari* fold. "Who else? Who do you think?"

Vikram was not thinking at all. He leaned back on the tree, struggling with great inner turmoil.

At the soft nudge he had woken, the moon across his eyes, and there in the blast of the moonlight was a woman, kneeling close enough that it seemed she had been about to embrace him. Close enough, too, to be easily seen. For an instant he thought it was a dream, but then he knew it could not be, and he was frightened. A poet, he had often read and written of the creatures of the forests, the demons, the nymphs. Her hair was a foaming cloud, her body, traced by silver, flowed and curved, inviting the hands to rest and to journey upon it. Her face had truly the loveliness of something inhuman, an image sculpted from a poreless almond-coloured material that lived, reigned over by two eyes like great black stars.

And then she spoke of her husband. Her husband would be returning. How would it seem? Somehow Vikram had fallen asleep and woken by this gorgeous one, whose spouse would shortly approach and find them. Compromised, attacked, slain—what else could follow? Then he recollected Gita. And then the gorgeous one began to refer to her husband by Vikram's own name, a coincidence that seemed peculiar. He had put on his glasses, to see if she would look differently, but her splendor was only increased. And then she had shouted in fear, and Vikram had seen that she lacked the upper left canine, just as his Gita did. His fat, ugly Gita. And that Gita, fat ugly Gita, finding the nymph had also lost a tooth just as she had, and the same tooth at that, being kind, had gifted the nymph with her garments before running away.

But now the beautiful, the fantastical one wept and shuddered in Gita's *sari* fold, and he wished only to console her, drinking the tears of her eyes like nectar. Gita? No, this was not Gita. Although she had snarled at him. *Who else?*

He did not dare lay a finger on such excellence. It was the stuff of fantasy and of poetry. And yet—and yet, in those seconds of her gaze, it had seemed to him that she too saw—

Vikram had not forgotten his demented semi-conscious prayer to the moon. It was solely that the memory was preposterous. In the end, however, he took a deep breath of the perfumed night. He fixed the demon-girl with his impaired vision that somehow consistently beheld her clearly, and said, "Gita, look at me. Look at me and tell me what you see.'' At which she slapped the earth in a fury with one hand, over and over. So he took the hand, to calm it, and sure enough the hand relaxed. "Gita," he said, "I will tell you firstly—when I look at you— you are beautiful, Gita."

It was possible, he knew, she might berate him, might go mad and tear at him. She had been ugly so long, and unloved always. And if, when she looked at him she beheld the complement of what he beheld, looking at her— She did not know, as he did, what he had asked of the moon. Did not know it had been . . . granted?

But there was knowledge, after all. The moon had filled the darkness with it. Presently, she raised her head and her eyes, and out of her glory she gazed at him. And timidly, but hopefully, she said, "I—*also?*"

Vikram laughed. *"Also."*

He laughed louder and she laughed too, and both their hands met, and their voices went up like a song into the tops of the forest.

In the dawn, as she had said, it was no trouble to find a way through the trees and thickets. The station appeared against the freshly-lit sky, huddled over by the flocks of people who had had to spend the night there.

They walked closely, Vikram and Gita. Sometimes they glanced shyly aside at each other. The burning arrows of day had had no power over the enduring gift of the moon, and the spell had not faded at sunrise. Each of them stole onward with a supernatural being at their side, tender and accessible, a dream that was also a beloved. And, though they did not yet know, a third person went with them now, who was to be the first of their sons.

The refugees on the platform paid them little heed, the skinny squinting man and his fat ungainly wife. There was nothing remarkable about them, except perhaps the profundity of their intimate silence.

In the eyes of others, then, in the mirrors on their walls, reflective surfaces of all types, they saw the truth, or one truth of two. But in the expression of Vikram when he looked at her, Gita saw the second truth, and he, in her eyes, beheld it also. They were, for each other, the one true mirror.

"Well, it is a good marriage," said the relatives and friends, with some surprise.

The book business was booming, the house was a wealthy one. And yes, Vikram had gained some flesh, Gita's cooking, no doubt. Though strangely Gita had lost weight, despite her childbearing. She would never be a comely woman, even without a gap in her teeth, and yet there was something, her walk, her gestures; not unpleasing. And her happiness was gratifying to those who thought they had aided it. He was a solid proposition, was Vikram, and had added dignity to himself as his fortunes steadied. He no longer squinted, but looked levelly through his spectacles. Authority, yes, Vikram had authority. One could ask his advice. And the poetry had won prizes, of course. Who had inspired some of those passages? Well, best not to worry about that. Gita was happy, and there were plenty of children.

And the children really were a miracle. Like gods and goddesses they stalked the lawns and the rooms, turning to their parents with looks of love one all too rarely noted in these unsettled times. Handsome sons, dark as Krishna, and dark amber daughters, all set with jewels for eyes. It was, the relatives and friends observed privately, something of a curiosity, this. For how could offspring of so much—one must say exceptional—*beauty*, have grown from such a very beautiless match . . . ?

The Fire at
Sarah Siddons

Robert Thurston

TWO WEEKS AFTER the death of his wife Linda, William Stoller
arranged to have his psychic friend Osgood conduct a séance.
He told Osgood he wanted Linda to tell him her last thoughts
before her sudden death, which had occurred during a mild June
afternoon when a teenager, drunkenly celebrating his imminent
graduation from high school, crashed his speeding car through
the front of a Lerner Shop, landing right where Linda was
comparison-pricing wraparound skirts. William said to Osgood
that he also could use whatever leftover endearments she could
transmit from the other side, anything to help him through his
period of loss. He had become fond of that phrase, period of
loss, and he used it several times during his conversations with
Osgood.

During the séance Linda did appear, in a rather hazy, somewhat bloated way, looking like an instant photograph just before
the chemicals started to effect resolution, but William got from
her spirit none of what he sought. Later he described her brief
appearance at the séance as a cameo. She said several times that
their son Edward was destined for great things, and that William
should do whatever seemed necessary to help Eddie seek his
fame. At the time Eddie was only eight years old. Although he
acquitted himself creditably in a school known for its easy teachers, he had shown little that could be taken as signs of future
greatness. Nevertheless, after Linda's ghost-image had reverted
to coaxing, William promised to do as she asked. She disappeared immediately, which he interpreted as a sign she was sat-
isfied. While they were having a post-séance drink, William
asked Osgood if there were any chance their unearthly visitor

had perhaps not been Linda; it could possibly have been another similar hazy and bloated lady caught in some kind of crossed line from the hereafter. Osgood assured him it had been Linda.

"God, I wish she'd said something comforting to me," William commented, a few healthy tears in his eyes. "Something for me, something about me, about my future. I didn't want to hear about Eddie. It was always Eddie with her. That last year, whatever she gave me, it felt like second-hand toys. Why didn't she say anything to comfort *me*?"

"Spirits are like that," Osgood said laconically.

"Like what?"

"Indifferent. Bitter. Most of them don't like being dead at first."

When Edward was ten years old, William moved the two of them into Seven Arts Estates, a just-completed housing complex located two miles outside of their city. Seven Arts featured a suburban layout in which no two adjoining houses were alike, although only a total of six architectural house designs were used throughout the complex. It was a kind of theme village, which keyed its street and place names to famous people in the arts. No one among the planners or management had ever taken care to find out what the seven arts were supposed to be. It is likely even they knew that television was not one of them, but that did not stop the planners from assigning several TV names to the landscape. The shopping center, for instance, was located on Cheyenne Bodie Plaza. William, always more inclined toward literary things, chose a home on Dickens Lane. The street signs marking Dickens Lane displayed a bearded man writing on a piece of scrolled paper with a quill pen.

During their first year on Dickens Lane, a disgruntled man whose application to live in Seven Arts Estates had been turned down engaged briefly on a program of sabotage, blowing up homes and parts of homes, plus the refreshment stand at Jackson Pollock Park. William's home narrowly escaped the man's vengeance. The house next to his blew up on a sunny afternoon. Its occupants, a nice middle-aged couple who both taught at the local community college, were killed. Apparently the saboteur had not known they would both be home that afternoon because their school allowed them time off for Jewish holidays. When the explosion occurred, Edward was playing with toy cars in his backyard and a piece of flying debris hit him in the left cheek. Although the wound was easily seen to by an emergency-room doctor, Edward was left with a permanent jagged scar on his cheek. The bomber was tracked down a day later at his home in town, a rather picturesque late-nineteenth-century homestead, but he blew up himself and the homestead before the police could arrest him.

After workers had cleared away the debris and boarded over the cellar of the house next to William's, the lot was left abandoned for a long while. It seemed no new buyer could be found. The middle-aged couple had been the only fatalities of the bomber's vengeful rampage, and so people seemed to fear putting up a new home on the lot. William took to standing at a picture window facing the lot. He enjoyed studying the weeds and thick high grass that now covered the earth except for where the cellar had been, an area where his neighbors began to dump trash. A year or so after the explosion, with still no buyers in sight, the developers had the cellar filled in, and some earth planted over it, and they began to send their maintenance crew around to tend the lot from time to time.

William left his job as assistant principal of the city's high school because one day he noticed that his gestures were becoming too fussy and that his voice cracked when his anger became unreasonable. He took a job managing the bookstore at Cheyenne Bodie Plaza. The store was named Shakespeare and Co., after the famous store in Paris. William had visited the original and remembered finding an out-of-print Erskine Caldwell which he had taken to a narrow second-floor reading room and read quickly on a decaying couch. The plaza's Shakespeare and Co. also had a reading room, installed there at William's suggestion, but customers rarely used it.

William took to decorating his home with house plants and found quickly that his taste inclined toward succulents, mostly because they needed the least care. He had a very tactile relationship with his plants. He stroked soft cactus spikes gently, let the harder needles almost prick his skin, tickled the beardlike growth of the old men cacti. He would run his fingers around the rosette of an aloe, tap against the hard surface of agave. Edward had little interest in his father's hobby, although he did show some affection for a sedum, but then only because it reminded him of jelly beans.

Edward did well at school and play but, in spite of his father's encouragement, never quite rose to the top of anything. He was class treasurer for a couple of years, after elections which he won by narrow margins. He managed to sneak into the honor society during his senior year because of a marked improvement in his grades. A second-string quarterback, he almost won the big game with a long hail-mary pass which dropped gently into his receiver's hands. It looked like a sure touchdown, but a free safety caught up with the rather slow-footed receiver at the one-yard line just as the game-ending gun went off. Edward did not do well with girls, even though he was on the football team, though William did see him once in town, his arm around a short, slightly pudgy, girl who, when William had been assistant principal of the high school, was already acquiring some reputation at the junior high for being easy.

"You were there," William said one day to Osgood, when Osgood came into the store seeking a book about Edgar Cayce. "She said Eddie would be somebody."

"That's what she said."

"He still seems to be looking for his category. Do spirits really know the future?"

"Who knows?"

"Osgood, you're supposed to be an authority on this subject."

"Some predictions are true, some aren't."

"And that means?"

"Spirits are people. They lie."

"You're a great help."

"Look, does it really make a difference what Eddie does?"

"Yes. Yes, it does. I'm not living this particular life for his self-indulgence. He better pay off."

For a while William took an interest in a young woman, a girl from the city who worked in sales at the Emily Bronte Boutique. Her name was Catherine, which he found wonderfully appropriate although it took a long time for her to understand why. After she had read *Wuthering Heights* she began greeting William by saying, "I am Heathcliff." Their ritual drew many stares from customers, most of whom lived in Seven Arts Estates without knowing much about the people who were memorialized in its street, shop, and place names. Except for the television stars. (In later years one of the fiercest political battles in the complex would result in the name change from Cheyenne Bodie Plaza to John Ritter Mall. At that time William belonged to a splinter group of cheerful dissidents who maintained that Tex Ritter Mall had a better chance for historical permanency. His group sent a query letter to the Chamber of Commerce of Truth or Consequences, New Mexico, to see how the residents there had responded to the fleetingness of fame, but the letter was never answered.)

Catherine stayed overnight with William a few times. She had been reluctant about it at first, fearful that it might offend Edward, but, when Edward (at William's insistence) had a chat with her about it, her objections were gently removed. Edward really did not mind; he was happy to have someone different doing the cooking. He liked Catherine best when she wore off-the-shoulder dresses or bathing suits, for such outfits exposed the rather large burn mark on her right shoulder, the scar of a childhood episode wherein she had tried to make cocoa on a stove and instead had set the kitchen on fire. Her burn scar reminded Edward of the jagged scar on his cheek from the bomber's flying debris. The mutual scars seemed to link them in former pain, and even tragedy, since Catherine had lost her dog in her fire and had never owned a pet since.

"You hardly ever leave Seven Arts," Catherine said to William one night when they were sitting cosily by the living room fire, "I mean, you're either here and down at the store or at Pollock Park or down at the Siddons Center. When was the last time you were in town except to visit me? And then we never went anywhere."

She was wearing an off-the-shoulder blouse. It seemed that William liked such an outfit as well as Edward, although for different reasons. In the firelight her burn scar looked made-up, sexy, a failed beauty mark.

"I don't like to go to town. My life used to be there. It's not there any more."

"I guess I can accept that. Your friend Osgood called me and asked how you were."

"How'd he get your number? How'd he get your name?"

"He called here one day when you were out shopping. He told me not to tell you he'd called. He said you didn't seem to want to talk to him any more."

"No. I don't."

"That's why he asked *me* how you were, and I told him fine, and he gave me a message. I'm not sure I should tell you the message."

"Tell me."

She shifted position, sat up, and her burn scar seemed to change shape in the flickering light.

"He said Linda appeared at one of his séances. It was a surprise. Unbidden, he called it."

"I'm not sure I want to hear this."

"All right."

"Don't do that to me. Tell me."

"He said she said not to forget Edward, what she told you about Edward."

A few moments later, after she tired of watching William stare into the fading firelight, Catherine asked him:

"Are you ever going to talk to me again."

"I'm not sure."

Catherine continued to work at the Bronte Boutique, but the skin around her eyes became quite dark and her figure became matronly. From time to time Edward dropped in to say hello to her, but all she ever wanted to talk about was how his father would no longer see her, even talk to her. Edward thought she whined too much, and he stopped stopping at the Bronte.

Edward was having his own problems, with college mainly. He could not grasp mathematical theory, history put him to sleep, languages made his tongue thick, and he despised the whole concept of metaphor. However, his grades were not bad. He called them gentlemen's grades until his father became enraged when he used the phrase and told him to get his act together or punt his goddamned life away.

William spent more and more time with his succulents, and on looking out at the empty lot next door. The maintenance crew was coming around less and less frequently, and there was beginning to be a scraggly appearance to the grounds. The children who played there seemed more intent on tearing up the earth than on sportsmanship, and all the dogs within miles chose the lot for their droppings. When people asked William what were they ever going to do with that lot, William suggested an animal bank. Animal bank, they asked. Yes, he said, with night deposit slots for dogs. He stopped using the joke when he found he had to explain it every time.

Edward struggled to finish college. He almost did not finish. For a while he became head of a college radical group. His timing seemed fortuitous since it was a time of campus uprisings. He let his hair grow a bit, which William didn't mind too much although he cringed somewhat at the greasy look at the tips. He was also pleased at Eddie's ability to seize microphones, and at the extensive coverage his tense little speeches got.

He began to wonder if his son's future greatness would be achieved through politics. Even though Edward did not get good political science grades, the dream seemed reasonable. Certainly others had achieved office without too much on the ball.

Then Edward's group became involved in an exam-stealing

scandal. While Eddie was not implicated, and indeed knew nothing about it, the story ruined his group's creditability. He gave up on radical politics and faded back into normal academic life. He achieved a quite normal graduation with quite normal marks, and William was loathe to admit, quite normal intelligence.

"He's never going to amount to a hill of beans," William commented bitterly to Osgood. They were speaking to each other again. They always spoke when it was convenient to, or appealing for, William.

"He seems like a good kid to me," Osgood said. "I think he'll do well."

"What do you know?"

"Well, I am supposed to have some psychic intuition."

"I don't see how you can be psychic and dippy at the same time."

"For some, that's a valid combination."

"So you say he's a good kid. He is. He's thinking of going into insurance. They've even offered him a job at the Wallace Stevens Agency."

"A suitable profession."

"Or he'll teach, he says."

"Also suitable."

"But they're not jobs people ordinarily become famous at."

"Anything is possible."

"And he shows no aptitude for either profession."

Edward passed on both jobs and became manager of the local fast-food hamburger spot. It was very much a college hangout, and Eddie seemed to enjoy chatting with its clientele. Even the older people found him charming, especially after he established a section all their own, the Senior Citizens' Sit-Down Spot, where they were allowed to stay as long as they wanted, even if their only purchase was a cardboard cup of coffee. Some of the older seniors stayed most of the day at the restaurant. In gratitude they kept purchasing coffees. They would put cardboard cups inside cardboard cups, piling up cups the way customers in French cafes pile up saucers. Sometimes Edward served the old people, even though it was a self-service restaurant.

One night William was awakened by the first of five phone calls from friends and associates telling him that the bookstore, Shakespeare and Co., was on fire. At first William didn't want to go to the fire and actually see his place of work in ruins, but the phone calls annoyed him. By the time he got to the scene, the fire was pretty much over, so he stood with the crowd staring at the smoldering remains. One of the two owners came over to him and said she was sorry but she and her partner had decided not to rebuild. They planned to collect the insurance money from the Stevens Agency and go to Europe. The people in Seven Arts just didn't read, she said with a genuine sadness in her voice. People should read, she said.

William was out of work for only a short time, enough for only two visits to the unemployment office. On one of the visits he saw Catherine in another line, but he didn't say anything to her and she didn't notice him. He thought she looked worn out.

His new job was as house manager for the Sarah Siddons Arts Center. The Center had once been bankrupt, the Seven Arts management had stuck with it, and now it was making a marginal profit. William enjoyed running the house and took pleasure in the fact that audiences increased soon after he took command. He hoped that at least part of the Center's new success was due to his program of carpet-cleaning, seat-repairing, and repainting of certain decorative architectural features which had deteriorated over years. He felt that making sure light bulbs were replaced immediately on all fixtures markedly improved the environment in all locations within the building. Edward was pleased with his father's new job, and he made several jokes about both of them now being in the managerial profession.

Edward had taken up with a steady girl friend whose name was Margery. She was a tiny girl whom William judged to be inadequate in all the important respects. She had a large nose and talked fluently about soap operas, daytime and primetime. One early morning, while wandering through the house in an insomniac state, William discovered Eddie and Margery in an intimate but chaste position on the living room sofa. Unaware of William's presence, Margery traced with quite delicate strokes the uneven scar on Eddie's cheek, the old scar from the mad bomber's explosion. William felt that he wanted to blow up the two of them right that minute, but instead he sneaked out of the room and returned to his bed, still wide awake.

The next morning he called Catherine. As he had suspected, she had been laid off from the Emily Bronte Boutique. She told William that she slept quite late every morning, except on the days when she was expected at unemployment.

"Marry me, Catherine," William said. She noted that his voice was tired, scratchy. He sounded unhappy. For a brief moment she wondered whether she should accept a proposal spoken in an unhappy voice. But she wanted no more boutiques, no more unemployment offices, no more people muttering about too-expensive designer clothing, no more clerks asking what have you done to look for work this week. She accepted.

"Good," William said, his voice still weary.

"Do you know what I look like these days?"

"I have a good idea."

"It's that bad. Does it matter?"

"No."

Osgood was best man at the wedding. He and Margery were the only ones at the ceremony who seemed genuinely happy. Edward was not unhappy, but he could not work up much enthusiasm for two tired-looking old people who, at the altar, could barely work up the energy for the exchange of vows. However, he did provide the facilities of his restaurant for the reception. He arranged for champagne to come out of the soft-drink nozzles and placed a massive amount of hors d'oeuvres in between the banks of cash registers. The hot foods were mainly the products of the franchise, which would have shamed Edward just a little, except that William had requested them. He even insisted that the sandwiches arrive at the tables and booths in the company paper wrappings. Many guests remarked it was probably the best reception they had ever attended. Later, when the company's main office found out that Edward used the franchise facilities without the proper authorization, he was properly admonished. Nobody in the company threatened to fire him because they already had on file many efficiency reports, which contained the information that, under Edward's managerial aegis, there was a fantastic amount of repeat business in his restaurant.

William returned from the honeymoon looking much better. He and Catherine had gone to a Caribbean island, and he had found that sitting on the beach without thinking a single thought suited him, even exhilarated him. Catherine unfortunately contracted some kind of stomach disease, probably from an island virus, and arrived home looking quite peaked.

Three days after his return William phoned Osgood. As he listened to the phone's rings, he glanced out the window at his new neighbors' backyard. These strange people, interlopers from some other state, had built their home on the old lot in record time, and the house looked, with its false-stone front and rocky canopied patio, like a fleeting thought. The family was sitting on lawn chairs reading what looked like the Sunday papers. It was Monday.

When Osgood answered, William told him to arrange a séance. Osgood said he'd given that sort of thing up. William said nobody gives up being psychic. Osgood claimed it was a habit and could be broken, but, after William's insistent pleadings, he agreed he could handle one more séance.

Osgood collected a couple of his peculiar friends, ones he didn't ordinarily introduce to William, keeping them as separate segments of his social life. He had many segments to his social and personal life, most of which William never knew about. Osgood and William had originally met in the army, and Osgood, who was footloose at the time, had moved to William's city after their discharge.

William arrived at the séance alone, but Osgood chose not to mention Catherine's absence, since William had said, after all, that he wanted to contact Linda. The sight of the peculiar friends, both sitting in unnatural postures and appearing quite vacant-eyed, almost made William leave. What if I died now, he thought, and everyone knew I died in the company of these freaks? People would realize they were just Osgood's friends, hired to help for the séance, wouldn't they?

During the séance Osgood had to work extra hard to dispel William's tension and establish the proper mood, but he always had had a good lulling effect on his friend, and eventually the mood was set.

Instead of appearing, as she had at the first séance, Linda took possession of Osgood. She said she had too much pride to materialize in front of William just after his new marriage.

"You keep track of me out there, up there, back there, wherever you are?" William asked.

"I know generally what you do, my dear."

Osgood's voice, while still retaining masculine timbre, sounded very much like Linda's. Osgood had known Linda well, of course, and, if one were looking for a fraud, one could suspect Osgood of impersonatory powers. But William was convinced that Osgood was Linda, simple as that. After all these years, he still knew Linda when he heard her.

"Eddie's managing a fast-food joint," William said.

"I know."

"You said he was going to be famous."

"I know. He will be."

Osgood's hand squeezed his affectionately, just the way Linda used to.

"Well, he's on his own," William said. "I'm not going to help him anymore."

"You won't have to. You never had to."

"But I devoted my life to him."

"That was your choice. You didn't do a bad job."

"I thought he'd turn out different."

"A common fear, but he's turned out just the way he should."

"I don't want to listen to him talk about the fast-food business any more, Linda, I don't want to look at Margery the rest of my life, I don't want to—"

"There, there, Billy. Take it easy."

His eyes closed, and he felt Osgood's arms embrace him, tenderly, while Osgood still muttered in Linda's voice. He felt Osgood's exceedingly-wet lips kiss him repeatedly on the cheek. Osgood held him quietly for a long time. When he opened his eyes, the peculiar friends were gone, and Osgood still had tears streaming from his eyes. Later, over coffee, Osgood insisted that the tears had not been his own. William would never be certain about that.

He went home and held Catherine for a long time. After that, he realized the odd tense feelings that had, it seemed, been a part of his everyday life since Linda's death, had now left him. Edward now seemed properly in place in William's emotional context. That night William told several jokes that made Catherine laugh. Before going to bed, Catherine, a glass of rosé in her hand, told him for the first time in years that she was Heathcliff. She was recovering well from the island disease. Color was returning to her cheeks, and she was looking healthy for the first time in years.

A week later a For Sale sign went up in front of the new house next door. Curious, William stopped the woman of the house, whom he had only talked to twice previously, in the street and asked her why she and her family were leaving Seven Arts. She said they weren't leaving Seven Arts, that in fact that had arranged for a nice new place over on the new street, Gide Boulevard. They were leaving the house because they'd never felt comfortable there. There were suggestions of ghosts there, she said, although no one in the family had ever actually seen one. She knew about the Jewish couple who'd been blown up in the former house and sometimes suspected, she said, their spirits were trying to invade the new house. It was an absurd fantasy, she said, but they had decided to move out anyway. She wished him well and said in parting they liked his son very much; they went to the fast-food place at least once a week and Eddie was terrific to them. When they did leave the house a month or so later, they forgot to take some blue and white polka dot curtains off a second floor window, and William meant to tell them about it the next time he saw them but he forgot. Even though real estate agents showed new people through the house, the curtains stayed up.

Edward originated a contest for the fast-foods company, and it was copied in several eastern seaboard outlets. In each local contest customers were awarded points for their purchases, and those who accumulated sufficient points could sponsor a young child, one of their own or one picked from welfare care, in attending some entertainment event, with the fast-food company paying for the tickets. Since the contest encouraged patronage and made the company appear generous, the main office was especially pleased with Edward this time. Their pleasure more than offset their earlier dissatisfaction with him about the wedding reception. For his franchise's big prize, Edward chose a small indoor circus that was coming to the Sarah Siddons Art Center that spring. It made him very happy to arrange all the details of the event with his own father, and he made several remarks to William that this was the first time they'd worked together professionally.

On circus night father and son stood in the back of the auditorium and counted the house. Edward was pleased to discover that about two-thirds of the audience were the children sponsored by his customers, plus several of the sponsors as guardians. When the band struck up the overture, Edward went to one of the worst seats in the auditorium while William returned to the lobby to rustle in the latecomers. Edward made William shake hands with him before they split up.

William, who hated circuses, had decided to take Catherine to the E. A. Poe Lounge for a drink. Since the circus had been playing the Center for two days and four performances, he knew just when it would break for intermission, and so he could easily get back to the Center from the lounge, which was located nearby. Catherine came into the lobby wearing a new dress, which she proudly announced she had bought in town and not in the Bronte boutique.

"You look smashing," William said to her as they went out the glass-doored main entrance of the Center.

"I don't look bad these days, do I?"

"You look very smashing."

The fire in the auditorium broke out during a trapeze act in which the artist performed daring gymnastic feats while swinging out above the audience. The cause of the fire was never established, although a flaw in the Center's heating system was strongly suspected by the investigators.

Edward had very nearly fallen asleep in his seat, worn out by his excitement and by late nights at the restaurant. He and Margery had been working hard at getting the place into the kind of shape that would allow them to leave it for a week's honeymoon. At first the smell of smoke made him think he was back working, lurking behind the griddles, watching his transient teenaged employees cook burgers and breaded chicken patties. He came fully awake at the sounds of screaming and hysteria. People were already beginning to congest the aisles. Standing up quickly and blocking the path of the nearest group of nearly-panicking adults, Edward told them to calm down and follow him. Walking with a careful deliberation, he led that group up the aisle to the lobby where he yelled at them to get the kids outside and then come back to the lobby to help. Returning to the auditorium, in time to see the trapeze artist fall to his death from a tall collapsing pole, Edward started directing the crowds toward the lobby and the safe side-exits, then he worked his way down the aisle to where a large group of children were clumped together, too scared to move. The conflagration reached the main curtain, which had been assumed to be fireproof. It erupted in flames. Sparks from the curtain jumped to various theater seats, spreading the fire. Edward led the scared children back up the aisle as smoke increased and thickened. In the lobby newly-arrived firemen took charge of the children. Behind him, he heard several bloodcurdling screams from the auditorium. A fireman tried to shuffle him outside, saying, "You've done well, fella, now get the hell outta here." At the glass doors one of the Center's women employees, a ticket-taker, handed him a towel. He quickly dabbed at his face with it, but could not go out the door she was holding open, could not make himself leave the building. He turned around and, pushing his way through the swiftly exiting crowd and advancing firemen, ran back into the auditorium. Less than a minute later he emerged with another group of children. A fireman grabbed at him, but he evaded the man's hands and went back into the auditorium. After he disappeared into the smoke, people in the lobby were certain they heard him coughing. Many of them waited outside tensely, waiting for Edward to come out again. He did not.

William, informed of the fire by the manager of the Poe Lounge, who came apologetically to the table and whispered the news, rushed back to the Center with Catherine, who had a small artery problem in her legs, trailing not far behind. The color of the fire and smoke against the overcast night sky, with the shadowed trees and houses in the foreground, seemed like something painted by one of the latterday painters whose names adorned streets, circles, and buildings in the Seven Arts settlement.

Osgood was already in the crowd when William reached its fringe. He lived nearby and had run here as soon as he heard the sound of the firetrucks. The crowd had already told him about Eddie's heroism and, running his words together so that William only understood half of what he said, he told William about it. Catherine reached them just as Osgood was describing Eddie's last venture into the auditorium.

William pushed his way forward through the crowd. He was conscious that people who recognized him drew back abruptly and gave him extra space. An officer among the firemen intersected William's path before he could push his way into the lobby, which was drenched in water but untouched by flames. The officer stayed with William as his colleagues continued their battle against the fire.

Later one of the firemen came out of the lobby and whispered to the officer. In a sympathetic but official voice the officer said the fire was under control but that no one had emerged from the auditorium for some time. It seemed as if, in spite of the heroic lifesaving efforts of Eddie and the firemen, many people had died, many children. Edward must have died, too, the officer informed William, his voice descending into a whisper.

With Catherine and Osgood watchful servants at either side of him, William held up rather well. He tried not to see the sympathetic looks that were coming from almost everyone in the crowd. The officer told him that his son had been very brave. William asked the man to call Margery, hoping he would treat her as gently and compassionately as he had treated William. He said she had already been informed and was on her way to the Center.

William felt the tears were finally about to fall from his eyes when one of the people in the crowd screamed alarmingly. Looking up, hoping to see Edward alive, he saw instead one of his employees emerging from the front line of the crowd. She was carrying a towel and speaking incoherently. She handed the towel to a fireman, whose eyebrows raised when he looked closely at it. Holding it out for the officer and William, at an angle from which the gasping crowd could see it too, they all saw that the towel bore an image of Eddie's face. It was very natural looking, in vivid colors. The officer touched it to see if it were perhaps a hastily-executed painting (experts would later be unable to find a trace of artistic materials in the threads or woven sections of the towel), while the woman said she had given it to Eddie to wipe off his face just before he returned to the fire for the second-to-last time. Even the scar from the mad-bomber's explosion could be made out on Edward's cheek. William grabbed the hands of Osgood and Catherine for safety.

The Rim of the Wheel

Lillian Stewart Carl

"LOOK UPON IT as an adventure," she said. "Maybe this dust we're breathing contains some essence of Alexander, the beauty of Mumtaz Mahal, a few molecules of Gautama Buddha's physical body—"

Richard reached into his bag and pulled out his light meter. Frowning, he glanced from it to the elephant pacing with ponderous grace just outside the window of the car. The gray bulk was somehow insubstantial in the dusk, the children that sat on its back only blots of shadow.

"Too dark," he said, and he thrust the meter back into the bag. "If we were on schedule—"

"Try to enjoy yourself," she said between her teeth.

"Sharon, I'm on assignment. I'm taking pictures of India on assignment for the Foundation. And we're not going to get to the Foundation guesthouse in time for me to do any work tonight."

She closed her eyes and for a moment succumbed to weariness. It would be so easy to sleep, to surrender to a dream—She opened her eyes and focused on the intricately folded turban of the Sikh driver.

"Mussoorie has been there for a long time; it'll still be there tomorrow," she said, trying again. "You know, I'm from Mussoorie and you have to show me—"

His snort was humorless. With a sigh she turned to stare at the crowds thronging the street. The stench, the dust and smoke eddied in slow whorls through the window, coating her skin with sludge. Her hair straggled in annoying damp ringlets across her forehead. A beggar, a shapeless heap of rags, thrust a scrawny hand into the car and whined some incomprehensible Hindi epithet.

The Sikh accelerated, following the car ahead. "Shouldn't you turn on the headlights?" Sharon asked faintly.

The turbaned head nodded. "So sorry. Lights not working. Following car ahead, you see."

"That figures," Richard groaned. "Car broke down three times. Waited in Saharanpur for hours with a bloody flat tire, shut up in a bloody hot car with beggars like vultures waiting—"

In Tibet, Sharon thought, the vultures are sacred. The Tibetans practice celestial burial, dismembering the bodies of the dead and feeding them to the carrion birds, freeing the soul for reincarnation, another trip around the wheel of life—Her neck crawled. Stop it, she ordered herself. Stop it. Surely here, on the other side of the world—

"That's India for you," she said, with a brittle brightness. "No parts for the car, no one to fix them. The locals have learned acceptance, I guess. But we're almost there, and dinner'll be waiting."

Richard muttered skepticism. The dusk thickened. The city of Dehra Dun dematerialized behind them. The driver turned at a fork in the road, following close behind the tail lights of another car. And there, suddenly, were the mountains that had all day receded before them, a mirage closing the edge of the Punjabi plain.

These were only the foothills of the Himalayas, but to Sharon's Midwestern American eyes they were themselves mountains. At the top, where the basalt cleaved the sky, flickered rows of yellow and white lights like Christmas decorations on some unimaginably tall tree.

"Mussoorie," the Sikh announced, pointing. "Up there."

Between here and there were strung tangled lengths of gray thread, twin headlights crawling around an acute angle—The road. They were going up the road, in the dark, without lights. Sharon gulped and leaned back against the seat. Look upon it as a change in perspective, as a chance to get away from teaching World Civ to kids who cared only about their cars, as an opportunity to observe Richard in his natural habitat and not in the artificial light of a suburban fern bar—

When he'd asked her to come to India with him, she'd jumped at the chance, hoping to escape the black disillusionment that had been haunting her. But she carried it with her, it seemed.

The car swung to the right. Sharon was pulled to the left, toward the window, and she looked in reluctant fascination out and down. The last glimmer of the sun lingered over the Indian plain, tinting its pall of dusk and smoke with an ironic rosy pink; a new moon floated just at the horizon. The sky overhead was a crystalline indigo, holding one bright star.

The car swung back in the other direction and approached even closer to the non-existent shoulder of the road. Headlights flashed by on the inside lane. Sharon's face was drawn by some centrifugal force into a grimace of fear, lips tight, eyes wide, as if she no longer inhabited her own body. Shapes swirled in the gloom beyond the edge of the precipice, great carrion birds slipping through the air, eyes glinting. From their beaks trailed— bits of fabric, pale silk scarves—

She blinked. No, no birds. Ancient dust in her eyes; taut nerves and a moment of dream. Richard huddled silent at the other end of the seat.

Half a lifetime later the cars emerged from the road and stopped on a wide ledge in the hillside. The yellow and white lights danced and sparkled at the top of a cliff scaled by a rickety stairway.

Sharon shook off her malaise, opened the car door, found that she could still stand erect. The air she gulped was cool. Wordlessly she accepted one of Richard's camera bags.

The car ahead disgorged an Indian family, children looking curiously at the Americans. The sari-clad matriarch gestured into the gulf of darkness below them, indicating anything from the parking lot itself to a distant glimmer that could well have been New York, pointedly ignoring them. A swarm of dark figures eddied around the cars, their heads barely reaching Richard's shoulder; a few coins changed hands and the figures began to lash suitcases and boxes onto their backs.

"Like pack animals," Richard said under his breath, counting his change.

"I'm sure," retorted Sharon, "that they're poor just to spite you."

He turned to her, brows slanted. "Hey, I know I've been acting like a real bastard today, but can't you give me credit for a little compassion?"

The Sikh driver disappeared. The Indian family straggled up the staircase. Sharon stared at Richard, open-mouthed. He was always doing that, surprising her with understanding when she anticipated a shrug of indifference—but then, he was probably just some fragment of her fevered imagination, some dream of peace and acceptance—

The hand he planted firmly in the small of her back was real enough; he urged her into motion, and she shut her mouth and moved.

The lights swung like banners in the wind. Beyond them was a gravel path. Fir trees arched overhead, their needles the delicate brushstroked patterns of a Chinese block print. The sky grew hazy, softening the stars to milky glimmers; the moon disappeared over the western rim of the world.

"No cars allowed," said Richard. "We walk." The bearers pattered away with the luggage, winking from one pool of lamplight to the next and the next, dwindling into a point of perspective like a singularity in spacetime.

"I could use a walk," Sharon said.

Richard took her hand, offered her a faint smile. "Are you all right? I'll try to behave myself—"

She squeezed his hand. "No, it's not you; it's never you."

"Culture shock, this time?"

"I suppose so—" But she said to herself, I wish it were that simple.

Swift, deliberate footsteps crunched from behind. Sharon tensed, pulling Richard to a halt in the stark white glow of a streetlamp. A Buddhist monk, his bald head shining, his orange robes drained of color by the harsh light, strode by them and paced on into the night. His eyes blinked, once, to register their presence. An odor of incense remained briefly in the bubble of light and then dissipated.

Sharon exhaled, suddenly dizzy, slipping down the smooth slope of a wave—She set her teeth against the plunge.

Richard guided her back into shadow. In a few moments a long red and white house appeared, nestling into the side of the hill; the path was at the level of its second story, and a bridge led onto the veranda. The windows were dark and cold. "Dinner'll be waiting," muttered Sharon. "Figures."

"They never got the message we were coming," Richard groaned. "At least we have a key, and our own food."

Dinner was cold, tough sandwiches of some unnamed meat, cold hard-boiled eggs, packaged cookies and Kool-aid. Sharon forced it down, telling herself that her body needed fuel, too dispirited for appetite.

The bedroom was spartan. Tile floor, bare walls, ancient creaking bedstead. The bathroom would have served as a meat locker. The bottom of the dresser drawer was lined with a yellowed sheet of newspaper; the headlined story was about a plane crash killing a group of Indian generals. A small patch of print in the corner casually mentioned that U.S. President Kennedy had been assassinated. And so much for that, Sharon told herself. She slammed the drawer on it.

She huddled mournfully under the clammy sheets, hating Richard for falling so easily into sleep. Her nose dripped and she mopped it with one of her precious store of tissues. The change in altitude was as good as a change in climate—a change in perspective—what did she think she would find here—heading East like an aging hippie searching for an enlightenment not found in a college class in transcendental meditation—release from the cosmic merry-go-round, the wheel of life and rebirth—Nirvana gained by renunciation of desire—a desire for purpose, for warmth—some Tibetan monks could raise their body temperature through meditation—in this climate they would need such an ability.

The bathroom light emitted as much wattage as a firefly, but she had kept it on. The wind from the Himalayas tapped at the windows. Shadows moved in the hall, murmuring in a mysterious language. Slow footsteps, felt boots, passed along the terrace outside.

Sharon clasped herself as tightly as possible to Richard's familiar body.

She couldn't have slept. But evidently she had, for she awoke from a dream of bright-colored banners streaming in a wind to hear running feet, shouts and explosions on the terrace. A Red Chinese invasion—she leaped up.

Richard stood at the window, outlined in pale sunlight, laughing. "Look. Monkeys came up on the terrace looking for food, and the servants are using cap guns to drive them away."

"What? Oh—" She looked out. The missing servants had appeared, and they were conducting their defense against the local macaques with great relish. Only the tops of trees showed beyond the low stone wall edging the terrace; brown shapes bounded from branch to branch, chattering with eerily human laughter, and the foliage waved. It was absurd, and Sharon laughed too.

One of the servants turned and saw the couple at the window. White teeth sparked beneath a swooping black moustache. "Good morning, Memsahib," he said.

Goodness, she thought, did they still talk in such a Colonel Blimp idiom? Or was the man making fun of her?

"I smell food," Richard stated. "Let's get dressed."

Sharon stood cradling a hot cup of Darjeeling tea, leaning against the window in the upper hall and rather enjoying the melancholy induced by a change of season—or climate, in this case. Yes, it was an adventure. Her dark dream of the night before was just part of her recurring nightmare, her disillusionment with her world. To a Buddhist, she thought, the world is a dream, shaped by the perceptions of the participant, neither real nor unreal.

They had come up the Indian side of the ridge where Mussoorie was built, this morning she had a view over the other side, to the north and east. Brown hills matted with mist climbed to a beetling smudge, a suggestion of mountain peaks. The sky seemed to flow away behind soft wind-borne clouds, as if the earth turned perceptibly before her eyes.

And there, on one of the trails that laced the hills, a caravan picked its way upwards. Yaks pulled a cart with a crimson canopy; outriders on horseback held streaming banners. The figures were tiny, distant, immaterial—a ray of sun struck them and their robes glinted with blue and silver. Was it a living person in the cart, or an image lacquered in gold?

Even as she watched, the mist gathered again around the yaks and the cart and the horsemen; they crested the hill and were gone. To the roof of the world, Tibet, the Forbidden Kingdom, timeless Shangri-La. *This center of heaven*, went a sixth-century poem. *This core of the earth, this heart of the world fenced round with snow*—

Richard was standing at her shoulder, looking at her doubtfully. He held that infernal British invention, a toast-rack, between thumb and forefinger. "I guess they ate cold toast every morning," he said, "to make them mean enough to rule the Empire in the afternoon."

There is some corner of a foreign field that is forever England;—this little world, this precious stone set in the silver sea—

"Sharon," Richard said, "would you care to join me for breakfast?"

She shook herself. "Sorry."

But his smile was quite gentle. "More tea, ma'am?" He filled her outstretched cup and said, "I thought we should begin with the Tibetan school. Refugee children; the Foundation wants pictures for its journal.''

"Oh yes, we hauled those magazines all the way from Delhi for them. Certainly.'' The tea left a faint herbal tang in her mouth. A cloud brushed the window pane with mist, making of it a steel mirror; she grimaced wryly at her reflection. Taking yourself seriously these days, aren't you?

It wasn't quite her own face that grimaced back.

Sharon crunched along the gravel path, carrying the back issues of *National Geographic* and *Smithsonian*. Richard was just beyond the guesthouse bridge; he had spotted a tiger skin staked out on a rooftop just below. He was crooning contentedly over his cameras and lenses, taking one picture in thin sunlight, another as a cloud tripped over its own shadow and fell against the ridge, spilling water vapor across the town. "Think you'll do any good with that thing?'' he called, seeing Sharon's Polaroid dangling from her wrist.

"Just snapshots,'' she returned. "Not art.''

He flashed her a quick smile. "Let's go, then.''

Now, in daylight, Sharon could see the entire mountainside, red roofs and trees and gardens like a painted fabric flung over the upthrust bones of the earth. Here was not a single straight line, no stark horizontals like the Punjabi plain or the American plain of her birth; here the world was designed in segments of circles, curving between earth and sky.

Another Buddhist monk strode past, prayer beads flowing from his fingers, intent on his own vision. A group of little boys playing ball parted before him like the bow wave of a ship. Sharon's stomach went hollow; she turned, and the monk turned at the same instant, as if startled from his contemplation. Their eyes met. "Sharon?'' Richard called, and Sharon spun about, rejecting the man's knowing look and the unease in her stomach.

The school was on another ridge, facing the guesthouse. The gate was opened by a plump, middle-aged woman dressed in a shapeless Tibetan robe. She smiled and bowed; Richard bowed in turn, as gracious as a medieval grandee. The woman led them down a stone-banked path to a jumble of plaster and wood buildings, row upon row of potted plants, tall fir trees. A wide courtyard ended abruptly at a wall; children sat against the sun-warmed stone eating from small bowls. Beyond them the land fell away, disappeared, and in the distance rose again in tiers of rock and brush. They left the boxes of magazines in a dim, low-ceilinged room where a cooking stove shed wisps of smoke over an opened CARE package. An ornate churn sat nearby. The woman handed Richard a steaming cup; Richard handed it on to Sharon, who took it and returned hastily to the open air.

Tea, strong as a liquor, churned with butter and salt. She coughed, and put a hand over her mouth to quiet herself. The voices continued unperturbed inside. A couple of the children, returning their bowls to the kitchen, giggled at the strange lady.

She tried another sip. It was familiar, somehow; perhaps she had tasted it in another life—A movement caught the corner of her eye, and she turned—a woman, dressed in rich brocade, a headdress of gold flowers and tinkling bells—

No. It was a young man, looking at her with a quiet curiosity. He was dressed in a European white shirt, pullover gray sweater, dark trousers, but he wore a Tibetan turquoise and silver necklace at his throat, and the planes of his face and eyes had been sculpted by the free wind of the mountains. He belonged on horseback, wearing robes of fur and felt, galloping across the high plateau of Tibet—

Sharon set her jaw against the importunities of her own mind. "Hello," she said. "I'm more or less with the Foundation."

"Ah, yes. One of our corporate benefactors." He had almost no accent, his intonation not the British-Hindi singsong of India, but American, flat. He smiled politely, sensing her puzzlement. "I was born in Lhasa, but left as a small child; my parents were political exiles. I studied in Switzerland and New York. Allow me—I am Trisong, schoolteacher."

The buttered tea seared her throat, drawing the blood into her cheeks. "Sharon Gardner," she said.

His smile widened. "The rose of Sharon, the lily of the valley—"

"You're familiar with the Bible?" she blurted.

"World civilization," he returned. "Would you like a tour of the school?"

"Thank you," A flash lit up the interior of the house; Richard was working. Might as well wander off for a while. She raised her camera, targeting the one small boy who remained sitting pensively against the mountain fastnesses. Trisong as a child, she thought. Exiled, his back to his homeland—how sad.

The picture emerged, a greenish-gray fluid; she thrust it into her purse before the image developed, as if she feared he had heard her thought. His dignity did not permit pity.

A small temple perched on a spur of the hillside, almost suspended in space. Sharon stood on the narrow path, dazzled; intricately carved and colored beams, scrollwork curling upwards to a tile roof, bright flags snapping prayers into the wind. "It's lovely," she said. She took another picture.

"I am told," said Trisong, "that this is only a pale image of the great temples of Tibet." He spun the prayer wheel that stood outside the gateway. Inscribed papers rustled inside the great cylinder as it turned.

"Hail to the jewel in the heart of the lotus," Sharon murmured, translating the words of the prayer to the Buddha.

He glanced back at her, surprised, flattered.

"World civilization," she told him.

The temple was dark, redolent of incense and dust. Long bolts of fabric hung from ceiling to floor, painted with fabulous beasts, legendary kings and monks, swirling demons. *"Thangka,"* Trisong said. "Buddhist images on cloth."

Sharon considered one seated figure, a crowned woman serene among the circling, garish colors, preserved in an attitude of meditation. Her world seemed very much in control. Perhaps Trisong's was as well—"Your pilgrimage was in the wrong direction," she told him. "The East is full of young Westerners seeking inner peace along the Eightfold Path of Buddhism."

Trisong nodded solemnly. "The elimination of the desire which causes suffering, a release from the turning of the wheel— a tempting goal. And yet Westerners also say that the elimination of desire has kept us from progress."

"It depends on your definition of progress, doesn't it? Nuclear weapons, pollution, the extinction of species—including perhaps our own. I feel as I'm clinging desperately to the rim of the wheel, screaming, as it spins out of control."

"Stop screaming and climb into the center."

"The center cannot hold . . ."

"And the beast is slouching towards Bethlehem? Yeats, too, was afflicted with the Western malaise." Trisong's dark eyes were cool, opaque, she fancied he was mocking her, and she bridled.

"You're a Bodhisattva?" she demanded sarcastically. "You've achieved enlightenment, and have come back from Nirvana to help us disillusioned wretches . . ." She stopped, bit her lip.

"No," he stated. A frown stirred from the depths of his eyes; his mouth tightened, cracking the calm mask of his face. "I have come here seeking my own balance between desire and pain, a spot between the rim and the center."

`So you're a lost soul, too. A coincidence?

A stranger. She looked around, saw a stack of long, flat books, changed the subject. "Holy Scripture?"

"Yes," he said, exhaling. "Rescued from the Red Guards, the Cultural Revolution, by—secret workers." And the frown intensified.

"Ah," she said. This was difficult—she raised her camera like a shield before her, set the flash, and took a picture of the slender young man surrounded by gods and saints and demons.

A gilded clay statue sat in the place of honor at the end of the room, a row of butter lamps flickering before it—Sakyamuni, the Buddha, features smoothed with wisdom and with peace, one hand raised in blessing. Long silk scarves lay as offerings across the lap.

Sharon continued taking pictures, unable to speak. The flashes glanced off the gold statue, hissed in the dim corners. The clouds outside the door gathered thick above the valley, churned by an invisible hand. A cold blast of wind howled around the building, a predator seeking the warm flesh inside; the *thangka* rustled, painted dragons stirring into life . . . Sharon clutched the small camera so hard the plastic cracked beneath her fingers.

Trisong stepped forward, extending his hands in supplication over the guttering flames of the butter lamps. The tiny fires steadied. The day was calm, the clouds pale fleecy blots of water vapor.

Sharon took a deep breath. Stop it, stop it now—With trembling hands she put her pictures into her purse. She forced herself to look at Trisong; he still struggled with some thought. "Thank you," she croaked.

And yet he seemed to sense nothing wrong with her, as if he, too, had such visions. "Will you come back tomorrow? I could show you the *thangka* I am painting."

"So you're an artist as well as a philosopher." Her impulse was to run. But she walked out the door, pausing to spin the prayer wheel. It clicked over, whirring gently. "Yes," she said, "I'll come back tomorrow."

"Didn't you look at any of these?" Richard called.

Sharon groped for the towel, collided with the bottle of drinking water, knocked her toothbrush clattering into the sink. "I was too embarrassed," she returned. "I felt—like an intruder in his private world."

"I think your world lines crossed today."

Sharon emerged from the bathroom. Richard lay across the bed, the cardboard squares of her snapshots arranged before him. "Seal of approval?" she asked.

"Competent," he stated. "Good composition here and here; if you ever figure out how to set film speed you might make a decent photographer—with a decent camera, of course." He shook his head over the cracked body of the Polaroid.

"Damned with faint praise, as usual," Sharon said with a smile, and Richard looked up to throw her a wink. It was a moment of companionship; she really could trust him—

She sat down beside him to look at the pictures. And immediately she slipped again down that long, smooth, curve; her head spun, dizzy, her breath stopped short in her throat. "These aren't the pictures I took," she said.

"What?"

"I mean . . ." She groped for words. "Here, this wall and landscape—there was a child sitting there. Cute little guy, black hair, like Trisong. And here, this tapestry. Trisong was standing in front of it."

"Good clear focus on the painting," Richard said quickly, attempting to intercept her panic. "The face of this woman—a queen?—looks almost alive. So you didn't focus the others properly."

"But . . ." She fell back on the bed, her fist pressed to her mouth. If Trisong had stepped aside just as she raised the camera—if the lens had been smudged somehow—It came out in a rush. "I'm going crazy. Seeing things that aren't there, sensing, imagining . . ."

Richard laid the pictures down with a sigh. "Come on. Let's go for a walk before dinner. I'll even leave my cameras here."

She strolled up the path, clasping Richard's arm as if he were the only steady object in a reeling world. "Tell me about it," he said, and she did.

"And what if," he said at last, "what if your emotional overload of the last months has become focused here—we Westerners would call it an eddy in time, perhaps. A quantum wavefront, changed by your perception of it, causing an altered state of consciousness."

"The wheel," she said. "Turning by reincarnation, by the illusion of history—however you want to look at it. The universe as a dream, created by my own desire for—another reality." She laid her head against his shoulder; his arm tightened around her waist. And yet you could be my center, she thought. You could anchor this reality—But that might well be too much to ask.

A cemetery lay on the slope of the mountain, weathered markers jumbled in the sod like natural outcroppings of rock. The late afternoon sunlight was thick honey between the brush-stroked shadows of the fir trees. The wind whispered through banks of gladioli and impatiens. "Fitzroy, Walker, Smalley," Sharon read. "They never made it Home, did they?"

"This was Home," returned Richard. "The weather, the lush vegetation—it reminded them of England."

" 'There is some corner of a foreign field . . .' " she sighed. "Remember Benet's poem? 'You may bury my body in Sussex grass, You may bury my tongue at Champmedy. I shall not be there. I shall rise and pass. Bury my heart at Wounded Knee.' "

" 'American Names,' " he nodded. "Is Home, then, the center?"

"Now we're Americans. Our ancestors were English. Maybe our remoter ancestors lived here. Reincarnation, history—"

He glanced at her, a quick sideways grin. "Well, those monkeys—"

"Richard," she began reprovingly, but in spite of herself she laughed. "All right. How do you cope so well?"

He grimaced. "I see the world through a camera lens—composition, color, light; maybe I make my own altered state. Maybe the Buddhists are right, and it's all just a magic show, an elaborate joke."

"Yes, maybe." The sun dipped behind the mountain; twilight flooded the cemetery. A raven screeched overhead and Sharon started. Sharp beaks tore her flesh from her bones, her blood spattered across the rocks—it was a mistake, she still lived in this body. "Can we go in now?" she said. "I'm very, very tired."

"Sure." He put his arm around her, shook her with gentle exasperation, guided her back up the path to the guesthouse.

Sharon awoke from a dreamless sleep—the dream, it seemed, was a waking one—to see a moving form just at the edge of the bed. A wizened little man crouched over a whisk broom and a dust pan, cleaning the floor.

Richard muttered something, nuzzling into her hair; she jabbed his ribs with her elbow and he awoke with an indignant snort. The sweeper continued across the tiles, inch by painful inch, as impersonal as if the couple in the bed were painted figures in an Ajanta fresco.

"Culture shock," Sharon whispered.

"Me too, honey; me too."

But the day had dawned clear and bright, the clouds swept away by a freshening breeze. The brown foothills were striped with the deep umber of their own shadows, as clean and precise and illusory as an Escher print. Beyond them shone the blue and silver of the Himalayas, a stained glass buttress supporting the curvature of the sky.

Sharon stood beside Richard as he changed lenses on his camera. "Breathtaking," she sighed. "One hell of a magic show."

"Mmm," he said, in a purr of satisfaction.

And there was the caravan, wending its way up a path, spearpoints glittering, banners snapping with scarlet and purple. A tiny figure leaned out of the litter and beckoned; its hands held something that caught the sunlight, reflecting a white flare into Sharon's eyes.

The back of her neck crawled. She made an about-face into the house. It would be interesting, she told herself, grasping at the rim of sanity, to see if Richard's pictures showed the litter, the horses and yaks of the caravan. Later. Much later. Back Home.

After breakfast Richard announced he wanted to take pictures of the town. Shopping, Sharon thought. A harmless enough activity. And the school later, when her nerves were steadier.

Mussoorie had been a British hill-station, and a British hill-station it remained. Gingerbreaded timber and brick buildings, Blue Willow tea sets in the shop windows, the fragrance of curry—a timeless Raj preserved under a Victorian bell jar. Sharon, in her present state of mind, fully expected to see Kipling's phantom rickshaw emerge from an alley.

She bought silk for a sari, an embroidered bedspread, carved shesham-wood trivets. She felt almost cheerful as she haggled with the merchants. Then Richard led her up the creaking steps of a Tibetan store.

With a chill of apprehension she ducked into the entrance. But the goods laid out for sale did not seem threatening, and her attention was drawn to a group of water-colors along one wall.

"Painted by the students at the Tibetan school," the shopkeeper told her. "Tibetan mythology, some historical tableaux."

It was the woman in the gold headdress, sitting next to a crowned man; another woman sat on his other side. The three made identical gestures of peace and reassurance. Silk scarves and clouds and crazily tilted mountains swirled around them, but their serenity was the calm in the eye of the storm.

Sharon took a step backwards, her lips tight with denial. She crashed against a string of brass bells, knocking them off the rack, and they rang harshly, voices pealing in the waves of sound. "Sharon," Richard began, reaching out for her.

Sharon turned, and came face to face with a steel mirror. Her own features were reflected in the polished metal, fair, genetically European—no. Even as she watched the smooth surface wavered, rippled, changed. Her eyes lengthened into almond-shaped darkness, her skin blushed deep gold, the bones of her cheeks and forehead molded themselves into flatter, smoother features. Her hair plunged down over her shoulders, straight, black, glossy—

Her hand moved of its own accord, knocking the mirror to the floor. It rolled crazily across the wooden planks and wobbled, clanging, to rest.

The shop was silent. The proprietor shrank back behind his counter. Richard stood with his mouth open, horrified. Sharon looked frantically around—the paintings, the Tibetan school—God Richard, forgive me—She thrust her packages into his hands and ran.

The streets heaved beneath her feet, passersby turned with the glaring eyes and bared fangs of demons, the clouds followed her, howling—

Beyond the gate the path was quiet in the morning sun, and the soothing murmur of students busy at their lessons lay over the courtyard. This then, was the eye of the storm. Sharon slowed to a walk, leaned on the wall, caught her breath. The valley sloped away before her; she reached out over the dizzying gulf of air, sliding down the curve of the wheel and off the rim, into space, into timelessness—Surrender to madness, she thought, and rest quietly forever.

"You would just come back again," Trisong said. "Reincarnated for another trip around the wheel."

She straightened, turned slowly around. Somehow she'd thought he wouldn't be there. But he was there, watching her, dark eyes unblinking, not smiling, not joking. "I came to see your painting," she said.

He led her to a whitewashed room littered with paper and brushes and splotches of bright paint, illuminated by a large window facing northeast to the mountains; he indicated the bolt of cloth spread over a table. The picture was almost completed. A caravan camped in a mountain pass, beside a lake whose surface was as smooth and clear as polished metal. The flags of the outriders, the gilding of the litter and the pavilion, the hulking shapes of the yaks, were all reflected in a double, dreamlike image. The sky was filled with an intricate pattern of clouds, the surrounding hills teemed with fantastic beasts, dragons and snow leopards and great antlered deer.

Only the central image was left unpainted, a dim gray sketch suggesting a woman's robed figure, a crown—

Sharon dropped onto a stool by the table. Trisong offered her a cup of buttered tea; she took it mutely from his hand and sipped, rolled the liquid around her mouth, swallowed. The taste and smell were echoes deep within her mind. An unnatural calm possessed her as she slipped away—another reality. Madness, and an eternity on the rim of the wheel.

"It is Princess Wen Cheng," Trisong said at her elbow. "She came from China in the seventh century to marry Songsten Gampo, the ruler of Tibet; he was converted to Buddhism by Wen Cheng and by his other wife, a princess of Nepal.

"According to tradition, the most sacred Buddhist image in the Jokhang temple at Lhasa, which represents the Buddha Gautama not as a monk but as a crowned Bodhisattva, was brought to Tibet by Wen Cheng." He paused. "I have never seen it."

I have, Sharon thought. The lacquered image in the cart—

He shrugged away his thought, picked up a pencil, drew a round shape in the woman's hand. "The princess carried a mirror in which she could see visions of her home. But on her journey she broke the mirror, and it became the mountains of the Sun and Moon. And she gave up her homeland, and journeyed on to Tibet. Renunciation, the elimination of desire, the center of the wheel."

The delicate pencil strokes shifted, forming the lines of a face—Sharon's own face, looking back at her from the cloth. "She must have been a Bodhisattva herself," Sharon murmured.

"She made a decision, and the deciding brought her peace."

Decision . . . yes—Sharon clenched her teeth so tightly that her jaw ached. "Is it possible," she asked, "to know our previous incarnations?"

"The Dalai Lama knows. He has the wisdom to deal with it. Perhaps it is merciful that the rest of us do not know."

"But if there were an eddy of time at the rim of the wheel, if somehow I knew, and could choose—'' The circle in the woman's hand exploded, showering encampment, animals, mountains and lake with shards that gleamed more brightly than the thin northern light of the room—the mountains shifted, rocks tumbling, trees falling with roots in the air—dragons coiled and snapped and horses fled in terror—the princess with Sharon's face watched, impassive, as the world spun like a kaleidoscope around her, sliding into a new pattern—

No. Sharon slammed the tea down on the table and it slopped over the edge of the cup. "No, I am not her. She was a Bodhisattva, and she was released from the cycle of rebirth. I knew her, yes; I admired her. But I couldn't make her decision. I was caught between two lives, between two illusions, bound to the wheel and yearning for another reality—''

Trisong watched her, expressionless, as still and stiff as the statue in the temple. "I too,'' he murmured. "Caught between two lives—''

She inhaled, trembling, weak. "It's over now. I have this reality, this life—I surrender to that, and I won't be tempted by madness any more. I choose myself.''

The painting was only that, two-dimensional colors on a cloth, the penciled figure of a woman holding a penciled mirror. Sharon leaned across the table, rummaged through a box of pens and brushes until she found an eraser. With a few deliberate strokes she blotted out the woman's face and removed the circle from her hand. She wetted her fingertip, picked up each particle of graphite that littered the cloth, shook it away.

And the smudged place on the cloth remained only a smudge, a quick sketch of a mannequin in fancy-dress robes, faceless, holding nothing. The beasts were stylized fantasies, the lake a thin sheen of northern sun.

Trisong laid his pencil on the table. "In deciding, peace,'' he said. "Surrender to my own life—''

"Yes.'' Sharon exhaled, unclenched her teeth, straightened. It was an adventure, a change of perspective. In the end, she had the strength to choose sanity. "And you?'' she asked.

He said, "I had thought I was the only displaced soul, wandering the world, searching. Then you came, here to the eye of the storm. More than a coincidence, I think.'' He took the eraser from her fingers and turned it in his hand, contemplating his drawing. "Thank you for showing me the path.''

"Me? Showing you?'' But their world lines diverged, and he

remained silent, contemplating the drawing. "Well, whatever," she whispered. She turned and tiptoed from the room.

Richard waited out of breath at the gate. "Hey, are you all right?"

"Yes," Sharon replied. "Yes, I'm all right. Thank you for riding out the storm."

It was their last morning in Mussoorie. Richard stood in the courtyard, scanning the surrounding hills with his camera while the schoolchildren lined up for a picture. "What do you see?" Sharon asked.

"Just what's there," he answered. "I lack your peripheral vision, it seems."

"And that," she told him, "is what makes you so refreshing to have around." She raised her Polaroid and took a picture of him taking a picture, wheels within wheels—

The children were ready, two rows of shining cheeks and crinkled dark eyes. Sharon turned to the middle-aged lady and the old man beside her. "I had hoped to say good-bye to Trisong. Is he working somewhere?"

The woman frowned slightly. "Who?"

"Trisong. A teacher . . ."

The couple exchanged a calculatedly puzzled glance. The old man cleared his throat before speaking. "Miss, we have no teachers here of that name."

Sharon shrugged away the sudden rush of fear. No. That was over. "A young man, sweater, necklace—he was painting a new tapestry."

The couple continued shaking their heads. The children broke formation and ran shrieking around the courtyard. Richard replaced his camera in its case. "Let me guess," he said. "You're the only one who's seen him." His hand closed firmly on Sharon's arm.

She shook her head. "No—I understand."

They took polite leave of the man and woman, and Sharon led Richard along the mountainside to the temple. The prayer flags snapped in the wind, the wheel creaked faintly as she turned it. She drew a long silk scarf from her purse and placed it in the lap of the golden image.

Richard was waiting, poised, for her to lapse into hysteria. "No," she said, to him and to the serene features of the Buddha as well, "No. No more of that. It's quite simple."

"Yes," Richard said encouragingly.

"Trisong said something about 'secret workers' in Tibet; he said he had never seen the Jokhang Buddha; he said something about a decision."

"So he went back, secretly, and the others are covering his tracks?"

"I think so." She turned. "See? That's real." There was the new *thangka*, its colors fresh and glistening; lake, mountain, caravan, princess—she was lovely, with her almond-shaped eyes and high cheekbones, brocade robes and crown. An ancient Chinese princess—holding a Polaroid camera.

"You tested me," Sharon smiled. "But I knew who I was. And who I am, and why. . . . Good-bye, now. I, too have work to do." She took Richard's arm, leading him from the temple, and she didn't look back.

Hand in hand they strolled toward the parking lot. A Buddhist monk, dignity in orange robes, walked with measured tread past them; he looked through them as if they did not exist in his spacetime.

"Richard," Sharon said.

"Yes?"

"I think it's time we got married."

He considered that a moment, smiling. "We could do a pretty good balancing act together, couldn't we? That's the way it should be; the essence of Buddhism, after all, is not in trying to find something you don't have, but in realizing something you've had all along—"

For just a moment she was giddy, but his hand was steady on hers, and the car was waiting to take them home.

Pan Am One left New Delhi at dawn. Sharon leaned against the window, watching as India receded into a gilded haze of sunlight, dust and smoke. Receded into memory, and there was held timeless.

Richard yawned and stretched. "Tokyo. The camera stores on the Ginza. Then home."

"Home," Sharon repeated. "I do want to go Home now; but someday I'd like to come back here, when I'm ready."

"You were ready this time," he told her.

The staticked voice of the pilot spoke. "Mt. Everest can be seen off the tip of the left wing." She turned, and Richard looked over her shoulder.

Massed snow and cloud anchored the northern horizon. The

earth was a shadow licking at Everest's feet, the arch of the sky a taut blue membrane pierced by the waxing moon.

And the same mass of snow and cloud anchored the southern horizon of Tibet; the great mountain called Chomolungma, too shy to show its face except on such a fine morning. Trisong's eyes were dark below the rim of a fur hat, the strap of a rifle crossed his chest, his pony moved restively as he paused to contemplate the dawn. A nomad again, like his ancestors, guarding the boundary between desire and pain—

I thank you, Sharon thought. She lay back, safe against Richard's shoulder, and the wheel of the world turned around her.

The Laughter of Elves

Juleen Brantingham

THERE IS SOMETHING strange about children of a certain age: a kind of light that glows from the skin, an air of grace, the memory of a scent. They are the silence that is almost sound after the laughter has died away, after the door has closed, after the mourners have expressed their sorrow. Their beauty stabs the heart with knives of ice.

There is . . . an attraction. I can feel it myself, so I can almost understand that man—though not what he did—wanted to do. Not ever that. But to be near her, yes. To glimpse another world through her eyes, to be touched without touching. To wonder.

The moonlight through the open window gilded her face as she slept. I stood in the doorway as I had done ten times a night, every night for two weeks. Holding my breath. Watching for something I had never seen. Waiting . . .

I don't understand. No one can give me answers, not answers that make any sense. All I have are images: that place, the man, the blood. And Tracy naked, not a spot of blood on her, too bewildered to be frightened.

Can't anyone tell me why?

I close her door with a sound as soft as a sigh and steal back to my bed, careful not to disturb the man who shares it with me. But I think my eyes will never close.

I wait.

It is late afternoon and Tracy is on the front porch playing with her dolls and her trucks. The sun filtering through the trees strikes sparks of gold in her hair and turns her skin a pale, delicate green. She speaks to her dolls, sings snatches of a song, and surely her words are English but the heavy summer air turns them into something my ears strain to make sense of.

I watch from the living room, hidden by the drapes. I'd been warned not to hover, not to make her fearful with my own imaginings and guilt but how could I stop?

By the calendar my daughter is four years and five months old but she gets upset if I say four or even four and a half. She is, she insists, four-going-on-five. I am thirty-going-on-ninety.

There is more traffic on the street now, the cars moving at cautious speeds through this neighborhood of children. When our gold Chevette turned the corner I hurried to the kitchen, to the clutter of meal preparations I'd abandoned when Tracy left her swing set outside the kitchen window to go out front and watch for Daddy.

I heard the murmur of their voices and a burst of laughter scalloped by a silvery giggle. The screen door banged and footsteps galloped down the hall. He burst into the kitchen with Tracy in his arms. Two identical pairs of hazel eyes sparkled. Two mouths smiled and kissed me. Tracy must do everything just like Daddy.

My knot of fear loosened slightly. Changing of the guard.

"Time enough to change before supper?"

"Of course. Make sure Tracy washes. Check her fingernails."

When they leave the kitchen is emptier than it was before. But the house is alive again. I am. Waiting is the death I have passed through one more time.

Chairs scrape across the floor. Silverware clinks. Around and through these sounds are the threads of conversation that tie us together, the glances that say more than words.

"So who *is* your new manager?"

"—and he's nine, Daddy."

"Nobody," Jack says, laughing. "The whole department was—"

"He's got a big dog and a two-wheeler—"

"Eat your peas, Tracy."

"—dropped right off the reorganization chart and—"

"—and cowboy boots. Oh!" Tracy was struck by a thought so startling it made her drop her fork. I smiled as I picked it up and wiped it off for her. With Tracy "struck by a thought" is a literal expression. Everything stops, her eyes get wide, and her face lights up.

"Daddy!" She tugged at his arm to be sure she had his full attention. "Daddy, he can even cross *streets* by himself!"

Jack looked at me and we laughed, silently, on the parental channel. "Imagine that!" he said.

"Why can't I do that? I'm as big as he is and he can do it. Why can't I?"

"You know why, chick. There are safety rules about crossing streets and you don't always remember them."

"I do mostly."

"*Mostly* isn't good enough. You have to remember all the time."

Tracy's stubbornness crept out with her lower lip. Some of the light died out of Jack's eyes. He was never very good at this part of parenting.

"I think I missed something. Who is this Wonder Boy with the dog and the two-wheeler and the cowboy boots?"

"Boots," Tracy repeated impatiently.

"The new boy in the neighborhood," Jack explained. "I understand his nickname is Boots. Didn't you meet him?"

I shook my head. "I haven't heard anything about a new family moving in. When did you meet him, Tracy?"

"Today. He came and played with me on my swing set."

"Tracy, you played alone today." Such a little thing, but suddenly I was afraid again. Sometimes I don't understand my daughter, the things she says, and I know—I'm almost sure that if I could just unravel those things I could stop being afraid. But Tracy—

"I was *not* alone! Boots was here! He pushed me on the swing and he showed me how to go down the slide on my tummy and he told me about his dog and his house and—"

"All right, settle down now," Jack said, putting his hand on her arm. "No yelling at the table. I guess Boots was here while your mother was busy and she didn't see him, okay? Now eat your baby cabbages."

She looked at him, then down at her plate. "Daddy, these aren't baby cabbages. They're peas."

"Are you sure?" Jack picked one up and examined it. "They look just like baby cabbages only with skins all over so you can't see the leaves. I thought maybe your mother went to the dolls' grocery store by mistake and—"

Tracy giggled. "Mommy couldn't go in the dolls' grocery store. She's too big. She'd smash it all apart and then the dolls wouldn't have anything to eat."

She hadn't been out of my sight more than thirty seconds all day.

* * *

"Jack, there was no boy here today. Nobody new has moved into the neighborhood since the Schillers came, six months ago."

We were on the back steps enjoying the breeze and the sunset. Tracy was on the swing set at the far side of the yard. She could see us and probably she could hear our voices but I was certain she couldn't make out what I was saying.

He shrugged, reached for his beer. "Maybe it happened yesterday. You know she gets the days mixed up sometimes."

"Yesterday morning she played with Melissa and Randy. After lunch it looked like rain so I made her stay inside. She watched TV."

"That's it, then. She saw someone on TV, a boy with a dog and a two-wheeler and she liked him so she pretends that he's real and came to see her."

"No." I'd been in the room every minute. I watched what she watched. There was no boy named Boots, no visitors yesterday or the day before, no one new in the neighborhood. Tracy wasn't mixed up. She was lying.

Jack shrugged.

The chains on the swing made a harsh cricket sound that slowed and died away. I looked and found her staring at me. The light was so dim she might have been looking at both of us but I knew she wasn't. Tracy knew all my secrets.

Jack and the doctor had warned me. I couldn't tell him why I was so sure. She knew that, too.

I shivered.

She was warm from her bath. The color in her face made her look more real than the frail green child I'd watched this afternoon. I popped the nightgown over her head, patted her on the behind, and turned her over to her father, waiting at the bathroom door.

He swung her up, making her giggle.

"What will it be tonight, Princess? Elves or buried treasure or magic wishes? Or maybe you'd like me to tell you why the Easter Bunny has nine pockets in his vest."

"Wishes, Daddy! Tell me a story about magic wishes. Wishing makes things come true, doesn't it, Daddy?"

"That's right, chick. If you wish for something hard enough—"

"Jack!" My voice was so loud it startled even me. "The new

storybook I bought is on her bedside table," I managed more quietly. "Why don't you read that tonight?"

Downstairs it was cool. The only light in the living room was from the waxing moon shining through the front windows. I walked through the house, locking doors, pulling shades, and turning on lights. I don't like moonlight. It hides things instead of revealing them. The shadows outside . . .

A touch on my arm made me jump.

"What are you looking at?"

"Nothing." I let the drape fall. "I thought I saw someone. Did she like the book?"

He groaned. "Love of my life, I adore you. But you have no taste when it comes to choosing storybooks."

"It's about animals. Tracy loves animal stories."

"It was written by a *zoologist*," he said, scorn wrapped around every syllable. He was at the bookcase, looking through the odd-sized books on the top shelf.

"Who could write a better book about animals?"

"A poet. Where's that photo album Mom sent?"

"Right next to your hand. If it was a snake it would bite you. What do you want it for? I burned all the pictures of your old girlfriends."

"Very funny. My mother didn't know her darling boy even *had* girlfriends until I took you home to meet her. Ever see this before?"

He handed me a snapshot of a gnome with ancient eyes, almost lost in a shirt and booties made to fit a bigger baby. "That's the picture your father took the day they brought you home from the hospital. You were a preemie, weren't you?"

He nodded, pointing to the booties that came half-way up the legs of the baby in the picture.

"Boots," I said.

"Yeah, that's what everyone called me up until the time I started school. I'd almost forgotten."

"You must have mentioned it to Tracy."

"Must have," he shrugged. "So there's your mystery boy. Kind of flattering, really. She liked the name so when she invented this imaginary playmate—"

I made a sound. He glared at me, lips thinned with irritation.

"Look, it's *normal*. I had one myself."

"It was different for you. Living out on that farm you never even saw another child until you started school. Tracy doesn't have to invent a friend. This neighborhood is full of kids."

"Then why did she do it? If she did. You're the one who claims this boy doesn't exist."

I just looked at him.

"No." He turned his back and walked away. "No."

"That doctor we took her to, he said she's not even sure yet what happened. He said the problems would show up later."

"*No*, dammit! He said *if* there were problems they would show up later. He also said that *if* we handle it right she can forget it ever happened."

"I don't *want* her to forget it happened. The details, yes." The blood. So much blood. Why . . . "But not that it happened. I want to teach her—"

"To be afraid."

"No! I want to teach her to be careful. There are other people like that old man."

We glared at each other, a couple of hissing cats. Pretending. He was always making up games and telling her stories. He made her believe that nothing bad could happen to good little girls, that the world was made of laughter and parties and happily ever after.

I couldn't stay mad at him. The anger was wiped out in the rush of memories. That ugly room in a burned-out house by the tracks—the blood—his mutilated body—and Tracy looking up at me with the eyes of an angel in the middle of hell.

I was there. I saw it. I knew how close we had come to losing her forever. Tracy and I had memories that all Jack's pretending couldn't erase.

How had it happened? Why? He took her away, coaxed her into that room and then . . . changed his mind. A fit of remorse, one of the cops told me. Maybe a multiple personality, one side a pervert, another believing sins must be punished.

If thy right eye offend thee . . .

No. I couldn't accept that. And they'd never found the knife.

I hadn't screamed when I found her there and carried her away in sheer blind panic. I wouldn't scream now. But I began to shake from the effort of holding it back. Once I started I was afraid I could never stop.

Jack's arms were around me, his breath in my hair.

"It'll be all right," he whispered. "We had a bad scare but it turned out okay. It will always be okay as long as we have each other."

Tracy wishes on stars. But it was very good to have his arms around me.

* * *

The nightfears are the worst. I never had them before. Just the normal maternal fears about speeding cars and rabid animals and pneumonia. The nightfears are different. Like the way moonlight changes the neighborhood, turns it into an alien landscape filled with unknown dangers, the nightfears are familiar things that have become shadowy and strange.

Her hair was fanned out on the pillow and her hands clutched the sheet up under her chin. I had meant only to look at her from the doorway but I found myself kneeling by the bed, studying her face as if I must memorize it. Or as if I had never seen it before.

She looked so delicate, just a sketch of a child, a few lines. Under her eyelids I could see her eyes moving, moving, never still.

What are you dreaming, baby? What beautiful world do you see? Or is it an ugly one, a nightmare world? I would follow you if I could. I would protect you . . .

Some expression flickered briefly on her face. In daylight I would have called it a smile. But shadows and moonlight—

I pulled back from her, shuddering. A child shouldn't smile that way.

The nightfears are the worst.

"Tracy, there's no house at the end of Lucas Street. I've driven past that corner a hundred times."

She hugged Raggedy Ann and refused to look at me. "They just builded it. Boots told me."

"There's nothing there but trees."

"That's why you can't see it. The trees hide it. Boots likes it that way."

"*Boots* likes it. I suppose his parents have nothing to say about it." Sarcasm is wasted on a child. Why did I bother?

"He doesn't have a mommy and daddy. He lives by himself."

Wishful thinking, maybe. Tracy might like to live alone, or at least without a mother who was always making her do things she didn't want to do, asking questions she didn't want to answer.

Twice this morning I'd looked up to find she wasn't playing where she was supposed to be. Twice I'd run outside in a panic and found her half-way down the block, going to see Boots.

Lock her in her room? She was my child, not my prisoner.

"Put your doll down. Come with me."

She looked up, instantly wary. That hurt added fire to the anger I was trying not to show, trying not to feel.

"Where are we going?"

"To see Boots." To prove there's no house on that corner. To make you admit there's no little boy who comes to see you when I'm not looking.

"He said he might go see his grandma today."

"Then we'll just take a look at his house."

"Maybe we can't find it. There's lots of trees."

It was three blocks to the end of Lucas Street, a long walk for short legs in the summer heat. The first block she dragged her feet, whined, and made excuses. The second block she walked carefully, not stepping on any cracks. She skipped down the third block, stopped to say hello to a toad in the gutter, and asked if we were having ice cream for supper.

I wasn't angry any more. I only wanted to get this over with. We turned the last corner and walked into the shade of the trees.

"Now, where is it?"

"Where is what, Mommy?"

"Boots's house. You said it was here, at the end of the street."

She pulled her hand out of mine and sat down to poke a finger through a hole in the toe of her sneaker. "Maybe he said it was the other end."

"Tracy, stop telling stories. There is no house here. There's no little boy. Now tell the truth. You made it all up, didn't you?"

There was a sound, a bird call, I was almost certain. Tracy turned to look, her eyes wide. "Boots!" she cried. She scrambled to her feet and ran away from me.

It was a rotten, miserable afternoon. One minute I felt like a wicked step-mother, the next like a martyred saint. Tracy was in her room, sobbing pitifully for a while, then storming around making crashing noises that I was too wise to investigate. Silence didn't come to the house until almost five o'clock. I tiptoed up the stairs and eased the door open, expecting to find that she'd nodded off.

She was in her rocking chair, sucking her thumb. She hadn't done that for over a year. She looked up at me with tear-reddened eyes. Then she was in my arms and both of us were crying.

"I'm sorry I spanked you so hard. You scared me, baby."

"I'm sorry, too, Mommy. Boots wanted to—"

"Don't. Please. Let's not talk about Boots."

It couldn't have been more than ten minutes that I spent chasing Tracy around that wooded lot but at the time I thought I was caught in a never ending nightmare. There couldn't have been many hiding places but she'd flickered in and out of my sight as if she could turn invisible at will. I would hear a giggle from behind a bush and then, impossibly, from the opposite direction. The woods had seemed to be filled with hidden children, their laughter, their footsteps.

She curled up in my arms, her forehead resting on my neck, one hand stroking my cheek. Tracy is not a cuddly child. Except when one of us has gone too far.

"Would you like to go out to the porch and watch for Daddy? He should be home soon."

She was slipping out of my arms before I'd finished the question. She was cheerful again, her wounds healed. I listened to her footsteps on the stairs and waited for the stretcher-bearers to come and carry me off the field. I'm too old to heal that quickly.

Jack was on the porch with her for almost ten minutes. I wondered if she would tell him about our troubles this afternoon. Probably not, I decided. Tracy almost never stops to look back.

He came into the kitchen alone and sniffed at the pan simmering on the back burner. "Wow! Homemade vegetable soup. I don't know how you manage it on a day like today."

"Yes, idiot. Just like Mother used to make. Straight out of the can. How was your day?" The other words were on the tip of my tongue but I held them back. Of course she was still on the porch. I didn't need another lecture on the dangers of hovering over her.

"What was Tracy bending your ear about?"

He laughed as he picked up the mail and sorted through it. "Didn't she tell you? She wants a dog, just like Boots's. Next it'll be a two-wheeler."

Boots again. I'd hoped we'd put that ghost to rest.

When I was little my father used to take me fishing. I never caught anything because I kept pulling the line out of the water to see if the worm was still on the hook. Where *was* she? There wasn't a sound from the front porch. A rat was chewing holes in my stomach.

He looked up. "You know, a dog might not be such a bad idea at that. It would be company for her and we certainly have enough room here. What do you think?"

What was he talking about? I felt split in two. Of *course* she was on the porch. Where else would she be this close to supper time? Why couldn't I hear the rattle of her trucks or the creak of floorboards?

"I don't know," I said distractedly. "Dogs are a lot of trouble."

He made an impatient sound. "You mean housebreaking and training and all that. Jeeze, why do you always think of the problems whenever I suggest something? Can't you ever look on the good side?"

"The good side?" I was setting the table, my hands shaking so badly the silverware rattled. Where was Tracy? "Why can't you ever look at the practical side?" My voice was sharper than I wanted it to be. Where was Tracy? "Dogs get sick. They dig holes and chew things—" This was wrong. I didn't want another. argument. But where was Tracy? "—and bite people and—" *Where was Tracy?*

His annoyance was changing to concern. "Lynne—"

I shook my head, took a breath. "I'm sorry. Please, can we talk about it another time? I had a really bad day."

"Of course we can."

He was so gracious. So generous. I had to grit my teeth.

"It was just an idea. Maybe after you've had time to think about it." He picked up the mail again, his concern forgotten.

Damn him. What was this? A test? Was he trying to find out how long I could go without running out to check on her? He stood there flipping through a magazine as if he didn't have a care in the world. As if he didn't have a daughter. Had he forgotten her? It was more than ten minutes since he'd come inside. Dammit, she'd run off three times already—

"Will you call Tracy, please? Tell her to wash her hands."

He looked at me but his eyes said he was somewhere else. "What? Oh, I guess we'd better start without her. She wanted to go see someone and I said she could for a few minutes." He turned back to the magazine—

—and left me falling apart. I couldn't catch my breath to get the words out normally.

"You. Let. Her. Go . . . alone."

"For Pete's sake. She's just down the block."

It seemed to be happening in slow motion. To someone else. I could almost see it: my face twisting into a grotesque mask, my shoulders bowed, my hands curling into claws. *He* was doing this to me. I hated him. Couldn't he feel anything? There was a scream locked inside me, but the only sound I could force from my throat was a whisper, like ashes.

"It's over for you, isn't it? You didn't see her there in the middle of that horror. You don't have questions . . . fears. It's all Disneyland and fairy tales—wishing makes it so—isn't that right?" I hated him. Hated. I wanted to hurt him as much as his unconcern hurt me, but how could I when I couldn't even reach him? She was his daughter, too. Why wasn't he afraid?

He was moving toward me, his hand out, his mouth shaping words I couldn't hear.

I twisted away. "Don't touch me!" I screamed. "Don't you ever touch me again! I *hate* you!"

Shattering silence, crystalline mocking laughter—ending. Inside my head . . . Inside . . . far away . . .

He looked bewildered. His eyes were just like Tracy's eyes that day when my world began to fall apart. I had never turned away from him before. No matter what was wrong, no matter what hurt us or disappointed us, we had always taken comfort from each other. We were strong together. But not ever again. The strength and the love had been an illusion, one of his pretty dreams.

Not ever again. He couldn't take me in his arms and wish away this pain.

"You don't *know* she's all right. I *need* to know, Jack. I need to know every *minute*. I need to *see* her."

A small, scared voice from the doorway said, "Mommy, I'm here."

I opened my eyes in silent darkness. But it hadn't been silence that wakened me. I reached for memory and found no trace of nightmare, only—laughter.

There it was again. Faint but clear, like distant bells.

I almost fell getting up from the sofa for I'd forgotten that was where I had chosen to sleep. Jack hadn't even tried to talk me out of it when I brought a sheet and pillow downstairs. All evening he'd watched me out of the corner of his eye as if I'd come down with a sudden disfiguring illness and he didn't want me to catch him rudely staring.

Laughter again. The faint patter of footsteps.

I went to the window and pulled back the drape. The moon illuminated nothing. Deep shadows moved and breathed and threatened. I began to shiver, though the night was almost as hot as the day had been. There was a smell in the heavy air, a scent as strange as moonlight.

No. I let the drape fall, backed away from the window. The

danger was not out there. It was here. I felt the eyes watching me. I turned.

They stood at the front of the stairs, holding hands. Two frail and beautiful children with faintly glowing skin.

"Tracy—"

But she wasn't Tracy. Not my child. Never mine.

And the other one. With hazel eyes and solemn mouth.

They stared at me for a timeless time. Then they laughed and ran away. Across the floor and . . . away. Where I could never follow. They ran into the night and the strangeness and my feet were too heavy to follow for I was of the earth and they were not.

Their laughter floated back to haunt me. The laughter of terrible things that had never been human.

I sat at the foot of the stairs until the sun's light touched me and still I could not move, could not force myself to walk up those steps.

I couldn't bear to see what they'd left behind.

Closing Time

George R.R. Martin

THE WORLD ENDED on a slow Tuesday night.

The rain had been coming down heavily since mid-afternoon, and trade was lousy. Hank was washing some beer steins and listening to Barney Dale relate his marital woes. He had heard all of Barney's marital woes before, but there was nothing else to do. The Happy Hour crowd had departed early tonight, and Barney was the only customer in the joint.

"Nothing I do pleases her," Barney was mumbling into his draft. He was a short, balding, elderly fellow whose wife had been brow-beating him for forty years now. Hank had been ear-witness to at least five of those years. "I'll really catch it to-night," Barney said. "Out drinking beer, she hates that, and she's *bigger* than me. She—"

That was when the door swung open and Milton stalked in, wet and angry. He stood in the open door, rain pattering on the asphalt of the parking lot behind him, while his eyes swept back and forth across the dim, empty barroom. "Where is he?" he said loudly. "I'm going to kill the bastid, I swear I am."

Hank signed. It was going to be another one of those nights. "First close the door, Milt," he called out. "The rain's coming in."

"Oh," said Milton. Underneath his temper, he was actually kind of a sweetheart, though you'd never know it to look at him. He stood six-foot-seven, with fists the size of cinder blocks, and twice as hard. "Sorry," he said, a bit abashed. He closed the door carefully and came striding over to the bar, working on his glower with every step. He was drenched, and his shoes squished when he walked. His anger was so palpable you almost expected the moisture to come boiling off as steam.

"The usual, Milt?" Hank asked. He flicked water off a stein, wiped it desultorily with his towel, and put it next to the others.

"Yeah," said Milton. He yanked out a barstool and sat down next to Barney, who was blinking at him in mildly inebriated astonishment. "And you tell me where that jiveass turkey has got himself to," he added.

"Who is it has you so worked up?" Hank asked, as he pulled out the creme de menthe and set to work on the grasshopper.

"Sleazy Pete," Milton growled. "I'm going to wring his skinny lil' neck for him. Where the hell is he? He hangs around here Tuesdays, don't he? I know he does. You tell that bastid he ain't gonna duck me, no way."

Hank spun a coaster onto the bar and placed the grasshopper on top of it. Milton wrapped one huge meaty hand around it and glared over at Barney Dale, as if daring him to make a comment. Barney suddenly discovered something of enormous interest in the bottom of his stein.

"You're too early," Hank said. "Pete will be in a little over four hours from now."

Milton sipped his grasshopper and grunted.

Barney raised his stein and smiled tentatively. Hank took it and drew him another. As he set it down, Barney said, "Now how do you know just when he's going to be in, Hank? You one of them ESP fellows my missus is always reading me about from the *Enquirer*?"

Hank smiled. "ESP don't come into it. Pete's a regular. I know my regulars. I know where they live and what they do for a buck and how many kids they got and what kind of cars they drive. And I sure as hell know when they come in. Pete usually comes in early, except for Tuesdays during the summers. He always goes to a movie or a ball game on Tuesdays. He'll be in a couple hours before closing time." Hank picked up another stein and dipped it into the dishwater.

"I'll wait," Milton said. "When that sumbitch comes in, I'll bust his goddam head, you wait and see."

"Sure thing," Hank agreed. He didn't like trouble in his place, but he wasn't too worried. He knew his regulars. Milton couldn't hold his grasshoppers, and he was a maudlin, amiable drunk. By the time Sleazy Pete wandered in, Milt would be a pussycat.

"Why are you so corked off at Pete?" Hank asked conversationally. Anything was better than Barney's marital woes. "I thought you two were buddies."

"*Buddies!*" Milton roared. "I'll kill that bastid. He gypped me. Here, take a look at this." He pulled something out of his pocket and tossed it onto the bar.

Barney Dale sipped his beer and stared at the thing curiously, not bold enough to reach for it. Hank set down the stein he was washing and picked it up. It was a round amulet on a heavy metal chain. He held it up to the light, and it twisted slowly. "Gold?" he asked.

"Hell, no," Milton said. "Brass. Even Pete ain't stupid enough to sell it if it was gold."

The amulet had a nice heft to it. Hank examined it more closely. All around the outside rim were little carvings of animals, all kinds of animals. In the center was a milky white stone of some sort. Thin lines ran in from the animals to the stone, like spokes on a wheel. "Interesting," Hank said. "What's the crystal in the middle?"

"Glass," said Milton. "Milkglass. Sleazy Pete said it was moonstone, whatever the hell that is, but it ain't."

Hank put the amulet back on the bar. "Can I look at it?" Barney asked, timidly. Milton stared at him and nodded.

"Pete sold it to you?" Hank said. Sleazy Pete ran a little used bookstore and bric-a-brac shop a few blocks away, and he was always coming in with one piece of junk or another and trying to sell it to some drunk. This wouldn't be the first time it had gotten him in trouble.

"Damn right," Milton said. "Lying lil' weasel. Got fifty bucks out of me for that ugly thing. I mean to get it back if I got to take it out of his hide."

"Why'd you buy it? Think it was gold?"

Milton frowned, finished his grasshopper, and signalled for another. "Hell, no," he said. "Do I look stupid or something? Knew it weren't no gold. Only I was drunk, and Pete said the damn thing was magic. You know. A goddam magic amulet."

"Ah," said Hank. "So you bought it because you thought it was magic, and it wasn't."

Milton looked pained. He stared morosely at the bar, shredding his coaster in his big hands. Hank gave him another with his grasshopper. "That ain't it, exactly," Milton said finally, with a touch of reluctance. "It's magic all right, but not like Pete said it'd be."

Hank looked up from his dishwater. "What?" he said. Barney

Dale was staring too, looking from the amulet to Milton and then down again, blinking his watery blue eyes as if he couldn't believe what he was hearing.

"You heard me," Milton said, frowning again. "The damn thing works. Only . . ." He paused, a bit perplexed. "Maybe I ought to start at the beginning."

"That's generally a good place to start," Hank said. He was thinking that maybe it would be an interesting night after all, at least for a Tuesday.

"It was a couple weeks back," Milton said. "Right in here, this very damn place. I had a bit to drink, you know, and Sleazy Pete comes over and shows me that thing and gives me this pitch about its powers. It was supposed to be, like, a thing for *changing*."

"Changing?" Hank said.

Milton waved his hand irritably. "Shiftin' shape, that's what that bastid Pete called it. You know, werewolf stuff, like in them old movies. Only this thing don't change you into no wolf, Pete says, which was fine with me, 'cause I didn't see no sense in running around ripping out anybody's throat, you know? He says it'll change me into a bird. Says he used it himself, during the full moon, which is the only time it works, and he changed into this big hawk, flew around all night. Only Pete has got this thing about heights, you know, so he didn't want the change. Only it ain't something you got any choice about, he says. If you own the goddam amulet, when that ol' moon comes pokin' up, you change.

"Well, hell *I* ain't got no thing about heights, and I always wanted to fly, you know, only I never had the money. Sounded like it'd be a lot of fun. So we dickered over the price for a bit, and finally I bought the thing and took it home and waited for the next full moon."

Barney had the amulet in his hand. "Last night was the first night of the full moon," he said, peering cautiously over at Milton.

"Damn right it was," Milton said.

"And you didn't change?" Hank asked.

"Shit, I *changed* all right, but not into no goddam hawk. I'm gonna kill that lying sumbitch, I tell you. He really sold me a bill of goods. Worst night of my life."

There was a brief silence. Neither one of them wanted to press him. Finally Barney Dale cleared his throat and said, "If you don't mind me asking, exactly what kind of change did you experience?''

Milton took a long sip from his grasshopper, then turned slowly and deliberately on his stool to face Barney. Beneath his thick, bushy eyebrows, his eyes were squinty and mean. "What's your name again, little man?"

Barney swallowed. "Er, Barney. Barney Dale."

Milton smiled. "Listen up good, Mister Barney Dale. I'm gonna answer your question, you hear. But you better not laugh. I'm telling you out front. You laugh and I'm gonna twist your little head clean off and drop-kick it about fifty yards down the goddam street. You got that?"

"Er," said Barney. "Yes. Sure. I wouldn't dream of laughing."

"Real good," said Milton. "Well, the thing of it is, I turned into a rabbit."

Barney didn't laugh, Hank had to give him that. He was too scared to laugh. Hank didn't laugh either, but he found himself fighting to suppress a grin. "A rabbit?" he said.

"A rabbit. You know, a goddam Easter bunny. Hippidy-hop, hippidy-hop. One of *them*."

"Oh," said Barney. He peered down at the amulet again and adjusted his glasses.

"A rabbit ain't no hawk," Milton said.

"That's true," Hank agreed.

"It was a goddam nightmare, I tell you, and that bastid is going to pay for every minute of hell I went through. City ain't no place for no rabbit."

"Not even a wererabbit," Hank said, smiling.

"No, sir. Nearly got run down by cars, and this one cat cornered me in this alley, and I was lucky to get out with my skin, and later on there was this dog chased me for miles, I swear. And the kids, the stinkin' little brats, they were the worst. Some of 'em threw stones, and some wanted to catch me and make me a pet. All night it was just hop, hop, hop, and one goddam thing after another." He shuddered. "My legs are sore as hell, too. I swear, when Pete comes in, I'm going to take this amulet of his and shove it up where the sun don't shine."

Barney Dale was turning the amulet round and round in his hands. "There's no rabbit on here." he said.

"What?" Milton snapped.

Barney put the disc on the bar between them. "Look," he said, "there's no rabbit. I thought perhaps these pictures here along the rim gave some indication of how it worked. You see? If there was a hawk, and then a rabbit, well, that would make sense, wouldn't it? Then we could see what followed, and no doubt the next bearer of the amulet would turn into that, whatever it might be. Only there's no rabbit, see? Here's a bird,"— he pointed—"and there's a wolf, and some kind of big cat, and all kinds of other predators, but there's no rabbit. I think these are just decorative."

Milton grunted. "Decorative. So what? Hell, I bet Pete turned into a rabbit too. Them pictures don't mean nothing. He knew what he was gettin' rid of, you bet he did. I'm going to kill him."

Barney glanced at his watch. "Er," he said, "pardon me, but you will run into a little problem there."

Milton looked over, incredulous. "You think I'm going to have a *problem* beating the hell out of a lil' nothing like Sleazy Pete?"

"I'm afraid you are," said Barney. "Hank said that Pete won't be in until a few hours before closing." He looked at his watch again. "And, if I have the correct time, moonrise will be along in about forty minutes or so. Long before closing time. You'll be a rabbit when Pete arrives."

Milton winced as if struck. "Oh, shit," he said. He looked around wildly. "Hank," he squealed, "you've gotta help me. Keep me here till dawn. Don't let no kids get me."

Hank shrugged. He was enjoying this immensely. "Anything for a regular," he said. "I got some lettuce in the fridge, too. And we can probably win a few bar bets with you."

Barney hefted the amulet in his hand. "I've got a better idea," he said. "I'll buy this from you."

Milton stared. "You'll *what*?"

"I'll buy it," Barney repeated, amiably. "Fifty dollars, you said? Here." He pulled out his wallet, extracted two twenties and a ten, and laid them on the bar. "Go on, pick it up. Then the amulet will be off your hands. You won't change, and when your friend comes in, you can beat him to a bloody pulp." He hefted the amulet again. It looked like a tiny golden wheel in his hand, with a cloudy white dented hubcap. "What do you say?"

Milton looked at Barney for a long moment, then gave a whoop of laughter and snatched up the money. "Brother, you're on!" he said. "Hell, I don't know what your game is, but I don't figure on spending no more time as no rabbit if I can help it. Hell, I'll even buy you a beer."

Barney slid the amulet into his pocket and stood up. "Thank you, but I'll have to decline, I'm afraid. I have to get home. My wife will kill me." He smiled slyly and started for the door.

"Barney," Hank called out, "wait a sec." He was unbearably curious. "What are you figuring?"

Barney smiled broadly. "It's a nice piece of brasswork, you know. I bet it's worth a lot more than fifty dollars, even if it isn't magic."

"But what if it is?" Hank asked. "Aren't you worried about changing?"

Barney shrugged. "Not especially. I'm going to give it to my wife, you see. She'll make a *wonderful* rabbit." He chuckled. "Good evening, gentlemen. I'll see you tomorrow."

They listened to him drive off. "Poor woman's got quite a surprise coming," said Milton. He handed Hank one of Barney's twenties. "Set me up with another."

"You still waiting for Pete?"

"Sure am," Milton said. "I figure I'll kill him anyway, just on account of last night. That's fair, ain't it?"

Hank smiled and shrugged. Three grasshoppers already. By the time Sleazy Pete made his appearance, Milton would be all sweetness and light.

A little over a half hour later, though, Milton looked up from his drink and said, "Hey, listen up! The rain stopped."

Hank listened. "I believe you're right," he said. Then, still listening, he got a cold feeling all of a sudden as he heard the sound of a car pulling up outside. It was a very distinctive sound, the putt-putt-putt of an old car with a muffler that has long ago ceased muffling. It came to a halt with a screech of worn brakes and a dull cough. Hank knew it instantly: Sleazy Pete's clunker. "So much for ESP," he said.

Milton looked at him curiously, but he didn't have time to inquire, for just then the door opened and Pete came sauntering in, all skin and bones and tattered denim and long blonde hair. "Hey, guys," he called out cheerfully. "What's happening? Game got rained out tonight. Hi, Hank. Hi, Milt."

Milton turned on his stool. "You," he said. "You are going to die." He got up and roared and started across the barroom, waving a fist the size of a wrecking ball. Sleazy Pete gave one long look before he broke and spun and raced for the parking lot. Milton followed, bellowing with rage.

Hank sighed and reached under the bar for his Louisville slugger. What a business, he thought. He followed them outside, prepared to subdue Milton by force if he threatened any real bodily harm to Pete.

Pete was sprinting for his car, but Milton was bigger and faster. He caught Pete just as he was opening the door, yanked him back and spun him around, seized his shirtfront and lifted him into the air. Sleazy Pete screamed and kicked. "I'm going to kill you, you bastid," Milton said, and he slammed Pete down across the hood of his car, hard.

"Now, Milton," Hank said. "Cut it out. You know I can't allow this."

"Think it's fun to turn me into a rabbit, huh?" Milton said. "Maybe I'll just turn you into chopmeat and we'll see how much fun that is, huh?"

"Milton," Hank said, a little more forcefully. "Stop. I mean it now."

"Let me alone!" Pete yelled. "You're crazy! I don't know nothing about no rabbit!"

Milton smiled and balled up a huge fist.

"Milton!" Hank shouted, and he brought his baseball bat down hard on the fender of Pete's car. There was a satisfying loud thunk.

Milton, startled, looked over at Hank.

"Let him go," Hank said. He hefted the bat.

Milton frowned and released his hold on Sleazy Pete. "Oh, hell," he said. "I wasn't gonna hurt him, just muss him up a little."

"He's mussed enough," Hank observed drily. Sleazy Pete had earned his name. His denims were ragged and patched and dirty, his hair was a wild scraggle, and even his car was a twenty-year-old wreck, partly faded red and mostly primer grey. Pete had never gotten around to finishing his paint job.

Pete sat up on the hood of his car, panting. "Jesus," he said. "You're one crazy dude. What the hell's wrong?"

"He says the magic amulet you sold him turned him into a rabbit," Hank said, before Milton could reply. "He didn't like it."

"Damn right I didn't," said Milton.

"A *rabbit*? That can't be right. A werehawk, that's what it was for. I used it myself. It turned you into a bird. It had to."

"I know birds, and I know rabbits. It turned me into a goddam bunny rabbit!"

Sleazy Pete scratched at his beard and looked perplexed. "That's interesting," he said. "I guess it works different on everyone who owns it. Maybe that pattern of animals on the rim . . ."

"Hell, no," Milton said. "We looked at it. Just decorative. Ain't no rabbits on there."

Pete looked even more puzzled. "Then I don't get it . . . I . . . wait, wait a sec, maybe it's like a mystic key to your true nature, you know. I'm a sort of freewheeling dude, so I turned into a hawk, and you—" He saw where that was heading and stopped abruptly.

Milton made an ominous growling noise and grabbed him again. "You telling me I'm a *rabbit*? Damn it, you *are* going to die!"

Hank swore under his breath and slammed the bat down on the fender again. "Cut it *out*!" he said.

They stopped. Milton grunted and let go. Pete shook his head. "Look at whatcha done to my *car*!" he wailed. The second blow had left a big dent in the fender. "Jesus, Hank."

"Sorry," the barman said. "I'll stand you to one on the house. No one is going to notice one more dent on this thing anyhow. It's an old piece of junk and you know it."

"It's a *classic*," Pete insisted. He ran his hand over the fender, frowning. Then he climbed off the hood and stood up. "Three free rounds, I insist. A real classic."

"One," said Hank. "I saved your life, and the car's a death-trap. What the hell is it, anyhow?"

"You don't know your classic automobiles," Pete said, affronted. "This is a Falcon, one of the first. Ford. Wonderful little car."

Hank had stopped listening all of a sudden. He looked around. The parking lot was dark, the asphalt still slick with the recent rain, but he could make out his own van down by the corner of the building. There was only one other car in the lot. He pointed to it with his bat. "That's yours, isn't it?" he said to Milton.

"Yeah," Milton said, frowning suspiciously.

"VW?"

"Yeah," said Milton. "Brand new. A Rabbit. It gets real good . . ." He stopped, and awareness dawned in his eyes.

Hank laughed.

Pete looked from one car to another. "Oh, Jesus," he said, cradling his head in his hands. "Where the hell is that thing now? We got to keep it safe. There are all kinds of . . . Cougars, Bobcats, hell, they could *kill* somebody. . . .''

"What does he drive, Hank?" Milton demanded. "You know him, right? What kind of car has he got?"

Hank shook his head ruefully. "Poor Barney. We're safe enough. He's got a VW too. Only his is older."

Milton nodded. "A Beetle."

"What a night he's going to have," said Milton.

Hank sighed and turned to go back into his establishment. But he stopped when he heard Sleazy Pete say, "Hey, look."

"The moon," Milton said, with a glance. Off where Pete was pointing, the sky was beginning to lighten. "The full moon. Guess it's started for the poor bastid. Hope his wife don't step on him."

That was when Hank went cold all over. He dropped the bat. It clattered on the pavement and rolled. Then he pulled out his key and turned and locked the door to his bar.

"Hey," said Milton, "it ain't closing time."

"Oh, yes, it is," Hank replied. He pointed to where the sky was growing brighter and brighter. "That isn't the moon. It's too overcast to see the moon, and anyhow that's the wrong direction." But by then none of them could mistake the glow for moonlight. It was swelling visibly, eating up half the sky, and its heart burned like the noonday sun, too bright to look upon.

"Oh, shit," Milton said, shielding his eyes and staggering back against the wall.

"He bought it for his wife," Hank said sadly.

Pete asked the last question. "What does she . . ." he began, but the flesh had melted off his bones before he could finish, and he ended with a terrible shrill scream.

Hank had only seen it once, the night that Barney's wife had come to drag him home. Barney had been so plastered that she'd needed help getting him to the car, so Hank had obliged, and he remembered. He had a good memory for things like that.

"A Nova," he said, as the world turned incandescent.

And Who Would Pity a Swan?

Connie Willis

ONE DAY WHEN the prince was out hunting, he came upon a
pool, and on its still surface sat three white swans, like flowers
on a mirror. Two of the swans were large and proud, and they
dipped their necks forward, looking for fish in the black water,
but the third was small and held its head up bravely on its curved
neck, and the prince thought suddenly of a little girl riding behind him on a large horse, and he felt a sudden pain, as though
an arrow, or a memory, had pierced his heart, and he cried,
"Emelie," and would have fallen.

But in that moment, he heard a splash and a sound that was
like a swan's trumpeting or a child's cry, and when he looked
up, the swans were gone and there were two men struggling with
something in the water. The prince thought, with an anger more
sudden than the pain, "They have come to steal the little swan,"
and he leaped off his horse and drew his sword.

"Let her go," he said, but the two men gave no sign that they
had heard him. They were bending over a maiden. They pulled
her to her feet, and taking an arm on either side, began to wade
toward the shore, but she struggled against them so that she went
down on one knee with a great splash.

The prince ran into the water and would have fought the men,
but when the girl saw him she stood up and looked at him in
wonder. She was very young, and her long dark hair hung wet
around her face like water weeds. Her white dress was streaked
with black mud, but for all that she was very beautiful.

The men still held her arms, though whether to hold her or to
aid her, he could not tell, and he saw that they, too, were richly
attired, but that their clothes were black with mud.

"Who are you?" the prince said. "What would you with this maiden?"

"She is our sister," the elder of the young men said, and then looked at her as if in wonder that it was so.

"We have been under a spell," the younger brother said.

"A spell?" the prince said.

"We were a king's children," said the elder brother. He spoke as if he were carrying a message that he himself had not understood until now. "A witch laid a spell on us that we should be swans till one remembered us and took pity on us, but we feared we should never be rescued, for who would pity a swan?"

"Swans," the maiden said. "We were swans."

"Who was your father?" the prince said kindly to her. She took a step backward, as if she were afraid of him. "I do not remember," she said.

"We have been swans too long to remember even our names," her brother said.

"Then I shall call her Cygnelle," the prince said, "and I shall call you all welcome. My father's castle lies but a little way from here."

Cygnelle turned and looked back at the black pool. "We were swans," she said, and she stumbled against her brother, who caught her and held her fast against him.

"Our sister has taken a chill," he said. "See how she shivers." He made as if to take his wet cloak from his back. The prince sprang forward and put his own dry cloak about her shoulders.

"Ride with her to your father's castle, and we will follow," her brother said.

And the prince set her before him on his horse and rode with her through the forest until they came to the path that led to his father's castle. The path was wide and straight, and the prince would have turned onto it, but Cygnelle said, "What lies this way?" and pointed toward another path, so overgrown with briars that it was nearly hidden.

"Nothing," the prince said, and turned away so sharply that his horse jerked his head in protest, and Cygnelle shivered. "It is only a ruined castle," the prince said more kindly. "No one has lived in it for years."

And he spurred his horse and brought Cygnelle to his father's castle, and his father the king came out to greet them.

"Father," the prince said, "this maiden and her brothers were placed under a spell by a witch that they should be swans."

"A witch," the king said, and it was as if he spoke to himself. "There was a witch who lived . . ."

"I do not know this maiden's name nor aught of her, but that I wish to make her my bride," the prince said.

"Swans," the king said. "Could it be . . . my child," the king said kindly and took Cygnelle's hand, "I thought that murderers had . . ."

And the prince felt a pain like an arrow, and he said, "She remembers nothing, not even her name. I have called her Cygnelle."

Then the prince had her dressed in rich clothing and her dark hair bound up with flowers, and they were married that very day.

They were taken to the bridal chamber with much merriment and joy, but when they were left alone together, she sat down before her mirror and took the flowers from her hair and looked at them. "One spring when we flew north," she said, "I saw a tree bending over a wall and on the tree white flowers, like these, and I remembered . . ." she held the flowers as if she had forgotten what they were and looked into her mirror and through and beyond it, holding herself still and silent, as if she were treading the dark waters of the pool.

"Forget that," the prince said in a voice he had never used before, not even to a servingman, "come to bed."

She did not start in fear of him, or tremble. She put down the flowers and came and stood before him so that he said more gently, "Come to bed," and she smiled and lifted up her arms to fasten them about his neck.

But the next morning when he awoke, he saw that she had risen early, and when he went out to seek her he found her in the great hall where the wedding breakfast was to be given, talking with her brothers.

"I have remembered something," her brother said. "One spring day, when we flew home from the south, we flew over a path, much overgrown with briars and a wall and a gate, and I thought, I know this place. It was our father's castle."

"A wall, and a tree with white flowers," Cygnelle said and took a step backward, as if she were afraid of him. "I remember . . ."

"It is our wedding breakfast," the prince said, and took her arm, though whether to help her or to hold her he did not know, and led her into the feast.

But when they had feasted and the king had toasted the prince and his bride, Cygnelle's brother raised his goblet and said, "May our sister have happy memories always."

Cygnelle smiled and raised her goblet in both hands to return the toast, but her hands shook and her wide white sleeves fell away from her arms like wings, and the prince thought, "She will never forget so long as her brothers are here."

And he said loudly, before Cygnelle had sat down, "Good brothers, when do you depart for your own kingdom?"

Cygnelle set the goblet down carefully, but her hand trembled, and wine spilled out on the table.

"You have remembered your father's kingdom," he said loudly. "My father will give you horses and gold, that you may go and seek it. Is that not so, Father?"

But the king said, as if he had not heard, "Where is this kingdom?"

"May it be so far from here that we shall never be troubled with seeing them again," he said, and went out from the marriage feast. His father followed him and put his hand on his arm.

"Where is their kingdom?" the king said.

"I know not. And I care not. I only wish them gone."

"Where did you find them?" the king said, as if he had not heard him. "Was it near King Gudrain's castle?"

"Yes," the prince said. "And would that I had left them there, for all they do is talk to Cygnelle of the days when they were swans."

"What would you have them speak of?" the king said, as if at last he had heard him. "They do not remember anything else."

"Why must they remember at all? Why can they not forget the past and go on? That is why I would send her brothers away. Cygnelle and I cannot be happy until she forgets her past."

"Will you be happy then, when she remembers nothing?" the king said. "Her brothers mean her no harm. They are only trying to help her remember who she was." He took his hand away from the prince's arm. "My son, when King Gudrain was murdered and his children taken . . ."

"They talk of the past and you talk of the past. If you will not help me, I will send them away myself," he said, and he went out into the garden to find Cygnelle and lead her away from her brothers, but when he came up to her she was standing all alone, and she looked up at him sadly, and said, "I have bidden my brothers depart for their own kingdom, and they have gone."

"Now we can be happy," the prince said, and took her arm. "Come and walk with me in the garden."

They walked along the paths of the garden until they came to a little pond set about with bricks. There was a tree of white flowers bending over the pond, and the prince stopped and picked a spray of blossoms for Cygnelle. She buried her face in the blossoms, and when she raised her face to him, he saw that she had left bright tears on the white petals.

"Cygnelle," he said, and would have bent to kiss her, but there was a sudden sound like trumpets blowing, and when he looked up he saw that it was a flock of wild swans flying overhead, their great wings spread like wide white sleeves against the sky.

"No," he said, and turned to look at Cygnelle. She had dropped the flowers and stood watching the swans.

"One day we flew along a wall and I saw a boy riding upon a horse, and I remembered . . ."

The prince put his hand under his ribs as if to a wound. "Forget them," he said, gritting his teeth against some pain. "Forget you were ever a swan."

"I cannot," she said, and looked at him in despair. "Help me to remember."

"No!" the prince said.

"Then let me go with my brothers. If you will not help me to remember, perhaps they may."

"No!" the prince said, and took her by the shoulders and shook her. "You say you cannot forget," he said. "Were you so happy when you were a swan?"

"Happy?" she said.

"Did you have swan lovers? Is it them you refuse to forget?" He pushed her from him. "I am going hunting."

The prince stayed out hunting all that day and the day after and the day after that, and when he rode in he found Cygnelle sitting by the pond looking into the dark water. She was holding a white flower in her hand, and her head was bent, so that he could see the curve of her long neck.

"I have been out hunting," the prince said.

She did not look up at him. She held the flower as if she had forgotten what it was, and she looked into the water and through it and past it. "Let me go to see my brothers," she said.

"No," he said. "I have brought you something."

But still she did not look at him.

"You cannot forget your swan lovers," he said, "so I have

brought them to you," and he drew forth a pair of wild swans, each with an arrow through its heart, and laid them beside her on the brick edge of the pool.

Cygnelle stood and took a step back away from him and stumbled a little, but he did not reach out his hand to steady her.

"I wish you had not come, that day in the forest," she said.

"So you could be a swan still?" he said bitterly, and went in to find his father.

"I have had good hunting, Father," he said. "A pair of wild swans."

The king had been looking out the window into the garden, and he turned and looked at the prince with great sadness. "Do you think you can kill the past then?" he said. "You cannot. I know. I have tried."

"Would you speak to me of King Gudrain again?" the prince said harshly.

"No," the kind said. "For you would not listen. I would speak to you of Cygnelle. You must let her go to her brothers. I have had word from them. They have found their father's castle, as I thought they would." He looked sadly at the prince. "Will you not ask me where it lies?"

The prince gasped, a terrible sound as if someone had tried to pull an arrow from his side. "No," he said, holding his breath against the pain. "I care not where their father's castle is, so long as it is far from here." He took a step back and stumbled, but the king did not reach out his hand to steady him. "You spoke of a witch, Father. Tell me where she lives."

"What would you with this witch?" the king said. "The spell is broken."

"I would have her lay a new spell upon Cygnelle that she should forget she was ever a swan. Tell me where she lives."

"No," the king said.

"Then I will find her myself," he said, and went out and saddled his horse and rode out to find the witch, but when he came to the pool where he had seen the swans, he thought, "While I am gone, she will go to see her brothers," and he turned his horse and went back to shut her in her room and set a watch at her door.

But when he came to the castle he found Cygnelle lying by the little pond, and his father the king kneeling beside her. Her dark hair was wet and lay about her still face like water weeds, and her white dress was streaked with black mud. The king gripped her hand and looked anxiously into her still face. "She has tried to drown herself," he said, as if to himself.

She lay as one dead, and as the prince looked down at her he saw that there were shadows under her eyes as black as a swan's mask. "Perhaps she thought she was still a swan," he said, "and tried to swim away."

The king looked up at him. "The witch lives near King Gudrain's castle," he said. "Take the path that leads from this castle till it meets a path so overgrown with briars it is nearly hidden. You have taken that path before. Take it again, and you will come to a wall and a gate, and at last you will lose the path and come to the witch. Or it may be," he said, holding tightly to Cygnelle's hand, "it may be that you will come to yourself."

"I will go to find the witch and make her put a spell upon Cygnelle that she will forget she was ever a swan," the prince said, "but you must first give me your word that you will not let Cygnelle go to see her brothers."

His father did not answer. He took off his own cloak and wrapped it around Cygnelle, and the prince saw that she shivered.

"I will not go unless you give your word," the prince said.

The king looked up at him and said, in a voice the prince had never heard him use, not even to a servingman, "I give it then, for I would do anything to have you gone from this place," and the prince rode out to find the witch.

He rode along the path that led from the castle and before long he came to the place where it met the path that Cygnelle had asked about. It was half-hidden and overgrown with briars, and when he saw it the prince felt a fluttering of memory like the beating of a bird's wings at his breast.

"No," he thought. "This is a snare of the witch's. She would stop me with memories."

And he put his hand to his side and held it there and rode on, and by and by he came to a wall. It was made of red brick and had once been so tall he could not see over it, but now the wall had tumbled down and briars had grown up around it. But among the briars was a tree of white flowers, and when the prince saw it he felt the knocking of memory in his heart, like the tapping of a bird's beak.

"No!" he thought. "The witch would have me stop here, lost in memories that can only bring me pain."

And he took out a kerchief from inside his shirt and held it to his side and rode on, and by and by he came to a gate. It was rusted, and the garden beyond it overgrown with briars, and the castle tumbling down, and when he saw it the prince felt memory, like the weight of a dead bird, against his heart.

"No!" the prince shouted, and he took off his shirt and tore it into strips and bound it under his ribs and rode on that day, and the day after, and the day after that, till he had lost the path, and at last he came to the witch.

She was standing amid a pile of red bricks, and at first the prince thought it was a ruined castle, but as she moved among the bricks, picking them up and putting them down, he saw that it was instead something unfinished, a stair here, a wall there, a part of an arch, as if the witch had forgotten what she was making. She was wearing a white dress, and her dark hair hung about her face like water weeds.

"Witch," the prince said, "I have come to ask you to help me."

She did not look up. She picked up a brick and carried it over to the unfinished stair.

"Witch," the prince said. "You must help me."

"Who are you?" she said. She set the brick down on the top of the last unfinished step. "What are you doing in my forest?"

"A king's children were put under a spell that they should be swans till one remembered them and took pity on them. I want you . . ."

The witch sat down on the stair. "To break the spell?" she said.

"No," the prince said. "That spell is broken. I wish a new spell to be . . ."

"Ravens, did you say?" the witch said, as if she had not heard him. "I put a spell upon a princess once that she should be a raven till a prince should love her for her sweet voice."

"Swans," the prince said. "But the spell is broken. I have need of another spell."

"It was a good spell," the witch said. "She flapped her black wings and said, 'caw' and 'caw', but who would say to a raven, 'What a sweet voice!' so she was never rescued. How did you break the spell," she said, "when you do not remember them?"

The prince felt a sharp and twisting pain, as if someone pulled an arrow from his side, and he swayed and would have fallen, but the witch had turned back to her bricks and was piling them now by the unfinished wall. The prince got down from his horse and went and stood by her.

"Witch!" he said, "the maiden I rescued cannot forget she

was a swan. I would have you place a spell of forgetfulness on her."

The witch picked up a brick and put it down again. "That she might forget you?" she said, and looked at him.

He had thought she would be old, but she was not, and when he saw her face he thought for a moment that she was younger even than Cygnelle, but then he saw that her face was only unfinished, like her castle, the features laid upon it without shape or purpose.

"I would have her forget she was a swan," the prince said harshly. "Will you help me?"

"I laid a spell on a king once," the witch said, as if she could not remember. "I thought and thought what sort of spell to bind him with, for I wished him to be cold and hungry, to huddle against the frost and grub in the mud for worms and mate in a cruel flapping of wings, and I thought, 'I will make him a swan, and he shall never be rescued until someone shall remember and pity him, and who would pity a swan?' "

"And was he rescued?" the prince said.

The witch looked down at the unfinished wall and past and through it, as if she had forgotten what it was. "He had three children, two sons and a daughter, and I made them swans also, and I made them forget that they were ever human, but him I made remember that he might suffer the more."

"What were the children's names?" the prince said.

"I wanted him to live till there was none to remember him," the witch said, "past memory, past pity, to be a swan forever. But as he flew with his children out of their own garden, a hunter passing by shot him through the heart with an arrow, and he fell dead at his own gate."

"What was the king's name?" the prince said, and took the witch by the shoulders and shook her. "Was it Gudrain?"

"I do not know," the witch said. "It may have been."

The prince let go of her shoulders and took a step back away from her. "Why did you wish the king so ill that you would lay such an evil spell on him?"

"I do not remember," the witch said, and it seemed to him more terrible than the cruel spells that she had told him of that she did not remember why she had made them or even the names of those she had laid on them.

"What of the children?" he said. "Did you lay some spell on those who loved them that they would not remember them?"

She put down a brick and picked it up again. "No. For they

lay already under a spell better than any I could devise. A spell of guilt and sorrow, that they would not remember for the pain of it. And refusing to remember, they could not pity, and failing to pity, the children could never be rescued. It is the best spell of all.''

And the prince looked at her face and the dark hair hanging about it like water weeds, and he thought of Cygnelle lying nearly dead by the pond because he would not let her remember. ''How did you come to be a witch?'' he said in wonder.

The witch put her hand to her side, under her ribs, but absently, as if she had long since forgotten whatever would lay there. After a moment she took her hand away and bent to pick up another brick, and as she straightened, she stopped and looked up at the prince and said, ''Who are you? What are you doing in my forest?''

And the prince called to his horse and rode back the way he had come. The way was narrow and choked with briars, so that the prince had to lead his horse by the bridle, and his clothes were torn by the briars, and his hands were cut by the sharp thorns. He could not find the path, and darkness came, and he fell into a muddy pool and let go of the bridle, and when he had struggled to his feet in the waist-high water and stumbled to the edge of the pool, he lay down beside it, shivering with cold under his wet cloak, and fell asleep.

And in the morning his horse came and nudged him gently awake, and he saw that it was the pool where he had found the swans, and he mounted his horse and rode with all haste until he came again to the place where the two paths met, the wide one leading to his father's castle and the other that led to King Gudrain's castle. ''I have taken this path before,'' he thought, looking at the half-hidden path. ''My father and I took this path together,'' and he sat as still upon his horse as a flower on a mirror and tried to remember.

The path had been wide and edged with red stone, and he had been so young that his feet had hardly reached the stirrups, but he had felt tall and proud to be riding with his father. ''We go to meet King Gudrain's daughter,'' his father had said. ''She is only a very little girl. You must be kind and watch over her carefully, for she will be your bride one day.''

The prince had let fall the reins and sat looking at the path, not seeing it. His horse tossed his head, and the prince came to himself and rode on, and by and by he came to the wall and the tree of white flowers. ''I have ridden this way before,'' he thought, "with Emelie," and he sat and waited on his horse like a swan on the water, trying to remember.

His father had said, "King Gudrain and I have much to talk of," and he had set Emelie before the prince on his horse and bade him take her riding along the path by the wall. She was only a very little girl, much younger than he, but she had sat up straight before him, not touching him, though her little hands clutched the pommel of the saddle, and she shivered when he kicked the horse forward. He had ridden with her as far as the end of the wall, where a tree covered in white flowers bent down, and he had picked her a bunch of the white flowers, and they had ridden back with her clutching the flowers in her little hands.

The prince had gotten down from his horse and was standing by the tree, looking at the white flowers, seeing nothing. His horse stamped its feet impatiently, and the prince came to himself and rode on, and by and by he came to the gate.

"It was here that I found him," he thought, and he sat upon his horse, still as the dead swans on the edge of the pond, already remembering.

"I fear for Gudrain," the king had said. "There is a witch in that forest who means him ill. I must warn him," but the prince had begged his father to let him take the warning to King Gudrain, and at last his father had let him go, and he had ridden hard as far as the place where the two paths met, eager to prove his worth to his father, but as he turned aside onto the path that led to King Gudrain's castle, he heard the trumpeting of a swan, and at the sound of it he forgot his father's warning and he drew his bow and followed it.

Its cry led him deeper and deeper into the forest, though now it sounded more like a man's cry for help, and the way became narrow and choked with briars, so that the prince had to lead his horse by the bridle, and he tore his clothes, but though he listened, he did not hear the swans again.

But at last he caught sight of a gate through the trees, and when he saw it he thought of his father's warning to King Gudrain, and he ran toward it and found King Gudrain lying on the ground, shot through the heart with an arrow. He had sat down on the ground beside the dead king and held his hand, afraid to go and seek for the bodies of Emelie and her brothers, until his father came seeking for him. But when they had gone into the garden they had found the children gone.

The prince had gotten down from his horse and was standing

looking at the ground, seeing nothing. And his horse blew and whinnied, and the prince came to himself and would have opened the gate, but his father barred his way.

"I have broken my word to you and brought her here to see her brothers," his father said. "I could not do otherwise, I feared that the next time I pulled her from the pond, I would be too late."

"As I was too late, carrying the warning to King Gudrain," the prince said. And the king looked at his torn clothes and his wet cloak.

"She is in the garden," he said, and opened the gate.

And the prince would have gone into the garden, but her brothers barred his way. "We will not let you take our sister away from here," the elder brother said, and drew his sword.

"Only let me speak to her," the prince said.

"What would you speak of then?" the younger brother said. "The swans you have killed?"

"I would speak to her of her father, and yours. It was I who killed Gudrain," he said. "I did not bring the warning in time." And they looked at his mud-streaked clothes and his cut and bleeding hands, and the younger brother said, "You will find her by the lily pond," and let him pass.

And the prince came into the garden. It was overgrown with briars, and the lily pond was choked with water weeds, but on its surface, like a flower on a mirror, sat a little swan, and on the other side of the pond, looking at the swan, sat Cygnelle. Her head was bent, so that he could see the brave curve of her neck, and she smiled at the little swan, but when she spoke her voice was filled with sadness.

"One day in spring we flew above an open ride," she said, "And I saw a boy riding with a child before him on the saddle, and I thought, though I could not remember why, 'One still lives who will not forget me. And he will come and rescue us,' And you did."

She put her hand out to the little swan, and her wide white sleeve fell away from her arm, "But you did not remember me, or even know my name."

"I know it now," the prince said.

She looked up at him, and he saw that there were black shadows of sadness under her eyes. "I could remember nothing but that I had been a swan, and I saw that the spell was not broken after all, but only changed, and that you would never remember and pity me that I might be rescued, for who would pity a swan?"

"I remember now," he said, and held out his arms to her across the lily pond. "Emelie," he said.

And then the spell was well and truly broken, and she came into his arms and stayed there. And her brothers and the king came into the garden and embraced them, laughing and crying. And the prince set her before him on his horse and took her to his castle, and there they lived lives that only those who remember much may live, and at last they died.

But the witch lived on till all had forgotten her, past memory, past pity, and was never rescued.

Son of the Morning

Ian McDowell

I SAT ON the cold cliff and squinted out across the water, absentmindedly trying to drop stones on the heads of the squawking terns that nested on the tiny beach so very far below. I'd been waiting for a long time—my nose felt full of icicles and my backside was almost frozen numb. It was all a rather silly vigil: sea voyages being what they are, Arthur might not make landfall for the better part of a week. Still, I waited there, naively expecting to see the speck of his ship approaching over the dark swells. Time is nothing but an inconvenience when you're fourteen years old.

It was all so exciting. My uncle Arthur was coming to our island to do battle with a giant he'd driven out of his own realms the year before. My Da, King Lot of Orkney, had sent a rather sharp letter to his brother-in-law when Cado (that was the monster's name) turned up on our shores and started terrorizing the peasantry. Not being one to leave such things half done, Arthur responded with a promise to come to Orkney and settle Cado's hash just as soon as he was able.

Lot hadn't given much thought to Cado when his depredations were confined to the Pictish and Dalriadan Scottish peasantry, but that changed when the giant swam the eighteen miles or so of stormy water between those territories and our island and announced his presence on our shores by wiping out three entire farmsteads down on Scapa Bay. And although royal search parties had found the remains of over two dozen gnawed skeletons, they'd not come across a single skull. Cado evidently had the charming habit of collecting his victims' heads.

I thought about all of this as I sat on the cliff at Brough's head.

I'd never been particularly worried about the monster for he had confined himself to the less-settled end of the island—and what were a few rustic peasants more or less? And I enjoyed the embarrassment that my father suffered for being unable to cope with the menace, for I harbored little love for Lot. Still, I looked forward to Arthur's coming. His battle with Cado was sure to be more exciting than a mainland boar hunt. And I did love my uncle. I loved him very much.

Suddenly I spotted it, the tiny speck that could only be a distant ship. I rubbed my salt-stung eyes, but it stayed out there; not wishful thinking but the hoped-for reality. Beyond the toy-like sail, dark clouds tumbled low across a sky as cold and gray as old, unpolished iron. The ship seemed to be riding before a storm. Evidently, they'd decided to chance the weather and make for Orkney rather than turn back to the mainland coast they'd surely been hugging during their long trip up from Cornwall.

I leapt up with a whoop and started scrambling back away from the cliff. The jagged stones, wet and black and speckled with bird dung, gave me poor footing, and several times I stumbled and fell before reaching the sand and turf. Over the rise bulked Lot's palace, squatting there in the lee that gave it some scant protection from the sea and wind. It might not have been much by mainland standards, but it was the grandest building in all the Orkneys. A twenty-foot ditch and two earthworks encircled a horseshoe-shaped two-story stone and timber hall. I dashed across the plank bridge that spanned the ditch and waved up at the soldiers manning the outer earthwork. Those that weren't busy playing dice, sleeping on the job, or relieving themselves waved back.

Mother's tower was on the opposite side of the inner courtyard from the Great Hall. Picking my way through milling clusters of chattering serfs, grunting pigs, squawking chickens, honking geese, and other livestock, I skirted the deepest mud and the piles of fresh excrement until I arrived at the tower's slab-sided foundation. The brass knocker stuck out its tongue and leered at me. "Who goes there?" it demanded in a tinny soprano.

"Mordred mac Lot, Prince of Orkney," I snapped, trying to sound smart and military. The door made no response. "Open up, dammit, I said I'm the Prince!"

The knocker rolled its eyes nonsensically. "I heard you the first time," it trilled, "and I don't care if you're the Prince of Darkness himself, I'm not opening this door until you've wiped your filthy feet!"

It was futile to argue with something that wasn't even really alive. I scraped the heels of my boots against the doorstep while muttering a few choice curses. When I was finished, the door swung wide without further comment. But I knew that it was snickering at me behind my back.

The stairs were steep and winding, which was one reason why King Lot never came here, though they didn't bother Mother, who had the constitution of a plow horse. The room at the top was high and narrow and all of gray stone. It had one window, large and square, with an iron grille and heavy oaken shutters. A ladder connected with a trap door that opened up onto the roof. In one corner was a brick hearth with a chimney flue, not so much a fireplace as an alcove for the black iron brazier that squatted there like a three-legged toadstool. Flanking the alcove were imported cedar shelves lined with animal skulls, a few precious books, rather more scrolls, netted bunches of dried herbs, and small clay jars containing rendered animal fats and various esoteric powders. In the center of the floor was an inlaid tile mosaic depicting a circle decorated with runic and astrological symbols. Off to one side of the mosaic stood a low marble table where Mother sacrificed white doves, black goats, and the occasional slave who'd become too old, sick or just plain lazy to be worth his keep.

Today it was a goat. Queen Morgawse was bent over the spread-eagled carcass, absorbed in the tangle of entrails that she carefully and genteelly probed with the tip of her silver-bladed sacrificial dagger. From the expression on her sharp, high-cheekboned face, I knew she'd found a particularly interesting set of omens in the cooling guts.

"Hullo, Mother."

She looked up, straightening to her full, considerable height. I may have gotten her black hair and green eyes (I'd seemingly inherited nothing of Lot's appearance, thank the gods), but that impressive stature had all gone to my older brother Gawain, though he'd added to it a broad beefiness that contrasted with her willow slimness. She was dressed in her standard magical attire: an ankle-length black gown that left her arms bare. On her head was a silver circlet, and her long, straight hair was tied back with a blood-red ribbon.

She smiled. "What is it, sweets?"

"Arthur's here. I saw the ship."

She frowned. "Is he now? And me such an untidy mess." She wiped her bloody hands on the linen cloth she's laid out under the goat. "Do me a favor, love. Clean up this mess while I go change to greet our guests. Do you mind?"

"No, Mother."

After giving me a quick kiss on the cheek, she hurried down the stairs, leaving me alone in the room. I bundled the goat into the stained dropcloth and stumbled with it to the window. That side of the tower was built into the earth and timber wall that formed the fourth side of the courtyard square. With a heave I got my burden through the aperture. It landed on the other side of the wall. Immediately a battle for possession of the carcass broke out between a pack of the palace dogs and several of the serfs who had hovels there.

A wet whistling sound came from somewhere above me. "Hello, Young Master. Please give me something to eat."

I looked up at Gloam where he clung to the ceiling directly over the magic circle. "No, I don't have time. Arthur's here."

Gloam resembled nothing so much as a pancake-shaped mass of dough several feet in diameter, his pale surface moist and sweaty with small patches of yeasty slime. Offset from his center was a bruise-like discoloration about the size of a head of lettuce. Only when its round mouth puckered open and its wrinkled lids parted to reveal eyes like rotting oysters did it become recognizable as a face. Gloam wasn't much to look at, but then, few people keep demons for their beauty.

"I know all about Arthur," he gurgled in a voice like bubbles in a swamp. "Your mother and he . . ." He broke off, looking suddenly uncomfortable.

"What was that?" I asked, curious despite myself.

"Oh, nothing, nothing at all. Forget I even said it."

I sighed impatiently. "Are you trying to trick me, Gloam?"

He darkened to the color of old buttermilk and faded back to his normal pasty hue, always a sign that he was enjoying himself. "No, not at all. I just know something that I'm not allowed to tell you."

"Something about Arthur, I take it."

He whistled and expelled gas. "Well, yes, and rather more than that. Have you ever wondered who your father is?"

My patience was wearing thin. "He's the King of Orkney, you stupid twit."

"Haven't you ever considered the possibility that King Lot might not be your da?"

Hadn't I ever. I suddenly felt a strange gnawing in my guts, as if I'd swallowed something cold and hungry. Not that Lot not being my father would make for any great loss, but if he wasn't, just who was? Finding my voice again, I asked Gloam as much.

"I can't tell you that," he gurgled in reply. "Your mother doesn't want you to find out until after you've reached manhood."

"I'm fourteen, dammit," I snapped in my best regal manner.

"Well, yessss," he mused, "and there was the serving maid with whom you tried to . . ."

"Never mind that!"

"And that *is* one common definition of initiation into manhood," he continued. "Not that you managed it very well."

Enough was enough. "Listen, you stinking, slimy mollusk, if you don't tell me right this very moment what it is that you've been hinting at, I'll . . ."

"Oh, all right," he said before I could come up with an appropriate threat. "But you must find me something to eat first. A dog, perhaps. Or a cat. A child would be best, really. A tender little mild-fed babe."

"Oh, stuff it," I snapped, "I'll go catch you a chicken."

He smiled, never a pleasant sight. "A chicken would be very nice."

So I ended up chasing chickens through the deep mud of the inner courtyard for several frustrating minutes. Finally, I caught a fat rooster. Tying its legs together with a strip torn from the hem of my surtunic, I puffed and panted my way back up the stairs with the protesting cock tucked securely under one arm. It shat on me, of course, but my clothes were already so soiled that it hardly mattered.

I tossed the bird into the tiled circle. Gloam detached himself from the ceiling with a loud sucking noise and fell on the hapless fowl, his jellyfish-like substance hiding it from view. After a brief struggle, the thing that moved under that white surface lost all recognizable shape and there was only a sort of pale sac that quivered slightly beneath its coat of frothy perspiration. The inflamed face erupted from his upper surface and grinned at me, the toothless mouth slack and drooling.

"Well, out with it, you repulsive greaseball!"

Gloam frowned. "All right, Mordred. Arthur's your father."

I didn't understand. "But he's my uncle!"

"Oh yes, that too."

"Oh." My mind felt blank; I didn't know what to think or feel. "How?"

Gloam sighed. "You mother will have my arse for this."

"You don't have an arse. Now, tell me how it happened."

His face flushed from dark purple to bluish green. "Fifteen years ago Arthur was little more than a green boy with his first command. No one knew who his father was: he was a landless bastard of a soldier. But he was very handsome. It happened during the Yuletide feast at Colchester, when the King and Queen of Orkney were paying their seasonal visit to Uther's court. Arthur had just had his first taste of battle and it had gone very badly. He drank too much. Your mother was tired of her dry little stick of a king, so she paid a midnight visit to Arthur's tent. It was dark and he never knew that she was the Queen of Orkney, much less that she was his own sister. When they met some years later he thought it was the first time. That's all there is to tell."

Arthur was my father. It was dizzying to go from being the son of a cold and loveless island lord to being the son of the best man in the known world. What would he say if he knew he was my da? My understanding of his Christian morality was dim at best, and, foolish as it sounds, the incest taboo never entered my mind. I'd had no formal schooling in *any* religion, and had no idea what the followers of the crucified carpenter thought about such things.

Arthur had hardly ever spoken of his faith. That was understandable: he'd come to power in a realm that was at least half what he'd call pagan, and no doubt he'd had to learn tact. Certainly, he'd never been held a nonbeliever against my brother, nor had he tried to repress the worship of Mithras, the Roman soldier's god, among his mounted troops.

But tolerance of different religions hardly meant that he'd welcome an illegitimate (and incestuous, but I still wasn't thinking of that) son with proverbial and literal open arms. Still, there was the chance he might. I suddenly found myself wanting that very much. He was unmarried, and according to gossip had not left behind the usual string of bastards that would be expected of a thirty-two-year-old bachelor king and former soldier. Though it was said that he'd shown more than a passing interest in Guenevere, the reputedly stunning daughter of the Cornish lord Cador Constantius.

The sound of sudden commotion outside broke my reverie. "That would be Arthur's arrival," commented Gloam dryly, as he flopped over to the wall and began to climb it, leaving a sluglike trail across the tiles and flagstones.

I was out of the room and down the steps in a trice, for at

least action would keep me from having to think. Indeed, the yard was a confusion of babbling serfs, barking dogs, and clucking chickens, all frantically trying to stay clear of the muddy wake churned up by the two-dozen riders that came pounding under the fortified gatehouse. A trim man on a magnificent black gelding rode at their head, snapping off orders with the practiced ease of long command.

Arthur was dressed for rough travel in an iron-studded leather jerkin and knee-high doeskin boots. His head was protected by an iron-banded cap of padded leather, lighter than the conical helmet he'd wear on campaign, and a sopping cloak was draped around his shoulders and saddle like limp wings. Obviously, his ship had passed through the storm I'd seen brewing.

He was of medium height, with broad shoulders and a barrel chest. His brown hair was cut short and his face clean-shaven in the Roman manner. Although this tended to emphasize his rather large ears, he was still a handsome man. For the first time I realized that his slightly beaky nose was almost identical to my own.

He vaulted down from his tall horse and clapped me on the shoulder. With his crooked grin and easy manner, he was still more the soldier than the king.

"Hullo, laddy-buck, you've become quite the man since I saw you last." I started to bow, which was rather hard with him standing so close. "No need for that," he laughed, "we're all bloody royal here."

"Actually, they're always saying Gawain got all the height and I'm the puny one," I replied to his compliment.

"Are they now? Well, a lad's growth is measured in more than the distance from his head to his heels, and that's the truth of it."

I saw no sign of Gawain. "Did you bring my brother with you, sir?"

He shook his head. "His squadron's manning the Wall, keeping an eye on our Picti friends."

Lot's acid bark cut through the brouhaha. "Mordred, get the hell out of the way, you're as filthy as a Pict! Change before supper or eat in the stable: by Mannanan and Lir, I'll have no mud splattered brats in my hall."

I quickly stepped back out of reach as the thin, stooped form of my nominal father came gingerly through the clinging mud. Arthur's formal smile was as cold as the sea wind. "Give you good day, my Lord of Orkney." To me he whispered, "Run along now before your Da starts to foam at the mouth. We can talk later, when we're out of this forsaken gale."

"Gale, hell, this is a slight breeze for this place," grumbled one of his captains who'd overheard the last sentence.

I scurried through the crowd to the entrance of the Great Hall. Brushing past clucking servants, I entered the building, shut the stout oak doors behind me, and crossed the huge room to the stairwell, where I started bounding up the steps two and three at a time. As I ran down the hall to my room, I began stripping off my filthy clothes. Once in my chamber, I tossed the soiled garments out the narrow window, shouting down instructions to the slave whose head they landed on to have them patched and laundered and to send someone up with a bucket of hot water. After washing with more than my usual care, I donned a fresh linen shirt, cross-gartered wool breeches, a long-sleeved and high-necked undertunic, a short-sleeved and v-necked surtunic, and calfskin shoes. That done, I went downstairs to the feast.

Lot sat at the head of the table with his back to the roaring hearth, Mother at his right and Arthur at his left. The King of Orkney had dressed for the occasion in a purple robe trimmed with ermine fur and there was fresh black dye in his thinning hair. The beard that he wore to conceal his lack of a chin was more clipped and clean than usual, but the barbering only emphasized its sparse inadequacy.

By contrast, Arthur's garments were of plain wool and bare of any fashionable embroidery at the neck, sleeves, or hem of his surtunic. His brown breeches were cross-gartered with un-dyed strips of dull leather and he'd changed to a clean but far from new cloak that was fastened at the shoulder with a simple bronze brooch. Although he'd been on his throne for almost three years, he'd never learned to dress like a king.

Mother had saved a place for me on her left. Lot glared but said nothing as I sat down and Arthur winked. The first courses were just being served: salads of watercress and chickweed, heaping piles of raw garlic, leeks, and onions, hardboiled auk and puffin eggs, and smoked goat cheese. Usually Lot tended to serve guesting lords niggardly meals of boiled haddock, salt herring, and the occasional bit of mutton stewed in jellied ham-hocks, leading Mother to the frequent observation that we might be better off as Christians, for they observed their Lent only *once* a year. But he dared not be stingy with his royal brother-in-law, High King of all the Britons. This time there'd be real meat to come, and plenty of it.

Arthur's men and the household warriors sat on sturdy, rough-hewn benches, quaffing tankards of ale and wine while the palace dogs and a few favored pigs milled about, waiting patiently for the scraps they knew were soon to come. The wall tapestries had recently been cleaned, fresh rushes were strewn on the floor, and the long wooden table was spread with that ultimate luxury, a snow-white linen tablecloth. More courses began to arrive: dogfish and grayfish in pies, whale flesh simmered in wine, smoked plovers and shearwaters, and a whole roasted ox and boar. Individual servings were shoveled out onto trenchers of hard, crusty bread and each man was given several small clam-shells to use as table implements, though most preferred to stick with their knives and fingers. Most of the guests did respect the tablecloth and instead wiped their hands on their clothing or on the backs of passing dogs.

Lot was actually trying to keep up a polite facade. "Of course, good Artorius," he was saying (he always called Arthur by his formal Latin name), "I'll be more than happy to help fortify the northern coast of the mainland—assuming, of course, that you can force a treaty on the Picts."

Arthur nodded. "The Picti are half-naked savages, but they're natives just the same as us and we could use their help against the Saxons."

"Ach, I thought you'd finished them for once and all at Badon Hill, back before you'd even ascended to the throne."

Arthur shook his head. "Not by half, I didn't. Oh, it will take them a few years to mount a new invasion, but they'll be back. They can't get it out of their thick heads that this isn't their land; do you know what they're calling us now? *Welshmen*, their word for foreigners. Foreigners, in our own forsaken country! Well, either Briton and Picti will find a way to stand together, or they'll go down separately under the Saxon yoke!"

Lot sipped his wine. "Of course, as an outsider, I can see certain virtues in them that your folk can't. For instance, their kings are very brave."

Arthur looked at Lot sharply. He knew as well as I did that the King of Orkney wasn't one to be praising others unless he had an ulterior motive. "Lord of Orkney," he said softly, "I came here to rid your land of a dire menace, not to hear you sing the virtues of my enemies."

"Well spoken," replied Lot easily, "but I was simply re-marking on a fact. Take old Beowulf Grendelsbane, for instance. He took on the monster that was menacing his people alone, and with bare hands, besides. Grabbed the beastie by the arm and pulled it off as easily as I tear the wing off this bird's carcass.''

''I am familiar with the story,'' said Arthur dryly. ''What's the point?''

Lot smiled. ''Just this. Though you've never said as much, I do believe that it would please you to see these islands convert to Christianity.''

Arthur nodded warily. ''It would do my heart good to see my nephews and sister living in a Godly household.'' Mother cleared her throat and made a point of looking down at her hands.

''But you must understand,'' continued Lot, ''my people find it hard to be impressed with your faith when you must bring with you over a score of armored men to do the sort of job that Beowulf of the Geats was able to do with his good right arm.''

One of Arthur's men spoke up. ''Sire, this is boastful nonsense! That Saxon oaf could never have . . .''

Arthur silenced him with a gesture. He turned back to Lot. ''Lot MacConnaire, if I go against Cado tomorrow all alone, taking none of my men with me, and if I bring you back his head, do I have your word that you will accept Holy Baptism?''

Lot nodded. ''If you can manage that, I'll build a church on every island.''

I felt stunned. Such a deed would be appropriate to a classical hero, but it could hardly be expected of a flesh-and-blood man. I looked carefully at my father. He was clearly not a fool. ''Uncle Arthur,'' I said softly, ''you are the greatest warrior in all of Britain. But is this wise?''

He looked at me solemnly. ''You're a good lad, Mordred. Some day you'll be an excellent king. I would see you brought into the Faith.''

I felt uncomfortable under his gaze. ''I was thinking of your realm, sir. Your people need you. Such a risk puts them in danger, too.''

He grinned his lopsided grin. ''Well, they'll just have to cross their fingers and hold their breath, won't they? Don't be a worrywart, lad, I do know what I'm doing. My God defended Padriac against the serpents of Ireland, and Columba against the dragon of Loch Ness. He protected Daniel in the lion cage and lent needed strength to little Daffyd's good right arm. He will not fail me, not if I'm half the man I must needs be if I'm to call myself a king.''

Mother cleared her throat. ''Tell me, brother, has that kingship become a bore yet, or do you still like the office?''

Arthur laughed. "It's been far from dull. Before I learned of my paternity, I thought I'd be a simple soldier all my life and that all my difficulties would end once I beat the Saxons. Then came Badon Hill, where I did that very thing, and I dreamed that I might retire in peace and quiet." Several of his men snorted at that, but he ignored them. "Don't laugh; I even had visions of becoming some sort of gentleman farmer, as larky as that sounds. But then Uther opened his deathbed Pandora's box and there were suddenly at least ten thousand voices crying 'Artorius Imperator! We want Arthur for our king!' and who was I to say them nay? My first year on the throne was all fighting. The Picts had to be driven back across the Wall, the Irish were making pirate raids, and every local king with a cohort to his name thought it worth his while to challenge my right to rule. Such a bloody mess you never saw and I imagined I'd be old and dying like Uther before I had it straightened out."

He motioned for a slave to refill his goblet. "But that was just the easy part. The fighting's been over for two years this winter and since then I've spent half my days haggling like a fishmonger and the other half wearing as many masks as a dozen troupes of actors. But I can't complain. It's been fun for all of that."

Mother laughed sweetly. "I'm sure it has." She smiled icily at her husband. "Isn't it refreshing to listen to a ruler who takes his duties seriously and doesn't look upon his office as his godsgranted excuse for never having to sully himself with a day's honest work?" Lot's only reply was a belch. His flushed and sweaty face indicated that he was getting very drunk.

Mother turned back to Arthur. "You must have future plans."

He nodded. "Trite as it sounds, peace and prosperity are the first things that come to mind."

"That's a rather vague agenda."

The King of Britain smiled. "Isn't it just? I'm afraid that my ideas of good government are not particularly complex. I'll die happy if I can just maintain a nation ruled by the principles of Roman law and Christian virtue."

Lot hiccuped explosively. "I thought it was Roman law that nailed your Christian virtue to a bloody tree."

The room went very quiet. More than ever, I was glad that Lot was not my father, but I felt ashamed of him just the same. Arthur's face seemed to freeze over like a winter loch, but he kept his voice calm. "I'll ignore that remark, Lord of Orkney. Some men are always fools and others need a touch of strong drink to bring it out."

Once again, Mother saved the situation. She clapped her hands for Fergus, the court bard. The little Leinsterman strutted out, bowed, and began to pluck his gilded harp. Lot and Arthur's eyes gradually unlocked while they listened to those soothing melodies. Skillful harpsong can calm a Brit that way, and even when drunk Lot was too much the coward to meet Arthur's gaze for long. Arthur's men relaxed and took their hands away from their swordbelts, causing our household guardsmen to breath sighs of deep relief. Though the numbers were on their side, they knew full well that Arthur's crack troops could carve them up like so many feast-day bullocks. I understand that the Saxons consider it in bad taste to wear steel at the table, and in this regard I've come to suspect that they may be a bit more civilized than we are.

Soon it was time for all to say goodnight. Arthur's men trooped out to the barracks (in deep winter weather they'd have stretched out before the hearth, sharing the floor with the dogs and pigs and the household guard), while Arthur himself had been granted an apartment at the far end of the upper hall. I paid my respects, trudged up the stairs, and settled wearily into bed without bothering to remove my clothing.

I had the oddest dream. I was standing below the crest of a steep hill, where a tall wooden cross loomed against an inky sky. A corpse had been crucified there in the old Roman fashion. After awhile I somehow realized that it was the *Cristos*. Although the birds had had his eyes and lips, I still recognized his face as being Arthur's.

I awoke all drenched with sweat, and found it hard to relax and sleep again.

Despite my lack of rest I managed to rise before dawn and dress in new and heavier woolen clothing, to which I added otter-skin boots with the fur inside, a hooded cloak, and a leathern jerkin with protective bronze scales. Then I strapped on a shortsword and slung a bow and quiver over my shoulder. These might not be much protection against Cado, but only fools take extra chances when such monsters are about. I knew my way well enough to navigate the upper floor and the pitch-black stairwell, but right after reaching the lower landing I tripped over a sleeping boarhound, who put his considerable weight on my chest and began to wash my face with his enormous tongue. After I'd cuffed him in the nose several times, he finally realized that I didn't want to play and released me. There was nothing left of the fire but embers, but those gave me enough light to tiptoe through the sleeping forms until I reached the outer door.

The yard was empty, for all the livestock and the serfs were huddled in the barns, and the mud was frozen solid by the evening chill. The dawn was close at hand, and enough light leaked over the horizon to see by. Squaring off in front of one of the wooden practice posts that stood between the barracks and the stables, I drew my sword and began to hack away. Despite the cold and the usual fierce wind, I'd actually started to work up a sweat when the door to the great hall opened and Arthur emerged.

Like me, he'd dressed for travel in a fur-lined cloak and high boots. Instead of the iron-studded leather he'd worn the day before, he was now clad in a mail hauberk: a thigh-length coat of inch-wide steel rings, wherein each metal circlet was tightly interlocked with four others. This was the sophisticated modern gear that, along with the recent introduction of the stirrup, had made his mounted troops the terror of the Saxon infantry. On his head sat a conical helmet with lacquered leather cheekguards and a metal flange that projected down over his nose. The sword at his side was at least half again as long as the traditional German *spatha*, and it had a sharpened point like that of a spear, as well as an efficient double edge. He also carried a sturdy iron-headed cavalry spear and a circular white shield embossed with a writhing red dragon was slung across his back.

He seemed surprised to see me. "Practicing this early?"

"Every day," I gasped between strokes. "Gawain won't be the only warrior in the family."

He leaned on his spear and watched me with a critical eye. "Use the point, not the edge: a good thrust is worth a dozen cuts. That's it, boyo, but remember; a swordsman should move like a dancer, not like a clod-hopping farmer."

Exhausted, I sat down on the cold ground. The post was splintered and notched and my sword was considerably blunted. No matter, it was just a cheap practice weapon.

"I rather foolishly forgot to ask your father for directions to Cado's lair," Arthur was saying.

"I know," I panted. "I'll take you there. Folks say he's made himself a den out of the old burial cairn of Maes Howe, down on the shore of the Loch of Harray."

He shook his head. "It would be too dangerous for you to come along."

I'd known he'd say that. "You need a guide. I know the way,

because I used to play down there when I was just a kid." Time for the baited hook. "Don't you want me to witness the power of your God?"

He looked very grave. "Would the deed convince you of the correctness of my Faith?"

No, my faith in him and not his *Cristos*, but I could hardly say *that*. "It would be something to watch," I said truthfully, "and I'd like very much to see a miracle."

His frown finally worked itself into a grin, as I'd known it would. Even then I must have partially realized just how vain he was of his faith, for all that he tried not to show it. "Saddle up," he said, pointing towards the stable. I readied his horse and mine while he went back into the great hall to steal bread and smoked cheese from the kitchen. The sun was only beginning to peek over the horizon when we rode across the plank bridge and skirted the nearby village's earth-and-timber palisade.

We passed fallow fields strewn with dung and seaweed, thatch-roofed stone cottages where the crofters were just rising for their daily toil, and low hills bedecked with grazing sheep. The Royal Cattle ruminated unconcernedly in pastures surrounded by nothing but low dikes of turf and stone. On the mainland the local kings and lordlings considered cattle raids to be good sport and engaged in livestock robbery with the same gleeful abandon that they brought to deer or boar hunts, but our island status protected us from that sort of nuisance.

Keeping in sight of the ocean, we rode between wind-shaped dunes and rolling slopes carpeted with peat and stubby grass. The sun rose slowly into view and shone golden on the water.

There was a whale hunt in progress beyond the tip of Marwick Head. Men in boats chased the herd towards a sand bar while beating pitchers, rattling their oarlocks, and shouting in an attempt to terrify the creatures into beaching themselves. The women and children who waited in the shallows would then attack with harpoons and makeshift weapons that ranged from peatforks to roasting spits. As they died the whales made shrill, whistling cries and strange humming noises that sounded like distant pipes and drums. Ordinarily I would have stopped and made sure the royal share was put aside for the castle household, for whale flesh was always a welcome treat. However, today there wasn't time.

It was over six miles down the coast to the Bay of Skail. We soon passed all signs of human settlement. The tireless wind actually seemed to get fiercer as the morning warmed. My feet

itched from the otter fur inside my boots and not being able to
scratch made for a decided nuisance. For once, I could smell no
sign of rain. The great clouds that raced overhead were as white
as virgin snow.

"Arthur," I said, breaking a long silence, "were you glad to
find out that Uther was your father?"

He took no offense at what might have been an impertinent
question. "Yes, though the old sinner wasn't the sort I might
have chosen for my da. Still, I'd been conceived in wedlock,
and knowing that took many years' load off my mind."

"Why? Is that important to a Christian?"

"Very. Bastardy is a stain that does not wash off easily. Being
born that way just makes the struggle harder."

This was getting rather deep. "What struggle?"

"To keep some part of yourself pure. A man has to look
beyond the muck he's born in."

For some reason I wanted to keep making conversation. "Is
it hard, then?"

He was looking out at the waves but his gaze was focused on
something else entirely.

"Always. I remember my first battle. A fog had rolled in from
the coast and hid the fighting. Men would come stumbling out
of the mist waving bloody stumps or with their guts about their
feet."

I'd never heard war described that way. "But you won, didn't
you?"

He nodded. "The first of many 'glorious victories.' I was as
green as a March apple and could no more control my men than
I can command the sea. They burned three Saxon steadings with
the men still in them. British slaves and all. The women they
crucified upside down against a row of oak trees, after they'd
raped them half to death."

I didn't want to hear this, but he kept on. "There was a celebration at Colchester in honor of our triumph. Your parents
were there, I think, though my rank was too low for me to sit
at the royal table and so I didn't meet them. I messed with the
junior officers, got more drunk than I've ever been since, and
committed all the standard soldier's sins. When I sobered up and
decided I would live, I made a vow to never again become what
I was that day."

Later, we dismounted and devoured the bread and cheese while
taking shelter in one of the stone huts of Skara Brae, the ancient
remains of a Pictish village that stood half-buried in the sand

beside the Bay of Skail. The meal done, Arthur stood beside his
gelding and gazed inland, scanning the treeless horizon. Gesturing out at that rolling emptiness, he said, "For all its small-
ness, there's none that could accuse this island of being the most
crowded kingdom in the world. Not to worry; some day you'll
be lord of more than this."

"What do you mean?"

"The time will come when you take your father's place upon
the throne of Orkney."

"I don't know," I said doubtfully. "It's bound to go to Gawain, not me. After all, he's the oldest."

Arthur clapped me on the shoulder. "Not if I have anything
to say about it. Your brother's a good man and I love him dearly,
but he doesn't have the makings of a king. Too thick-headed.
The Saxons will return someday, and when they do I may be too
old or too tied down by royal duties to lead the war host into
battle. I'll need a good *Dux Bellorum*, and the role of warlord
fits your brother like a glove. Lot will proclaim you his heir if
he knows what's good for him, and that's the truth of it."

I gave up on all attempts at idle chatter as we rode inland for
the Loch of Harray. Arthur remained outwardly calm, but I was
beginning to feel the first gnawings of anticipation in my churn-
ing stomach. Ach, but I was so sure that I was about to see a
deed the like of which had not been witnessed since the days of
Hercules himself.

At last we spied Maes Howe. It was a huge green mound over
a hundred feet in diameter and as high as a two-story dwelling.
Here and there the great gray stones of the cairn's roof poked
their way above their covering of grass and soil. I knew from
my boyhood explorations that there was an exposed passage on
the other side of the barrow that led to a central chamber about
fifteen or twenty feet square. If Cado was as large as he was
reputed to be, he obviously did not object to cramped living
quarters. Of course, giants were probably used to things being
too small for them.

Arthur reined in his horse at the edge of the broad but shallow
ditch that surrounded the mound. "I assume that this is it, then."

"Aye. The only entrance that I know of is on the other side."

His eyes scanned the great mass of earth and rock. "I think
you'd best keep back a ways, so that if I should fail you'll have
time to wheel your horse around and escape."

And in that moment Cado walked around from behind the
ancient pile.

Arthur and I gasped in unison and I actually came close to shitting in my breeches. The giant was at least eight feet tall and tremendously broad, with ox-like shoulders and a barrel torso. In fact, he was so stumpy that if seen at a distance he might be mistaken for a dwarf. His filthy, mud-colored hair blended with his equally filthy beard and fell to his knees in matted waves. Woven into this tangled mass were the scalps and facial hair of his victims' severed heads, so that he wore over a dozen mummified skulls in a sort of ghastly robe. This served as his only clothing. From the mass of snarled locks and grinning eyeless faces protruded arms and legs as massive as tree trunks, all brown and leathery and pockmarked with scrapes and scratches that had festered into scabby craters. Even at thirty paces his stench was awful, a uniquely nauseating combination of the smells of the sick room, the privy, and the open grave. His appearance alone was so formidable that the weapon he held easily in one gnarled hand, a twenty-foot spear with an arm-length bronze head, seemed virtually superfluous.

Ignoring me, his gaze met Arthur's. "Ho, Centurion," he bloomed in surprisingly pure Latin. "How goes the Empire?"

This was the real thing, with no safe gloss of legendary unreality. I found myself wanting to be hunting or fishing or snatching birds' eggs from the cliffs, or doing anything as long as I was far away from here. It was a shameful feeling, and I did my best to ignore it. Arthur at least seemed to be keeping his cool.

"No more Empire, Cado, not for years. And I'm no centurion. You must know that."

Cado squinted at him with red-rimmed eyes the size of goose eggs. "Aye, the Empire's dead. And so are you, *Artorius Imperator*."

Arthur wasn't taken aback. "You know me, then. Good."

Cado snorted. "Oh, I know you well enough, Artorius. How could I not know the man whose soldiers have harried me across the length of Britain. You're mad to come here without them, *Imperator*. Do you wish your son to see you die?"

I was suddenly unable to breathe. How could Cado know? How could he *know*? By the very look in his eyes, I was suddenly sure that he did.

Arthur stiffened. "He is not my son. And I do not intend to die."

Cado's black-lipped mouth spread out in a face-splitting grin, exposing a double row of square yellow teeth that might have done justice to a plow horse. "I think he is, Artorius. I can smell you in his sweat and see you in his face. Like all immortal folk, my kind can sense things that humans cannot. He's your seed, or I'm the Holy Virgin."

Arthur looked at me. Afraid to meet his eyes, I tried to turn away, but I felt frozen by his expressionless gaze. Before I could speak, he turned back to Cado and laughed out loud.

"You can't confuse me with such paltry tricks, monster. And don't make it any harder on yourself with blasphemy. I don't profess to know whether or not you have a soul, but if you do you'd better make your peace with God."

Cado never stopped smiling. "Don't you know where giants came from? We're descended from the ancient *nephilim*, the sons of the unions between the *Elohim* and the daughters of Adam. I need no peace with God—my blood is part divine!"

Arthur lowered his lance and unslung his shield. "More blasphemy, Cado? You might face your ending with somewhat better grace."

Cado growled, a low rumbling that spooked my horse and made him difficult to control. "Tell me one thing," said the giant. "Why have you hounded me these many leagues? What am I to you now that I am no longer hunting in your lands?"

"You know full well what you are," said Arthur grimly. "Your actions have made you an abomination in the eyes of the Lord."

Cado began to laugh, an ear-splitting sound like a dozen asses braying all at once. "Little man, your puking Lord fathered all abomination. I see his world as it truly is and act accordingly."

Couching his lance, Arthur spurred his horse forward with what might have been a prayer and might have been a muttered curse. The sun gleamed on his polished mail as he emerged from the shadow of a wind-driven sweep of cloud. Lugh and Dagda, but he looked magnificent in that brief moment.

Cado casually lifted his spear and thrust out with the blunt haft, catching Arthur squarely in the midriff before he was close enough to use his lance. Torn from the saddle, he seemed to sit suspended in the air for a brief eternity. As he crashed to the sward, his horse shied past Cado and went galloping away in the direction of the distant loch.

Cado bent over him, reversing his spear so that his spear head just touched Arthur's throat. For a measureless time they seemed locked in that silent tableau. My brain screamed that I should do something, but my body showed no interest in responding. The two combatants were frozen and so was I, and I lost all sense of myself as my awareness shrank to nothing but those still and silent figures.

At last Cado spoke. "Now would be the time to look me in the eye and say 'kill me and be done'—I do believe that that's the standard challenge. But you can't say it, can you?" He laughed even more loudly than before. "They all tell themselves it's victory or death, but in the end they find those two limited alternatives not half so attractive as they'd thought."

Arthur hadn't moved. I was suddenly abnormally aware of my physical sensations: the itchy fur inside my boots, the sting of the cold air up on my raw nose, the spreading warmth at my crotch where I'd pissed in my breeches, and the mad pounding of my heart. Arthur was down. He wasn't moving. I knew that I must do something, and it seemed incredibly unfair for such responsibility to have fallen upon my puny shoulders.

I've always been good with horses. Urging my mare forward with my knees, I unslung my bow and drew an arrow from my quiver. The trick was not to think about it, but to act smoothly and mechanically. If I thought about it, I'd fumble. Cado was within range now. He looked up just as I pulled the string back to my ear and let the arrow fly. The feathered shaft seemed to sprout from his left eye socket. I'd already drawn it again, but all my instinctive skill left me and the arrow went wild. Not that it mattered. My impossibly lucky first shot had done the job.

Cado stiffened and groaned. He shivered all over, causing the heads in his hair and beard to clack together like dry and hollow gourds. When he fell over backwards it was like a tower going down.

As suddenly clumsy as a six-year-old, I half-fell out of my saddle and ran to Arthur. "Don't be dead," I pleaded like a stupid twit, "please Da, don't be dead."

He groaned. "Too big. Sometimes evil's just too damned big. And I'm too old for this."

"Are you all right?"

He sat up painfully. "Rib's broken, I think, but I can still stand." With my help he did. "My horse has run off."

I pointed to mine. "Take the mare. I'll search for your gelding."

He clapped me on the shoulder. "You're a good lad. I was an arrogant fool today—I hope you can forgive me."

I didn't know what he meant. "Of course," I muttered, cupping my hands and helping him into the saddle. From this vantage point, he surveyed Cado's corpse.

"Like Daffyd and Goliath. The Lord works his will: I'm taught humility and Cado is destroyed."

I looked him in the eye. "Are you saying that your god guided my arrow?"

He shrugged. "Perhaps. Not that it takes any of the credit away from you. I'm very proud, Mordred. I pray that someday the Lord will give me as fine a son as the one he gave to Lot."

I'd been trying to find an opening all day. My heart was in my mouth—this was more frightening than confronting Cado. "Arthur, there is something you must know."

Something in my voice must have warned him, for he looked at me very oddly. "And what would that be?"

No hope for a smooth tongue: I had to be blunt and open. "You're my father."

"What?"

"You're my father."

I knew it then: I'd blundered. His face wore no expression, but the words hung between us in the heavy air. I tried to laugh, but it was a forced, hollow sound. "I was just joking," I stammered, desperately trying to unsay my revelation. "I didn't mean . . ."

He reached out and gripped my shoulder. His clutch was firm, painful. And his eyes were cold and hard as Lot's. "You're lying now. I know that much. And Cado called you my son, too. How could it be true?"

I tried to pull away, but he held me fast. Now my terror was of *him*, of the man himself. This was a side of Arthur that I'd never seen. "Please," I said. "it's all a mistake. I . . ."

He shook me. "What makes you think you are my son? Tell me now, the truth, and all of it."

I could no more refuse that command than I could up and fly away, though I would have been glad to do either. "Mother's familiar told me."

"A demon? And you believed such a creature?"

"I asked Mother, and she said that it was true."

He shook his head. "How? It's impossible. We've never . . ." He broke off then, but his eyes were still commanding.

"It was at Uther's court after your first battle. She came to your tent in disguise."

The silence that followed that statement was as cold and painful as the bitter wind. He mumbled something that might have been a prayer, and his expression resembled that of a man kicked by a horse. His hand slipped from my shoulder. "It's sin," he said at length, his eyes not meeting mine. "It's mortal sin."

This was worse than I'd feared. Bloody gods, but why couldn't I have kept my foolish mouth shut? "She didn't know you were her brother. It's not her fault."

"No, for she's a pagan, and lost anyway. I'm the one to blame."

"It wasn't your fault either. It wasn't anybody's fault."

He shook his head sadly. "Ach, no, it's always someone's fault. Always." Straightening up, he reined the mare towards Cado's still form. "You knew, monster. You knew what I was. Perhaps you should have killed me." His shoulders slumped, and he looked so *old* as he sat there swaying in the saddle. "But no, then I'd have died in ignorance, unshriven, with no chance at repentance. No wonder that I lost today. My own sin rode beside me."

"Don't talk like that!" I shouted, suddenly angry as well as hurt.

He ignored my protest. "Come up behind me. I won't leave you here, no matter what you are."

No matter what you are. Words that have haunted half my life.

"Go on with you," I snapped. "I said I'd find your god-damned horse."

He didn't react visibly to my profanity. He just sat there, slumped in the saddle, the wind tugging at his cloak. His eyes were focused in my direction, but it was as if he was looking through me at something else. At length he spoke. "All right, Mordred, suit yourself." With that he spurred the mare into a gallop. I suppose that in that moment I became the only thing he ever fled from, but that distinction does not make me proud. I stood there, watching him ride away, while the wind whispered in the grass.

"Throw it all away, then!" I shouted when he was well beyond hearing. "Damn you, Da, it wasn't my fault either!"

I never did find his bloody horse.

And so, the end of this testament. Why did I tell him, when even the young fool I was then might have guessed how he'd react? I don't know. It's all very well for Socrates to maunder on about how one should know oneself, but sometimes the water is just so deep and murky that you cannot see the bottom. I didn't hate Arthur, not then, but the love was all dried up. I'd never asked to be made the symbol of his own imagined sin.

It was a long walk home. A storm rolled in from the ocean long before I reached my destination. The rain was curiously warm, as if Arthur's god were pissing on his handiwork. Wrapped in my soggy cloak, I trudged back to Lot and Mother's world.

The Big Dream

John Kessel

THE LIGHTS OF the car Davin was trailing suddenly swerved right and dropped out of sight: it had run off the road and down the embankment. Davin jerked his Chevy to a stop on the shoulder. A splintered gap in the white wooden retaining fence showed in his headlights, and beyond them the lights of Los Angeles lay spread across the valley.

He slid down the slope, kicking up dust and catching his jacket on the brush. The 1928 Chrysler roadster lay overturned at the bottom, its lights still on. He smelled gasoline as he drew near. The driver had been thrown from the wreck but was already trying to get up; he crouched a few yards away, touching a hand to his head. Davin got his arm around the man's shoulders and helped him stand.

"You all right?" he asked.

The man's voice was thick with booze. "Sure I'm all right. I always take this shortcut."

Davin smiled in the darkness. "Me, I couldn't take the wear and tear."

"You get used to it."

The man was able to walk and together they managed to get back to Davin's car. They climbed in and Davin started down the mountain again.

"The cops will spot that break in the fence within a couple of hours," he said. "You want to see a doctor?"

"No. Just take me home. 2950 Leeward. I'll call the police from there." Davin kept his eyes on the winding road; the Chevy needed its brakes tightened. His passenger seemed to sober remarkably quickly. He sat straighter in the seat and brushed his hair back with his hands like a college kid before a date. Maybe the fact that he'd almost killed himself had actually made an impression on him. "I'm lucky you happened along," the man said. "What's your name?"

"Michael Davin."

"Irish, huh?" There was a casual contempt in his voice.

"On my father's side."

"My father was a swine. Mother was Irish. Not Catholic, though." The contempt flashed again.

"Maybe you ought to go a little easier," Davin said.

The man tensed as if about to take a poke at Davin, then relaxed. He seemed completely sober now. "Perhaps you're right," he said.

Davin recognized the accent: British, faded from long residence in the U.S. The wife hadn't told him that. They rode in silence until they hit the outskirts of the city. Town, really. Despite what the Chamber of Commerce and the Planning Commission and the Police Department could do about it, the neighborhoods still had some of the sleepy feel of Hutchinson, Kansas. Davin sometimes felt right at home helping a businessman keep track of his partner—they would do that in Kansas, too; that would just be good town sense. And that reminded him that no matter how sick he got of L.A., he couldn't stand to go back to the midwest.

Davin knew that the address the man gave him was not his home. It was a Spanish-style bungalow court apartment in a middle-class neighborhood; Davin had begun trailing him at his real home on West 12th Street earlier that evening. He pulled over against the curb. The man hesitated before getting out.

"I'm sorry about that remark. The Irish, I mean. My grandmother was a terrible snob."

"Don't worry about it. You better have someone take a look at that bump on your head."

"I'll have my wife look at it." The man stood holding the door open, leaning in. His fine features were thrown into relief by the streetlight ahead of them. "Thank you," he said. "You might have saved my life."

Davin suddenly felt dizzy. He seemed to be outside himself, floating two feet above his own shoulder, listening to himself talk and think.

"All in a day's work," I said, and watched as the philanderer turned and strode up the walk to the door of bungalow number seven. He let himself in with his own key. An attractive young

woman—his mistress—embraced him on the doorstep. They call
L.A. the City of Angels, but a private dick knows better.

It had started very quietly the day before, Friday. Before the
knock on his door, there had been no dizziness, no feeling of
doing things he did not want to say or do. Davin had been sitting
in his office in the late afternoon, legs up on the scarred desk
top and tie loosened against the stifling heat. Dust motes swirled
in the sunlight slicing through the window over his shoulder. In
the harsh light, the cheap sofa against the wall opposite him
seemed to be radiating dust into the room. The blinds cut the
light into parallel lances that slashed across the room like the
tines of a fork.

It was the second week of the heatwave. The days seemed
endless and thinking was more effort than his mind wanted to
make. He had remembered waking one morning that week and
imagining himself back in Wichita on one of those days that
dawn warm and moist in early August and you know that by
three o'clock there'll be reports of at least four old people dropping dead in airless apartments. That was how hot it had been
in L.A. during the last two weeks.

He had the bottle of bootleg bourbon out and the glass beside
it was half empty. Then the knock sounded on the door.

Davin drained the glass and stashed it and the bottle in the
bottom desk drawer. "Come in," he said. "It's not locked."

A young woman entered.

Davin was tugging his tie straight when he realized the woman
wasn't young after all. She sat in the chair opposite him and
crossed her legs coquettishly, but worn hands and the tired line
of her jaw gave her away. She wore a cloche hat and sunglasses—
probably to mask crows feet around her eyes—and a white silk
dress cut just above the knee. The hair curling out from under
the hat was bleached blonde. Maybe it didn't work anymore, but
Davin could tell that she was a woman who had become used to
men's attention at an early age.

"How may I help you, ma'am?"

She fluttered for about five seconds, then answered in a voice
so alluring it made him shiver. He wanted to close his eyes and
simply listen to the voice.

"I need to speak to you about my husband, Mr. Davin. I'm
terribly worried about him. He's been behaving in a way I can
only describe as destructive. He's threatening our marriage, and
I am afraid that he may eventually hurt himself."

"What would you like me to do, Mrs. . . . ."

"Chandler. Mrs. Raymond Chandler." She smiled, and more lines showed around her mouth. "You may call me Cecily."

"Keeping people's husbands from hurting themselves is not normally in my line of business, Mrs. Chandler."

"That's not exactly what I want you to do." She hesitated. "I want you to follow him and find out where he's going. Sometimes he disappears and I don't know where he is. I call his office and they say he isn't there. They say they don't know where he is."

So far it was something short of self destruction. "How often does this happen, and how long is he gone?"

Cecily Chandler bit her lip. "It's been more and more frequent. Two or three times a month—in addition to the times he comes home late. Sometimes he's gone for days."

Davin reacted to her story as if she had handed him a script and told him to start reading.

I could have told her the problem was probably blonde. "Where does he work?" I asked.

"The South Basin Oil Company. The office is on South Olive Street. He's the vice president."

I told myself to bump the fee to $25 a day. "Okay," I said. "I'll keep tabs on your husband for a week, Mrs. Chandler, but I'll be blunt with you. It's a common thing in this town for husbands to stray. There's too much bad money and too many eager starlets out for a percentage of the gross. One way or the other, no matter what I find out, you're going to have to work this problem out with him yourself."

Instead of taking offense, the woman smiled. "You don't need to treat me like an ingenue, Mr. Davin . . ."

McKinley had been president when she was an ingenue.

"Wives stray, too," she continued, her voice like sunlight on silk. "I won't be surprised if you come to me with that kind of news. I only want Raymond to be happy."

Sure, I thought. Me too. Then I thought about my bank account. This smelled like divorce, but a couple of hundred dollars would go a long way toward sweetening my outlook on life. We talked terms and I asked a few more questions.

Somewhere in the middle of this conversation the script got lost, and bemused, Davin fell back into his own person.

"How long have you been married?"

"Five years."

"What kind of car does your husband drive?"

"He has two. A Hupmobile for business and a Chrysler roadster for his own."

"Do you have a picture of him?"

Cecily Chandler opened her tiny purse and pulled out a two-by-three Kodak. It showed a dark-haired man with a strong chin, lips slightly pursed, penetrating dark eyes. A good-looking man, maybe in his late thirties—at least fifteen years younger than the woman in Davin's office.

Davin sat in his car outside the Leeward bungalow and waited. He had driven off after Chandler went inside, cruised around the neighborhood for five minutes and come back to park down the street, in the dark between two streetlights, where he could watch the door to number seven and not be spotted easily.

It seemed that he spent a great deal of time watching things—people's houses, men at Santa Anita, an orange grove so far out Main Street you couldn't smell City Hall, people's cars, waitresses in restaurants, the light fixture over his bed, young men and women at the botanical gardens—and almost as much time making sure he wasn't spotted. That was how you found out things. You watched and waited and sometimes they came to you. Davin wondered why the hell he'd started acting wise to the Chandler woman. He didn't do that. He'd always been the type of man who became inconspicuous when the trouble started. Maybe all the watching was getting to him.

It hadn't taken long after Cecily Chandler had hired him for Davin to find out about the mistress in number seven. He had followed Chandler after he left work at the Bank of Italy building that afternoon. The woman had met him at a restaurant not far away and they had gone right to her bungalow.

So it was a simple case of infidelity, as he had known the minute the wife had talked about her husband's disappearances. Davin hated the smell of marriages going bad: tell her and let her get some other sucker to follow it up. That was the logical next step. But something kept Davin from writing it off at that. First, Chandler's wife had clearly known he was seeing some other woman before she came to see Davin. She had not hired him for that information.

A Ford with the top down and a couple of sailors in it drove by slowly, and Davin slid lower in his seat as the headlights flashed over the front seat of his car. The sailors seemed to be looking for an address. Maybe Chandler's girlfriend—M. Peterson according to the name on her mailbox—took in boarders.

Second, there was the question of why Chandler had married a woman old enough to be his mother. Money was the usual answer. But South Basin was one of the strongest companies to come out of the Signal Hill strikes, and a vice president had to have a lot of scratch in his own name. He could have married her for love. But there was another possibility: Cecily Chandler had something she could use against her husband, and that was how they got married. And that was why he wasn't faithful, and that led to the third thing that kept Davin from ending his investigation there.

Chandler *was* acting as if he wanted to kill himself. Davin had started following him again Saturday morning, had stuck with Chandler as he opened the day with lunch at a cheap restaurant and had gone home to Cecily in the afternoon. Davin ate a sandwich in his car. He'd picked Chandler up again as he headed to an airfield with another man of about his age and they went for an airplane ride. Someone in the family had to have money.

Davin had loitered around the hangar until they returned. A kid working on the oilpan of a Pierce Arrow told him that Chandler and his friend, Philleo, came out to go flying every month or so. When the plane landed the pilot jumped out, cussing Chandler, and stalked toward the office; Philleo was helping Chandler walk and Chandler was laughing. A mechanic asked what was going on, and the pilot told him loudly that Chandler had unbuckled himself when they were doing a series of barrel rolls and stood up in his seat.

Chandler got a bottle of gin out of the back seat of his roadster. Philleo tried to stop him but soon they were pals again. After that they'd driven up into the hills to a roadhouse speakeasy outside the city limits. When Chandler left in his white Chrysler, Davin had followed him down the winding road until he'd run through the fence.

The Ford with the sailors in it passed him going the other way, now. Other than that there was little traffic in the neighborhood. Chandler was sure to stay put for the night. Davin thought about getting something to eat. He thought about getting some sleep in a real bed. He was getting stiff from all the time he had spent sitting in his car. The heat made his shirt stick to his back. Worst of all, this kind of work got you in the kidneys. He tried to remember why he'd gotten into it.

After the war, being with the Pinkertons had been easy. At least until he'd gotten his fill of busting the heads of the union organizers during the Red Scare. The city had to keep its good business reputation and Davin had done his part until one night when he caught a man in a railyard and realized that he liked using a club on an unconscious man. If one of the other cops had not pulled Davin off, he would have beaten the man to death. He'd woken up feeling great the next day and only began to tremble when he remembered why he felt so good. It scared him. He didn't want to kill anybody but after that night he realized that he could do it easily, and enjoy it. So he quit the Pinkertons, but he couldn't quite quit the work. He was his own agent now. He sat and watched and waited for that violence to happen again, and in the meantime stirred up other people's dirt at twenty bucks a day.

Davin had enough dirt for two days' work. As he was about to start the car, he noticed, in the rear-view mirror, the flare of light as someone lit a cigarette in a parked car some distance behind him on the other side of the street. The car had been there some time and he had neither heard nor seen anyone come or go.

Davin got out, crossed the street and walked down the sidewalk toward the car. A woman sat inside, leaning sideways against the door, smoking. She was watching the apartments where Chandler had met his girlfriend. She glanced briefly at Davin as he approached but made no effort to hide. As he came abreast of the car he pulled out a cigarette and fumbled in his jacket as if looking for a match.

"Say, miss, do you have a light?"

She looked up at him and without a word handed him a book of matches. He lit up.

"Thanks." Her hair looked black in the faint light of the street. It was cut very short; her lips were full and her nose straight. She looked serious.

"Are you waiting for someone?" Davin asked.

"Not you."

Davin took a guess. "Chandler's not going to be out again tonight, you know."

Bulls-eye. The girl looked from the bungalow toward him, upset. She ground out her cigarette.

"I don't know what you're talking about."

"Chandler and the Peterson woman are having a party right now. Too bad we weren't invited, though I bet you'd like to be. Maybe we ought to get a cup of coffee and figure out why."

The girl reached for the ignition and Davin put a hand through the open window to stop her. She tensed, then relaxed.

"All right," she said. "Get in."

She drove to an all-night diner on Wilshire. In the bright light Davin saw that she was small and very tired. Slender, well-dressed, she did not look like a woman who was used to following married men around. Davin wondered if he looked like the kind of man who was.

"My name is Michael Davin, Miss . . . ?"

"Estelle Lloyd." She looked worried.

"Miss Lloyd. I have some business with Mr. Chandler and that makes me want to know why you're watching him."

"Cissy hired you." It was not a question.

Davin was momentarily surprised. "Who's Cissy?"

"Cissy is his wife. I know she wants to know what he's been doing. He's killing himself."

"What difference should that make to you?"

Estelle looked at him steadily for a few seconds. She was young, but she was no kid.

"I love him too," she said.

Estelle's father, Warren Lloyd, was a philosophy professor, and her uncle Ralph was a partner of Joseph Dabney, founder of the South Basin Oil Company. She told Davin that when she was just a girl her father and mother had been friends with Julian and Cissy Pascal, and that the two families had helped out a young man from England named Raymond Chandler when he arrived in California before the war.

Estelle had had a crush on the young man from the time she reached her teens, and he in turn had treated her like his favorite girl. It was all very romantic, the kind of play where men and women pretended there was no such thing as sex. When Chandler had gone away to the war, Estelle had worried and prayed, and when he came back she had not been the only one to expect a romance to develop. One did: between Chandler and Cissy Pascal, eighteen years his senior.

Cissy filed for divorce. Estelle was confused and hurt, and Chandler would have nothing to do with her. The minute she had become old enough for real love, he had abandoned her.

Chandler's mother did not like Cissy and so Raymond did not marry her right away. Instead he took an apartment for Cissy at Hermosa Beach and another for his mother in Redondo Beach. Despite the scandal, Estelle's uncle helped Chandler get a job in the oil business, and he rose rapidly in the company. Estelle kept her opinions to herself, but although she dated some nice young men, she was never serious. Davin wanted to like her. Looking into her open face, he wasn't sure he could keep himself from doing so.

"So why are you waiting around outside his girlfriend's apartment?"

Estelle looked at him speculatively. "Did Cissy hire you to watch him or do you like peeking in bedroom windows?"

He did like her. "*Touché*. I won't ask any more rude questions."

"I'll tell you anyway. I just don't want to see him hurt himself. I know there's no chance for me anymore—I knew it a long time ago." She hesitated, and when she spoke there was a trace of scorn in her voice. "There's something wrong with Raymond anyway. He's not made Cissy happy and he would be making me miserable too if I were in her place."

"What do you think the problem is?"

She smiled sadly. "I don't think he likes women. He uses them, gets disgusted because they let themselves get used, and calls it love."

"Now you sound bitter."

"I'm not, really. He's a good man at heart."

Davin finished his coffee. Everyone was worried about Chandler. "It's late," he said. "It's time for you to take me back."

It was no cooler in the street than it had been in the diner. Davin lit a cigarette while Estelle drove, and when she spoke the strange mood of the last two days was on him again.

Hesitantly, softly, in a voice that promised more heat than the California night, she said to me, "You don't have to stay there watching all night. I have an apartment at the Bryson."

It was like she'd pulled a .38 on me. It was the last thing I expected. Her eyes flitted over me quickly as if she were measuring me for a suit of clothes. I could smell her faint perfume.

"No, thanks," I said. I almost gagged on the sweet scent of her. Ten minutes before, I had liked her, and now I saw her for what she really was. It was tough enough for a private eye to keep himself clean in this town; I'd expected better of this woman.

She let me off in the deserted street and drove away. I stood on the sidewalk watching the retreating lights of her car, inhaling deeply the scent of bougainvillea and night-blooming jasmine like overripe dreams, trying to figure out what Estelle's game might be.

A light was on in the Peterson bungalow. The curtains were partly drawn and the eucalyptus outside the window obscured his view. The night had cooled and a breeze that still held something of the sea rustled the trees as it wafted heavy, sweet air from the courtyard garden. A few clouds were sliding north toward the hills where Chandler's roadster lay at the bottom of an embankment; the high full moon turned Leeward Street into a scene in silver and black. Davin wondered at his own prudishness. He had not been propositioned so readily in a long time and had not turned down an offer like that in a longer one. As he reached his car he noticed a Ford with its top down parked in front of him. The sailors had found their address.

Something kept him from leaving. Instead he circled around the back of the bungalows until he reached number seven. The rear windows were unlit. Remembering Estelle's taunt, he crept to the side and looked in the lighted window. Through the gap in the curtains he could see a woman curled in the corner of a sofa beside a chintzy table lamp. She wore scarlet lounging pajamas. Her hair curled around her face in blonde Mary Pickford ringlets; her lips were a bright red cupid's bow and she was painting her toenails fastidiously in the same color. Davin could not tell if there was anyone else in the room, but the woman did not act like she expected to be interrupted. Sometimes that was the best time to interrupt.

He walked around to the front and rang the bell. The scent of jasmine was even stronger. The door opened a crack, fastened by a chain, and the red lips spoke to him.

"Do you know what time it is? Who are you?"

"My name is Michael Davin. You're awake. I'd like to talk to you."

"We're talking."

"Pardon me. I thought we were playing peek-a-boo with a door between us."

The red lips smiled. The eyes—startling blue—didn't.

"All right, Davin. Come in and be a tough guy in the light where I can get a look at you." She unchained the door. That meant Chandler was gone. "Don't get the idea I'm in the habit of letting strange men in to see me in the middle of the night."

"Sure." She led him into the small living room. The pajamas were silk, with the name "May" stitched in gold over her left breast, and had probably cost more than the chair she offered Davin.

He sat on the sofa next to her instead. She ignored him and

returned to painting her nails. The room was furnished with cheap imitations of expensive furniture: the curtains that looked like plush velvet the color of dark blood were too readily disturbed by the slight breeze through the window to be the real thing; the Spanish-style carpet was more Tijuana than Barcelona. May Peterson held her chin high to show off a fine profile and the clear white skin of her shoulders and breasts, but the blonde hair had been brown once. The figure, however, was genuine.

"You like this color?" she asked him.

"It's very nice."

She shifted position, crossing her right foot in front of her, and leaned on his shoulder.

"Watch your balance," he said.

She pulled away and looked at him. "You're really here to talk? So talk." May's boldness surprised and attracted him. It was not just brass, she acted as if she knew what she was doing and had nothing to hide. As if she knew exactly who she was at every moment. As if she didn't have time for lying, as if the idea of lying never crossed her mind.

"Where's Chandler?" he asked her.

She did not flinch; her eyes were steady on his. "Gone. Sometimes he doesn't stay all night. You should try his wife."

"Maybe I should. Apparently he doesn't anymore."

"That's not my fault."

"Didn't say it was. But I bet you make it easier for him to forget where he lives."

May dipped the brush in the polish and finished off a perfect baby toe.

"You don't know Ray very well if you think I had to seduce him. Sure, he likes to think it was out of his control—lotsa men do. But before me he was all over half the girls in the office."

"You work in his office?"

"Six months in accounting. He hired me himself. Maybe he didn't think the hired me because I got a nice figure, but I figured out pretty quick that was in the back of his mind." She smiled. "Pretty soon it was in front."

If May was worried about what Davin was after, who he was or why he was asking questions, she did not show it. That didn't make sense. Maybe she was setting him up for some fall, or maybe he was in detective's paradise, where all the questions had answers and all the women wanted to go to bed.

May removed the cotton balls from between her toes and closed the bottle of polish. *"There,"* she said, *snuggling up against me. "Doesn't that look fine?"*

Beneath the smell of the nail polish was the musky odor of woman and perfume. It seemed to be my night for propositions; I felt unclean. I needed to plunge into cold salt water to peel away the smell of my own flesh and hers. The world revolves by people rutting away like monkeys in the zoo, but I had enough self-respect to keep away from the cage. As much as I wanted to sometimes, I couldn't let myself be drawn down into the mire; I had to keep free because I had a job to do.

Wait a minute, Davin thought. Even if May knew he was a detective, she had to realize that bedding him wouldn't protect Chandler. So why be a monk? Cold salt water? Rutting in the zoo?

I didn't move an eyelash. The pajamas fit her like rainwater. Lloyds of London probably carried the insurance on her perfect breasts. The nipples were beautifully erect. I got up.

"All right, May, pack it up for the night; I'm not in the market. Tell your friend Raymond that he's going to find himself in trouble if he keeps playing hookey. And you can bring your sailor pals back into the slip as soon as I leave."

"Sailor pals? What are you talking about?"

"Don't forget your manners, now. You're the hostess."

She looked at me as if I'd turned to white marble by an Italian master. Davin, rampant.

"Look, I'm not stupid," she said. *"I figure you must be working for his wife. Big deal."*

I looked down into her very blue eyes: maybe she was just a girl who worked in an office after all, one who got involved with the boss and didn't want any trouble. Maybe she was okay. But a voice whispered to me to see her the way she was—that a woman who looked like May, who said the things she said, was a whore.

"Sure, you're not stupid, May. Sure you're not. But some people take marriage seriously. Good night."

She stayed on the sofa, watching him; as soon as he closed the door behind him, he felt lost. He had just exited on some line about the sanctity of marriage. He'd pulled away from her as if she had leprosy, as if she had tempted him to jump off a cliff. He wasn't a kid and this wasn't some Boy Scout story. He had a job to do, but he wasn't a member of the Better Business Bureau. He was talking like a smart aleck and acting like an undergraduate at a Baptist college.

He drew a deep breath and fumbled in his pocket for his cigarettes. The moon was gone and morning would not be long in coming. It was as cool as it was going to get in any twenty-four hours and it still felt like ninety-five and climbing; the heat wave would not let up.

He started up the walk toward the street and a blow like someone dropping a cinder block on the back of his neck knocked him senseless.

The jasmine smelled good, but lying under a bush in a flower bed dimmed your appreciation. Davin rolled over and started to look for the back of his skull. It was not in plain sight. He got to his knees, then shakily stood. He didn't know how long he'd been out. It was still dark, but the eastern sky was smoked glass turning to mother-of-pearl. The door to May Peterson's bungalow was ajar and her light was still on. Head throbbing, Davin pushed the door slowly open and stepped in.

The lounging pajamas were torn open and she lay on the floor with one leg part way under the sofa and the other twisted awkwardly at the knee. Her neck had not gone purple from the bruises yet. All in all, she had died without putting up much of a struggle. The shade of the chintzy table lamp was awry but the bottle of nail polish was just where she'd left it. Someone had taken the trouble to pull the phony curtains completely closed.

Davin knelt over her and brushed the hair back from her forehead. Her hair was soft and thick and still fragrant. A deep cut on her scalp left the back of her head dark and wet with blood. The very blue eyes were open and staring as if she were trying to comprehend what had happened to her.

Davin shuddered. Light was beginning to seep in through the curtains. The small kitchen was in immaculate order, the two-burner gas stove spotless in the dim morning light; the bed-clothes of the large bed in the back room were disordered but nothing else was disturbed. A cut-glass decanter of bourbon stood on the dressing table with its stopper and two glasses beside it. David felt a hundred years old. He rubbed the swelling at the back of his neck where he'd been slugged—the pain shot through his temples—and left May Peterson's apartment quietly and quickly.

He drove down to use the pay phone at the diner where he and Estelle had had coffee. Fumbling to find the number in his wallet—whoever had hit him hadn't bothered to rob him—he dialed the Chandler home. A sleepy woman answered the phone.

"Mrs. Chandler?"

"Yes?"

"This is Michael Davin. Is your husband at home?"

A pause. He could see her debating whether to try to save her pride. "No," she said. "I haven't seen him since he went out with Milton Philleo yesterday afternoon."

"Okay. Listen to me carefully. Your husband is in serious trouble, and he needs your help. The police are going to try to connect him with a murder. I don't think he had anything to do with it. Tell them the truth about him but don't tell them about me."

"Have you found out what Raymond has been involved in?"

Davin hesitated.

"Mr. Davin—I'm paying for your information. Don't leave me in the dark." The voice that had been so thrillingly sexy two days before was that of a worried old woman.

The light in the telephone booth seemed cruelly harsh; the air in the cramped space smelled of stale cigarette smoke. Behind the counter of the diner a waitress in white was refilling the stainless steel coffee urn.

"The less you know right now the easier it will go when the police call you," Davin said. There was no immediate answer. He felt sorry for her, and he thought about the hurt look in Estelle's eyes. "It's pretty much what I told you I suspected in my office."

"Oh."

Davin shook his head to dispel his weariness. "There's one more thing. Do you know of anyone who has it in for your husband? Anyone who'd like to see him in trouble?"

"John Abrams." There was certainty in her voice.

"Who is he?"

"He works for South Basin, in the Signal Hill field. He and Raymond have never gotten along. He's a petty man. He resents Raymond's ability."

"Do you know where he lives?"

"In Santa Monica. If you'll wait a minute I can see whether Raymond has his address in his book."

"Don't bother. Remember now—when the police call, say nothing about me. Raymond is not involved in this."

Davin hung up and opened the door of the booth, but did not get up immediately. It was full day outside; the waitress was drawing coffee for herself and the dayside short-order cook. Davin considered a cup. He decided against it but made himself eat two eggs over easy, with toast, then headed home for a couple of hours of sleep. He wished he were as certain that Chandler hadn't killed May as he'd told Cissy.

The sun was shining in his eyes when Davin woke the next morning; the sun never came in through his bedroom window that early. The sheets, sticky with sweat, were twisted around his legs. The air was stifling and his mouth felt like a dustpan. He fumbled for the clock on the bedside table and saw it was already one-thirty. The phone rang.

"Is this Mr. Michael Davin?"

"What is it, Cissy?"

"The police just left here a few minutes ago. I have to thank you for warning me. They told me about May Peterson."

She stopped as if waiting for some response. He was still half asleep and the back of his head was suing for divorce. After a moment she went on.

"I didn't tell them anything, as you suggested, but in the course of their questions they told me the neighbor who found Miss Peterson's body saw a man leave her apartment in the early morning. Was it Raymond? Do you know?"

"It was me," Davin said tiredly. "Have you heard anything from him?"

"No."

"Then why don't you let me do the investigating, Cissy—Mrs. Chandler."

There was an offended silence, then the phone clicked. Davin let the dial tone mock him for a moment before he hung up. He ought not to have been so blunt, but what did the woman expect? He wondered if Cissy had had any doubts before divorcing Pascal for Chandler. Pascal was a concert cellist, Estelle had told him. Older than Cissy. She had married for love that time. Davin imagined her as a woman who had always been beautiful, bright, the center of attention. He supposed it was hard for such a woman to grow old: she would become reclusive, self-doubting, alternating between attempts to be youthful and knowledge that she wasn't anymore. He wondered what Chandler thought about her.

The speculations tasted worse than his cotton mouth. Men and women—over and over again Davin's job rubbed his nose in cases of them fouling each other up. Maybe beating up union men for a living was cleaner work after all. He pulled himself out of bed and into the bathroom. He felt hung over but without the compensation of having been drunk the night before.

A shower helped and a shave made him look almost alert. Measuring his narrow jaw and long nose in the mirror, he tried to imagine what had gotten those women so hot the previous night. What had moved May to let him into her apartment so easily? Maybe that had only been a pleasant fantasy; fantasies sometimes were called upon to serve for a sex life, as Cissy Chandler and Davin both knew. His revulsion toward both May and Estelle had been a less pleasant fantasy.

The memory of May Peterson's dead, bemused stare—that was neither pleasant nor fantasy.

While he dressed he turned on the radio and heard a report about the brutal murder that had taken place on Leeward Avenue the previous night. The weather forecast was for a high of 100 that afternoon. Davin pawed through the drawer in the table beside his bed until he found a black notebook and his phony horn-rimmed glasses. His Harold Lloyd glasses, he called them. He sat down and called the Santa Monica operator. There was a John Abrams on Harvard Street.

It was a white frame house that might have been shipped in from Des Moines. The wide porch was shaded by a slanting roof. Carefully tended poinsettias fronted the porch, and a lawn only slightly better kept than the Wilshire Country Club sloped down to a sidewalk so white that the reflected sunlight hurt Davin's eyes. The leaded glass window in the front door was cut in a large oval with diamond-shaped prisms in the corners. Davin pressed the button and heard a bell ring inside.

The man who came to the door was large; his face was broad, with the high cheekbones and big nose of an Indian. He wore khaki pants and suspenders and a good dress shirt, collarless, the top buttons undone.

"Are you Mr. John Abrams? You work for the Dabney Oil Syndicate?"

The blunt face stayed blunt. "Yes."

Davin held out his hand. "My name is Albert Parker, Mr. Abrams. I'm with Mutual Assurance of Hartford. We're running an investigation on another employee of South Basin Oil and would like to ask you a few questions. Anything you say will be held strictly confidential, of course."

"Who are you investigating?"

"A Mr. Raymond Chandler."

Abrams' eyebrows flicked a fraction of an inch. "Come in," he said. He ushered Davin into the living room. They sat down, Davin got out his notebook, and Abrams looked him over—the kind of look Davin suspected was supposed to make employees stiffen and try to look dependable.

Abrams leaned forward. "Is this about any litigation he's started lately? I wouldn't want to talk about anything that's in court."

"No. This is entirely a matter between Mutual and Mr. Chandler. We are seeking information about his character. In your opinion, is Mr. Chandler a reliable man?"

"I don't consider him reliable," Abrams said, watching for Davin's reaction. Davin gave him nothing.

"We've got a hundred wells out on Signal Hill and I'm the field manager," Abrams continued. "I like working for Mr. Dabney. He's a good man." He paused, and the silence stretched.

"Look, I don't know who told you to talk to me, but I'll tell you right now I don't like Chandler. He's a martinet and a hypocrite: he'll flatter Mr. Dabney on Tuesday morning and cuss him out for not backing one of his lawsuits on Tuesday afternoon. He runs that office like his little harem. If you'd watch him for a week you'd know."

"Yes."

Abrams got up and began pacing. "I've got no stomach for talking about a man behind his back," he said. "But Chandler is hurting the company and Mr. Dabney. He's dragged us into lawsuits just to prove how tough he is; he had us in court last year on a personal injury suit that the insurance company was ready to settle on, and then after he won—he did win—he turned around and cancelled the policy. That soured a lot of people on South Basin Oil.

"The only reason he was hired was because he had an in with Ralph Lloyd. He started in accounting. So he sucks up to Bartlett, the auditor, and gets the reputation for being some kind of fair-haired college boy. A year later Bartlett gets arrested for embezzling $30,000. Tried and convicted.

"Now it gets real interesting. Instead of promoting Chandler, Dabney goes out and hires a man named John Ballantine from a private accounting firm. This suits Chandler just fine because Ballantine's from Scotland and Chandler impresses the hell out of him with his British upper-crust manners. Ballantine makes Chandler his assistant. A year later Ballantine drops dead in the office. Chandler helps the coroner and the coroner decides it was a heart attack. Mr. Dabney gives up and makes Chandler the new auditor, and within another year he's office manager and vice-president. Very neat, huh?''

Abrams had worked himself into a lather. Davin could have let him run on with just a few more neutral questions, but instead, as if someone else had taken over and was using his body like a ventriloquist's dummy, he said:

"You really hate him, don't you?"

Abrams froze. After a moment his big shoulders relaxed and his voice was back under control. "You've got to admit the story smells like a day-old mackerel."

"To hear you tell it."

"You don't have to believe me. Ask anyone on Olive Street. Check it with the coroner or the cops."

"If the cops thought there was anything to it I wouldn't have to check with them. Chandler would be spending his weekends in the exercise yard instead of with those girls you tell me about."

Abrams' brow furrowed. He looked like a theologian trying to fathom Aimee Semple McPherson. "Cops aren't always too smart," he said.

"A startling revelation." I was getting to like Abrams. He reduced the moral complexities of this case. He reminded me of a hand grenade ready to explode, and I was going to throw my body at him to save Raymond Chandler. "Mostly they aren't smart when somebody pays them not to be," I said. "Does the vice-president of an oil company have that kind of money?"

"Don't overestimate a cop's integrity."

"Who, me? I'm just an insurance investigator. You're the one who knows what it costs to bribe cops."

The big shoulders were getting tense again, but the voice was under control. "Look, I didn't start this talk about bribes. You asked me my opinion. I gave it; let's leave it at that."

He was right; I should have left it at that. Instead I pushed on like a fighter who knows the fix is on and it's only a matter of time before the other guy takes a dive.

"So Chandler killed Ballantine?" I said. "What about May Peterson?" I felt good. I was baiting a man who could wring me out like a dishrag and who looked like he was ready to.

"Peterson? Never heard of her. What kind of insurance man are you, anyway?"

"I'm investigating an accident. Maybe you were out a little late last night?"

Abrams took a step toward me. "Let's see your credentials, pal."

I got up. "You wouldn't hit a man with glasses on, Abrams. Let me turn my back."

"Get the hell out of here."

A woman wearing a gardening apron and gloves had come into the room. The house, which had seemed so cool when I'd entered, felt like an inferno. I slid the notebook into my pocket and left. The porch swing hung steady as a candle flame in a tomb; the sun on the sidewalk reawakened my headache. Abrams stood in the doorway watching as I walked down to the car. When I reached it he went back inside.

Davin shuddered convulsively, loosened his tie, leaned against the car. He squinted and focused on the street to keep the fear down: he was a sick man. He'd totally lost control of himself in Abrams' house. He wondered if that was what it felt like to go crazy—to do and say things as if you were drunk and watching yourself in a movie. He lifted his hand, looked at the hairy backs of his knuckles. He touched his thumb to each of his fingertips. His hand did exactly what he told it to. He seemed to be able to do whatever he wanted; he could call Cissy Chandler and tell her to sweat out her marriage by herself. He could drive home and sleep for twelve hours and wake up alone and free. What was to stop him?

Davin was about to get into the car when he noticed a piece of wire lying on the pavement below his running board. Just a piece of wire. The freshly-clipped end glinted in the sunlight. He bent over and tried to pick it up: it was attached to something beneath the car. Getting down on one knee, he saw the trailing wires where someone had cut each of his brake cables.

He rode the interurban east on Santa Monica Boulevard. Along the way he enjoyed what little breeze the streetcar's passage gave to the hot, syrupy air. He got off at Cahuenga and walked north toward his office on Ivar and Hollywood Boulevard, trying to piece together what had happened.

Abrams could have told his wife to take the pruning shears and cut the cables as soon as he recognized Davin on the porch. Abrams would have recognized Davin only if he was the one who had slugged Davin and gone on to murder May Peterson. He might have done it out of some misplaced desire to get back at Chandler.

But there was a problem with his theory. Why would Abrams

go on to slander Chandler so badly? It would look better if he hid any hostility he felt.

When Davin considered the picture of a middle-aged woman in gardening gloves crawling under a car on a residential street in broad daylight to cut brake cables, the whole card house collapsed. It couldn't be done, and not only that—Abrams simply had no reason to try such a stupid thing.

Then there was the question of why Davin had been slugged in the first place. Something about that had bothered him all day, and now he knew what it was: whoever killed May had no reason to knock out Davin. Davin had been on his way out, and sapping him only meant he would be around to find her dead. It didn't make any sense.

Near the corner of Cahuenga and the boulevard he spotted a penny lying on the sidewalk. The bright copper shone in the late afternoon sun like a chip of heaven dropped at his feet. Normally he would have stopped to pick it up; one of the habits bred of a boyhood spent in a small town where a penny meant your pick of the best candies on display in Sudlow's Dry Goods. Instead he crossed the street.

But his mind bemused by the puzzles of the cut brake cables and the senseless blow on the head, got stuck on this new mystery. If he'd paused to pick up the penny, he would have been a little later getting to the office. The whole sequence of events afterwards would be subtly different; it was as if stopping or not stopping marked a fork in the chain of happenings that made his life.

The strange frame of mind refused to leave him. Normally he *would* have stopped, so by not stopping he had set himself down a track of possibilities he would not normally have followed. Why hadn't he stopped? What had pushed him down this particular path? The incident expanded frighteningly in his mind until it swept away all other thoughts. Something had hold of him. It was just like the conversation with Abrams where he'd gone for the jugular—something was changing every decision he made, no matter how minor. With a conviction that chilled him on this hottest of days, he knew that he was being manipulated and that there was nothing he could do about it. He wondered how long it had been happening without his knowing it. He should have picked up that penny.

After a moment the conviction went away. No. To think that way was insane. He was tired and needed a drink. He could talk himself into all kinds of doubts if he let himself. He ought to

take a good punch at the next passerby just to prove he could do
whatever he wanted.

He didn't punch anybody.

Davin took the elevator up seven floors to his office. Quintanella and Sanderson from Homicide were in the waiting room.

"You don't keep your door locked," Sanderson said.

"I can't afford to turn away business."

Sanderson mashed his cigarette out in the standing ashtray and
got up from the sofa. "Let's have a talk," he said.

Davin led them into the inner room. "What brings you two
out to see me on a Sunday?"

"A dead woman," Quintanella said. His face, pocked with
acne scars, was stiff as a pine board.

Davin lit a cigarette, shook out the wooden match, broke it in
half and dropped the pieces into an ashtray. They pinged as they
hit the glass. The afternoon sun was shooting into the room at
the same angle it had taken when Cissy Chandler had come into
his office.

I'd had about enough of them already.

*"That's too bad," I said. "It's a rough business you're in.
You going to try to find out who killed this one?"*

*Sanderson belched. "We are," he said. "And you're gonna
help us. You're gonna start by telling us where Raymond Chandler is."*

*"Don't know the man. Sure you've got the right Davin?
There's a couple in the book."*

*"Will you tell this guy to cut the crap, Dutch?" Quintanella
said to Sanderson. "He makes me sick."*

*"I didn't think they ran to delicate stomachs down at Homi-
cide," I said. "You have to swallow so many lies and keep your
mouth shut."*

"Tell him to shut up, Dutch."

"Calm down, Davin," Sanderson said.

*"You tell me to talk, he tells me to shut up. Every time you
guys get a burr in your paws, you make guys like me pull it out
for you. Call me Androcles."*

*"We can do this downtown," Sanderson said. "It's a lot less
comfortable down there."*

*"You got a subpoena in that ugly suit?" The words were roll-
ing out now and I was riding them. "If you don't," I said, "save
the back room and the hose for some poor greaser. You want
any answers from me, you've got to tell me what's going on. I'm*

not going to get bruised telling you things you've got no business knowing.''

Quintanella flexed his hands. "C'mon Dutch, let's take him in."

"Shut up, Tony." Sanderson looked pained. "Don't try to kid us, Davin. We got a call from Mrs. Chandler this afternoon telling us she hired you last week. She said you knew about the murder of this call girl last night."

Call girl. The words momentarily shook Davin out of it. That was what Cissy would say, and guys like Sanderson would figure that was the only kind of woman who got murdered.

"Cissy Chandler's not the most reliable source," Davin said.

"That's why we came to you. The neighbor lady at the Rosinante Apartments said she saw a man who looked like you hanging around there last night. So why don't you tell us what's going on. Or should we let Tony take care of it?"

Davin watched them watch him. Quintanella was in the chair near the door, rubbing his left wrist with his other hand. This case was getting beyond him fast. He had no reason to protect Chandler when for all he knew the man had killed May.

"Jesus," Davin said. "You're crazy if you think I need this kind of heat. I'm not in this business to draw fire. I'll talk." He loosened his collar. "Will you let me get a drink out of this desk? No guns, just a little bourbon."

Sanderson came over behind the desk; Quintanella tensed. "You let me get it," Sanderson said. "Which drawer?"

"Bottom right."

Do it. Do it now. It was like Davin's blood talking to him, like the night in the freight yard with the club in his hand. He couldn't stop to pick up the penny.

When Sanderson opened the drawer and reached for the bottle, I punched him in the side of the throat. He fell back, hitting the corner of the desk, and Quintanella, fumbling for his gun, leapt toward me. I slipped around the other side of the desk and out the door before the big man could get the heater out. I was down the stairs and out the exit to the alley before they hit the lobby; I zig-zagged half a block between the buildings that backed the alley, crossed the street and slipped into the rear of an apartment building on the opposite side of Ivar. I had just thrown away my investigator's license. I caught my breath and wondered what the hell I was going to do next.

* * *

Davin called Estelle from the lobby of the Bryson and she told him to come up. Although it was only early evening, she was in her robe. Her dark hair shone; her face was calm, with a trace of insouciance. She looked like Louise Brooks.

"I've got some trouble," Davin said. "Can I stay here for awhile?"

"Yes."

She offered him coffee. They sat facing each other in the small living room. The two windows that fronted the street were open and a hot, humid wind waved the curtains like a tired maid shaking out bedsheets. The air smelled like coming rain. Maybe the heatwave would be broken. Davin told her about his talk with Abrams.

"You don't believe those things he said." There was an urgency in Estelle's voice that Davin supposed came from her love for Chandler. He realized that he didn't want her to care about Chandler at all.

"Did they happen?"

"Bartlett was convicted of embezzling. Ballantine died of a heart attack. Raymond had nothing to do with either of those things."

"He was just lucky."

Estelle exhaled cigarette smoke sharply. "I wouldn't use that word."

"I'm not trying to be sarcastic," Davin said. He hadn't had to try at all lately. "But you have to admit that it all has worked out nicely for him. He meets the right people, makes the right impression, and events break just the way you'd expect them to break if he was in the business of planning embezzlements and heart attacks. I can't blame a guy like Abrams for taking it the wrong way."

"Things don't always work out for Raymond. I know him better than you do. Look at his marriage."

"Okay, let's. Why did he marry her?"

Her brow knit. "He loves her, I guess."

"Why did he wait until his mother died?"

"She didn't approve."

"I'm not surprised. Age difference. But he was pretty old to still be listening to Mom."

Estelle took a last pull on her cigarette, then snuffed it out. Her dark eyes watched him. "I don't know. I don't know if I care anymore."

Davin wanted not to care about the whole case. But he had

been hired to watch a man and he had lost that man. In the process a woman had been killed, and he couldn't bring himself to think she deserved it. *It was a matter of professional ethics.*

Ethics? He wasn't some white knight on a horse. The idea of ethics in his business was ludicrous; it made him mad that such an idea had worked its way into his head. Only a schoolboy would expect ethics from a private eye. Only a schoolboy would think less of May Peterson because she had slept with Chandler. Only a schoolboy would have turned Estelle down the previous night.

"I was surprised you asked me here last night," he said.

"That sounds sarcastic, too."

"Not necessarily."

The wind had strengthened and it was blissfully cool. With a sound of distant thunder, the rain started. Estelle got up to close the windows. She drew her robe tighter about her as she stood in the breeze; Davin watched her slender shoulders and hips as she pulled the windows shut. When she came back she folded her legs up under her on the sofa. The line of her neck and shoulders against the darkness of the next room was as pure as the sweep of a child's sparkler through a Fourth of July night. She spoke somberly.

"I used to be a good girl. Being in love with a married man made me think that over. I'm not a good or bad girl anymore; I'm not any kind of girl." She paused. "You don't look to me like you're really the kind of man you're supposed to be."

Davin felt free of compulsion for the first time in the last three days.

"I'm not," he said, in wonder. "I feel like I've been playing some kid's game—or more like dreaming some kid's dream. I feel like I'm just waking."

Estelle simply watched him.

"I'd like to stay with you tonight," Davin said.

She smiled. "Not a very romantic pickup line. Raymond would do it funnier, or more poetic."

"He would?"

"Certainly. He's very poetic. He even wrote poetry—still does, as far as I know. You didn't know that?"

"I haven't been on this case for very long. Is it any good?"

"When I was nineteen I loved it. Now I think it'd be too sentimental for me."

"That's too bad."

Estelle came to Davin, sat on the arm of his chair, kissed him. She pulled away, a little out of breath.

"No it isn't," she said.

All during their lovemaking he felt something trying to make him pull away, like a voice whispering over and over, *get up and leave. Go now. She will push you, she will absorb you. Doesn't she smell bad? Isn't she an animal?*

It wasn't conscience. It was something outside him, alien, the same thing that had pulled him away from May Peterson. But Davin had finally picked up that penny, and he felt better, as he lay on the border of sleep, than he had in as long as he could remember. Being with Estelle was the first really good thing that he had done on his own since Friday afternoon. He felt that they were breaking a pattern merely by lying together, tired, limbs entwined. Estelle's breathing was regular, and Davin, listening to the rain, fell asleep.

Davin dreamt there had been a shipwreck and that he and the other passengers were floundering among the debris, trying to keep afloat. There was no sound. He knew the others in the water: Estelle was there, and Cissy, and Abrams and May Peterson and some others he could not make out—and Chandler. Chandler could not swim, and he clutched at them, one after the other, as if they were pieces of wreckage that he could climb up on in order to keep afloat. They might have made it themselves, but they were all being shoved beneath the waves by the desperate man, and they would drown trying to save him. But Chandler never would drown, and would never understand the people dying around him. He could not even see them. He fumbled for Davin's head, his fingers in Davin's eyes, and Davin found he did not have the strength to shove him away. Davin coughed and sputtered and struggled toward the surface. Fighting against him in the salt sea, Davin saw that for Chandler, he was little more than a broken spar, an inanimate thing to be used without compunction because it was never alive. Drowning, Davin saw that Chandler had forced him under without even realizing what he had done.

He woke. It was still dark. Estelle still slept; some noise from the other room had stirred him. The rain had stopped and streetlights threw a pale wedge of light against the ceiling. Through the doorway, Davin saw something move. Two men slipped quietly into the room.

In the faint light Davin saw that they wore sailors' uniforms and that the smaller of the two had a sap in his hand. Davin snatched the bedside clock and threw it at him.

The man ducked and it glanced off his shoulder. Davin leapt out of the bed, dragging the bedclothes after him. He heard Estelle gasp behind him as he hit the smaller sailor full in the chest. They slammed into the wall and the man hit his head against the doorjamb. He slumped to the floor. Davin struggled to his feet, still tangled in the sheets, and turned to see that the big man had Estelle by the arm, a hand the size of a baseball glove smothering her cries. He dragged her out of bed.

"Quiet now, buddy," the big sailor said in a soft voice. "Else I wring the little girl's neck."

The man on the floor moaned.

"What's the deal?" Davin asked. Estelle's frightened eyes glinted in the dark.

"No deal. We just got some business to take care of."

Davin stood there naked, helpless. He was no Houdini. All he had to keep them alive was words.

"You killed May Peterson," he said. "Why?"

"We had to. To get at that bastard Chandler. He makes a good impression. We wanna see what kind of impression he makes on the cops."

Davin shifted his feet and stepped on something hard. The sap.

"What have you got against him?"

The big man seemed content to stand there all night with his arm around Estelle. He gasped, almost a chuckle. "Personal injury is what. Ten thousand bucks he cheated us outa. We hadda accident with one of his oil trucks. We had it as good as won until he made 'em go to court."

The man at Davin's feet rolled over, started to get up. "Be quiet, Lou," he said.

"What difference's it make," the big sailor said. "They're dead already."

"Be quiet and let's do it. There's other people in this place."

Davin's thoughts raced. "It makes no sense to kill us. I'm no friend of Chandler's. I've been tailing him."

"You was there last night," the small sailor said, poking around the floor in the dark for the sap. "That's good enough. We've got to get rid of you."

"Who says?"

Neither one answered.

"What the hell are you looking for?" Davin asked.

"You'll know soon enough," the short one said.

"Damn, you guys are stupid. This doesn't make any sense. How do you expect to get away with this?"

Big Lou jerked back on his arm and Estelle struggled ineffectually. "It was you two that got caught in the bed together, right? Like a coupla animals? You don't deserve to live." He spoke with wounded innocence, as if he had explained everything. As if, Davin realized, he was hearing the same voice that had whispered to him. Davin trembled, furious, holding himself back, feeling himself ready to fight and afraid of what might happen if he did. Don't move, he thought.

Move.

The shorter sailor was still obsessed with finding his weapon, shuffling through the sheets on the floor, picking Estelle's discarded camisole with two fingers as if it were a dead carp.

"Let me help," I said; I snatched the sap from beneath my foot and laid the sailor out with a blow across the temple. The small man hit the floor like the loser in a prelim. At the same time I heard Lou yell. Estelle had bitten his hand. Lou threw her aside, shook the pain away, and catlike, quickly for such a big man, moved toward him.

Lou wasn't too big. Tunney could have taken him in twelve. I tried to dance out of his way, but he cut me off and worked me toward the corner of the room. I swung the sap at his head; Lou caught the blow on his forearm and I tried to knee him in the groin. He danced back a half-step. I stumbled forward like a rodeo clown who missed the bull. As I tried to get up I got hit in the ear with a fist that felt like a baseball bat. Just to show there were no hard feelings, Lou kicked me in the ribs.

"Stop!" Estelle yelled. "I've got a gun."

Lou turned slowly. Estelle was kneeling on the bed, shaking. She had a small automatic pointed at him.

Lou charged her. Two shots, painfully loud in the small room, sounded before he got there. He knocked the gun away, grabbed Estelle's head in one hand and smashed it against the brass bedstead once, twice, and she was still. I was on him by then. Oh yes, I was real quick. Lou shook me off his back and onto the floor, grunting now with the effort and the realization that he was shot. He shook his head as if dazed and stumbled toward me again. When he hit me I stood and heaved him over my shoulder. There was a crash and a rush of air into the room: Lou had gone through the window. Six stories to the street.

Davin shuddered with pain and rage—not at what Lou had

done, but at himself. The other sailor was still out. Estelle lay half off the bed, her head hanging, mouth open. Her straight, short hair brushed the floor. Davin lifted her onto the bed. He listened for her heartbeat and heard nothing. He touched her throat and felt no pulse. He lay his cheek against her lips and felt no wisp of breath.

A great anger, an anger close to despair, was building in him. He knew who had killed Estelle, and why, and it was not the sailors.

No one had yet responded to the shots or the dead man in the street. Davin pulled on his clothes and left.

Davin didn't know how much time he would have. He burned with rage and impatience—and with fear. Estelle was dead. He shouldn't have moved. He was not a hero. Somebody had made him. Somebody had made him walk by that penny on the sidewalk, too, and as damp night gave way to dawn his confusion gave way to cold certainty: Chandler was his man. And, Davin realized, laughing aloud, he was Chandler's.

He took the streetcar downtown, past the construction site of the new civic center. He got off at Seventh and Hill and walked a block to South Olive. He was hungry but would not eat; he wondered if it was Chandler who decided whether he should become hungry. He watched the officeworkers come in for the beginning of the new week and wondered who was trapped in Chandler's web and who wasn't. In the men's room of the Bank of Italy building he washed the crusted trickle of blood from his ear, combed his hair, straightened his clothes.

Nothing that had happened in the last three days had made sense. Cissy hiring Davin, Chandler running off the road, Davin getting knocked out at May's apartment, the sailors killing May and then Estelle, the cutting of Davin's brake cables, Sanderson and Quintanella letting him get away so easily—and the crazy way things fit together, coincidence straight out of a bad novel. All of these things ought not to have happened in any sensible world. The only way they could have was if he were being pulled from his own life into a nightmare, and that was what Davin had realized. The nightmare was Chandler's.

Somehow, probably without his even knowing it, whatever Chandler wanted to happen, happened. Lives got jerked into new patterns, and his fantasies came true. Maybe it went back to Bartlett's embezzlement and Ballantine's heart attack; maybe it went back to Chandler's childhood. Whatever, the things that had been happening to Cissy and May and Estelle and even Big Lou and his partner, even the things Davin could not imagine any man consciously wanting to come true—were all what Chandler wanted to happen. Estelle was dead because of the situation the sailors and Davin had contrived to trap her in, and they had contrived this without knowing it because they were doing what Chandler wanted. There was no place in Chandler's world for women who liked sex and weren't afraid to go out and get it. There was no place in Chandler's world for the ordinary kind of private detective that Davin was. He had to find Chandler before the next disaster occurred.

He waited until he saw Philleo show up for work at South Basin Oil and followed him up to the fourth floor. Most of the staff was there already and talking about May Peterson. They stared at Davin as if he were an apparition—he felt like one—and Philleo turned to face him.

"May I help you?"

"Let's talk in your office, Mr. Philleo."

The man eyed him darkly, then motioned toward the corner room. They shut the door. Davin refused to sit down.

"Where's Raymond?" he asked.

"I talked to the police yesterday. You're no policeman."

"That's right. Where is he?"

"I have no idea," Philleo said. "And I'm not going—"

The phone rang. Philleo looked irritated, then picked it up. "Yes?" he said. There was a silence and Philleo looked as if he had swallowed a stone. "Put him on," he said.

Davin smiled grimly: yet another improbable coincidence. He had known the moment the phone rang who was calling. Philleo listened; he looked distressed. After a moment Davin took the receiver from his unresisting hand.

The man on the phone spoke in a voice choked with emotion and slurred by alcohol, with a trace of a British accent.

". . . swear to God I'll do it this time, Milt, I can't bear to think what a rat I am and what I'm doing to Cissy—"

"Where are you?" Davin said softly.

"Milt?"

"This isn't Milt. This is Michael Davin. I'm the man who helped you the other night when you ran off the road. Where are you?"

There was a pause, and Chandler's voice came back, more sober. "I want to talk to Milt."

"He doesn't want to talk to you anymore, Raymond. He's sick of you. He wants me to help you out instead."

Another silence.

"Well, you can tell that bastard that I'm in the Mayfair Hotel and if he wants to help me he can identify my body when they pull it off the sidewalk because I'm going to do it this time."

"No you won't. I'll be there in ten minutes." Davin gave the phone back to Philleo, who looked ashen. "He says he's going to kill himself."

"He's threatened before. I could tell you stories—"

"Just talk to him."

Davin ignored the elevator and ran down to the lobby, flagged a cab that took him speeding down Seventh Street. He didn't know what he was going to do when he got there, but he knew he had to reach Chandler. The ride seemed maddeningly slow. He peered out the window at the buildings and pedestrians, the sunlight flashing on storefronts and cars, searching for a sign that something had changed. Nothing happened. When Chandler died, would any of them who were controlled by him feel the difference? Would Davin collapse in the back seat of the taxi like a discarded puppet, leaving the driver with a ticking meter and a comatose man to pay the fare? Or would Chandler's death instead set Davin free? If Davin could only be sure of that, he would kill Chandler himself. Maybe he would kill him anyway. He needed to stay mad to keep from thinking about whether he could have saved Estelle. If Davin had walked out of her apartment instead of asking to stay, if she had kicked him out, then she would probably still be alive. She'd be a good girl, and he'd be a strong man. If May had slammed the door in his face—

They reached the Mayfair and Davin threw a couple of dollars at the driver. The desk clerk had a Mr. Chandler in room 712.

The door was not locked. The room stank of tobacco smoke and sweat and booze. Chandler had to have his own private bootlegger to stay drunk so consistently. The man was sitting in the opened window wearing rumpled trousers, shoes without socks, and a sleeveless T-shirt. He had his back against one side and one leg propped against the opposite. An almost-empty bottle stood on the sill in the crook of his knee. The phone lay on its side on the bedside table with the receiver dangling and a voice sounding tinnily from it. A book was opened face down on the bed, which looked as if it hadn't been made up in a couple of days. Beside the book lay a pulp magazine. *Black Mask*. Above a lurid picture of a man pointing a gun at another man who held a blonde in front of him as a shield, was the slogan, "Smashing Detective Stories."

Chandler did not notice him enter. Davin crossed to the phone, stood it up, and quietly hung up the receiver. The silencing of the voice seemed to rouse Chandler. He lifted his head.

"Who are you?"

Davin's weariness suddenly caught up with him, and he sat down on the edge of the bed. He had felt some sympathy for Chandler even up to that moment, but seeing the man, and remembering Estelle's startled dead eyes, he now knew only disgust. Everyone who loved this man defended him, and he remained oblivious to it all, self-pitying and innocent when he ought to be guilty.

"You're the guy—" Chandler started.

"I'm the guy who pulled you out of the wreck. I'm the private detective hired by Cissy to keep you from hurting yourself. She didn't say anything about keeping you from hurting anyone else, and I was too stupid to catch on. Before Friday I had a life of my own, but now I'm the man you want me to be. I get beat up for twenty bucks a day and say please and thank you. I'm a regular guy and a strange one. I talk sex with the ladies and never follow through, I crack wise to the cops. I'm the best man in your world and good enough for any world. I go down these mean streets and don't get tarnished and I'm not afraid. I'm the hero."

"What are you talking about?"

"You're mystified, huh? Before Friday I could touch a woman and not have to worry about her getting killed for it. Now I'm busy taking care of a sleazy momma's boy."

Chandler pointed a shaking finger at him. "Don't you mock me," he said. "I know what I've done. I know—"

Davin was raging inside. "What have you done?" he said grimly. "You sound like you've got a big conscience. So tell me."

Chandler's weeping had turned into anger. "I've betrayed my wife. I'm not surprised she put you onto me—I would have told her to do that myself, in her situation. I've—" his voice became choked, "I've consorted with women who aren't any good. Women with death in their eyes and bedrooms that smell of too much cheap perfume."

"Are you serious?" Davin wanted to laugh but couldn't. "Where do you get all this malarkey? May and Estelle are dead. Really dead—not perfume dead."

Chandler jerked as if electrically shocked. He knocked the bottle out the window, and seconds later came the crash.

His face set in a sour expression. "I'm not surprised about May. She led a fast life." He paused, and his voice became philosophical. "Even Estelle—it doesn't surprise me. I finally figured out that she wasn't the innocent she pretended to be."

Davin's rage grew. He got up from the bed; the book beside him fell off and closed itself. *The Great Gatsby*, the cover read.

"May and Estelle were killed by those sailors you fought in the insurance suit. They said they were out to get revenge against you."

Chandler shook again. "That makes no sense," he said. "May and Estelle had nothing to do with that. Anyone out to get me should come for me. There must have been some other reason they were killed."

Davin grabbed Chandler by the arm. He wanted to push him out the window; it would be easy, easier than the night in the railyard. Nobody would know. For the first time, Chandler looked him in the eye. Davin saw desperation there and something more frightening: Chandler seemed to know what he was thinking, was granting him permission, was making an appeal. He did not try to escape Davin's grasp. Davin fought the desire to give one quick shove that would end it; the frustrated need, the rage of the years of keeping himself sane, pushed him toward it. The whole struggle was the matter of an instant. He pulled Chandler into the room.

"Quit the suicide act. What have you been doing since you left May?"

If Chandler had felt anything of the communication that had passed between them, he did not show it. "What does it look like?" he said. "I couldn't stay with her; when I first met her I thought she was innocent, defenseless, but I learned the kind she was quick. I couldn't go home and face Cissy. I came here."

He looked toward the window. "If I had any guts it wouldn't be an act."

"Those sailors had no reason to kill except you. They did it in the stupidest way possible. Not for revenge. Just so things could work out the way you want them to."

Chandler pushed by him and went into the bathroom; Davin heard the sound of running water. He was getting ready to shave. He seemed to be sobering fast.

"You're crazy," Chandler said as he lathered his face. "The way *I* wanted? Look, I feel like the bastard I am, but what did

I have to do with any of this? Am I supposed to stop defending the company when we're in the right? I've got to try to do the right thing, don't I?''

Davin said nothing. After a few minutes, Chandler came out of the bathroom. Hair combed, freshly shaven, he seemed already to be on the way to becoming an executive again. The news of the deaths, the struggle on the windowsill, had knocked the booze out of him; knocked the guilt down in him, too. He picked up his shirt and began buttoning it.

Davin felt he was going to be sick.

"You know, that credo you spouted—you were just joking, I realize—but there's something to it," Chandler said seriously. " 'Down these mean streets.' I'd like to believe in that; I'd like to be able to live up to that code—if we could only get all the other bastards to.''

Davin rushed into the bathroom and vomited into the toilet.

Chandler stuck his head into the room. "Are you all right?"

Davin gasped for breath. He wet a towel and rubbed his face.

Chandler had his tie knotted and put on the jacket of his rumpled summer suit. "You should take better care of yourself," he said. "You look awful. What's your name?"

"Michael Davin."

"Irish, huh?"

"I guess so."

"I'll bet being a private investigator is interesting work. There's a kind of honor to it. You ought to write up your experiences some day."

Estelle was dead, lying upside down with her hair brushing the dusty floor. Her mouth was open. "I don't want to," Davin said.

Chandler took the copy of *Black Mask* from the bed. Davin felt hollow, but the way Chandler held the magazine, so reverently, sparked his anger again.

"You actually read that junk?"

The other man ignored him. He bent over, a little unsteadiness the only evidence of his bender and the fact he'd been ready to launch himself out the window half an hour earlier. He picked up the copy of *Gatsby*.

"I've always wanted to be a writer," he said. "I used to write essays—even some poetry."

"Estelle told me that."

Chandler looked only momentarily uncomfortable. He motioned with the book in his hand. "So you don't like detective stories. Have you tried Fitzgerald?"

"No."

"Best damn writer in America. Best damn book. About a man chasing his dream."

"Does he catch it?"

Sadly, Chandler replied, "No. He doesn't."

"He ought to quit dreaming, then."

Chandler put his hand on Davin's shoulder. "We can't do that. We've got nothing else."

Davin wanted to tell him what a load of crap that was, but Chandler had turned his back and walked out of the room.